MORE PRAISE FOR THE MAZE

"One of my favorite authors. You guys have to read this book." —*Jesse Watters Primetime*

"A tough, unsolved murder case with interlocking crimes and suspects that ends in a fiery finish. . . . A well-done crime yarn." —*Kirkus Reviews*

"It's easy to make the argument that Nelson DeMille is the most influential genre novelist of the last fifty years. . . . *The Maze* is as twisty and labyrinthine as the title indicates. No other modern novelist has penned more seminal tales than DeMille, and his latest adds to that list." —*Providence Journal*

"Whether you like Corey or not, his perspective is sharply presented through writing that is tight, clean, evocative, and provocative. . . . The story [has] a high emotional intelligence quotient as well as a cerebral one." —*New York Journal of Books*

"DeMille is one of those writers who rarely has a misfire. The Corey novels (this is the eighth) have been uniformly strong, mostly due to his lead character, a deeply complex, compelling, and unpredictable fellow. A complete success." —*Booklist*

"A treacherous maze of vice, graft, and blackmail." —*Publishers Weekly*

NOVELS BY NELSON DeMILLE

By the Rivers of Babylon
Cathedral
The Talbot Odyssey
Word of Honor
The Charm School
The Gold Coast
The General's Daughter
Spencerville
Up Country
The Gate House
The Quest
The Cuban Affair

John Corey Novels
Plum Island
The Lion's Game
Night Fall
Wild Fire
The Lion
The Panther
Radiant Angel

With Alex DeMille
The Deserter
Blood Lines

With Thomas Block
Mayday

Ebooks
The Book Case
Death Benefits
Rendezvous
Getaway (with Lisa Scottoline)

THE
MAZE

A JOHN COREY NOVEL

NELSON DeMILLE

POCKET BOOKS
New York   London   Toronto   Sydney   New Delhi

Pocket Books
An Imprint of Simon & Schuster, LLC
1230 Avenue of the Americas
New York, NY 10020

This book is a work of fiction. Any references to historical events, real people, or real places are used fictitiously. Other names, characters, places, and events are products of the author's imagination, and any resemblance to actual events or places or persons, living or dead, is entirely coincidental.

This Pocket Books paperback edition July 2024

POCKET and colophon are registered trademarks of Simon & Schuster, LLC

Simon & Schuster: Celebrating 100 Years of Publishing in 2024

For information about special discounts for bulk purchases, please contact Simon & Schuster Special Sales at 1-866-506-1949 or business@simonandschuster.com.

The Simon & Schuster Speakers Bureau can bring authors to your live event. For more information or to book an event, contact the Simon & Schuster Speakers Bureau at 1-866-248-3049 or visit our website at www.simonspeakers.com.

Manufactured in the United States of America

10 9 8 7 6 5 4 3 2 1

ISBN 978-1-5011-0179-3
ISBN 978-1-5011-0180-9 (ebook)

AUTHOR'S NOTE

The Maze is a work of fiction, but it was inspired partly by the true and previously unsolved case known as the Gilgo Beach murders, which I have fictionalized in this book (with generous portions of literary license and dramatic liberties) as the Fire Island murders.

To my granddaughters,
Vera DeMille Halasz and
Margot Sørina Madsen DeMille.
Mudgie loves you.

THE
MAZE

CHAPTER 1

You can't drink all day unless you start in the morning.

It was 11 A.M. on a sunny June day, and I was sitting with a cold Bud in a deep wicker chair on the back porch of my uncle Harry's big Victorian house overlooking the Great Peconic Bay. The uniform of the day—every day—was shorts and T-shirt. My bare feet were propped on the porch rail, and on my lap were a pair of old binoculars and the *New York Times* crossword puzzle.

I'd been chilling here for about three weeks, and as I'd said the last time I was borrowing Harry's summer house, the problem with doing nothing is not knowing when you're finished.

I put my beer down on a side table next to my 9mm Glock.

It was a cool day with a nice salty breeze coming off the water. I'm a city boy, but I can get used to nature in small doses. I focused my binocs on a cabin cruiser out in the bay, a few hundred feet from shore. The boat was not running, but neither was it at anchor. It was drifting, and the incoming tide and wind were taking it toward the rocky beach at the end of the sloping lawn. No one was visible in the wheelhouse or on deck. Odd. I put the Glock on my lap.

If they were coming for me, they'd probably come at night. But a surprise daytime attack was also possible. For all I knew, the hit team was already inside the empty house, in cell phone contact with the boat, which had fixed my position. *My* cell phone, unfortunately, was sitting on the kitchen counter, charging.

My only escape would be to grab my gun, vault over the porch rail, and sprint across the lawn to the bay, then start swimming along the shoreline, where the water was too shallow for the cabin cruiser to get close. The hit team in my kitchen would not have anticipated my dash to the sea, and they'd be frantically trying to figure out what to do as they charged out of the house onto the porch and saw me swimming, then coming ashore and disappearing into the thick bulrushes.

And then what? Make my way to safety? Or execute a flanking maneuver to come around their rear and take them out one by one? They wouldn't expect that. But they should know that John Corey does the unexpected.

After the hit team were all dead on the back lawn, I'd flip the bird to their backup team on the boat, then go in the house and call the police and the town dump. Why the dump? Because, as we used to say in the NYPD: A single death is a tragedy; multiple deaths are a sanitation problem.

Clearly, I was going nuts. In fact, people often ask me, "Are you crazy?" I was glad there was still some doubt.

Anyway, as I said, I'm John Corey, former NYPD Homicide detective. After I left the job on a line-of-duty three-quarter disability—the result of three bullet wounds—I took a job as a contract agent with the Federal Anti-Terrorist Task Force. I left the ATTF under unusual circumstances and landed another Federal gig, this one with the Diplomatic Surveillance Group, which terminated last month—also under unusual circumstances. I was also once an adjunct professor at JJC—John Jay

College of Criminal Justice in Manhattan. Now I am NYU—New York Unemployed.

I put my Glock back on the side table, took a swig of beer, and glanced at the newspaper on my lap. Today was June 21, the summer solstice and the longest day of the year. The sun was still in the eastern sky and the migrating birds were mostly settled in, as were the odd ducks from the city who had weekend homes around here.

I noticed the cabin cruiser was now at anchor, and two couples were fishing. That's what assassins do before they strike.

I'm not totally nuts, by the way, or unreasonably paranoid. I have acquired a number of enemies over the years, including my former FBI bosses in the ATTF, and also my former colleagues in the CIA. Most recently, I have pissed off my superiors in the Diplomatic Surveillance Group. Going way back, I guess I also pissed off some of my NYPD bosses. But I didn't think any of those people actually wanted me dead . . . well, maybe the CIA did. I know too much.

Aside from my former colleagues, I have some real enemies, starting with the perps who I'd put behind bars in my NYPD days. Then there were the Islamic terrorists whose pals I had capped or captured when I was with ATTF. Those A-holes definitely wanted my head separated from my body. But perps and terrorists are mostly stupid, and I didn't lose any sleep worrying about them. The real pros were the guys I tangled with when I was with the Diplomatic Surveillance Group—the guys from SVR, the Russian Foreign Intelligence Service, the equivalent of our CIA, and the successors of the Soviet KGB. Those bastards are tough and they're good at what they do. And what they do is kill people. Which a few of them tried to do to yours truly. I'm still here. They're not. The SVR would like to settle that score. And I'd like to see them try it.

Also on my enemies list are two unknown gentlemen who pumped fourteen or fifteen rounds at me on West 102nd Street seven years ago, when I was an NYPD detective working a homicide case. Those myopic A-holes managed only three hits at thirty feet and would not have qualified at the Police Academy pistol range. Not that I'm complaining. Anyway, I spent a month at Columbia-Presbyterian Hospital and a few weeks at my Manhattan condo before I accepted Uncle Harry's kind offer to convalesce here at his waterfront summer house, which he rarely uses. And here I am again, not convalescing this time but decompressing, which is a lot better than decomposing.

In the category of my frenemies are my ex-wife, Robin, and my future ex-wife, Kate Mayfield.

Robin, a successful criminal defense attorney, came to visit me when I was at Columbia-Pres, even though we were then separated. She once stepped on my oxygen hose, but I'm sure that was an accident. The second time I'm not so sure. FYI, Robin has reclaimed her maiden name, which is Paine, and which is so her. Robin has never remarried, but every time I run into her in New York, she has a new guy, making me think she's had more fresh mounts than a Pony Express rider.

As for FBI Special Agent Kate Mayfield, my estranged wife, I haven't seen her since last October, when she transferred from the Anti-Terrorist Task Force office at 26 Federal Plaza in New York to FBI Headquarters in DC. But we keep in touch by text and e-mail, and even phone now and then. Neither of us has actually filed for divorce, meaning, I guess, that a reconciliation is possible, though not probable, given that she's probably fucking Tom Walsh, our former FBI boss at ATTF, who has also conveniently transferred to DC.

I should have had Walsh brought up on misconduct charges, but that would have hurt Kate's career, so I didn't. I will, however, settle with Mr. Walsh at the first opportunity. Or should I thank him?

Also regarding my love life, there is Tess Faraday, who was my partner when I was working what turned out to be my last assignment with the Diplomatic Surveillance Group: the case of the killer Russians. Tess, who was undercover for State Department Intel, got under the covers for John Corey, but unfortunately, our relationship has transitioned from romantic to platonic. Not sure how that happened, but it happens, though she sometimes hints that benefits are still available if I were divorced or in the process thereof. Meanwhile, I haven't had sex in so long I can't remember who brings the handcuffs.

I worked on the *Times* crossword awhile—a seven-letter word starting with "u" that means ointment . . . "Up yours"? No, "unguent." I finished my beer and contemplated lunch. Or did I just drink lunch?

I looked south, out at the bay, sparkling in the sunlight. Uncle Harry's summer house is located in the hamlet of Mattituck, Town of Southold, which is on the North Fork of Long Island, about a hundred road miles east of Manhattan. Across the bay is the South Fork, the trendy Hamptons, populated every summer by A-listers, many of whom are actually A-holes. Here on the North Fork, the full-time residents are fairly normal people—farmers, fishermen, butchers, bakers, and candlestick makers. Also, in recent years, vineyards have sprung up on what were once potato farms. The wineries attract tourists who like to talk about wine. I mean, do I talk about beer? It's beer. Drink it and shut up.

Anyway, property values have skyrocketed here, so Uncle Harry's house and land are worth about a million bucks. Harry had actually sold this place after my convalescent stay here, but the deal fell through, and he took that as a sign that he should keep the house. Good move. It's now worth double what it was then. He keeps offering to sell it to me, like I have a million bucks. He wants to "keep it in the family." Wrong family, Harry.

Harry lives in the city, Upper East Side, not far from my condo. If you ask him what he does for a living, he says, "I'm in organized crime," then adds, "Wall Street." Gets a laugh every time.

When I was a kid, Uncle Harry, who is my mother's brother, and Harry's late wife, June, would invite his poor city relatives out here for two weeks every summer—me, my parents, and my brother and sister. This was a nice break from our tenement on the Lower East Side. I have a lot of good memories here, and lots of great photos of those summers with my cousins, Harry Jr. and Barbara. As for me buying this place, I recall what the local Southold police chief, Sylvester Maxwell, once advised: "If it flies, floats, or fucks, rent it."

Max, as he's called by his friends, gave me this good advice right here on this back porch when I was convalescing from my gunshot wounds. He'd stopped by to see if the legendary John Corey was interested in helping him on a double homicide that had just landed in his lap. I wasn't. But the victims were Tom and Judy Gordon, an attractive married couple who I knew and liked. The Gordons were PhDs, biologists who worked at nearby Plum Island, a.k.a. Anthrax Island, where the Department of Agriculture does research on animal diseases. It's also a place where people say that biological warfare research is on the secret agenda. So that got my attention.

Anyway, I had agreed to go with Chief Maxwell to the Gordons' house, which was the scene of the crime. And before I knew it, I was up to my Glock in some strange and dangerous stuff. No good deed goes unpunished. But, on the plus side, the Plum Island case gave me the opportunity to meet two nice women—Emma Whitestone, a local girl, and Detective Beth Penrose of the Suffolk County Homicide Squad. But that's another story. A complicated story.

Flash-forward seven years and Uncle Harry had just informed me that he'd rented this house to another Wall Street guy and his wife for July and August—for sixty large. I would have liked to stay for the summer, but I couldn't match that offer, so it was time to move on. Maybe back to my condo on East 72nd. Summer in the city.

Now I had to make an important decision. Should I get up and grab another beer? Or sit here until I have to pee?

The decision was made for me when I heard a noise through the open kitchen window behind me. I grabbed my Glock as I stood and faced the door, my butt on the porch rail in case I had to do a backflip into the rosebushes and come up firing. My adrenaline pump kicked in and I was ready for action.

CHAPTER 2

The aforementioned Detective Beth Penrose stepped out on the porch and took in the view. "Nice." She looked at me as I slipped my Glock in my pocket. "Sorry to just barge in," she said, "but I called your cell and you didn't answer."

"How did you know I was here?"

"I saw your Jeep in the driveway."

"I mean *here*, in Mattituck?"

"Oh . . . Max told me." She asked, "Do you have a minute?"

I didn't pursue the Max line of questioning and inquired, "Is this business or pleasure?"

"Business."

"Then I have a minute. For pleasure, I have all day."

She smiled, and we made eye contact. Bumping into an ex-lover can be awkward. Having one show up at your door is usually trouble.

I motioned to a wicker chair.

She sat and I sat beside her. She kicked off her sensible shoes and put her feet on the rail, giving me a view of her good legs and reminding me of what lay north of the hemline. I try not to have impure thoughts, but my dick has been unemployed longer than I have.

Beth stared at the tranquil bay. She was wearing a tailored tan suit and a white blouse, and I deduced that she was on duty. Somewhere under her form-fitting jacket was a forty-caliber Glock, with room left over for her big guns. Sorry.

Anyway, Beth is a pretty woman—and don't let me forget intelligent—with medium-length copper-colored hair, blue-green eyes, and pouty lips. As I said, we met— or, more accurately, butted heads—on the Gordon homicide case. Despite the bad start, we connected and were together for almost a year. Then, when I was with ATTF, I met FBI Special Agent Kate Mayfield on the job. I used to play the horses a lot, and the best advice I ever got from an old handicapper was "Never change your bet at the window," which is also good advice in the dating game.

Bottom line, I broke up with Beth and married Kate, but Beth and I met by chance last October when she was assigned to the Russian case I was working on in Southampton. She was unattached then, and I would have stayed in touch with her, but I wound up getting involved with my Diplomatic Surveillance Group partner, Tess Faraday. This was after Kate transferred to Washington to further her career—and maybe to be near Tom Walsh. "Timing is everything," as my mother used to say after watching an episode of "As the World Turns."

Beth looked out at the cabin cruiser. "Fluke and flounder are running."

"Right." The favorite fish of Russian assassins.

"Max said you've been here a few weeks."

"Yeah . . . I would have called you, but—"

"You came here to be alone."

"Right."

"How's that working out?" she asked.

"Great, until about three minutes ago."

"Still a smart-ass."

"That's how I hide my insecurity."

No reply.

"Can I get you something?"

She glanced at my morning beer on the side table. "No, but you go ahead."

"I'm good."

She nodded, then said, "I got a very edited briefing memo from the FBI on the Russian case. " She asked, "What happened after I saw you?"

"I'm not at liberty to discuss that."

"Okay. But are you still with DSG?"

I had been put on paid administrative leave from the Diplomatic Surveillance Group while the very sensitive Russian case was under investigation—which was the Feds' way of keeping me under their control and quiet until they got their cover-up straight. I was released from paid leave last month, and in exchange for my letter of resignation, I got a letter of commendation put in my file. I signed the usual confidentiality statements, collected my last paycheck, and presto, became a private citizen. But as someone wisely said, "You are who you were," and who I was, was John Corey, NYPD, ATTF, and DSG. Have gun, will travel.

"John?"

"What did Max tell you?"

"He wasn't sure of your current status." She hesitated, then said, "He did say that your wife has transferred to DC."

"It was a great opportunity."

"It must have been."

I didn't reply.

"Are you thinking about relocating to DC?"

"No."

We sat in silence, looking out at the bay. It's best not to discuss your troubled marriage with a former girlfriend. You don't want to give her the idea that you have regrets about what happened or that you want to reconnect. I asked, "So . . . what can I do for you? Or vice versa?"

"I guess my one minute is up."

"Can't you see I'm busy?"

She smiled, then said, seriously, "Are you . . . chilling out, or . . ." she pointed to the Glock in my pocket ". . . hiding out?"

"You know I don't hide."

"Do you have reason to believe you are the target of a person or persons who would harm you?"

"Other than you?" We both got a laugh at that and I asked, "Does that cabin cruiser look suspicious to you?"

"No. But maybe I shouldn't be sitting so close to you."

I smiled, then asked, "Do you have any specific information for me?"

"No, but I would advise you to keep your doors locked." She added, "If I were here to kill you, you'd be dead."

"For sure one of us would be dead," I agreed.

"I'll ask Max to have a Southold PD do a drive-by on a regular basis."

"Not necessary," I assured her.

"If you change your mind, my cell number is the same, as you'll see when you pick up your messages."

I actually still had her number in my phone. "Okay. So . . . is that the business?"

"No. Max asked me to deliver a message to you."

Max, of course, could deliver it himself. I asked, "When did you talk to Max?"

"Last night." She added, "We had dinner."

Max is sort of a ladies' man and I asked her, "Are you seeing him?"

"No. We have a professional relationship."

"Right." Same as I had with Robin, Beth, Kate, and Tess before I had sex with them. I need to stop doing that.

On that subject, Beth asked me, "What ever happened to your DSG partner? Bess?"

"Tess." Sounded like a loaded question. "Don't know. You seeing anyone?"

"No. Okay, let me ask you—"

"Do you still have that weekend cottage out here?" The one where we used to screw our brains out?

"I do. So—"

"Probably worth a million bucks now," I said.

"Not quite. So, are you—?"

"You get many murders out here?"

"I'm considering one right now."

"Rage is one of the seven motives for murder, as we both know. Jealousy is another. There's a thin line between love and hate."

She glanced at her watch. "I need to get back to Yaphank."

Yaphank is a small town with a weird name—American Indian, I guess—about thirty miles west of here, where Beth works out of Suffolk County Police Headquarters. She is a detective sergeant in the twenty-person Homicide Squad, making her second-in-command after the lieutenant who runs the show. Not bad for a young woman working in a traditionally male job. Not to mention a job that can do things to your head after seeing your first dozen murder victims. I guess that's what we had in common.

Anyway, Beth lives in Huntington, a town about thirty miles farther west of Yaphank, so she probably stayed in her nearby cottage last night. With Max? I asked, "What brings you out here?"

"I came here to check on my place and have dinner with Max. He mentioned that you were out here, and he asked me to deliver a message to you. That's why I'm here."

"Okay, I'm ready to receive a message."

"Good. First, let me ask you, are you officially unemployed?"

"As of last month."

"Are you looking for work?"

"Not with Chief Maxwell."

"It's not with Max."

"Good. But I'd take a position with the county PD as your superior officer."

"Not in this lifetime."

"Okay, what's the deal?"

"Here's the deal—just listen. Max knows a guy, Steve Landowski, who I know slightly, and who is a former Suffolk County detective. Steve now owns a private investigation firm near Riverhead called Security Solutions. One of Steve's PIs is a retired NYPD detective named Lou Santangelo, who you might remember."

"I do. We worked Missing Persons together."

"Lou thinks you were the best detective he ever worked with, and he would be honored if you'd consider a job with Security Solutions." She added, "Steve Landowski would love to speak to you about a position."

Well, I didn't see that coming. John Corey, private eye. "I don't think so."

"Why not?"

"I'm exploring other opportunities."

"There are no other opportunities." She reminded me, "You have a three-quarter NYPD disability—"

"That's for pay purposes. I am one hundred percent physically fit, as you may remember."

She ignored my innuendo and continued, "You can never return to the NYPD with a three-quarter disability. If you wanted to be a cop again, the best you could hope for would be a small-town deputy police chief in some upstate burg in the middle of nowhere surrounded by bears."

So she remembered my bear phobia. That's what happens when you confide your irrational fears to your wife or girlfriend. They use it against you. "I'm okay with bears now."

She stood and put her butt on the rail, facing me. We made eye contact and she said, "You will never get another job in Federal law enforcement."

"You don't know that."

"I know *you*. You don't play well with the Feds. You buck authority, and you don't like rules and regulations."

This was all true. Cops say that FBI means "fabulously boring individuals," and my time with them on the Anti-Terrorist Task Force and the Diplomatic Surveillance Group was a study in culture clashes. The Feds didn't appreciate my direct NYPD approach to a problem or my politically incorrect jokes about the world of Islam. All the NYPD people assigned to the ATTF had this attitude, but I think I was the ringleader. "What's the definition of a moderate Arab?"

"John—"

"A guy who ran out of ammunition." I admitted, "Working with the Feds was a challenge. But I'll have you know that I have several letters of commendation in my file."

"All of which will disappear if you try to reapply for a Federal job. They don't want you back, John. And you don't want to work with the Feds anyway."

"Not my first choice. But that's where the action is, and I can adjust—"

"You want to be a cop again. And this—working with PIs who are mostly former cops—is as close as you can get to that." She added, "Locker room talk, sexist attitudes, hard drinking—"

"Where do I sign?"

"And very little supervision or chain of command."

"Okay, I get all that. But—"

"And you'll be your own man." She looked at me. "Max thought this would be perfect for you." She added, "And it could be profitable. Some of these guys do okay if they get the right clients." She let me know: "I dated a PI once—former Suffolk County detective. He drove a Mercedes."

"Probably borrowed it for dates."

"Do me a favor and Max a favor. Just go talk to these guys."

"Do me a favor and tell Max thanks but no thanks."

"Tell him yourself." She slid her butt off the rail. "I have to go." She slipped into her shoes.

I asked, "You on duty?"

"I am."

"Time for lunch?"

She hesitated. "I'll take a raincheck."

I stood. "Dinner tonight?"

"I have a . . . meeting."

"Okay." I let her know: "I have to clear out of here by July one. My uncle rented the place for the summer."

She didn't reply.

"I'm heading back to the city." Gee, I wish I had a cottage out here where I could spend the summer instead of staying in the city.

"Good luck, John." She extended her hand and I took it.

I said, "Even if I wanted to take this job, I couldn't make the commute from Manhattan every day."

"You could rent something here."

"Summer rentals are crazy expensive out here. And my Manhattan condo"—which was signed over to me by Robin, my financially successful defense-attorney ex-wife—"costs a fortune to maintain. But thanks for—"

"Why don't you go talk to these people? If you get the job, which you will . . . maybe we can work something out with my cottage." She added, "It has two bedrooms, as you may or may not remember."

There you go. Eventually, you get there. We made eye contact again and I said, "Thanks."

"You'll call them?"

Thinking with my dick now, I replied, "I will."

She pulled a business card from her pocket and handed it to me. "That's the office number. The receptionist is Amy. She'll expect your call. Ask for Steve or Lou."

I put the card in my pocket with my Glock.

She suggested, "Call Max first. He'll brief you about Security Solutions."

"The last time I did Max a favor, I almost got killed."

"That was your own fault."

Empathy is not Beth's strongest trait. At least she didn't remind me that I almost got her killed too. Beth is a class act.

"You go off on your own, half-cocked, the way you did with the Russian case, which also almost got you killed. Do you see a pattern?"

"Now that you mention it."

"At least with a PI agency, you won't be involved in dangerous situations."

"That's not a selling point."

"Tough guy." She looked at me. "Call me. Let me know how it works out."

"Will do."

"I'll let myself out."

We did a quick, former-fornicators hug, then she turned and went back in the house, calling out, "Keep your phone with you, Detective."

I wouldn't want to work for *her*.

I looked out at the bay, where a sailboat disappeared into a rain squall. I recalled something the late Tom Gordon once said to me: "A boat in the harbor is a safe boat. But that's not what boats are made for."

John Corey, private investigator. Sort of a safe harbor, but I wasn't made for that. Maybe, though, this job came with benefits. A little cottage in the country. Maybe the rekindling of an old flame.

But a man can't swim in the same river twice, because it's not the same river and he's not the same man.

I need to think about this.

CHAPTER 3

I stood at the rail with my beer and recalled that day seven years ago when Police Chief Sylvester Maxwell appeared on this porch to tell me about the murder of Tom and Judy Gordon and asked me if I would assist him in the investigation. The Southold Town PD had about sixty personnel, and even a few detectives, but they didn't have a John Corey. The township, Max told me, had approved a hundred-dollar-a-day consulting fee. I'd laughed at the money and feigned no interest in the case, but in truth I guess I was flattered, bored, and ready to get off my convalescing ass and put my detective skills to work. I had no idea, of course, that I would be sailing into a shitstorm. Well, maybe I did. I actually like shitstorms.

And now, all these years later, Detective Beth Penrose shows up on this same porch with another, perhaps more lucrative job prospect from Chief Maxwell. This time I didn't have to *feign* no interest. I had zero interest in becoming a private investigator. Not that PI work is beneath me—it's an honorable profession. But for John Corey, this would be like a rock star taking a gig in a piano lounge.

Also, it did not escape my notice that Max had sent my former lover in his place. Why? Maybe he was busy, or maybe he knew that Beth could be more convincing. Or maybe Beth, on hearing about this job from Max, had actually *asked* to be the messenger. Why? Maybe she wanted to reconnect. Or maybe she got perverse pleasure out of visiting unemployed ex-boyfriends.

Now and then, however, things are as they appear: People who cared about me were acting in my best interest. Which I can do for myself, thank you. And what was in my best interest? Well, I needed a summer job, a summer house, and summer love, so maybe this could work. But probably not.

It was time for my morning swim, so I went down to the swimming platform, a sort of floating dock, stripped down to my tighty-whities, and dove in.

The water was cold on this first day of summer, but it cleared my head, allowing me to think rationally. My first thought was that if Max had come to me instead of Beth, the conversation would have lasted the allotted one minute.

I swam out toward the cabin cruiser, whose name I could see now—*Dilly Dally*. The four Russian SVR agents were pretending to be angling for fluke and flounder while they discussed how to kill or kidnap me. Make my day, assholes.

Meanwhile, my phone was in the kitchen and my gun was on the swimming platform. If anyone was really looking to pop me, I was a sitting duck. Why do I tempt Fate? That's what Beth wanted to know, and what Dr. Wilkes— the FBI shrink—asked me. Doctor Wilkes concluded that I had a subconscious death wish, which I do not, and he totally missed that I was a danger junkie, addicted to risk and peril.

Aside from my personal needs, my past government careers—NYPD, ATTF, DSG—were important to society and to the country, and I always had the satisfying sense that I was part of a team guarding the ramparts of civilization against the barbarians at the gates.

PI work wouldn't do that, and it wasn't usually dangerous—except when you were on a matrimonial case and the husband who you caught with the girlfriend came at you with a blunt object.

Anyway, my options for suitable employment were narrowing, so maybe I should consider this offer, which may come with housing for me and a weekend room-mate. Very nice of Beth to offer. I, of course, would offer to pay, or do some work around the house, or let her take sexual advantage of me. You gotta earn your keep.

I swam for about half an hour in the buoyant salt water, then, mind and body refreshed, I headed back to shore.

———

Back in the house, reunited with my clothes, gun, and cell phone, I popped open a can of Budweiser and heated a can of Hormel chili. Spoon or fork? Spoon.

I sat at the table in the bay window of the old farm-style kitchen and ate and drank as I checked my messages.

There was a text from Tess, asking how I was doing. This was not an idle question. We had both seen things on the Russian case that the CIA didn't want us to see, and done things that the SVR wanted us to pay for. So Tess and I check in now and then to see if we're alive and well.

I replied to Tess: GREAT NEWS! I WON A TRIP TO MOSCOW FOR TWO FROM A TRAVEL AGENCY CALLED SVR! ARE YOU FREE TO TRAVEL NEXT WEEK?

There was also a text from Kate, asking if I was still in Mattituck or back at the NYC condo.

Kate, a lawyer and FBI agent, is careful never to explain or reveal too much in e-mails or texts—even to me, when we were happily married—so I had no idea why she was asking. Maybe she needed to let the process server know where to deliver the divorce papers.

I replied: I'M CURRENTLY AT BELLEVUE HOSP FOR PSYCHIATRIC EVALUATION. I'm sure I'll see that text at my divorce proceedings.

There were a few other texts, mostly junk, and one from Robin, also asking if I was still in Mattituck, and if so could she use my garage space in the condo. I thought she traveled by broomstick.

I replied: WAS THAT IN OUR DIVORCE SETTLE-MENT? NOT SURE OF MY SUMMER PLANS YET.

On to the e-mails. My condo board was voting on a maintenance increase due to rising blah, blah, blah. Maybe I could sublease my garage space to Robin.

I checked my voice mail and heard Beth's missed message: "Hello, John, I'm in the area and I'd like to stop by. Hope you're well. See you shortly."

So, Beth, Kate, Tess, and Robin. Coincidence? My lucky day? Great cosmic joke?

There were framed photos scattered around the kitchen, and I looked at one: me, my parents, and my brother and sister, along with my cousins, Harry Jr. and Barbara. We're all on the floating platform in swimsuits with the bay behind us. I look to be about fourteen. There is no bullet wound on my chest.

My parents are now in God's waiting room—Florida—and my brother, Jim, lives in Westchester County with his wife and two kids. My sister, Lynne, has relocated with her A-hole husband to the West Coast—wherever that is. We don't see much of each other, but we keep in touch and try to get together for Thanksgiving or Christmas, usually at Jim's house in the aptly named village of Sleepy Hollow.

My father had the idea of having a family reunion at

Harry's house this summer—what he called a Blast from the Past and what I call a Civil War Reenactment. This could actually be fun—if I forgot to tell my family that another family would be living here.

I got a Good Humor bar out of the freezer and went out on the porch and dialed Sylvester Maxwell.

This was Max's private cell and he answered, "Hey, John."

"You busy?"

"Yeah, I'm at a wine tasting, then my pedicure."

"Hate to interrupt that. Beth asked me to call you."

"Glad she got hold of you."

"She came by for a few minutes."

"Good. So what do you think?"

"I need more info."

"Okay. How about a few beers at Claudio's? Maybe dinner. Five o'clock?"

"Sounds good," I said.

"See you then."

I hung up and bit into my ice cream bar, which brought back memories of my summers here and also on the boardwalk at Coney Island. I had a fairly typical New York City childhood despite the city being on the verge of chaos and bankruptcy. Race relations were tense, street crime and drugs were rampant, organized crime was thriving, official corruption was entrenched, people were fleeing to the suburbs, and Wall Street was threatening to move to New Jersey. Even the NYPD—the Thin Blue Line—was tainted and demoralized. The Greatest City in the World was a shithole. But if you grow up in a graffiti-covered shithole, shit and graffiti seem normal. It was my two weeks out here every summer that made me realize there was another world outside the streets of New York. So when I graduated from my shit high school, did I come out here to live? No, I stayed in the belly of the beast and became a city cop. Target Blue, as we used to say. Go figure.

I finished dessert and went back inside to the big vestibule and climbed the staircase to Uncle Harry's den, a sunny room formed by the corner turret. I sat at his desk, checked the business card that Beth had given me, and fired up his computer.

Security Solutions Investigative Services had a website, but in the PI business, discretion and privacy are selling points, so that limits what you can advertise to potential clients. Apparently, though, you can show some anonymous testimonials, such as this: "I suspected my wife of cheating, but I didn't know how to prove it until a friend suggested Security Solutions. I met with the owner, Steve, and he spent an hour with me in his office, then called in one of his investigators, who took careful notes. A week later, I met with them again and they had all the evidence I needed that my wife was being unfaithful. Sincerely, L.K., East Hampton."

Another marriage headed for divorce court. Exhibit A: Photos of the Ram-it Inn. Exhibit B: Video of the suspected cheaters entering the hot-sheet motel. And so forth. Half the marriages in America end in divorce, and then there are the really unhappy ones.

The website had no photos, and it didn't list the names of the PIs, but it did give the name of the owner, Steve Landowski: a twenty-year retired Suffolk County detective, who Beth had said she knew slightly. The website also assured potential clients that all the agency's private investigators were licensed and bonded and were former law enforcement officers with experience, training, and extensive knowledge of the law regarding courtroom testimony. Also, investigators were prepared to travel anywhere. Maybe I should hire them to surveil my wayward wife in Washington.

Security Solutions, I saw, did not limit its scope to marital cases. They also offered a wider range of services, including background checks, workplace theft, drug use, missing persons, location and recovery of lost or stolen property, trial prep, and criminal investigations for victims who felt that the police were not making enough progress on their case.

When I was working Missing Persons—before I transferred to Homicide—I'd run into a few PIs who had been hired by victims' families to "assist" in the investigation. PIs are mostly former cops, so you give them respect, and you also respect the wishes of the victim's family. But unlike in crime novels or movies and TV shows, these cases for the most part are solved by old-fashioned police work. Not PIs.

So . . . is this what I want to do? Well . . . the marital cases could be fun. And certainly I had firsthand experience.

Anyway, as per the website, Security Solutions also did personal security, meaning bodyguards for people who need, or think they need, protection. And here the website did reveal a client's name—Billy Joel, a Long Islander, who used the protective services of Security Solutions at a Hamptons charity fundraiser.

Some distance down from protecting A-listers, S.S. also provided premises security—bouncers—for nightclubs and rowdy bars. And, knowing my former brothers in blue, I was sure there were nights when it was hard to tell the difference between the bouncers and the bouncees.

A lot of PI agencies had this side business of offering premises and personal security, and the PI firm acted as a sort of temp employment agency for retired and moon-lighting cops on a per-hour basis. So it appeared that Security Solutions was a full-service PI agency, filling a need in American society—like the original PI firm, the Pinkertons—that government didn't always provide. And making a few honest bucks along the way. God bless free enterprise.

Anyway, there was no mention that Security Solutions personnel had carry permits, but that was implicit. You wouldn't want your bodyguard armed with a Nerf gun.

And finally, this PI agency had in-house counsel, meaning a lawyer on the premises, which, theoretically, kept things honest. And I stress "theoretically."

Well, it seemed I was qualified to be a PI, except I'd need to take a test for a state-issued license, which would be like James Bond applying for a license to snoop.

Actually, I was overqualified for this job, but as they say on Broadway, "There are no small parts, only small actors."

I worked my way through the site, reading a few more unintentionally funny testimonials. The misspellings and similar grammatical errors made me suspect that my former colleague Lou Santangelo had written the testimonials himself with half a bag on.

As for contact information, they listed a phone number, an e-mail address, and a fax number, which were the same as on the business card that Beth had given me. But no street address, just a town, Riverhead, and a P.O. box. Apparently, Security Solutions did not want walk-in customers or drive-by shooters.

As for a fee schedule, the website stated: *Fees starting at fifty dollars an hour for security guards. Fees for other professional services and travel expenses vary. Bend over and spread your cheeks.*

It didn't actually say that; it said checks and credit cards accepted. More importantly, for those who wanted no paper trails, cash was good. Receipts on request.

So, I thought about all this. The professional life of a PI is not much different from the job that the ex-cop retired from: odd hours, unpleasant stakeouts and surveillances, court appearances, and sometimes an element of personal danger if, for instance, you were on bodyguard duty—or if you had a confrontation with that cheatin' husband.

And all of this without having the legal status of a sworn law enforcement officer or having the powers of arrest. On the other hand, as Beth pointed out, a PI agency would still look and sound like the locker room in a precinct house. If nothing else, these guys would talk the same talk as me, and we had all walked the same beat once.

As for the money, this could be a job you had to save up for, notwithstanding Beth's Mercedes-driving boyfriend. Fortunately, my three-quarter disability pension gave me a cushion. I'd actually be solvent right now if Robin hadn't generously signed over the big, expensive condo to me. I'd dump this albatross, but the women like it. Good south view from the balcony. Used to be able to see the Twin Towers. Also, it's a hassle to move.

I shut down the computer, went to the master bathroom, and showered off the salt water, then dressed for drinks with Max—khaki slacks, blue polo shirt, docksiders, pancake holster, and Glock—then returned to the den.

Uncle Harry had a nice library that I'd been using to expand my mind, and I found an appropriate book: a Nero Wolfe, the fat, reclusive armchair detective who grew orchids in his Manhattan brownstone. Nero Wolfe, like John Corey, drank beer and not wine, and he was a self-confessed genius, which I can relate to. As a kid, I loved these books until I realized that Nero Wolfe never got laid.

I sat in a comfortable leather armchair and opened *The Rubber Band*, which I'd never read, hoping to be inspired by Mr. Wolfe to work up some enthusiasm for private detective work. If this eccentric, orchid-loving fat boy could find purpose and fulfillment without sex or danger, why couldn't I?

Well . . . based on the past, there is hope for the future. No matter how routine an assignment I've ever had, danger seems to follow, and romance blossoms like adolescent acne.

The Gordon murders are a good case in point. And so was my last case with the Diplomatic Surveillance Group—a routine day of following some Russian diplomats that suddenly went literally nuclear.

My mother used to say that my middle name is Trouble. It's actually Aloysius (thanks, Mom), but she perceived early on that shitstorms and I seem to find each other.

So far, she's been right.

CHAPTER 4

I put on my blue blazer, slipped an extra mag in my pocket, bolted the kitchen door, and exited the house through the front door, which I locked behind me.

Beth's entry into the house had introduced some reality into my boredom-induced fantasies. Reality one: The Russian SVR had a contract out on me. Reality two: Islamic terrorists saw killing me as a portal to Paradise. I stepped off the front porch and walked toward my Jeep in the circular driveway, practicing situational awareness.

It occurred to me that I had an obligation to tell the couple who had just rented this house that I, the previous occupant, was the target of Islamic terrorists and Russian assassins. If the renters backed out, Uncle Harry would understand and reward me for doing the right thing by giving me the house for the summer. Maybe not.

I climbed into my vintage Jeep Grand Cherokee and hit the ignition, which did not detonate a bomb, so I should make it to Claudio's on time. I turned out of the driveway onto Great Peconic Bay Boulevard, a country road that was smaller than its name, then got onto Main Road and headed east toward Greenport, where Claudio's was located.

I turned on my radio, which could barely pick up NYC stations but could pick up Connecticut across the Sound, and I tuned in to a New London country-western station.

If you think you've got problems with a cheatin' spouse or lover, listen to some of this shit.

Anyway, I was more curious than I was interested in what Max had to tell me about Security Solutions. Why would he think I'd want the job? Well, I would soon find out. I passed through the quaint hamlet of Mattituck and continued on through farmland and vineyards. The full-time residents of the North Fork number about thirty thousand, probably less than the population of East 72nd Street. It was a weekday and not quite tourist season, so traffic was light.

This area of Long Island was settled not long after the Plymouth Rock landing, and the settlers came mostly from New England, not old England. This was according to Emma Whitestone, who was born here and had lived in the city for many years. She had come back here to find inner peace, but found me instead.

I passed through the historic hamlet of Cutchogue, where Beth had her cottage, and I tried to picture myself living there for the summer. But the picture, like the radio station, was not coming in clear.

I noticed a lot of American flags and other expressions of seasonal patriotism in anticipation of the July Fourth holiday. Actually, the folks around here tend to be patriotic all year long, in contrast, say the locals, to the glitterati and literati of the South Fork—the Hamptons. I don't believe that's true, but it shows that the two forks are separated by more than a body of water.

Anyway, if I took the PI job, I'd probably also get the guest room in Beth's cottage, and if I got that, would I also get Beth? Do I want Beth? Gotta think about all that.

I was deep in wine country now, with vineyards and wineries on both sides of the road covering the flat fields where Long Island potatoes grew when I was a kid. Personally, I think it would've made more sense to turn the potatoes into vodka, which is something I can drink. Screw the wine. Right?

I drove through the hamlet of Southold, after which the land between the Sound and the bay narrowed, so everything was more windswept, making it unsuitable for viniculture but apparently hospitable to big birds—like gulls who like to shit on cars. Which is why I never open my sunroof around here. No one shits on John Corey.

The country-western station faded out, and I found an NPR talk show probably called *Fall Asleep Behind the Wheel.* Two androids were having a discussion of a new exhibit at the Guggenheim. Kill me. I shut off the radio.

A half hour after I left Uncle Harry's house, I approached the village of Greenport, population about three thousand, an old fishing town in the throes of gentrification.

As for Sylvester Maxwell, I'd seen him twice since I'd been here: once for dinner and once for sundowners on my back porch. As brothers in blue, we'd bonded, but Max is acutely aware that our respective law enforcement careers have little in common, so he sometimes makes self-deprecating remarks about his job—like the crack about him being at a wine tasting followed by a pedicure.

Well, to be more charitable to him, his job might seem easy, but policing a gentrifying tourist area with a small force has its challenges, especially with the summer population and the wine-loving day-trippers from the city and from the Hamptons who, patriotic or not, tend to be egotistical assholes. And I was sure that it was those summer people from NYC—not the locals—who were the clientele of Security Solutions: the privileged rich, the obnoxiously famous, and the famously obnoxious, like artists, actors, and especially writers, along with their guests, retinues, and friends. Half a year of hell, according to Max, who complains that the autumn harvest season is getting just as crazy and crowded as the summer. The locals hate the invasion, though they like the money. But the money brings problems. And problems bring the need for Security Solutions. PI agencies were once unknown out here, but apparently, there are now clients.

Was this my fate? Hopefully not. But I'd listen to Max, because as every detective knows, listening to bullshit is part of the journey toward enlightenment. Beers help. Also, listening to Max was the first step toward a few drinks with Beth Penrose. If that's what I wanted. You don't know until you know.

CHAPTER 5

Claudio's Restaurant was at the end of Main Street at the foot of a long wharf that jutted into the bay. About twenty fishing and pleasure boats—big and small, sail and motor—were tied up, and I looked for the *Dilly Dally*, the Russian assassins' boat, but it wasn't there, which was disappointing. What is there to live for if no one wants to kill you?

The sun was still high on this longest day, the bay was calm, and squawking gulls soared in a cloudless sky. A few couples strolled hand in hand along the wide wharf, and I remembered doing that with Emma, Beth, Tess, and Kate. Though not at the same time.

Parking was ten bucks, which I handed over to a guy who should have been wearing a pirate hat. I could have tinned him, but I save my retired-NYPD ID for moving violations.

I exited the Jeep and walked toward Claudio's, a big two-story wooden building that began life as a whalers' and sailors' tavern about a century and a half ago. Max likes this place because they treat him like a celebrity. It's good to be the top cop in a small town.

I walked into the restaurant a few minutes past five, but Max was not at the bar. His pedicure must have run late. I stood at the rail and ordered a bottle of Bud from the barmaid.

The antique bar and liquor cabinets were imported

from somewhere, all mahogany, marble, and etched glass, very out of place in an old sailors' saloon but probably a big draw in the days when whale blubber was big money.

The barroom and restaurant were already half full, a mixture of locals and tourists. I recalled trying to pick up Judy Gordon at this bar, and I'd been making good time until her husband showed up. Anyway, it was the beginning of a warm friendship that ended with their double homicide. The things I've seen : . . and as we say, none of it can be unseen. But in their case, I also saw justice done—and it was done by me.

The barmaid, a forty-something blonde with hoop earrings and a ponytail, put a bottle of Budweiser in front of me. "Glass?"

"It comes in a glass."

She smiled.

I said, "I was in here the other night, and the barmaid said to me, 'If you lost a few pounds, had a shave and a haircut, you'd look all right.' And I said, 'If I did all that, I'd be talking to the chick at the end of the bar instead of you.'"

She laughed. "You live around here?"

"Aquebogue." I don't give personal info that could get into the wrong hands.

"What brings you here?"

"Meeting someone." I added, "Chief Maxwell."

"Yeah? He likes to sit at his table. He called. You wanna sit?"

"I'll wait." I asked, "What's your name?"

"Flo."

"Hi, Flo. I'm Jim. Chief Maxwell's emotional support coach."

She processed that, and since I was with the chief, or because I'm so charming, she stuck around. I said, "When

I was in here last time, there was a really big lady dancing on a table, and I said to her, 'Great legs,' and she smiled and said, 'Do you really think so?' And I said, 'Definitely. Most tables would have collapsed by now.'"

"You're funny."

"Right. So I think the chief was in here last night."

"Yeah."

"With his girlfriend."

"He's got lots of lady friends."

"I think I know this one. Kinda scrawny and maybe not so good-looking."

"No. This one was a looker."

I asked, "Did the chief keep her waiting, as usual?"

"No . . . he got here first."

"I'm glad he's listening to my advice. I hope he walked her to her car."

"No . . . she left . . . he stayed."

Well, it didn't sound like Max and Beth were sharing a bed. Also, Flo didn't know she'd been interrogated. And I didn't know why I cared if Max was banging Beth. Maybe I'm just nosy out of habit. Detective and all that.

Flo excused herself and moved down the bar to an arriving customer.

Or maybe Beth and Max's relationship *was* relevant. You don't know until you hear what the next person says.

And right on cue, Chief Sylvester Maxwell walked in wearing civvies similar to mine and looking like he'd had a long day.

Sylvester Maxwell had put on a few pounds over the years, but he still had a full head of wavy blond hair and a ruddy complexion. To me, he looked like a middle-aged frat boy, but the ladies found him attractive. Must be the gun and the shield—and the steady paycheck.

We shook and he said, "Sorry I'm late."

"You're a busy man."

"Yeah. Busy with bullshit."

"What're you drinking?"

"Let's go to my table."

"I like the bar."

"Chief of Police can't stand at the bar, John."

"Right. You're never off-duty."

"Tell me about it."

I threw a twenty on the bar for Flo, and I took my beer and followed Max to the restaurant side, a big sunny room with lots of windows looking out at the wharf and bay. The hostess smiled and waved to the chief as he led me to his reserved table in a corner, where he sat with his back to the wall so he could surveil the room. I sat opposite, and before I was settled in my chair, a young waiter scurried over. Max said to him, "I'll have an Amstel Light, Jason. Get my friend another Bud."

"No problem." He scurried off.

The next young waiter who says "No problem" or "You got it" gets my foot up his ass. Whatever happened to "Yes, sir"?

Max scanned the room and looked out the windows. You'd think it was *he* who had to worry about getting whacked. In fact, he asked me, "You carrying?"

I nodded.

He had no comment and asked, "How was it when you saw Beth?"

I feigned stupidity and asked, "What do you mean?"

"You know . . . you dumped her."

"She was too good for me."

"What does that make your wife?"

"Not good enough."

He smiled. "You know why I never married?"

"Because same-sex marriages weren't legal."

He smiled again. "No. Because if it flies, floats, or fucks—"

"Rent it."

"Right. Also, this job is hard on marriages. Cops, as you may know, have a high divorce rate." He added, "Too many temptations on this job. Easy pickin's."

I assumed he was talking about women and not bribes.

Jason brought the beers with a bowl of beer nuts, and Max said, "Thanks."

"No problem. You wanna see a menu?"

I replied, "If it's not a problem."

"No problem." Jason moved off.

Max and I touched beer bottles. He said, "It doesn't work even when both people are in law enforcement. Like you and Kate. What happened there?"

"Not sure, and don't want to talk about it."

But he did. "Maybe she felt she was in an unequal relationship. Like she's an FBI agent with a law degree. And you're just ex-NYPD. But then you became a superstar at the ATTF, and she resented that."

"I think it had more to do with me leaving the toilet seat up."

He continued, "To the NYPD detectives in the ATTF, you were a hero. Bucking the Feds, giving the FBI shit, speaking your mind, and getting the job done. Maybe she was jealous. And maybe your attitude was hurting her career."

"Max, if I did a postmortem on all my failed relationships, I'd be in therapy most of the week."

"It's important to know what happened."

What happened was that Kate got involved—sexually, emotionally, or both—with her FBI supervisor, Tom Walsh, who had also been my ATTF boss. Why? Don't know, don't care. Not my circus, not my clowns. I said, "Well, if my next relationship doesn't work out, maybe it *is* me. Let's talk about Security Solutions."

"Okay, but first tell me what happened with that Russian case."

That went down in Southampton—the South Fork—and thus was out of Max's jurisdiction and way beyond his need to know, but he knew something. Maybe from Beth, who should know better. "I'm not at liberty to even acknowledge that there *was* a Russian case."

"Okay . . . but why aren't you still with the Diplomatic Surveillance Group?"

Obviously, he'd spoken to Beth. "Not at liberty to discuss."

"You wanna know what I think?"

"No, but I'm about to find out."

He looked at me. "Based on a few things you said and what I've heard, Kate's boss, Walsh, who was also your boss, hated you, and the feeling was mutual. So maybe Walsh—and maybe Kate—got you transferred from ATTF to DSG so you'd be out of their way but still employed by the Feds, where they could keep you under the eye and busy and with no loss of pay—which Kate would want. Then, after Walsh got himself and Kate transferred to Washington, he got you fired from DSG." Max added, "A final fuck-you."

Max is smarter than he looks, and he's been on the job long enough to put things together and come up with plausible scenarios and insights. But I'd never tell him that. I replied, "I actually resigned."

"I'm sure you were complying with a request to—"

"Also, Max, I resent your suggestion that my wife engaged in a conspiracy with our boss to get rid of me. Your

analysis doesn't fit the facts." Well . . . maybe from a distance, it could appear to an outside observer that this is
what happened. It may have crossed my mind too.

But that presupposes that Kate Mayfield and Tom
Walsh—two FBI nerds—would be bold enough and creative enough to come up with such a plan. I mean, those
two would report themselves if they took a box of paper-
clips home by mistake. And intraoffice adultery is a career
buster in the FBI. On the other hand, lust has no rules. As
for Kate . . . don't know. She claims her relationship with
Walsh is not romantic, and she has her own apartment in
DC, which looks good for appearances and also for the
FBI Office of Professional Responsibility. The problem,
she says, is not Walsh. The problem is me. Well, of course
it is. And yet she hasn't filed for divorce. I should file
while I'm unemployed and see if I can get alimony.

Max finished his Amstel Light. "Sorry if I offended
you. But a guy like you will do okay, professionally and
romantically." He assured me, "Women are like buses—
there'll be another one along in fifteen minutes." He
asked, "Hey, what happened to that DSG lady you were
involved with?"

Max could know about Tess only from Beth. I wished
I'd been a fly in the clam chowder at last night's dinner.
"She joined a convent."

He laughed. "You do that to women."

"Right." Or they get on with their lives and careers, as
Robin did and Beth did. And as Kate was doing. And as
I'm sure Tess will. Meanwhile, Max needed to get on with
his pitch so I could get home and watch "Swamp People."
I prompted, "So, Security Solutions. You're on, Max."

"Okay . . . but you should know that I think Beth is
interested in you."

I had no reply.

"That's why she wanted to pitch the PI job to you. To see you."

Was he baiting me? Or fishing? "She told me you asked her to deliver the message to me."

"Yeah . . . I did."

Jason came over with two menus and announced, "The special tonight is fresh-caught flounder."

Max, without looking at the menu, said, "Catch me a cheeseburger, rare, with fries and another round."

"You got it."

I glanced at the menu, which had gone upscale and foodie from my last visit a few years ago. "I'll have the same. If it's not a problem."

"No problem." Jason headed for the kitchen.

Chief Maxwell observed, "You got some bad hands dealt to you, John, and yet you want to get back into the same game." He looked at me. "You got to know when to hold 'em and when to fold 'em."

"You're losing me, Max." But not really.

"You got screwed by the Feds. But they did you a favor. These law enforcement jobs—Federal, state, local—come with some perks, privileges, and prestige, but not with a lot of dough. If you go private, you can do better." He added, "The best revenge is living well."

I didn't reply, but I thought of Robin, who was once a prosecutor for the city, making peanuts with her law degree. I'd met her on the job when I was working Homicide and she was doing God's work, putting criminal scum behind bars. Then the Devil—a well-known criminal defense attorney named Richard Shlofmitz—noticed her in court and was attracted to her legal genius and probably her ass, and he made her an offer she couldn't refuse. Needless to say, I wasn't happy about my wife switching sides and defending the felons I was trying to put away. And neither were my brothers in blue. If you asked me to put a price tag on selling your soul, I'd say about four hundred thousand dollars a year, which was what Robin was making defending criminals.

Max was saying, "Aside from good money, there wouldn't be any politically correct bullshit like I have to put up with."

"You want those beer nuts?"

"No." He continued, "Politicians up my ass every day. Civilian groups second-guessing everything I do. Media assholes snooping around. They should all spend a day in my shoes." He took a chug of beer. "Sometimes I think I should pack it in. I have over twenty-five years on the job."

"You could get a gig with Security Solutions."

"Not the worst thing."

"But then when you walked into a place like this, you'd have to wait for a table and pay for your beers like everyone else."

"I always pay for everything."

"Did you pay for parking?"

"No . . . I'm on duty."

"Good. Your expense account can buy me dinner."

He circled back to the revenge theme, which he saw as a Corey motivator. "Whoever screwed you in Fedland will be jealous that you're free of the government bureaucracy and bullshit and making more money than them by taking your skills to the private sector."

Before I could reply, Jason brought the beers, and Max asked him, "You catch that cow yet?"

"Sorry, Chief, the kitchen is shorthanded tonight."

"That's because I have half of them in jail."

Jason forced a smile and ran off to check on our order,

and Max returned to his advice about revenge and living well.

Revenge in my world is up close and personal. Living well is something else. I asked, "Whose bright idea was this?"

"Your former NYPD colleague Lou Santangelo. I was at a retirement dinner for a Suffolk PD captain, and your name came up."

"How and who?"

"Can't remember. I think Santangelo. Telling stories about his days with Missing Persons."

"What was Santangelo doing there?"

"He was there with Steve Landowski, the guy who owns Security Solutions." He explained, "Security Solutions goes to lots of police functions. Good for business. Landowski has good contacts in the Suffolk PD. Santangelo in the NYPD. They got a guy, Chip Quinlan, who was also NYPD. And they got a new guy, Joseph Ferrara, who is former Nassau County PD." He added, "They all have good contacts at their former jobs. They're plugged in."

"Good. But Lou Santangelo's bulb burned out a long time ago."

He ignored that and said, "The smart PIs show their faces at retirement and promotion parties. And funerals. Stuff like that." He assured me, "You'd enjoy all that."

"Love funerals."

He continued, "As you know, almost all PIs are former cops, and they treat the police with respect and vice versa. All that stuff in books and movies about the smart PI who butts heads with the dumb police chief or the clueless detective is bullshit."

"You ever read Nero Wolfe?"

"Yeah . . . I think."

"Wolfe and his sidekick, Archie Goodwin, were never cops, and they're always butting heads with the police. Especially with Inspector Cramer, head of Manhattan Homicide, and Lieutenant Rowcliff, who's a real asshole."

"Yeah, but that's not the way it really is. So—"

"So my name came up, and you said you knew me—small world—and Lou Santangelo said, 'What's he doing now?' and you said, 'Day drinking,' and Lou said, 'We'll take him on for a hundred Gs a year.' And you said, 'I'll talk to him.'"

"They didn't mention money. You need to talk to them."

"Are they expanding into counterterrorism?"

"No, but—"

Jason appeared with the burgers, apologizing for the delay.

I assured him, "No problem. You got ketchup?"

"You got it."

"Where?"

"I'm on it." He hurried off.

Maybe I should see this postverbal babble as an expression of old-fashioned American can-do. "No problem." "You got it." "I'm on it." And my favorite—"It's all good." Even when it isn't. Optimism is good.

Max was tucking into his burger and fries with gusto, but without ketchup.

I looked around the room. It was filling up, and I tried to imagine this place a hundred and fifty years ago, without electricity, and without Jason, filled with seafarers—men without cell phones who risked their lives to pull a living out of the unforgiving sea. I could imagine an old whaler standing at the bar with a nineteenth-century Jason who was worried about his future, and the whaler puts his hand on the boy's shoulder and says, "Whale blubber. That is the future, my boy," and Jason replies, "I'm on it."

"You thinking about what I said?"

"No."

Jason delivered my vegetable course, the ketchup. "Enjoy!"

"I'm on it."

Max continued his pitch. "PI agencies are about connections. Police connections, political connections, court connections. People who can do you favors and who you can do favors for in return." He added, "It's a world of networking."

"I know that, Max."

"As for the clients—where the money comes from—it's no different than any business. Satisfied customers. People who'll recommend you to their friends."

I bit into my burger. Good beef, good cheese, good bun. "It's all good."

"Good." He continued, "PI agencies are for the most part problem-solvers. People who *have* money fix problems *with* money. They need a fixer. Sometimes they need things to go away. Sometimes they just need answers. Like, is my wife or girlfriend banging the tennis pro?"

"The answer is yes."

"Yeah. If you ask the question, you know the answer. But you need to document it. The average schlub tries to play detective and get the goods on his wife or girlfriend, and usually he steps on his dick or gets himself hurt. But the guy with the bucks hires somebody else to do it— ex-cops with lots of experience. Private investigators."

"Max, just tell me what Santangelo said. Please."

"Okay . . . It was actually Steve Landowski. He wants to add a superstar to his letterhead. Basically, he wants to use your name and your résumé—John Corey, former

NYPD detective, medals and honors, wounded in the line of duty, Anti-Terrorist Task Force, top security clearance, Diplomatic Surveillance Group, former adjunct professor at John Jay College of Criminal Justice."

Even I was impressed.

"He also wants you for your connections to the NYPD and the FBI."

I didn't reply.

"Landowski is a bit of a wheeler-dealer, to tell you the truth, and he has a new bright idea every ten minutes. So he's convinced himself that John Corey can bring value to his business, and I think he's willing to pay for it."

"So I shouldn't tell him that I'm on the FBI's Do-Not-Resuscitate List."

Max looked at me. "That's up to you, John. Or you could say nothing and let him believe what he wants."

"That's not the way I work."

"Yeah, I know. But don't undersell yourself. You must still have good contacts in the NYPD and other law enforcement agencies that you worked with over the years."

"My police contacts were helpful when I was chasing terrorists. Don't know if they'd be as helpful if I was a private investigator."

"You know they would."

"Okay. Anything else from Landowski?"

"He's enthusiastic. He's willing to accommodate you. He says he'd understand if you didn't want to do routine fieldwork. He needs someone in the office who can examine the cases, talk to potential and existing clients, give advice and supervision to the guys in the field, and show up at events."

I pictured myself a year from now—three hundred pounds, growing orchids in the office.

"You could work in the field on any case that interested you. You'd report directly to Landowski."

"That's it?"

"That's all I remember. You need to talk to him. Go see his operation." He added, "His offices are in a big old farmhouse." He smiled. "They call it Animal House."

I didn't see that on their website.

Max said, "I was there a few times."

"Professionally?"

"Whatever."

I didn't pursue that and finished my beer.

Max remembered something else. "Lou Santangelo. He wants to have a beer with you and catch up. Talk about old times on the job." He added, "And your bachelor days together."

I doubted if either of us could recall anything that happened after Happy Hour ended. I asked Max the obvious question: "What's in this for you?"

Max seemed prepared for the question. "I owe you a favor. For the Gordon case."

"Can't you just send me a bottle of Scotch?"

Max smiled. "If you just go talk to Landowski, I'll do that." He admitted, "I kinda promised to deliver you, so do me this favor, and if you should ever need a favor from me, I'm here for you."

"Thank you, Godfather."

He smiled again, then said, "Beth thinks this would be good for you."

I didn't reply.

"She says you have to vacate your uncle's place by July one." He looked at me as though he had good news. "But if you take this job, I think she'll offer to share her cottage with you until after Labor Day, when you can afford a place of your own out here. Or go back to your uncle's place."

"Max, I don't need free housing. I have a luxury condo in the city."

"Hey, Sherlock, she could be offering you more than free housing."

"Really?" Well, apparently Max and Beth were not sleeping together, but if they were, the cottage could get crowded. I guess if I was interested in the job—or in Beth—I should say something positive that Max would pass on to Landowski and/or Beth. But I didn't need Sylvester Maxwell to play Godfather or Cupid, so I said, "I'll call you tomorrow."

"I'll tell Landowski you're thinking it over."

"Right."

"This could be a whole new life. Get rid of the expensive place in the city. Live here. Be happy."

"Right. From the city that never sleeps to the town that never wakes up."

"That's changing. We're getting more lively." He smiled.

"I've been here in the winter. The zombie apocalypse looks more lively."

"I like the winters. Quiet."

Jason came over and asked, "Coffee? Dessert?"

I replied, "Not for me, and I'll take the check."

Max said to him, "Leave the check open. I'm staying. Another Amstel."

"You got it." He dashed off.

Max said, "This is on me." Before I could stand, he said, "One more thing. If you go see Landowski, or speak to him on the phone, don't mention Beth's name."

"Why?"

"Don't know. She asked." He speculated, "Maybe something between them on the job."

Beth had said she knew him only slightly. But sometimes that's all it takes.

Max added, "I think Landowski just has a problem with women on the job."

"Okay. If I ever speak to Steve Landowski about a job, I'll be sure not to use Beth Penrose's name as a personal or professional reference."

"Give her a call."

I didn't respond. I stood and Max stood. We shook. I said, "Thanks for dinner."

He surprised me by saying, "Thanks for your service to the country, John. You did good. Now you should do something good for yourself. You deserve it."

I made my way out of the crowded restaurant and into the cool night air. The sun was setting into a fiery red sky, and it was party time on the big boats. People were out and about on Main Street and on the wharf, walking, fishing, violating the open-container law, and living fairly normal lives. The streetlights came on, which was Little Johnny's signal to go home.

I walked onto the wharf, where the pirate was still collecting ten bucks, found my Jeep, and drove it onto Main Street. I navigated through the small town and was soon on Route 25, in dark, open country, heading west toward my home away from home. Out of habit—and training—I pulled my Glock from the pancake holster and put it on the center console as I checked out my rear and sideview mirrors.

Well . . . on the surface, it looked like everyone would be happy if I took the job: Beth, Max, Landowski, Santangelo . . . and maybe me. Everyone wins.

And I'd be in a job where my reputation was appreciated—instead of 26 Federal Plaza, where it wasn't.

In a way—as Beth had said—I'd be home again.

Or was that a time and place—like Uncle Harry's house in past summers—that could never be relived?

As for revenge and living well, Max was projecting his own mind-set. Kate Mayfield and Tom Walsh would not be jealous to hear that John Corey was a private investigator, even if I was driving a Mercedes. You had to live and work with the Feds to understand their arrogance and superior attitudes.

Max was right about one thing—I had to do what was good for me.

Lots to think about. But first, "Swamp People." No P.C. bullshit on *that* job.

CHAPTER 6

Good episode of "Swamp People." But I'd like to see a spinoff called "Gators' Revenge."

I'd fallen asleep reading *The Rubber Band* and had a weird dream that Nero Wolfe was fat-shaming me, which motivated me to skip the pizza rolls for breakfast and go for a run. So I put on my belly band, which held my cell phone and Glock, and did a two-mile run on the surrounding country roads, hoping to run into at least one Russian assassin. But no luck. There's never a killer around when you need one. Anyway, during my run, I made the decision to call Security Solutions for a future appointment—like maybe next year.

Back in the kitchen, over coffee, I made the call, and the receptionist, Amy, seemed excited to hear from me. We chatted a few minutes, and she asked if I could come in at 10:30.

"Today?"

"Yes. I'll clear Steve's calendar."

"I'll have to cancel my pedicure."

She laughed, then gave me the address of Security Solutions and said, "See you at ten-thirty."

I hung up. Well, this would make Max and Beth happy. Me, not so sure.

I pulled up my cell phone messages.

A text from Robin said: YOU CAN PARK YOUR

JALOPY ON THE STREET. IT LOOKS LIKE A DUMPSTER.

Did she talk like that to her Mafia clients? I replied: I'LL LET YOU KNOW TOMORROW IF I'M STAYING HERE OR COMING BACK TO NYC.

Actually, I was fairly sure I'd be out of here June 30, but I didn't know where I was going.

Tess texted: YOU WON'T BELIEVE THIS, BUT I JUST WON THE SAME TRIP TO MOSCOW FROM THE SVR TRAVEL AGENCY. I'M EXCITED.

I replied: I HAVE A CONFLICT NOW. CIA INVITED ME TO A SECRET BRIEFING IN REDACTED. I LEAVE TONIGHT. ENJOY MOSCOW.

Tess and I are really into this dark humor. I mean, what's funnier than joking about people who want to kill you? You gotta laugh. Right?

Anyway, no text or e-mail from Kate, which is how she sends me a message. And the message is: YOU'RE NOT FUNNY. When they stop laughing at your jokes and move to another city with another guy, you know your marriage has some problems.

There were a few e-mails, including a summer-themed message from my mother, who is obsessed with me wearing sunscreen. When I went to Yemen to hunt down a terrorist, she reminded me to pack sunscreen.

I replied: *I have SPF 50 in spray, cream, and lotion. I'll call this weekend.* After I have two drinks.

Anyway, it was now 10 A.M., another sunny day, and I was in my green dumpster driving west on Route 25 toward Riverhead for my 10:30 meeting with Steve Landowski and maybe Lou Santangelo. Amy the receptionist wasn't sure about Detective Santangelo's whereabouts. Neither was I when I worked with him. I think he thought Missing Persons meant *be* one. No, Lou, it's *find* one.

Anyway, as with any job interview, you have to know how to dress. I guessed that the PIs working for Security Solutions dressed casually or wore assignment-appropriate clothing. But for a job interview, you wanted to make a good impression. Uncle Harry had left a lot of his late wife's clothing in the closet, and I considered Aunt June's blue cocktail dress. It always looked good on her, and I would explain to Steve and Lou that I was working undercover. Or maybe that I had recently self-identified as a party girl. Steve Landowski would thank me for my time and promise to get back to me, and Lou would not mention having that beer. This could work. But at the last minute I chickened out and put on my blazer and khakis and took my Glock out of Aunt June's handbag.

I continued west on Route 25, which passed through vineyards, tourist-priced farm stands, B&Bs, quaint shops and trendy restaurants, and now and then a newly planted field where green stuff grew. This place had one foot in its seafaring and agricultural past and the other foot in its touristy future. Could I live here? That was the question. In any case, I'd do Max the favor and go talk to Security Solutions, which would also satisfy Beth. Then, after listening to the deal from Steve Landowski, I could make an informed decision, which, after due consideration, was "No."

In fact, I had been thinking about global security firms, the modern equivalent of joining the French Foreign Legion. I'd already been to Yemen—the earth's anus—with the Anti-Terrorist Task Force, so I had combat creds, and a top-secret security clearance, and I could probably write my own ticket with a top global security company. The money was negotiable, the danger was manageable, and the overseas supervision was negligible. Have balls, will travel.

The downside—aside from the obvious risks of being

killed or kidnapped—was living in a shithole country. Another downside, as I saw in Yemen, was that the private security personnel had to interface with the CIA, whose arrogance made my arrogance look like Mr. Rogers. Plus, the CIA and John Corey had some scores to settle with each other. And on that subject, the Russian SVR—as well as various Islamic terrorist groups—would be delighted to discover that John Corey was out of the U.S. and working in Sandland or Shitland. Well, every job has a few problems. I'm on it.

So with my mind made up about Security Solutions and my résumé about to go global, I drove on.

Amy, who had a nice voice, had given me a description of the farmhouse if my GPS got confused, which Amy said it sometimes did around here. Look for a flagpole, she said.

I'd promised Beth and Max that I'd let them know if I was going to call Security Solutions, but Max, I was sure, had already heard from Landowski about my appointment, and Beth had surely heard that from Max, so neither of them needed to hear from me. I would, however, let them know I'd turned down the job and was exploring overseas opportunities.

As for Beth's offer of the extra bedroom in her summer cottage . . . well, that seemed to be connected to me working here. We'll see.

I continued on Route 25, and a road sign informed me that I was entering the Town of Riverhead, which meant I was leaving the Town of Southold—Max's bailiwick. I didn't know the Chief of Police here, so I slowed down, though basically I'm ticket-proof if I show my retired-NYPD ID. But if I show my retired-FBI creds to a cop, the fine is doubled. Just kidding. But maybe not.

My cell phone was in my cupholder and I punched

in the address that Amy had given me—10 Jacob's Path, Riverhead—and hit "Go." A male voice said, "Continue on Route 25." A voice in my head said, "Keep going until you get to Manhattan."

I mean, how did Max, Beth, Lou Santangelo, and Steve Landowski think I was going to work in a farmhouse in the middle of a frickin' potato field or wherever the hell this place was? Last time I saw Lou Santangelo, he'd never been east of Brooklyn Heights. I pictured him now in bib overalls, chewing on a piece of straw.

The guy in my cell phone told me to turn onto Route 58, then turn right onto Saw Mill Road. I wondered how he could see the road from the cupholder.

After a few minutes, I came to a fork in the road and the phone guy said bear right, like he'd been here before.

I was traveling north now, on Jacob's Path, toward the Long Island Sound, and the flat terrain spread out to the horizon. This was the end of wine country, and I could see that the agriculture around here was mostly shrubs and sod to supply landscapers and nurseries in the Hamptons and the NYC suburbs. I passed a pumpkin patch and a strawberry field, which, in the appropriate season, would be marked with signs that said: <u>PICK YOUR OWN!</u> Meaning you harvest someone else's stuff, then go pay for it. There's a sucker born every minute. Though I did pick strawberries once with Beth. The things you do when you're in heat.

My navigator announced that my destination was five hundred feet ahead on my right. I looked up the road and saw a large white two-story house surrounded by big trees, and as I approached, I saw an American flag fluttering on a tall pole on the front lawn.

The voice said, "You have arrived at your destination."

Wrong. This is just a detour before the expressway; a pit stop on the road of life.

CHAPTER 7

I pulled into the gravel driveway, which led to a grassy parking area on the side of the farmhouse, and stopped next to a black Escalade. I got out and saw that the other three vehicles were small rice-burners, and not a Mercedes in sight.

I surveyed my surroundings. Across Jacob's Path was a half-buried structure, like a bunker, with a rounded earthen roof and wide doors and which I recognized from my times out here as an old potato barn.

On this side of the road abutting the parking area was what looked like a strawberry field.

Behind the farmhouse I could see a small barn whose siding was aged to a silvery gray, and beyond the barn were rows of evergreens that would be expensive Christmas trees by December.

North of the farmhouse, at the end of a scraggly lawn, was a thick wall of hedges, about ten feet high, which probably marked the end of this property.

Well, this definitely had a different vibe from 26 Federal Plaza.

The air smelled of wildflowers and fresh earth, the sky was blue, and there wasn't a sound except the birds singing in the trees. A day like this makes me want to squeeze off nine rounds.

I looked at the big white clapboard house, which had a covered front porch. Above the porch was a surveillance camera pointed toward the road. I noticed another camera on this side of the house, pointing toward the parking area and me. I was sure the whole perimeter was covered.

Also mounted high on the house were security lights, which were probably activated by a photoelectric cell or by a motion detector after dark. Mr. Landowski was into security and surveillance.

The house itself looked in decent shape, but could have used a paint job. There was no PI shingle out front, and a potential client might wonder if he or she was in the right place. So would a prospective employee.

I adjusted my blue blazer and my attitude and walked up the porch steps to the front entrance, which was a steel security door with a keypad. There was an eyeball camera above the door, and I pushed the buzzer and got buzzed in.

The door opened into a large foyer, and ahead was a staircase and a wide hallway that led to the rear of the house, where I could see a kitchen. To the left were closed pocket doors, and to the right were open pocket doors that revealed what looked like the reception area. In fact, a young woman was coming around her desk, walking toward me.

She put out her hand and we shook. "Hi," she said, "I'm Amy Lang."

"John Corey." Amy was about mid-twenties, long blond hair, long legs, pretty face, nice smile, and big blue eyes. I was glad I didn't wear the dress.

"Thanks for coming. Steve's on a call."

"I can come back later." Maybe next year.

She escorted me into the reception area. "Have a seat." She indicated a black vinyl leather chair. "Can I get you anything? Coffee? Water?"

"No, thanks." I took a seat, and she surprised me by sitting across from me. Between us was a coffee table piled high with magazines and newspapers that looked like they'd come out of a recycling bin.

Based on Uncle Harry's house, this small room may have once been the front parlor or sitting room—a place where visitors were received. The furniture was cheap contemporary, and the floor was old wood planks. The walls were painted stark white, adorned with framed photos of what looked like local scenes—farms, vineyards, docks, boats, and so forth. Among the photos was a mirror; if it was a two-way mirror, there'd be a surveillance camera behind it.

Amy said, "I took those photos."

I asked, "Surveillance photos?"

She smiled. "We don't display those."

I looked at Amy, who was wearing a crisp blue-and-white-striped blouse, knee-length blue skirt, and sandals. Very nice smile. And nice voice. Local East End accent, which is best described as mellow, with a touch of New England.

"Do you have any questions while we're waiting for Steve?"

"Yes, what's a nice girl like you doing in a place like this?" Actually, I didn't say that. The other thing I was thinking was that Steve Landowski was not busy—he wanted me to suck up ten minutes of Amy Lang. I know how cops think.

"Mr. Corey?"

"Call me John."

"Okay. Any questions, John?"

"How long have you been with Security Solutions?" And are you sleeping with anyone here?

She seemed prepared to deliver her résumé. "I've been here two years, since I graduated from John Jay with a bachelor's degree in criminology."

"Congratulations." I added, "I used to teach at John Jay."

"I know that." She smiled. "I tried to get into one of your night classes, but they were always full."

Or she was full of shit. I returned the smile and almost said, "I give private lessons," but I said instead, "Small world."

She confessed, "I saw you once from a distance."

"Surrounded by admiring students?"

She smiled again and continued, "I've taken the NYPD entrance exam and scored well."

"I'm sure of that."

"I've been waiting for over a year to be called for my physical, psych test, and all that."

"Right." Then there's the PD investigator who does a background check, interviews with family and friends, and so forth. Then, finally, you get assigned to a class at the Academy. Amy would have had an easier time getting into law school, and I'm sure she knew that. It occurred to me that if I was applying to the NYPD today, I might not get past the psychological test. Or the family interviews. My mother would tell them, "He doesn't wear sunscreen."

"So," I said, "you're marking time here and getting some OJT."

She nodded. "Potential clients think I'm the receptionist. But I'm actually Steve's assistant, and his screener. I engage the prospective client in casual conversation. I try to get a feel for what type of person they are, how distraught or angry they are, what their appetite is for pursuing their problem—"

"Meaning how much can they afford."

She didn't respond and went on, "I try to determine which PI would be good for them, based partly on their particular problem and partly on their personality."

"Sounds like you may be overthinking the process." I let her know: "In a detective squad room, there's what we call a batting order, and who's up next catches the squeal."

She looked at me. "This is a service business," she said, then confided, "This is Steve's method."

The guy who has a new bright idea every ten minutes.

Amy further confessed, "I also interview potential employees."

"How am I doing?"

She smiled. "You're hired."

I changed the subject and asked, "Are you sure you want to be a cop?"

"I am sure."

"I would have thought that hanging around with all these retired cops would give you second thoughts."

"Everyone here has said that."

"Okay. Just checking."

Amy was used to being given unsolicited advice by older men and probably used to being hit on, so I changed the subject again and asked, "How many PIs work here?"

"Four full-time on the payroll, including Steve. We have dozens of contract and freelance people for surveillance, stakeouts, bodyguards, premises security, and whatever else comes up." She smiled again. "Lots of high school prom work this time of year."

"Like . . . white sport coat and a pink carnation?"

"Yes. Parents want moonlighting or retired cops to chaperone house parties, and drive. Stuff like that." She further explained, "To keep the kids from drinking and driving, drugs, drowning, fighting, and fucking."

The F-word sort of took me by surprise. "Did you have a cop at your prom?"

"I did. I got high with him and had sex. That's why I want to be a cop." She added, "Just kidding."

"I think you've been here too long."

"You may be right. But it's good training for the macho PD culture."

"Nothing will prepare you for that."

She smiled. "Any more questions?"

"Can I work the next prom?"

She smiled again. "Steve has bigger things in mind for you."

I didn't reply.

"Anything else you'd like to know about Security Solutions?"

"Why a farm?"

"Steve inherited it. No office rent, and he lives here. He can tell you about that."

"I think that's all I need to know. But let me ask you why someone referred to this place as Animal House."

"I have no idea. Never heard that before."

Which was bullshit.

She changed the subject. "So I'm sure you want to know about the other PIs here. You know Lou. There's also Joseph Ferrara—he prefers Joseph, not Joe—who joined us about six months ago. He's a former Nassau County detective. Great guy. And Chip Quinlan, NYPD retired detective. Like you. He's been here about four years." She continued, "We also have a legal consultant, Jack Berger, an older gentleman who works with our bookkeeper on billings. Jack is a lawyer." She added, "Disbarred."

"The best kind."

"That's what he says. There are also two full-time women—Judy and Kim—who are clerical."

"So no female PIs."

She hesitated, then replied, "We had one."

I sensed I shouldn't pursue that, and Amy continued,

"We sometimes need a female PI for certain situations, so if we don't have a female freelancer available, I take that job."

"Lou Santangelo would be happy to dress in drag."

She smiled. "You'll fit right in here."

As Beth had promised. I asked, "Are you a licensed PI?"

"No. But I can do some PI work under Steve's license. Sometimes, like, if he's doing a surveillance and he has to follow someone into a restaurant, then I'm his date. Or his wife. So he doesn't stand out."

"Right. You get overtime?"

"I get dinner."

"And some experience."

She nodded. "I've learned a lot. Like how to follow a cheating husband. Or boyfriend."

"That could come in handy someday." If it hasn't already.

"I hate those cases. They're soul-sucking . . . but they pay the bills." She looked at me, hesitated, then said, "You understand."

She seemed to have some knowledge of my marital status, probably from Landowski, who got it from Max. "I do."

"Sorry about your problem."

"No problem."

"Okay . . . So, I also do fieldwork with Lou and Chip now and then, but not Joseph yet." She looked at me.

I think I was supposed to say, "I look forward to being on a surveillance with you," or something like that. But, in fact, that was not going to happen. I did give Amy credit for being a good tease, though. She had a bright future. I asked, "You carry?"

"I have a permit." She added, "Smith & Wesson Bodyguard, fits in my purse. I hardly ever carry. Except on a date."

I smiled.

She looked at me. "Anything else you'd like to know about me?"

Did I say good tease? *Great* tease. I took the opening to ask, "Do you live around here?"

"I do. I live with my parents to save money. When I get the call to the Academy, I'm going to get an apartment in Manhattan and put these little-town blues behind me."

"Sounds like a plan."

"You live in Manhattan."

"I do."

"But you have a place out here."

"I do." Maybe.

"So there wouldn't be any commuting issues."

"Depends. Where's the closest subway stop?"

Amy laughed. Clearly she enjoyed my humor. She continued, "Most of our clients live in the city, but they have summer and weekend houses here on the North Fork or in the Hamptons, so your place in the city could make it easier for you to meet clients there if they wanted."

Amy—or Steve—had apparently thought about all the benefits that John Corey could bring to the job—if John Corey wanted the job, which he didn't. I replied ambiguously, "That's true."

"Good." She looked at me, and our eyes met. Talk about soul-sucking; you could drown in those liquid blue eyes. She said, "I know that Chief Maxwell has spoken to you about Security Solutions. Is there anything Max said that you'd like me to clarify before you speak to Steve?"

So, it's "Max," is it? That's interesting. And Max hadn't mentioned Amy Lang by name, or in any way—not even as an inducement for me to make this appointment. Max is the kind of guy who wouldn't tell you where the fish were running.

"John?"

"If you've heard from Max, then you might know that I had to be talked into coming here."

"Keep an open mind."

"I can't keep what I don't have."

She looked at me. "There's more here than meets the eye."

I didn't ask what that could be. Ducks? But I did ask, "Is Lou Santangelo here?"

"He'll be here soon. He wants to say hello."

I noticed that Amy didn't ask me for my résumé, or ask me the usual job interview questions, like "Why do you want to work here?" Or "Where do you see yourself in five years?" In fact, I was not here to be interviewed; I was here to be persuaded.

Amy understood this and said, "I almost turned down this job, but Steve said to hang out here for a few weeks. That was two years ago. So do me a favor and hang out for a few weeks. Then make a decision."

Well, Security Solutions might be a fun place to work. So is a carnival or a bordello. But neither looked good on your résumé—or your obit. In fact, this was sort of a happy dead end. I asked, "Why is this so important to Steve?"

"He's looking to step up his game, and you're part of that. He wants bigger and better clients and bigger and better cases."

"He might think about a better office."

She smiled. "We like it here. And it's close to the Hamptons and the expressway to Manhattan." She added, "Steve is thinking about opening a satellite office in Manhattan and maybe one in the Hamptons."

"Watch the overhead."

"Steve always says you have to spend money to make money."

Amy was obviously impressed with her boss. Or she was just being a loyal employee. Or she was sleeping with the boss. I can usually tell. But not always, as I found out the hard way. I asked, "Who belongs to the Escalade?"

"Not me." She looked at me. "I'm on straight salary, John. No extracurricular bonuses or benefits."

I nodded. "You'll make a good detective."

"I'm learning that detectives don't ask innocuous questions."

"Right. We trick people into confessing."

She smiled. "I'm sure I could learn a lot from you."

Well, yes. And maybe vice versa. But I don't work here and never will. I glanced at my watch.

Amy stood. "Let me see what's keeping him."

"Thank you."

She went out to the foyer and disappeared into the hallway.

Amy Lang was a pleasant surprise, and I was sure she earned her pay here, hooking prospective male clients and putting female clients at ease. Steve Landowski obviously understood sales and marketing. And Amy Lang understood public relations. It's a service business.

As for John Corey, he understood temptation. And what could be more tempting than just giving in and taking the job? I could picture me and Beth on the back patio of her cottage, sunbathing with a few beers. Also time at the beaches, maybe a little sailing or fishing, dinners at a few seaside restaurants. And a relatively stressless job here on the farm, a.k.a. Animal House. Plus, of course, beers with my colleagues after work, and maybe a business overnighter with Amy in the city. And, according to Max, Steve Landowski was willing to pay me for my résumé and my connections. Also, according to Amy Lang, there is more here than meets the eye. I doubted that, but my detective instincts were aroused by that statement.

Well . . . given a choice between all this and an overseas job in some disease-ridden shithole, the choice should be a no-brainer.

CHAPTER 8

While I waited for Steve to get briefed by Amy, I checked my phone messages. There was a text from Max: THANKS. I OWE YOU.

I texted: WE'RE EVEN.

A text from Beth said: CALL ME AFTER SECURITY SOLUTIONS. MAYBE WE CAN HAVE A DRINK.

Well, maybe we can. But we wouldn't be celebrating my new job.

I replied: SOUNDS GOOD. I'LL CALL LATER.

I realized that I still had feelings for Beth, so to keep my romantic options open when I saw her, I should say I was undecided about this job but seriously considering a blow job.

Meanwhile, I needed some alternate career options, so I e-mailed Dick Kearns, a former NYPD detective who worked with me on the Anti-Terrorist Task Force. Dick now owns Kearns Investigative Service, a company that does background checks for the FBI and other government agencies as well as for private corporations—including global security firms. Dick and I owed each other so many favors it was hard to keep track of who was at bat.

One benefit of working in law enforcement for over twenty years was that you were part of a network, a web—what we sometimes called The Wheel in the NYPD—and you only had to touch part of the web to get it sending signals to other parts.

I e-mailed Dick, asking him to reach out and get me some contacts with Blackwater-type firms. You don't always need to say why you want what you want, and sometimes you can't say, but in this case I told Dick I was looking for a high-paying job in Sandland or Shitland.

So Dick would reach out and, within a few days, get me what I needed. And if Dick's company happened to do the background checks for a firm I was interested in, Dick could verify to them that John Corey was a patriotic, solid, and sober citizen with a high security clearance, no financial or family problems, and certainly no mental health issues, and that Detective Corey had never been arrested, indicted, or incarcerated, and flossed daily. As for marital issues, Detective Corey's wife was an FBI Special Agent who fully supported his overseas career choice. And might even pay for his one-way ticket. Conclusion: No Negatives.

These global security firms didn't actually want to know too much, anyway, because they already knew that anyone who wanted that job was a head case.

As I was signing off with Dick Kearns, Steve Landowski strode into the room as though he was making a bust. "Hey! John!"

I almost put my hands up, but I stood instead.

"John! Really sorry I kept you waiting."

He thrust out his big hand and we shook.

"No problem," I assured him.

"Got tied up on a call. Sorry to make you spend all that time with Amy." He smiled, man-to-man.

Amy had not returned with him, so I said, "She's easy to talk to."

And right on cue, he replied, "And easy to look at."

"You got it." I should have worn the dress.

"She's unattached."

"I'm on it."

Landowski grinned. "Your reputation precedes you."

"You too."

Steve Landowski was a big guy with a big voice. He had sort of a square head, like he'd stuck it between the bars in his crib too many times, and his black hair was spiky, maybe evidence of a recent electric shock. If clothes make the man, Landowski needed a makeover. He wore an untucked Tony Soprano short-sleeve shirt whose color and pattern defied description. He had on black chinos and clunky brown work shoes, probably OSHA-approved.

"Thanks for coming, John."

"No problem, Steve."

"It's an honor."

"It's all good."

"Right. Hey, let me show you around."

"Not necessary. Let's get down to business."

"Take a minute."

He took my arm and steered me into the foyer and parted the pocket doors, which revealed what must have once been the living room and was now an open office area, crammed with messy desks, file cabinets, a copy machine, a fax, and tables piled high with papers. The walls were covered with bulletin boards, thick with notes, photos, memos, and Post-its. On one wall was a security monitor that showed four outside views. Also mounted on the wall was a surveillance camera that covered the office.

Landowski said, "This is the nerve center. This is where we run assignments for all our freelance PIs and our contract rent-a-cops." He added, "We're busy now because of graduations, weddings, and July Fourth parties coming up. Plus, city people are coming out to the Hamptons."

"Right." Among all this clutter were two middle-aged women at their desks, and Landowski called out, "Kim! Judy! This is John Corey. He's thinking about working with us."

The ladies smiled and waved politely, and I did the same.

He informed them, "John and Lou worked together at One Police Plaza. Missing Persons." He looked at me. "Right?"

Should I let everyone know that Lou Santangelo was the missing person at Police Plaza? No. I replied, "Right."

Landowski walked me toward the back of the long office and another set of pocket doors. Along the way, on the wall over the old fireplace, were three big grease-pencil assignment boards which showed client names, case numbers, location, the PI assigned to the case, and a column headed REMARKS, with words like SURVEIL-LANCE, COURT DATE, WIFE IN FLORIDA, and other cryptic notations.

This office looked like an old squad room before everyone had a computer on their desk. In fact, Land-owski said, "I still like paper. I like shit on the walls—charts, maps, photos, calendars."

"Take-out menus."

"Right. Computers are good, but they isolate the user and the information. People forget what they can't see. Shit on the walls is in your face."

I tended to agree with him, but later, when he was pitching me the job, I'd tell him his office should go paperless. Even the take-out menus.

When we were out of earshot of the ladies, Landowski said, "They're both divorced and horny."

Was that an inducement to work here? Or a warning?

Landowski pointed to a sign above the pocket doors

that led to the next room: <u>ABANDON ALL HOPE YE WHO ENTER HERE</u>.

I asked, "Customer billing?"

He laughed, but I know that laugh; it means "I make the jokes around here."

Anyway, he parted the doors, and I followed him into what was probably the former dining room. There was a ratty rug on the floor, and eight mismatched desks and chairs butted against the walls, which were covered with faded wallpaper and more bulletin boards. As in Kim and Judy's office, there was a surveillance camera mounted on one wall. This guy was really into keeping an eye on things.

"This is the PIs' office," he said unnecessarily. "Four desks are filled—Lou, Joseph Ferrara, Chip Quinlan, and my in-house lawyer, Jack Berger. The other four desks are for contract PIs when they're working a case for me." He added, "This is where you'll be working."

I've seen more squalid squad rooms, but not by much. A wave of nostalgia swept over me.

"Pick any desk you want."

I liked the one with the pizza box on it. I asked, "Where do you work?"

"I'll show you later. Follow me."

We exited the former dining room into a pantry whose shelves were piled with bulging manila folders—probably active case files. Maybe take-out menus.

The pantry led to a big country kitchen, like Uncle Harry's, except this one had the unmistakable look of a communal space, with every inch of countertop covered with stuff—paper products, Solo cups, bags of snacks and cookies, and, of course, boxes of donuts. Where there are cops, there are donuts.

Also competing for counter space were a coffeemaker,

a microwave, and a toaster oven, all of whose display screens were probably flashing: <u>CLEAN ME!</u>

There was also an oversized refrigerator with a bio-hazard warning sign on the door. Next to the fridge was a gas stove that could probably be implicated in a large number of murdered meals. At the far end of the kitchen was another surveillance camera, which made sense here if you wanted to see who was stealing other people's lunches.

I also noticed a door that I guessed led to the basement. There was a big padlock on the door, which, as a detective, always gets my interest. But maybe the explanation was the sign above the door which read: <u>A MEAL WITHOUT WINE IS BREAKFAST.</u> The wine cellar. I could ask Landowski, but you shouldn't ask people about locked doors—unless you have a search warrant.

Landowski did not comment on the padlocked door and said, "Everyone uses the kitchen. I live here, but I try to make it homey for everyone." He pointed to a round table. "We all meet here once or twice a week, usually at five, share a bottle or two of local wine, and discuss cases, workflow, ideas, gripes, and whatever." He added, "We're like family here."

"I hope things get better."

He didn't reply to that and asked, "You want something? Coffee, tea? A beer?"

"No, thanks. So—"

"Let me show you the rest."

No use arguing with a man who thinks I give a shit.

Landowski walked to the far end of the kitchen and opened a door that led to a dimly lit room at the back of the house.

He said, "This is the mudroom. You know? When they came in from farmwork. They came through here and took off their boots and stuff. So the lady of the house didn't have a fit." He added, "Now it's my equipment room."

"Right." There was a single barred window in the room which looked out at the barn in the back, and the rear entrance was a steel security door. Around the room's walls were steel shelving units and a big gray steel cabinet that I recognized as a gun safe.

There was an old zinc laundry tub against the wall which looked original, and next to it was a modern addition: a stacked washer and dryer, which you'd usually find in the basement. But the basement was apparently off-limits.

On the steel shelves were electronic equipment, video cameras, recording devices, telescopic lenses, binoculars, and other tools of the trade. A security camera scanned the room.

Landowski assured me, "We have the latest of everything. Cost a frickin' fortune."

"You have to spend money to make money."

"Absolutely. Not like when the taxpayers gave us everything we needed, including our paychecks. Right, John?"

"Right."

We went back into the kitchen, and I followed Landowski into the central hallway. He motioned to the staircase and said, "There are five bedrooms upstairs. One is mine, and one is my private office. But we'll sit in the office down here, where we meet clients."

"I don't want to take too much of your time."

"Don't worry about it."

Another idiotic expression I can't stand.

As we walked, he pointed to a small door under the staircase that had a unisex restroom sign on it. "Pissoir if you gotta go."

If there was a window in there, I could escape. But it was an interior room. "I'm okay."

"There's a full bath upstairs. Anyone can use the shower."

Except the clients, who get a hosing.

He continued, "One of the bedrooms upstairs is our recreation room. Full bar. The other two bedrooms are guest rooms. Sometimes somebody has to sleep over. Or sleep it off. Sometimes the PIs have company." He looked at me to see if I understood these employee benefits.

I said, "It's not every job where you get a full bar and a crash pad."

He smiled and added, "Thursdays we have a little party. We call it Thirsty Thursdays." He let me know: "I'm going through a divorce. Lou is separated. Joseph Ferrara and Chip Quinlan are divorced. A few of my contract PIs are unattached or wish they were."

Sounded like I'd fit right in.

"The only guy living with his wife is Jack Berger."

Not for much longer if he keeps working here.

He said, "I understand you're having some marital problems."

"No problem."

"Okay. Tomorrow is Thursday. We start at six."

"I don't have a date."

"You don't need one." He explained, "Tomorrow night is party girls who I know."

And probably arrested when he was on the job.

He further explained, "Another Thursday is regular date night. BYOB—Bring Your Own Broad. Girlfriend or whatever. One Thursday is stag night. A friendly poker game. And one Thursday a month is exotic dancers."

Well, the perks never ended at Security Solutions. So

this is what Max meant by Animal House. I said, "Maybe Chief Maxwell would like to join us."

"He comes by now and then." Landowski hesitated, then added, "Sometimes I invite a few cops. County and local. State troopers once in a while. Sometimes a few prominent citizens and pols. People you'd know if you lived out here."

Indeed, there was more here than met the eye. A PI agency on the ground floor and a party room and hot sheets on the second. Thank God for the shower. I said, "It's important to maintain good community relations."

"Yeah." He assured me, "There's nothing illegal goes on. No drugs, but it gets a little crazy sometimes."

"I hear you."

"No neighbors to worry about."

And even if someone called the police, the police were already here, having a beer. Exotic-dancer night must be a packed house.

I didn't think that Detective Sergeant Penrose knew any of this. But Max did. And Max should know better than to compromise himself with Steve Landowski. On the other hand, if it was actually all legit—no drugs, and if the exotic dancers were paid for their art and did not solicit extra money for sex, but did it for love—then Max was guilty of nothing more than bad judgment. Whereas the ladies who worked downstairs—Amy, Kim, and Judy—were more like the piano players in the brothel who claimed they didn't know what was going on upstairs. I was a little disappointed in Amy. But I'd forgive her.

Anyway, Steve Landowski wanted to let me know all this before he pitched the job, and for some guys, these perks were an inducement to sign on. For other guys, maybe not. Landowski sensed this and said, "If you're not okay with this, you don't have to go upstairs. That's okay too."

"My only concern is that my wife might have hired a PI to get evidence of my moral depravity."

I thought that was funny, but he didn't and said, "That's how I got caught. That bitch hired a PI."

"That's ironic."

"That sucks."

"That too. Okay, Steve, I—"

"Okay, you want to get down to business. To money. Let's sit."

He opened a door in the hallway that led to a room located between the reception area and the mudroom. He motioned for me to go first.

I'd seen and heard enough, so this was where I should end this interview. But how could I tell Max I'd turned down an offer if I hadn't heard it? And what would I say to Beth later, over cocktails? Well, I could mention my shock and disgust about the exotic dancers and the party girls. Would she believe I was shocked and disgusted? Maybe not.

"John?"

I was about to make my excuses and say good-bye, but Landowski's mention of his guests—police and politicians—made me think about blackmail and corruption. If you give a bloodhound a scent, he follows it.

"John?"

"Right." I walked into the room.

CHAPTER 9

Landowski introduced me to the room. "This is my show office where we bring clients. Used to be a storage room." He motioned me to a round mahogany table. "Have a seat."

I sat in a leather chair and he sat opposite me and said, "I hired a decorator to do the room. Looks classy. Right?"

The room was small, but big enough for a client to unload his or her troubles. There was a single window that looked out at the parked cars and the strawberry field. All three rice-burners were still there, so Amy was still here.

The walls and woodwork were painted a decorator gray, and there was an Oriental rug on the floor. One wall had a built-in bookshelf filled with leather-bound volumes that the decorator had probably bought by the yard, and if latent fingerprints had been lifted from the books, it would prove that Steve Landowski had never touched any of them.

On the other walls were framed citations, awards, and the usual stuff you collect after twenty years on the job. Steve Landowski seemed to have had a good career, and I wondered what division he'd worked in. Thinking about the boom-boom rooms upstairs, probably Vice Squad. There were also framed photographs on the walls, one of a young Patrolman Landowski in uniform and one with him and two teenagers, a boy and a girl who did not look like Steve Landowski.

"Those are my kids."

Adopted?

"Got my wife's looks."

Thank God.

"That's my wife."

I looked at the photograph he was pointing to—a surprisingly attractive, smiling woman, probably taken before she hired a PI to tail him.

All in all, the photos and PD stuff were a good balance of Landowski's professional and personal life, and a potential client would feel comfortable here, assured that former Suffolk County detective Steve Landowski had been a good cop and was a solid family man, and not a character out of a Dashiell Hammett novel.

Among the photos and stuff on the wall was a small framed mirror screwed to the paneling, similar to the mirror in the reception area. And again I'm thinking two-way mirror, behind which would be a video camera that sent images to a monitor and to a video recorder somewhere in the house. And where there's a video camera, there's also a hidden mic. Or, the mirror was just a mirror.

I noticed a bar cabinet in the corner, complete with ice bucket and crystal decanters. Landowski asked, "You want a drink?"

"I had a few on the drive here. But you go ahead."

"We'll have one later." He settled into his chair. "So what do you think of the setup here?"

"If it works, it's all good."

"Yeah. It works. Better than an office building. It's private."

"It's a farm."

"It's *disguised* as a farm."

"Fooled me."

"Until you got inside. Right?"

"Right. So—"

"I inherited this house from my mother, who inherited it from her old aunt Eva, who was from Poland." He added, "Almost all the potato farms around here were Polish or German."

"Right. So—"

"By the time my mother got this place, all the land was sold off—about three hundred acres. This house has five acres left."

"That's about right for a PI agency, Steve."

"Yeah. The other acres around me are, like, landscaping stuff and tourist shit, like pumpkins, strawberries, Christmas trees. No more in potatoes. So I own the strawberry field and the potato barn across the road where I have some farm equipment. That makes it a farm. Right?"

"Right."

"So I pay almost no property taxes. I pay farm taxes. But now these assholes in the town tax office are reassessing my tax status. They say it's not a farm because I have this office here. They're looking for a ten-G tax increase. So I got Jack Berger working on filing a tax grievance."

"Good luck."

He looked at me. "It's not about luck. It's about who you know."

Indeed it is. And maybe it's about who you've invited to the upstairs party. I glanced at my watch, but he didn't notice.

"Did you see that maze?"

"No."

"On the north side. The hedge maze."

"Right. Didn't know it was a maze."

"There's lots of corn mazes out here. Tourists come with their kids and pay five bucks to run around the corn maze."

"Children of the corn."

"Yeah? Anyway, the corn maze is, like, seasonal. October. November. So this guy next to me grows a hedge maze, and it's good all year. Fucking kids drive me nuts on weekends. The guy's got, like . . . mummies in there. Vampires. Stuff like that. Kids scream their asses off."

"I would too."

He forced a smile. "Just actors and dummies."

"Thank God."

"Yeah. So this guy next door is supposed to be growing shrubs and shit for sale. Agriculture. But that fucking maze has been there for ten years, and he pays farm taxes." He asked me, "Does that sound like agriculture?"

I was sure the question was rhetorical, but I replied, "Two things you can't avoid—death and taxes." I added, "I'm not a property tax lawyer, and I have a lunch date. So let's talk about Security Solutions. For a minute."

"Jack says I can win. If that asshole next door can—"

"You might want to check with a lawyer who is admitted to the bar."

"Jack's on retainer. He's also helping me with my divorce case."

I hope he doesn't get the tax case and marital case mixed up. "Steve. Listen. I need to get to lunch."

Landowski seemed not to hear and he suddenly stood and went to the bar. He put ice cubes in two tumblers, then poured from a decanter. "Scotch. Max said that's your drink. Right?"

"Right."

He carried the glasses to the table, handed one to me, and we clinked. "Welcome to Security Solutions." He took a gulp and sat. "Macallan, twenty years old."

Which reminded me. "Will Amy be joining us?"

"No."

"Lou?"

"Later. Drink up."

I took a sip.

"Okay, John, I think Max outlined some of this for you."

"He did. So—"

"But you want to hear it from me."

Not really.

"Here's the deal. You got three things I want. Your reputation, your résumé, and your Rolodex. Did Max make that clear?"

"Very clear. But let me make a few things clear to you. As for my reputation, it's not so good with the bosses."

"Fuck the bosses."

"I did. Which is why my reputation with them is not so good."

"I called around. I spoke to Lou. Your reputation with the guys you worked with is golden."

"Wonderful to hear." But it's not for sale.

"And here, you're the boss. No authority to buck." He smiled. "Except for me."

I didn't reply.

He continued, "You got creds. Homicide, Missing Persons, John Jay College. Then working with the Feds, which gave you top-secret clearance. That's big for a lot of clients." He smiled again. "I can raise my rates."

Again I didn't reply.

"And you got hit in the line of duty. I remember that. Made the news. You were famous."

I would rather have been famous for something else. But an NYPD detective hadn't been wounded in the line of duty for years, and the Detectives' Endowment Association kept the story alive for the good P.R.—and also because it was contract time.

Landowski assured me, "We're definitely gonna play that up with clients. You're a hero."

I was, but not for getting ambushed by the gang who couldn't shoot straight, and Detective Landowski knew that as well as I did. But PI Landowski knew a selling point when he saw one.

He went on, "And you have lots of NYPD contacts. Active duty and retired guys. And you worked with the State Police and local police in the metro area. Right?"

I nodded.

"You also worked with the CIA—but I don't think we should advertise that."

Especially since the CIA wanted me dead.

"Police contacts are important to a PI firm. I got contacts. Lou's got contacts, Chip's got contacts, and Joseph says he has contacts. And when we call, we get polite talk. But we don't always get callbacks." He looked at me. "They'd call you back."

Well, my contact on the Suffolk County Police Department, Beth Penrose, would probably call me back. But I wasn't supposed to mention her name here for some reason. I replied, "You may be exaggerating my celebrity star power."

"Yeah? We'll see." He continued, "And you got FBI contacts, and we don't."

I let him know: "I did not have a good relationship with the FBI." Especially with my supervisor, who may now be fucking my wife. On the other hand, maybe Tom Walsh owed me a favor. Maybe I owed *him* a favor.

"The thing is, you *know* these people."

"Steve, I don't think the FBI feels a need to help me or Security Solutions. As for the NYPD and the local police, I'm sure your contacts are as good as mine. So—"

"So even if that's true—and I don't think it is—that's

not what we tell the client." He looked at me again. "This is about the *client*. The guy—or the woman—who wants to hire us. Who pays our bills. These are the people you're gonna talk to. Because—and let me be honest here—you might come across better than me."

You think? "You're being too modest, Steve."

"I'm being honest. You're the professor at John Jay."

"Adjunct professor, retired."

He smiled. "We'll call you professor."

I smiled in return. "You better not. Okay, I get all this, so let me think about—"

"There's more."

I was afraid there was.

"The clients like that we have a lawyer here who they can talk to. This is a big plus for Security Solutions, and—"

"Do they know he's disbarred?"

"Jack's a great lawyer. Criminal defense. He knows your ex. By reputation. Maybe met her once."

Small world. I couldn't wait to meet a disbarred criminal defense attorney who knows my ex-wife.

Steve Landowski, ex-cop, shared my low opinion of criminal defense attorneys and assured me, "Jack never defended a scumbag violent offender or sex offender. Just scumbag white-collar defendants."

I wondered what got him disbarred. Robin could tell me, but Landowski said, "There was some irregularities with his billing practices. It was all bullshit. Nothing to do with the court. It's always about money."

"Right." Jack Berger sounded more than qualified to handle the billing here.

"I just wanted to clear the air about Jack."

"I appreciate that, Steve." It seemed to me that Security Solutions was less than the sum of its parts. "Okay, I think that between you, Amy, and Max, you've answered all my questions and addressed all my concerns. So I will consider your offer—"

"I didn't make an offer."

"Okay, make me an offer."

"First you have to know your job description."

"I'm all ears."

"Okay. You'll be my front man. You're a sharp dresser." He smiled. "You meet with or call our existing clients to keep them up-to-date and happy. That's billable hours. Also, you, and maybe Amy, will meet with potential clients. You'll sell Security Solutions to people who need help. You'll also have some supervisory duties. Keep an eye on our freelance PIs, and also work with Lou, Joseph, and Chip. You'll brainstorm with them once or twice a week, study the case files, make suggestions, and maybe take the lead on some cases and show how smart you are." He smiled, then continued, "If somebody's not performing, we can deal with that. If we need to hire a new PI, you and me will interview them together. You will draw top-notch applicants." He let me know: "I'm looking for a female at the moment."

Me too. "Okay. Sounds good."

He had more. "You can spend as little or as much time in the field as you want. You can work from this office, or from your city place or your place out here, as long as you're here for meetings and clients." He smiled again. "Thirsty Thursdays are optional." He asked, "How's it sound so far?"

"There's more?"

"Yeah. Last thing. You have to go to some police functions, here and in the city. Like retirement parties, promotion parties, cigar nights—"

"High school proms?"

"No . . . that's not police functions." He continued, "Also maybe a few political fundraisers. You need to get out and about. I'll usually be with you. Maybe Amy. Also, if you need clerical services or legal advice, Jack, Amy, Judy, and Kim are there for you. And last thing, you'll need a PI license at some point, and it's easy to get from this office."

Well, to give him credit, he'd thought this out, and it didn't sound half bad. For him. But not for me.

He asked, "You carry, right?"

I nodded. .

"Good license?"

"Good enough." Maybe I should pull my gun and back out of here.

"Okay. Any questions about the job?"

"If I have any, I'll e-mail them to you."

"Okay. So now the important part. The money." He looked at me. "It's a base pay of a thousand bucks a week, plus you get a nice expense account. All on the books. That's just for your name on the letterhead and for being here. If you personally work a case, you get half of the hourly. For you, I'll bill clients two or three hundred an hour. Plus, you get a ten percent override on any existing case that you work on, and twenty-five percent commission on any new case you bring to the agency. You could do easily a hundred fifty a year, maybe two or more."

Well, not bad, but Robin got four hundred for selling her soul. I should get at least that for my soul, even without a law degree.

He looked at me to see how I reacted, and when I didn't, he leaned toward me and threw in a sweetener. "There could be more. I'm looking to take Security Solutions to the next level. And you're part of that plan. I see an office in Manhattan and one in the Hamptons, then maybe Westchester—wherever there are people who have problems and the money to solve them. I'm also looking to expand my rent-a-cop business. Bodyguards and premises security. The premises thing can be big if we get corporate clients. Warehouses, factories. Stuff like that. And the bodyguard business in the Hamptons is big. Lots of high-profile people who need protection."

He asked, "Did you look at our website?"

"I did."

"Did you see that we provided personal security for Billy Joel?"

"I saw that."

"I took that job myself."

Bye-bye, Billy.

"Great guy. Got his autograph."

"On a check, I hope."

Steve laughed. "For my son. So I'm thinking that with you here—top-secret clearance, Anti-Terrorist Task Force— I can pick up some high-profile clients who need personal protection."

Maybe this is where I should tell him I was on several hit lists and needed protection myself.

"And you don't do the work. You sell the job."

"Right."

"Unless you want to do it. Like if we get Christy Turlington."

"I'm on it."

He smiled. "We can do it together."

"I'll give you Martha Stewart."

He laughed. We were having fun. I glanced at my watch.

He got serious and said, "If this all works out, you'll have a piece of it. We could be talking three, three-fifty for you. Maybe more. Depending on what you bring in. Plus, you got a nice three-quarter to add to that." He joked, "You could be doing better than me."

Well, Steve Landowski had a vision, and I hate to piss on people's visions. In fact, his vision may actually become reality, even without me. Also, maybe he wasn't as dense as he seemed—or, more likely, he overcame his intellectual challenges with cunning and drive. I've seen this with other cops—smarter cops—in their post-retirement careers. Like Dick Kearns, who was now making three or four times his cop salary. So why shouldn't I transfer my hard-earned skills and experience to the private sector? That's what I was thinking of doing with a global security firm. They pay about a hundred and fifty a year, but you earn every nickel of it. Especially if you get captured by jihadists.

"John?"

I could have said thanks but no thanks right then. But I didn't want Landowski calling Max and telling him I flat-out turned down the job. Max would call Beth, and I'd be drinking alone tonight. Also, what went on upstairs here might need some looking into. Not by me. But by the county police. I should talk to Beth about that.

"John?"

"Let me sleep on it."

"Okay . . . this is a pretty generous offer. But we can work on it."

"You should sleep on it too, Steve. Make sure you don't have buyer's remorse." I suggested, "Talk to Jack. And Lou. And Chip and Joseph. I don't want to cause any resentment."

"Yeah . . . Lou is excited. Jack thinks it's a good idea. So does Amy." He let me know: "She was impressed with you. Thinks I'm making the right move." He added, "She looks forward to working with you."

"I'm sure she also told you that I had to be talked into coming here."

He nodded. "Max told me. But now that you're here, you know a good deal when you see one."

"Right." I stood. "Talk to your PIs, Steve. I'll call you in the morning."

"You wanna wait for Lou?"

"I did that for two years in Missing Persons. Give him my regards." I stuck out my hand and we shook. "I'll let myself out."

Steve looked a little annoyed. Like a guy who's used to getting what he wants. And maybe he thought I was playing hard to get so he had to up the offer. To squash that, I said, "The offer is generous. Just not sure I'd be a good fit here."

"Let me worry about that."

"I'll call tomorrow."

I exited the room into the hallway and made my way to the foyer, where I stuck my head into the reception room to say good-bye to Amy—and maybe have a quick chat. But she wasn't at her desk. Probably in the kitchen, having lunch. Maybe we could share a box of donuts. Maybe not.

I headed for the front door, and within sixty seconds I was in my Jeep and on the road, putting distance between me and Animal House.

CHAPTER 10

After you leave a job interview, you replay it in your head. In this case, I pushed the "Erase" button. Even the Amy segment.

Now on to . . . where? Condo in Manhattan? Or hang around here and have drinks with Beth tonight? My head was telling me to go to Manhattan, but my pocket rocket was pointing toward Beth Penrose, whose unexpected visit had triggered some good memories.

As I headed back to Route 58, which would take me west to the Expressway and Manhattan, or east to the North Fork, I dialed her mobile. I'd play it by ear.

She answered. "Hi, John."

"Working?"

"In the office."

You don't want to talk to a Homicide detective if he or she is standing over a dead body.

She asked, "How did it go?"

"It was all I expected."

"Okay . . ."

"They're also looking for a female PI. You interested?"

"No offense, John, but I'd rather work in a massage parlor than work with you."

Funny. "That hurts."

"How did you leave it?"

"I'm sleeping on it." Care to join me?

"Okay . . . so . . ."

I was approaching my intersection. I'm a very decisive guy, but sometimes there are no good choices, and even the less bad choice has unintended consequences—like drinks with a woman who could complicate your life.

"John?"

"Are we on for drinks?"

"If you are. I can leave here by five."

"Where would you like to meet?"

"I'll come your way. Do you know aMano in Mattituck?"

"No, but I can find it."

"I'll pick you up. About six."

"Thanks. We can have a drink at my place." I asked, "Are you free for dinner?"

"I am. I'll make a reservation at aMano. Italian."

"Sounds good. Look forward to it."

"Me too," she said. "See you later."

I hung up. Well . . . the pocket rocket was in flight. I approached the intersection and headed east on Route 58. Within half an hour I was back at Uncle Harry's in time for my lunch date with hot chili and cold beer.

———

As I dined on the back porch, I read an e-mail from Uncle Harry, gently reminding me that my squat ended on June 30 and inviting me to dinner at Caravaggio for that night. Meaning, please be out by then.

I replied: *Thanks. I'll get back to you tomorrow about dinner.*

Dick Kearns had texted: ARE YOU CRAZY?

There's that question again. I replied: RE: CRAZY, I'M TRYING TO REMOVE ANY DOUBT. PLEASE DO ME THE FAVOR. I'LL BUY YOU DINNER AT ECCO.

Max, I noticed, hadn't texted or e-mailed, but I was sure that Landowski had called him a minute after I left and complained that I was playing hard to get.

I had a lot of balls in the air, a lot of moving parts that needed to fall into place.

But first things first. Like tidying up the house and changing the sheets on my bed in optimistic anticipation of an overnight guest. I can do this, but Charlotte—Uncle Harry's cleaning lady from East Germany or from Hell—could do it better, so I called her, but she said she was busy, even for fifty bucks an hour. So I said, "I have a *lady* sleeping over."

"It's about time," she said. Or did she say, "About what time?"

"About sex. Six."

"I be there for dirty."

I think she meant 4:30. "Thank you."

I hung up. Well, clean sheets are a good start. Think positive.

My Glock and I took a trip to town to get a bottle of Grey Goose, which Beth drinks—or used to drink—and also some cheese and crackers for the cocktail hour, which hopefully would last until bedtime. Is it still a date if you don't get laid?

I had time for a swim, during which I thought about how I should spend my summer. Life, I've decided, is like a video game, and every move has consequences, intended and unintended, which is followed by another move. And you don't play the game alone; there are other players, and you don't always know who they are or what their next move is. And then there are natural forces, like earthquakes and hurricanes, that can put an end to your pathetic plans. And finally, there is Fate or karma or divine intervention—if you believe in any of that. I once got stuck in traffic and was a few minutes late getting to an elevator to take me to a breakfast meeting in Windows on the World in the North Tower of the World Trade Center. All the people who took the elevators before me, including my former NYPD partner, Dom Fanelli, died.

Back in the house, I saw that I'd had a phone call from—of all people—Kate. The message was: "Hi, John. Just touching base. A few things to discuss. Please call me. Bye."

No specifics, as usual, and her tone was neutral—but with a touch of friendliness. Which, coming from an estranged wife, is not good.

I texted: CAN'T CALL TODAY. WILL CALL TO-MORROW.

I went upstairs and showered, which I should have done right after leaving Steve Landowski's office. What this guy was looking for was a celebrity salesman, like a superstar golf pro who pitches time-shares at a resort.

Well, I accuse the Feds of turning their sanctimonious noses up at crass commerce, but now and then I can be guilty of the same thing—though I call it principled behavior. In any case, my name wasn't for sale.

I needed to dress for my date. Beth would be coming here directly from work, so she'd be well dressed, and I was sure the restaurant was upscale. So I put on a white linen shirt and a pair of trousers that Kate had actually bought for me in Southampton, whose color was called Narragansett red, but which I called pink. Women, though, seem to like bright plumage on men.

I slipped on a pair of docksiders and slapped on a little Dior Sauvage, which also gets compliments from the ladies, and voilà, I was all dressed up for the mating game. I carried my Glock downstairs in the pancake holster and put it on the kitchen counter, then threw a newspaper over it so Detective Sergeant Penrose didn't give me a lecture.

———

Charlotte arrived promptly at 4:30, and I went into the kitchen and set up the hors d'oeuvres and glasses for cocktails which we'd have on the back porch, then I popped a beer and went out to the porch and stood at the rail.

It was a nice afternoon, fair-weather clouds, breeze from the south, golden ripples on the bay, and circling gulls looking for sushi. A romantic setting. I should score. Right?

———

Charlotte, I think, wanted to hang around to see if my lady friend was a looker, but I got her to the front door at quarter to six, gave her a hundred bucks, and thanked her.

She said, "You will come."

"I hope so." Or did she say, "You're welcome"?

Anyway, I decided to wait for Beth on the front porch, and a little after six she pulled into the circular driveway in a Ford Explorer.

She was wearing her usual tailored suit and carrying a shoulder bag that looked big enough to hold cosmetics, a toothbrush, an extra pair of panties, and a birth control product of her choice.

I met her in the driveway and we did a quick hug. "Nice cologne," she said.

"Thank you. Come on in."

She followed me onto the front porch and said, "Nice pants."

"Thanks." So far, so good. We went inside, and I locked the door before she reminded me, and I led her into the kitchen. "We can have a drink on the back porch. Grey Goose?"

"Please."

"On the rocks with a twist of lime."

She smiled.

As I made the drinks—Dewar's and soda for me— she looked around the kitchen as though it were a crime scene, noting the recycling bin filled with evidence of my criminally negligent diet. It also took her about five seconds to lift the newspaper and find my gun. But, to her credit, she didn't lecture me about the unsecured gun or my dining choices. That would come later, if we had sex. Or not at all if, when we discussed Security Solutions, she got frustrated with my evasiveness and left. Hard to guess what was going to happen tonight. But she liked my pants.

I handed her the vodka and we touched glasses. I said, "You look great."

"Thank you."

"I have some cheese and crackers."

"Maybe later."

"Okay." I took my Glock and we went out on the back porch, where I put the gun on the side table. We stood at the rail, looking out at the bay.

"This is such a beautiful spot," she said. "Too bad you have to leave."

"I had first dibs for sixty thousand."

She was silent a moment, then asked, "Did you ever think about selling your place in the city and coming out here?"

Beth had been an overnight guest in my condo a few

times, and she knew it was too big and too expensive. "I have." Not thought about it.

"And?"

"Well . . . this is a lot of house for one person."

"You could find something smaller."

"Right. But I don't want to completely give up the city."

"You could also find a smaller place in the city."

"I could." I wasn't sure where this was going, but I was sure that I had to watch what I said. I wanted to sleep with Beth tonight, but I didn't want to get involved tomorrow. On the other hand, sharing her cottage in Cutchogue sounded good, but that was a commitment—unless I made it clear that I was relocating overseas in September. I like to be honest, but I wasn't sure if I believed my own bright idea about the overseas job. And if I *really* wanted to be honest, there was Kate. What did she want? Life can go from sitting on your back porch, happily doing nothing, to super complicated in one day. Which it had. Also, I noticed that Beth hadn't mentioned her cottage guest room, which, if I understood her offer, was tied to my employment at Security Solutions.

"How did it go today?"

I finished my drink. "Well . . ." What's more important? Being honest? Or getting laid?

Beth helped me. "Be honest."

"Okay. To be honest, Steve Landowski is a little hard to take."

"I've met him a few times. On the job."

"And I've worked with Lou Santangelo, though I didn't see him today." I did, however, see Amy. Anyway, I had to finesse this, so I said, "I'm not in a position to critique Landowski's business, but I don't think I'm a good fit there."

"Does he?"

"He did. But maybe he's having second thoughts."

She looked at me. "Were you arrogant? Or condescending?"

"Well..." Both.

"You need to learn how to compromise a little."

"Actually, I don't."

"Okay... so what now?"

She seemed a bit annoyed, and I was now sure I'd be sleeping with Nero Wolfe tonight on clean sheets.

She asked, "Did he make you an offer?"

"You know he did."

She nodded.

"What else did Max tell you?"

She sipped her drink. "He said that Steve was surprised and annoyed that you didn't jump on his offer."

"I'm sure Max was not surprised."

"Max thought you could make it work for you and for Steve." She added, "But he understands."

"That's nice. And did Max also tell you about...?"

"What?"

The second-floor perks, which would offend Sergeant Penrose's sensibilities and strengthen my case. But I wasn't on trial, and I didn't need to say more than I already said. Also, it occurred to me that if I told her about the party girls and the cops and politicians, and told her to have this looked into, she'd tell me that I should take the job and do that myself, unofficially. But maybe Max *had* told her about Thirsty Thursdays. It also occurred to me that there was more going on here than I was being told. This was just like working for the Feds.

"John? About what?"

"Forget it."

"Okay. I will." She put her drink down, took her phone

out of her bag, called aMano, and canceled the dinner reservation.

Things were sorting themselves out, which they usually do when they go downhill. Well, we weren't going to cop-ulate tonight. "Okay," I said, "I'll walk you to your car."

"Are you kicking me out?"

"I thought you were leaving."

"I'm leaving the porch. Going to your bedroom."

Did she say bathroom?

"Kiss me first."

I put down my glass. "That's the best offer I've had today." And I wondered where it came from. There must be a catch. There always is.

She smiled, and we kissed. My off-duty pistol got very hard, which reminded me to grab my Glock, and we went inside where Beth grabbed her bag, and I moved quickly up the stairs. I was sleeping in the master bedroom and I got there first.

Beth followed and said, "I remember this room."

"Me too." It had a big four-poster bed, suitable for bondage if you're into that. A ceiling fan spun lazily overhead, and the open windows let in the sea breeze and the setting sun. I put my gun on the nightstand.

She took off her jacket and put her Glock and holster on the other nightstand, next to *The Rubber Band*, which reminded me that my condoms were in the nightstand drawer if I needed them.

I couldn't wait to get out of the pink pants, which I pulled off first while kicking off my docksiders, then my shirt and shorts, which I dropped on the floor.

Beth got out of her clothes, which she usually hangs neatly in the closet, but she threw them on a chair and turned toward me.

I looked at her naked body in the sunlight, remembering every inch of it, and happy to see it again. As we moved toward each other, I could see the scar on her left rib cage where the bullet had grazed her. Every physical scar that you carry is an everlasting reminder of how and where you got it. I was there when she got that one, and I was sure that every time she got dressed or took a shower, she remembered John Corey. And every time a lover asked about the scar, she had a story to tell, starring John Corey and Beth Penrose.

We embraced and kissed like it was our first time, and I lifted her onto the bed, then buried my face between her thighs, which she always enjoyed. Her body went into a spasm, then stiffened, then she came. Beth is a moaner, not a screamer like Tess, whose orgasms in my condo had the neighbors dialing 9-1-1.

I stood and pulled down the blanket, and she put her head on one pillow while I slid the other one under her butt, which she also liked. We had this down pretty good with lots of practice.

Afterwards, Beth rolled on her side and went to sleep. I ran my fingers along her scar. She'd actually saved my life that day, though we never spoke about it. I had said, "Thanks," and she'd said I owed her a favor, so, some weeks later I asked her out to dinner, which I guess I couldn't have done if I was dead. But, as I said, that moment when she saved my life never came up again. Even when I ended the relationship. Beth is a class act.

———

Later, we went downstairs in robes and had another drink on the back porch and watched the sun set. I was thinking about that cheese, but Beth surprised me by suggesting a moonlight swim.

We walked across the lawn to the floating platform in our robes with our Glocks and cell phones in our pockets.

Beth untied her robe and let it fall to her feet and stood naked in the moonlight. It's private here, but you can be seen on the platform from surrounding houses or from boats. I don't care who sees me hanging hog, but the Beth Penrose I remembered would have worn a bathing suit, or at least her bra and panties, and would have jumped into the water quickly. But this Beth Penrose just stood there stark naked, like a Greek goddess, under the stars and moon, the sea breeze streaming through her coppery hair, and the sparkling water spread out before her.

She glanced at me, smiled, then did a perfect dive into the bay. I ripped off my robe and followed.

We floated on our backs and looked up at the night sky. So, apparently, I didn't have to take the job to get laid. Right? Stay tuned.

We were in shallow water, so she stood, took my head in her hands, and gave me a long kiss as I floated on cloud nine. Then, suddenly, she pushed my head underwater and held it there, and I wasn't sure if she was being playful or if she was working for the Russians. She was incredibly strong, though I could have broken free, but I just held my breath. Finally, she let go and I popped to the surface.

As I caught my breath, I heard her say, "That's for leaving me. Don't do it again."

"Okay . . ." I looked at her to see if she was smiling, but she wasn't. In fact, she seemed on the verge of tears. Never saw that before.

Well, Johnny got what he wanted tonight, but John got more than he bargained for. Nevertheless, I knew what I was supposed to say, and I took her in my arms. "I'm here for as long as you want me." I added, "And I'm sorry." And I may have even meant it. We kissed.

There were night fishermen in the bay, and a few of them were in small boats close to us, so I put my arm around her shoulders and we waded ashore, then onto the platform, where we got into our robes and walked in silence to the porch. We refreshed our drinks and sat, holding hands, looking at the sea and night sky.

That was a good reconnect date.

She finished her drink and said, "I love you."

Which was the first line of a joke we used to share, and I replied, "Is that you talking or the vodka?"

She delivered the punch line. "It's me talking to the vodka."

We laughed. Good joke. Though the "L" word makes me nervous.

Beth took her cell phone and played Bobby Darin's "Beyond the Sea," which was a nice choice, though I might have chosen "Green, Green Grass of Home," about the guy walking to his execution. But . . . Hey, don't fight it. It's all good.

CHAPTER 11

It's good to start off the day with a bang, which we did as the sun came up.

Afterwards, Beth looked at the Nero Wolfe book on my night table. "I've read some of those." She smiled. "Are you learning anything about being a PI?"

"I am. But I've noticed that Nero Wolfe never has sex."

"Only you would notice that."

Was that a compliment?

Anyway, it was good to have her in this bed again. And surely there would be no complications or commitments. Right?

We went down to the kitchen, and while the coffee was brewing, Beth went out to her SUV, returning with an overnight bag. Women usually know if they're going to have sex on a date and pack accordingly; men can only hope. And be prepared. On that subject, I asked, "Are you using any kind of birth control?"

"I'm not seeing anyone. But I'll start the pill today."

Yesterday might have been even better. Meanwhile, pull and pray.

We took our coffee out to the back porch and sat in adjoining chairs. It looked like another perfect day with puffy clouds and circling gulls. A morning mist rose off the water, and out in the bay a few early fishermen in small boats were casting lines and dropping crab traps. This is a nice piece of the world, and, as everyone knows,

when you have a new lover—or one who's come back—
the world looks nicer and newer.

I asked, "Are you working today?"

"I can call in sexually exhausted."

"Your usual excusable absence."

She smiled. "To be completely honest, I already put in
for the day off."

Beth plans ahead.

She asked, "Did you have plans for today?"

I noticed the past tense, so I replied, "No. I hoped to
be with you today."

"That's nice. Or B.S."

Morning-after talk is part of the deal, but not the easiest part.

We did, however, have things to discuss. Hopefully,
Security Solutions was not one of them. But my summer plans and living arrangements were still up in the
air, including my possible overseas employment, which
maybe I shouldn't mention.

Beth had her own agenda and asked, "What's the situation with your wife?"

"Well . . . I suppose one of us has to file for divorce."

"Why haven't either of you done that?"

"Don't know."

"Is there a possibility of a reconciliation?"

"The odds of that, Beth, are about the same as for
peace on earth."

"Okay . . . I don't want to probe."

You already did, darling. I said, however, "You have a
right to know," meaning, I'd like to have a pleasant day
today and sleep with you tonight.

But Beth wasn't done and asked, "Do you hear from
your DSG partner?"

"Now and then." I explained to Beth about the mutual

concern that I and Ms. Tess Faraday had regarding retribution by the Russian SVR. Other than that professional problem, I assured her, my former partner and I had nothing to talk about. Sounded good to me.

Beth took my hand, and we sipped coffee and looked out at the bay and the birds. Ospreys mate for life. But are they happy?

She asked, "How seriously do you take this threat?"

I was happy to move on from ex-wives and -girlfriends to Beth's less urgent concern—my possible assassination. "These are serious people," I replied. "But, as you may know, the SVR hasn't ever assassinated an American, or anyone, on American soil." Which was not completely true. Also, considering that Tess Faraday and I had capped a few SVR agents here, the Russians might not feel any professional restraint about retaliating here.

"You should be careful if you travel out of the country."

"Right." So this might not be a good time to mention my overseas career option.

She asked, "What did you do to become a target of the SVR?"

"I'm not at liberty to say."

"Well . . . if you ever want to talk about it . . . I'm here."

"Thank you."

The agenda continued. "When are you supposed to get back to Steve?"

"This morning."

"And what are you going to tell him?"

"What would you like me to tell him?"

She hesitated, then replied, "I'd like you to tell him that you'll try the job for the summer, which is probably his busiest time. If it doesn't work for you, or for him, you're both free to part company."

Can I ask for that same summer arrangement with

Ms. Penrose? Well . . . thinking ahead, I would feel better if I were living in Beth's cottage as a gainfully employed lover than if I were living there as a beach bum. I mean, how bad could it be working for Steve Landowski for the summer? By September I'd know how it was going with Beth and what I wanted to do next. Also, I'd know what was going on with Kate. This would be like getting paid for buying time while marking time.

"John?"

But was all that enough reason to take the job? No. There were, however, other reasons, the first being that Max and Beth seemed very keen on my working for Security Solutions, and their reasons didn't seem clear. And then there was Landowski's second-floor playroom where he invited cops and politicians, and that reeked of corruption. And finally, Max had asked me not to mention Sergeant Penrose's name to Steve Landowski. You don't have to be a detective to find that suspicious. So . . . maybe I should check this place out.

I said, "Okay . . . I'll get back to him with my acceptance conditioned on the understanding that this summer is a trial period."

"Good. That will work."

"We'll see if Landowski thinks so."

"He will." Now that I was gainfully employed, she said, "I'm assuming you're moving into my cottage."

"I thought you'd never ask."

"Good. Let's do it this morning."

"We already did it."

"Moving."

"Right."

"Do you have a lot of stuff?"

"Everything I brought here fits in my Jeep."

"Except your ego."

We got a chuckle out of that. Beth, when she was relaxed, was easy to be with. Why did I leave? Well . . . let me think. Before I could, she said, "I'm going to live out here for most of the summer. The commute to Yaphank is about the same from here as it is from my condo in Huntington."

"Good."

"I'll take some serious time off. We can take a trip."

Beth had obviously thought this out. And it was good of her to let me know my plans. And, to be honest, my own plans weren't so thought out, and Beth, who was sometimes a control freak, was filling a vacuum. Also, to be honest with myself, I wanted to be with her. Yesterday I wanted Amy Lang. But that was as idiotic as wanting a dangerous job overseas. This morning . . . I was having an epiphany . . . and I wanted a summer of love with Beth Penrose.

She said, "We can go to Maine or Vermont for a week."

I reminded her, "I'm just starting a new job."

"Just start a week later." She assured me, "Steve Landowski will give you whatever you want."

"Maine sounds good."

"Or," she said, "we can go to Europe . . . Oh, you shouldn't leave the country."

"I'm okay with that."

"You take unnecessary risks."

"Risks are necessary to keep me feeling alive."

"Someday, John, your luck is going to run out."

"I got lucky last night."

"Seriously. According to Darwinian law, you should be extinct."

Not the first time I've heard that.

"Have you ever done one of those DNA ancestry tests?"

"No. Why?"

"I was wondering what percentage of Neanderthal you are."

Funny. "Higher is better . . . right?"

She didn't confirm that, and we sat in silence awhile, sipping our coffee. I said to her, "You told me you barely knew Landowski. Yet Max asked me not to mention your name to him." I asked, "Why is that?"

"It's nothing personal. It was a police matter." She explained, "It was a turf dispute between Homicide and Human Trafficking—that's what the Suffolk PD calls the Vice Squad. I had to give a statement to the commissioner's office that apparently didn't sit well with Detective Landowski."

"Okay . . . so Steve Landowski was Vice Squad?"

"Yes, I thought you knew that."

"Max didn't mention it." And neither did Landowski. But I'd guessed it—jokingly. For some reason, I found this amusing. I mean, who would be better equipped to throw a stag party with strippers? More importantly, who did Landowski invite to his parties? I asked, "Why didn't you—or Max—tell me there was some animosity between you and Steve Landowski?"

"It's irrelevant. I—and Max—just didn't want Landowski to know that you knew me." She added, "It might have prejudiced his thinking about hiring you."

Not as much as if I'd shown up in Aunt June's cocktail dress. I said to Beth, "If I ask you a question, will you be honest with me?"

"I will."

"Okay, did Steve Landowski bust you for prostitution?"

She laughed. "I knew you'd find out."

"They don't call me Detective for nothing."

So, I let the matter rest there—on a joke. But . . . there was more to this.

"Well," she said, "if you take this job, you'll be in a low-risk occupation. I'll sleep better at night. So will you."

I didn't reply.

She stood. "I'm going to shower and get dressed. Then we'll move your stuff to my place."

"Yes, dear."

She gave me a kiss on the cheek, moved toward the house, then came back and looked at me. "If . . . this is too much for you, let me know now, and I'll just leave."

Well . . . recalling my head underwater in the bay, and Beth's proficiency with a Glock, I knew I needed to answer carefully. I stood and put my hands on her arms and looked into her eyes. I said, sincerely, "I've missed you and thought about you. When you came here yesterday, I knew I wanted to be with you again. Thank you for making it happen." I added, "I should have called you when I first got here."

She kept looking into my eyes, the way a detective does with a suspect. Finally, she nodded. "This will be a good summer. Come September, we're both free to leave."

"I'm not going to make the same mistake twice."

She smiled, we hugged, and she went into the house.

I stood at the rail, staring into the mist. Last night was pure lust. This morning was something else.

This would be a good time, psychologically and post-coitally, to call Kate, and I walked across the lawn and down the rickety steps that led to the swimming platform. The bay was calm, and also calming, which is what I needed before I made this call. I dialed Kate Mayfield's cell number.

She answered, "Hello, John."

"Hello."

"Thanks for calling back."

"What's up?"

"Where are you?" she asked.

"I'm at Harry's place. Where are you?"

"Getting ready to go to work."

"I can call back."

"I can talk. How have you been?"

"Fine. What can I do for you?"

"I just wanted to catch up. See how you're doing."

"I'm still doing fine." I let her know, "I can't talk long."

"Okay ... Well, I was thinking of coming to New York. And I wondered if we could meet."

I knew that was coming. "For what purpose?"

"To discuss what's happening."

"There's not much to discuss."

"There is. I'm ... feeling sort of in limbo."

"You're actually in Washington."

"And that makes you angry."

"It did. Not anymore."

"You could have come with me."

True, she did offer. But it was a half-assed offer. And she knew that while I was on paid administrative leave with the DSG I was technically on duty and had to stay in New York. I could have gone to DC on weekends, but I was pissed, which fueled my relationship with Tess Faraday—which at that point was still platonic.

"John? You there?"

"I'm here."

"You could have asked for permission to live with your wife in DC during your leave. DSG would have granted permission."

"The point, Kate, is that *I* didn't want to live in DC. *You* did."

"You didn't even come to see me."

"The shuttle works both ways."

"You know I was busy getting set up here."

I could remind her that she'd spent the Christmas holidays with her family in the Midwest—but she was deep into rewriting history, so why bother? "Kate, there's no purpose in rehashing this."

"You never supported my career, and you didn't support me."

We didn't seem to be on the same page regarding career conflicts or geographic preferences. The words "irreconcilable differences" popped into my head.

"I'm sorry, John. That wasn't fair."

Beware of apologies from estranged wives. "I could see how you'd feel that way. Okay, so—"

"I'd like to come to New York and we can talk face-to-face. Clear the air."

How about video chat?

She offered, "I can come to you in Mattituck or Manhattan."

"Sorry, I don't see the purpose of a meeting."

"We need to do this, John. My . . . I'm seeing someone . . . a therapist. She says this is important. We need closure, or . . ."

"I'm also seeing someone." An old girlfriend. She says I need a divorce.

"You're seeing a therapist?"

"Sort of." Sex therapist.

"I'm surprised."

"I've come a long way." Considering my high Neanderthal score.

"That's good to hear. I'm sure your therapist would agree that a civilized meeting is important and necessary. So we can go forward."

"I'll ask her."

"You're seeing a woman?"

"I am."

"That might be good for you. I can come to New York this weekend. Or next. We can have dinner. Maybe we should meet in Manhattan. We could go to Ecco. Or, if you'd rather talk in a less public place, we could meet in our condo."

Our condo? I thought my ex-wife gave it to *me*.

"I'd like to see the place . . . for old times' sake. And I left some things there that I can use. I'll find a hotel. Or, if you're comfortable with me staying in the guest room, I can do that." She reminded me, "We're married."

Was I misinterpreting this conversation? I mean, yesterday I might have agreed to all this. I recalled that Robin and I had about six good-bye bangs. Seven, if you count the one after the divorce when she came to the condo to get her winter coats. Sex was not our problem. Same with Kate. Hot as a pizza right out of the microwave.

"If you're uncomfortable with that, I understand."

"This is a lot to think about."

Which was not the reply she'd expected. Nor was it an offer I'd expected. I mean, the six-hundred-pound gorilla in the room was Tom Walsh, whom I hadn't brought up, because if I did, it would send her into a long tirade about me accusing her of having an improper relationship with a man who is her supervisor, mentor, and friend, and all that bullshit.

During my mental absence from the phone call, Kate Mayfield had consulted with FBI Special Agent Mayfield, and one of them finally thought to ask me, "Are you seeing anyone?"

"I am." I added, "Not a therapist."

"Oh . . . well . . ." Silence, then: "I should have expected that."

Really? I haven't gotten laid since mid-January, when Tess announced that we should see other people—as the ladies say—but remain friends, of course. Tess seemed to be rethinking that, but that was the least of my problems at the moment.

"Is it serious?"

Sounded like she was asking about a medical condition. "I've reconnected with Beth Penrose."

"Who . . . ?"

"The lady I broke up with to be with you."

"Oh . . . well, that's ironic. Why didn't you say so sooner?"

"You didn't ask." And, to be honest, I was getting some perverse pleasure out of the conversation.

Silence, then, "I still think it would be a good idea to meet. So we can move forward." She added, "I'll book a hotel. Let me know when it's convenient for you."

How about never? Is never good for you? I looked back at the house and saw Beth on the porch, wearing jeans and a T-shirt. She waved to me. I waved back.

"John?"

"Yes?"

"I . . . think I made a mistake."

"And what would that be?"

"Agreeing to this transfer to Washington."

"I think, Kate, you *requested* the transfer."

"It was offered. It was a great opportunity to work at FBI Headquarters. But now I see that I was happier at Twenty-six Fed."

"I'm glad one of us was happy there."

"We should have discussed it more."

Total bullshit. We weren't discussing much of anything at that point. She was hot to trot to Washington with Walsh, and I was involved with my own career problems in the DSG. As for Tess Faraday, at that point in time she was just a minor pain in my ass—a seemingly clueless partner whom I'd been temporarily stuck with. The sexual relationship began long after Kate decamped. Well . . . maybe two weeks.

Beth was walking across the lawn toward me.

Kate informed me, "I'm thinking about asking to be transferred back."

Two possibilities here: Tom found a new girlfriend. Or Tom was being transferred back to New York. Well . . . third possibility—Kate wanted to get back together. And all she had to do was appeal to my forgiving nature, which is nonexistent.

"John?"

"You never liked New York. But it's your decision."

"I'll let you know." She changed the subject. "What are you doing at Harry's?"

"Celebrating my freedom from DSG."

"Do you have something lined up?"

"I'm exploring opportunities."

"Try ATTF again."

Maybe Tom could put in a good word for me. "I'd rather gut fish." Beth was approaching the deck. "Okay, I have to go."

"Okay . . . I'll let you know when I'm coming to New York."

"Please do. And please tell Tom to expect an unannounced visit from me." I hung up.

Beth walked barefoot onto the floating platform. "Who was that?"

"My future ex-wife."

She looked at me. "What did she want?"

"What she can't have."

She kept looking at me. "No, she can't."

"Ready to move?"

"I've already put most of your stuff on the front porch, stripped the bed, and took your Nero Wolfe book."

"Pinch me, I must be dreaming."

We locked arms, and as we walked, she asked, "Are you okay?"

"Couldn't be better."

"The best is yet to come."

"Can't wait."

So we packed both SUVs for our drive to her cute cottage in Cutchogue, where we would live happily ever after. Right? Well, if all this seems too good to be true, then it is.

CHAPTER 12

Before I left Uncle Harry's house—for what was probably the last time—I remembered to call Charlotte to arrange a thorough cleaning before the renters arrived. She wanted two hundred, which I said I'd leave in the bread box.

Charlotte asked, "Where you putzkie?"

I looked down at my crotch. "Right where it's always been."

"Where you puts key?"

"Oh . . . under the front mat."

"Tell uncle I clean his horse September."

"He'll be happy to hear that."

That taken care of, I seriously considered leaving a note for the renters to call my cell, and I asked Beth for her opinion.

She replied, "What would you say to them?"

"Well, I'd give them some helpful tips about the house, then I'd advise them to stick a note on the front door—in Russian and English—saying that John Corey has moved."

"This is actually not funny."

"Right."

"Let's talk to Max about this. Let him handle it as a local police matter."

"Okay." I was sure that Beth had already spoken to Max about this. Their shared hobby is John Corey.

Beth had laid out jeans for me and found my T-shirt that said INFIDEL in English and Arabic, which she thought was funny, though the Feds didn't, and had banned all their NYPD personnel from wearing any "culturally insensitive" T-shirts. Glad I'm outta there.

So I got in my Jeep and followed Beth to her cottage in the historic and too quaint hamlet of Cutchogue, which has a three-hundred-year-old village green and ye olde buildings. Beth's cottage was on a leafy lane, near an inlet called Wickham Creek, and I pulled into her gravel driveway and got out. Beth remained in her car on a phone call—probably to Max—so I looked around.

The small cottage was as I remembered it: a classic cedar-shingled Cape Cod with an open carport and a white picket fence and climbing rosebushes. Whenever I used to walk into this house, I always thought I'd see seven dwarfs in the living room.

Beth got off her call and out of her SUV, and we stood out front. She asked, "Bring back memories?"

"All good."

We unloaded my clothes and a six-pack of Bud from my Jeep and got everything inside.

The cottage was small, especially after Harry's place, but it was cozy and neat, with a fireplace and a sliding glass door that led to a brick patio. No sign of cats, which would have been a deal-breaker.

Beth asked, "Look different?"

Also, it used to have comfortable old furniture. "Looks great."

"I painted and furnished the whole place myself. No decorator. No boyfriends."

"I see only you here."

She looked at me. "You are the only man who's ever had closet space here."

And not much of it. "Let's unpack."

First things first, which was getting the beer in the fridge. There was room for me in Beth's bed, but no room for my clothes in her closet or bureau, so we put my stuff in the second bedroom, as I'd done the last time I was here. There was only one small bathroom, but I managed to find space for my toothbrush.

The move-in complete, Beth poured two glasses of something fizzy that was not beer, and we sat on the rear patio in the chaise longues. There were fruit trees out back and flower gardens, and the nearest backyard neighbor was about fifty yards away. Same with the adjacent neighbors, so there was some privacy, and I remembered taking a rain shower with Beth out here one hot summer night.

I noticed some new additions—two hammocks on the lawn and a hot tub in a corner of the patio. Also a table and chairs for outdoor dining and a Weber grill. I pictured us lying in the hammocks, reading and listening to music, or sitting in the hot tub with cold beers, then eating grilled burgers al fresco. *Idyllic. Summer. Love.* Good words.

I sipped the drink, which smelled off. "What is this?"

"Kombucha. Fermented tea. About one percent alcohol." She assured me, "It's good for you."

This could be a very long summer. Or a very short one.

Beth said, "I love it out here. I can relax. That hot tub is ecstasy in the winter."

I thought my contract was up in September.

I took her hand as we sat in the chaises, looking out at the gardens—birds, bees, butterflies, and dragonflies. In a week or so there'd be fireflies on hot summer nights, and the fireflies, like the summer people, would disappear in September. Maybe I would too.

Beth said, "I'm glad you took the job."

"Me too." Not really. "How much is the rent here?"

"Two hundred a week. But you can work it off."

We both got a chuckle.

She said, "Think about where you'd like to go for vacation."

"Anyplace with you is a vacation, darling."

"Is that you talking, or the kombucha?"

"It's me talking to you." I added, "I need a beer."

"Later." She asked, "How about an Alaskan cruise? We can see the midnight sun. The aurora borealis."

I see that in my head most nights after a few cocktails. But to get off on the right foot, I replied, "Sounds wonderful. What's for lunch?"

"I'll make a salad." She got up. "Relax." She went into the house.

There was a potted petunia or something next to my chair, and I poured the kombucha on it and the flowers wilted. Well . . . not right away. But they would.

I looked out at the fruit trees, gardens, lawn, and hammocks. I love the city, but there comes a time in your life when nature, surrounded by a white picket fence, looks good.

I wasn't sure I was in that time yet, but for now I was in this place—with Beth Penrose.

The summer of love.

What could possibly go wrong?

CHAPTER 13

We dined at the patio table. The fresh green salad and balsamic vinegar dressing tasted like battery acid over grass clippings. "This is wonderful," I said. To make conversation that didn't include the past or future, I asked, "How's the homicide business?"

She shrugged. "Mostly domestic mayhem. Family, neighbors, friends, and lovers."

Right. People had a statistically higher chance of getting killed by someone they knew than by a stranger. But not so with people in law enforcement.

She admitted, "Not a lot of detective work involved."

"Especially when the wife is standing over the deceased husband holding a smoking gun and grinning."

She smiled. "It gets a little depressing."

"Max says he gets busy here in the summer."

She nodded. "You have thousands of people coming to the Hamptons, and now the North Fork. There are the rich, and there are those who'd like to have what the rich have." She added, "It's mostly auto theft, con artists, a few house burglaries, and prostitution. I get maybe one or two high-profile homicides, usually having to do with a wild house party—drugs and alcohol. Or a husband, a wife, and a lover."

"Right." Max and his township PD could handle the small stuff, but homicide was where the county PD came in—as had happened with the Gordon murders, when I met Detective Penrose.

Beth poured sparkling water for both of us. I drank my sparkling beer.

I asked her, "Any problems with the Russians?" meaning the Russian oligarchs who'd taken a fancy to big mansions in the Hamptons.

"The usual. They don't go out much in public, but their house parties are off the charts." She looked at me. "Like the one you—and your DSG partner—crashed last summer."

"Right." Tess and I had crashed the party, posing as catering staff, and later we'd returned as Federal agents with Suffolk County PD backup, including Detective Penrose. We busted everyone at the party, but, being Feds, we didn't tell the police what it was about. Detective Penrose and her colleagues were resentful, of course, but they had to be satisfied with the two magic words— National Security. I can't say I don't miss all of that.

Beth asked again, "What happened after you left the Russian house?"

"Still can't say."

She stayed silent a moment, then said, "I thought you'd call me—to thank me for my assistance."

"I should have. Sorry."

She didn't respond.

I said, "Glad for a second chance."

She smiled.

I was still more than curious about why I shouldn't mention Beth's name at Security Solutions. Her and Max's explanation didn't hold water, and actually didn't comport, so I asked, "Have you ever had any interaction with Security Solutions?"

She glanced at me. "Not me personally. But I think Missing Persons has."

"Right." Homicide was not likely to be contacted by a PI agency or vice versa. But if you worked Missing Persons, you were more likely to be contacted by a PI who'd been hired to find a missing spouse, child, or whoever was MIA.

"Why do you ask?"

Because I was trying to clear up some bullshit. But I replied, "I just wondered if the county police would be a good resource for me at Security Solutions. I'm also thinking that when I'm a PI, I can find some business reason to visit you in Yaphank and take you to lunch."

She didn't reply to that.

"And maybe give your colleagues some helpful tips on how to investigate a homicide."

"I'm not sure they—or I—would appreciate that, John."

I smiled. "Just a thought."

She pulled her phone out of her pocket and texted someone, saying to me, "I'll find out who Missing Persons has dealt with from Security Solutions."

"Not important."

"You asked. Takes a sec." She pushed "Send" and put down her phone. "Okay, no more shop talk. How does Bermuda sound to you?"

It sounded like a practice honeymoon destination. "You pick."

She asked me, "Weren't you supposed to call Steve this morning?"

"It can wait."

"Are you having second thoughts?"

"No. But he could be."

She looked at me.

I assured her, "The job is mine if I want it."

"Okay. Can I ask you how much he offered?"

"What did Max tell you?"

"I would not discuss something like that with him."

"Why not? You've discussed my professional and personal life with him."

"Only for the best of reasons."

Right. Like, can we get this guy employed, divorced, and made available? "I appreciate that. I would also appreciate it if you and Max found something else to talk about." I also cautioned her, "Max and Steve Landowski seem to be in close communication."

She nodded, then made eye contact. "To clear the air about Max, if that's an issue, we are just work friends."

Like my wife and her boss?

She let me know, "He's not my type."

"You shouldn't be dating cops at all."

"Tell me about it."

Anyway, the good thing about summer jobs and summer romances was that they had a built-in end date. Hopefully, everyone understood that.

We made small talk, getting to know each other again.

In my business, which was also Beth's business, you develop a sixth sense for knowing when something is not as it seems. Like, the perfect alibi is too perfect, and what seems inconsequential is of the utmost importance.

There was something going on here with Beth and Max, something that seemed more scripted than serendipitous or coincidental. My trained brain kept whispering, "Something is off here." And I had no idea what that was. But it was.

To quote Georges Braque, as I used to do in my class, "Truth exists; only lies are invented."

CHAPTER 14

After lunch, back in the cottage, Beth said, "I'm going to sunbathe. Why don't you call Steve Landowski, then join me?"

"Okay."

She looked at me. "You don't need to compromise, John. You need to make it work—for both of you." She added, "You can help set a standard at Security Solutions."

If I could find where they hid their standard, I could help set it someplace.

She hesitated, then said, "You might also want to notify some other people—by text—of your new living arrangement."

I nodded.

She went into her—our—bedroom to change.

I took out my cell phone and sat on her new couch, which could use some pizza stains.

Before I called Landowski, I first needed to put my past life in order. And to be sure there was no turning back, I needed to burn all my bridges behind me. I texted Kate, Bridge One: OUR MARRIAGE IS OVER. I AM WITH A WOMAN I LOVE. I AM FILING FOR DIVORCE IN NEW YORK.

I think that covers all the issues. I hit "Send" and rewarded myself with a chug of beer.

Second bridge, Tess: I AM NOW LIVING WITH

DET. BETH PENROSE WHO YOU MET ON THE JOB IN SOUTHAMPTON. I WISH YOU ALL GOOD THINGS AND MUCH LUCK AND LOVE. NO NEED TO REPLY.

Surprisingly, that was a tougher bridge to burn than the Kate bridge. Maybe because I still liked her.

Now on to Robin Paine-in-the-ass. Who I also actually liked.

But Beth came into the living room wearing a tiny bikini bottom and no top. She had a beach towel draped over her shoulders and a bottle of sunscreen in her hand. She said, "Don't forget to tell Landowski you need a week before you start."

"Right."

"I put your bathing suit and a beach towel on our bed. See you outside." She opened the sliding door. "Good luck."

I finished my beer and texted Robin: AS OF TODAY, COUNSELOR, YOU WILL CEASE AND DESIST FROM CONTACTING ME IN ANY WAY, FOR ANYTHING. I hesitated, then hit "Send."

Landowski and I hadn't swapped cell numbers, so I dialed his office number, which would be answered by Amy, which I'm sure was Landowski's preference, and mine too.

Amy must have put my number in her caller ID when I'd first called, because instead of answering, "Security Solutions," she said, "Hi, John."

"Hi, Amy."

And instead of saying, "Would you like to speak to Steve?" she said, "I enjoyed meeting you yesterday."

I guess the job is still open. "Same here."

"Sorry I missed you before you left."

"I didn't see you at your desk."

"I was in the kitchen having lunch. Steve should have told you."

"I should have deduced that myself."

She laughed. "Your sleuthing skills are getting rusty."

Your teasing skills are getting sharper. "Actually, I had a lunch date."

"Hope you weren't late." She added, "Steve likes to talk."

"We had a lot to cover."

"I know." She said, "Before I put you on with him, are there any issues or questions that I can help you with?"

Too many to mention. But I replied, "Can't think of any."

She must have detected a different tone in my voice—the result of a lower sperm count since last we spoke—and she said, "Okay. Well, I hope you've given some serious thought to this."

I didn't have to. I'd rejected the idea before I got there. But . . . the world had changed since yesterday morning.

"John?"

"I hope Steve has also given this some thought." To the extent that he knew the difference between a serious thought and a bright idea.

"He and I spoke about it. But I'll let him talk to you."

"Good."

"Okay. Hope to see you soon."

Since Amy and I were most likely going to be colleagues for the summer, I replied pleasantly, "I hope so."

"Great. Hold for Steve." She added, "Bye."

I held for Steve, who had to get briefed by Amy. This guy probably didn't take a piss without running it by Amy Lang, screener extraordinaire, as well as his hired brain and resident femme fatale.

"Hey, John!"

"Hey, Steve."

"So have you thought about my offer?"

"I have some threshold issues."

"Okay. Like what?"

"Like I can't start until after July Fourth, and I want this to be for a trial period, ending Labor Day weekend."

"Okay . . . that's a good way to see if it's working for everybody."

"Right. And during that time, I will be a consultant, and Security Solutions will not carry me on the books as an employee, and you'll use my name only by mutual consent."

This was where Steve Landowski should say, "Go fuck yourself," but he was silent, and silence is agreement.

I continued, "I need this in writing."

"Okay . . . I can have Jack Berger draw up a consultant agreement."

"E-mail it to me." I would have had Robin look it over, but I'd just fired her.

"Jack will need some stuff from you. D.O.B., legal address—"

"I'll e-mail my résumé to your office."

"Okay. You and Jack can work it out. Anything else?"

Should I ask for Steve's Escalade for the summer? That might be pushing it. "No."

"Good. Why don't you come in tomorrow morning and we can sign some shit?"

"I'll be there at eleven."

"Okay. Good." He had another thought. "Tonight is Thirsty Thursday. Good time for you to meet Chip and Joseph, and see Lou and some other people." He reminded me: "It's party-girls night. Got some nice ladies tonight."

Whom he probably knew well from when he was on Vice. "I'm busy tonight."

"Okay. Next time."

I didn't reply.

"You drive a hard bargain, John."

Time to give him a bone. "Wait'll you see what I can get out of those rich assholes in the Hamptons."

He laughed. "Yeah. You can do it."

"I'm on it, Steve."

"Good. We'll have a little welcome lunch for you here tomorrow, and you can say hello to everybody."

"Okay."

"Anything else on your mind?"

Escalade? "No. See you tomorrow." I hung up and finished my beer.

So, I was now a consultant for a very tacky private investigative agency. And why was I doing that? Well, aside from the obvious—getting paid, getting laid, room and board, and all that—there could be something illicit going on at Security Solutions: Thirsty Thursdays, attended by local pols, cops, and who knew who else? I smelled corruption. And that was worth a look from the inside and a tipoff to the county police or the DA's office. I wondered why Max hadn't smelled the same thing. Maybe he'd only been there on poker night.

I went into the bedroom and got into my bathing trunks. I didn't know where or how Beth secured her gun, so I took mine with me, along with my cell phone and the beach towel, and went outside. Good to have a handgun handy anyway. Especially if people want to kill you.

Beth had moved the chaise longues onto the lawn, and she was soaking up the sun, bare-breasted, with her eyes closed. I walked toward her and said in a disguised voice, "Here to cut the grass, ma'am. Do you need your bush trimmed?"

She laughed.

I sat on the edge of my chaise, put my Glock on the grass, and looked at Beth Penrose, her skin glistening with lotion. She opened her eyes and turned her head toward me. "Did you speak to Steve?"

"I did. I go in tomorrow at eleven to do some paperwork, followed by lunch. I report for duty after July Fourth."

"Good. I'll go in tomorrow and put in for some unscheduled time off."

"Tell them something big came up."

She smiled.

I spread the beach towel on the chaise next to Beth's and lay back. The sun felt good. I could do this all summer. But not this summer.

Beth said, "If we agree on Bermuda, I'll book it and we can leave Saturday."

"Sounds good."

She asked, "Anything I should know about your conversation with Steve Landowski?"

"I told him I'm there for the summer as a consultant. Not an employee."

"All right . . . whatever works for you." She added, "In fact, that might work better. You can see and evaluate the whole operation before you decide if you want to stay."

"Right."

She was silent awhile, then asked, "Did you tie up your other loose ends?"

"I did."

"Any remorse?"

"Don't know that word."

She had no response.

"Can I have that sunscreen?"

She rolled off the chaise and knelt beside me with the bottle of lotion, which she rubbed on my face, then moved down to my chest. Her fingers passed over my bullet scar, and she asked, "Did you ever find those guys?"

"No. But I will." Though probably they were dead. Or doing hard time for something else. Life expectancy for violent felons on the street is very short. My partner, Dom Fanelli, had vowed to find them, and had he lived, I'm sure he would have. On the subject of scars and life expectancy, I said to her, "I wouldn't be here now if you hadn't shown up at the right time."

"You wouldn't have been in that situation if you weren't such an asshole."

"Well, thanks anyway."

"You can thank me by not being such a reckless asshole."

"My reckless asshole days are over."

"I'll hold you to that." She moved back to her chaise and lay down.

Well, here I was again with Beth Penrose, and we were sort of picking up where we left off.

Except this time . . . as I was lying there in the sun, I still had this feeling that I'd walked into a scripted play that had been in progress before I got here. Beth. Max. Security Solutions. An unlikely confluence of events. And *why* was I not supposed to mention Beth Penrose's name to Steve Landowski? Sometimes, what you see and hear is not what is really happening. Or what you see and hear really *is* happening, but you're drawing the wrong conclusions. The example I used to give in my John Jay class was the Great Plains Indians who saw puffs of smoke on the distant horizon, then for the first time in their lives saw a locomotive racing toward them. Conclusion: The smoke caused the locomotive. But really it's the other way around.

Detective Corey had to think about all this.

CHAPTER 15

Beth's shower stall was as I remembered it, full of feminine hygiene products, including a pink razor. I showered quickly, before I had an urge to shave my legs, and went into the guest bedroom. I sat on the bed wearing a towel and checked my messages. I was not at all surprised to see that neither Kate nor Robin had replied, and if they were surprised by my text, their surprise was that I hadn't told them sooner to buzz off.

Tess, however, had texted: I'M HAPPY FOR YOU. SHE'S A LOOKER. BUT MAYBE TOO SMART FOR YOU. GOOD LUCK. MUCH LOVE.

Class act. Good breeding. Glad I never married her.

I texted back: STAY SAFE.

I had an e-mail from Dick Kearns with the websites and direct contact info for three global security firms. Dick said he'd done background checks for all of them, and he also said: *I assume you have reasons for wanting this job. If it's your problem with Kate, getting killed in court is better than getting killed in Shitland. If it's money, I can help. If you just want a job, you got one here anytime. Good luck.*

You can always count on the blue bond.

I e-mailed Dick: *Thanks for the money offer and job offer. I've got a gig out East until Sept. And living with a lady. Kate is a non-issue. I'll put the overseas job on the back burner and reevaluate in Sept. Let's catch dinner next time I'm in NYC.*

Well, by keeping that door open, I was feeling a little

disloyal to Beth, who had invited me to live with her. But it takes two to tango, and it could be Beth who wanted me to cha-cha out in September. I'm not easy to live with, as I've been told.

Beth, fresh out of the shower and wearing nothing but a smile, came into the guest bedroom. She glanced at the phone in my hand. "Everything okay?"

"It is."

"Good. I'll call out for dinner. Chinese? Japanese? Italian? Your choice."

"I'll take you out. What was that place we both liked?"

She looked at me. "We need to stay here."

"Why?"

"Because we can't be seen together."

"You married?"

"We're not supposed to know each other." She further explained, "The North Fork is like a small town. Somebody who Landowski knows and who also knows me, maybe from the job, could see me with you."

"They don't know me."

"They might. Or they could snap a cell phone shot of us."

I asked her bluntly, "What's going on, Beth?"

"I told you." She assured me, "Once you have the job, maybe we can go out together."

It's easy to recognize bullshit, but not as easy to understand it. It also occurred to me that Beth Penrose had never intended for us to have drinks and dinner at aMano's last night, which was why she came to my place. Apparently, my employment at Security Solutions would be jeopardized if Steve Landowski knew that Beth Penrose and John Corey knew each other. And why was that? I couldn't imagine that Beth Penrose was ever romantically involved with a man like Steve Landowski.

But you never know. As for Beth's explanation that she and Landowski had butted heads on the job, that was possible, but it would have had to be a hell of a turf battle. So . . . something else.

"John?"

"Okay. But I'd like you to fill me in a bit more on this issue."

"I will. But not tonight."

Not tonight, dear. I have a headache. "Okay. How about a pepperoni pizza?"

"You got it."

She left, and I got into a pair of khakis and a blue polo shirt, then went to the kitchen and got a beer, then walked out to the patio and sat at the table.

I realized I'd be on vacation with Beth until past June 30, so I e-mailed Harry: *Sorry, can't make dinner. Starting a new job after the Fourth and I'll be away until then with a lady I'm living with out here. Charlotte will clean house for the renters. My treat.*

As for telling Harry that Russian assassins may be looking for me at his house, that would have to be a phone call after I spoke to Max.

Or was I being paranoid? Even if I was, paranoid people also have real enemies. Bottom line here, you underestimate the SVR at your own peril. Better to be safe than dead. Even better is to kill them before they kill you, which I'd already done. But there were more of them.

Next on my to-do list was to e-mail Jack Berger at Security Solutions. I forwarded to him my résumé, which contained all the info he needed—except for my new summer address, which was c/o Beth Penrose, a name not to be mentioned, so I'd have to fudge that. I concluded with: *Looking forward to meeting you tomorrow to work out the details.*

As I sipped my beer and waited for Beth, three e-mails popped up, one from Dick Kearns: *Glad to hear all that, especially new lady. Forget Shitland. Call when you're in NYC.*

The second e-mail was from Jack Berger, acknowledging receipt of résumé.

The other e-mail was from Uncle Harry: *Happy to hear you've found love, labor, and lodgings. You always do. Will miss you for dinner, but have a good holiday. Let's talk before you leave.*

For sure we needed to talk.

I finished my beer and watched two bluebirds trying to get it on. Maybe that's where the expression "I couldn't give a flying fuck" came from.

Beth came onto the patio carrying a tray, which she set down on the table. "Dewar's and soda for you. And some peanuts, which you like."

"Marry me." No, actually I said, "Thank you."

Beth sat and raised her vodka. "To our first day."

We touched glasses and drank.

She was wearing white pants, a navy blue top, and sandals. Beth wasn't into jewelry and she kept the makeup to a minimum, so to encourage low maintenance and short mirror time, I said, "You look like a model in a Nautica catalog."

"Thank you." She glanced at my phone on the side table. "Have you heard from anyone?"

"Tess. Wished me luck."

"Anyone else?"

"Jack Berger, at Security Solutions, confirming tomorrow. And my uncle. I'll call him about the other thing after we speak to Max." I added, "No one else."

She nodded and said, "I got a call from my contact in Missing Persons who I texted."

"About . . . ? Oh, right."

"The Security Solutions PI who made an inquiry at Missing Persons—this was sometime last summer—was a woman named Sharon Dolch Hite. Before she retired and took a job at Security Solutions, Sharon was a Suffolk County detective in the Third Precinct, which is located in Bay Shore, but I didn't know her."

I recalled that the Suffolk County PD had about 2,500 people, so everyone couldn't know everyone, but I'd always assumed that the smaller Detective Division was on a first-name basis. But I guess not. In any case, I assumed Sharon Hite was the same female PI who Amy had said used to work there.

Beth continued, "According to the detective I spoke to at Missing Persons, Sharon Hite took retirement in June last year and went to work at Security Solutions sometime after that."

And apparently didn't last too long there. And easy to guess why. I really didn't care about this, but I said, "Okay. Thanks."

Beth had more. "Sharon Hite had come to headquarters in Yaphank on behalf of a Security Solutions client to see what the Missing Persons Squad knew about a missing woman named Carolyn Sanders whose street name was Tiffany." She added, unnecessarily, "Carolyn, a.k.a. Tiffany, was a prostitute."

"Right." Why half of them named themselves after a jewelry store was a mystery even I couldn't solve. Better than Best Buy, I guess. "So Sharon Hite worked for Security Solutions, and she quit or was fired. Maybe I should talk to her to find out why." So I could quit for the same reason.

Beth didn't respond to that, but said, "I would advise you not to ask anyone at Security Solutions about Sharon Hite."

I glanced at her. "Why?"

"Let me get some more information for you, in case there was some unpleasantness."

"Okay . . ." But did it really matter why Sharon Hite left Security Solutions? I wasn't making this my career. Though maybe Beth thought I was, and she didn't want me to get off on the wrong foot.

As though reading my mind, she said, "I'd like you to go there tomorrow with a positive attitude. I'm telling you about Sharon Hite so you *don't* ask about the female PI who used to work there."

"I got that." I also had the thought that whatever Beth had just heard from her contact in Missing Persons was more than she was telling me. Or was I being . . . you know? "Okay. You'll get back to me."

"I will. I doubt if anyone at Security Solutions will bring up Sharon Hite, but if they do, just listen." She added, "It's easier to play dumb when you are."

"Right." So now there were two ladies' names I wasn't supposed to mention at Security Solutions—Beth Penrose, Suffolk County PD, and Sharon Hite, former Suffolk PD. Coincidence? I think not.

———

The pizza came and Beth had a slice, but left the rest for me and nibbled on a salad. She'd gotten herself a white wine and a brown beer for me and said, "You propose a toast."

The word "propose" gave me a momentary panic attack, but I recovered and said, "Okay . . . there is no place in the world I would rather be right now, and no one on earth I'd rather be with than you, and I hope you feel the same."

"I do," she said.

Two words I never want to hear again. We touched glasses and drank.

I was sure that the subject of vacation was on Beth's agenda, so to sound engaged—wrong word—*enthused*, I asked, "Have we decided on a vacation destination?"

"We're leaning toward Bermuda. Have you been there?"

Meaning, been there with a woman. "I haven't."

"Neither have I. But I hear it's romantic, and I'd like to go with you."

"Let's do it."

She squeezed my hand. "I'll book it tomorrow."

"I'll give you my credit card. It's on me."

"No. It was my idea, and it's on me."

She sounded sincere, but I said, "You just got me a job and a place to live. So this is my thanks."

"Okay . . . thanks." Beth asked, "Are you ready for tomorrow?"

"I can't wait to meet my new colleagues."

She looked at me. "Max tells me that Steve told him that you and the receptionist—Amy—hit it off."

That pissed me off and I replied, "I am not happy that you and Max—"

"I know. You said. But I'm sure you'd rather I tell you that Max and I talk about you than *not* tell you."

"I'd rather you discussed only police matters."

"We do." She looked at me. "And I'll share some of that with you shortly."

I didn't reply, but I was hoping she'd confirm that the smoke I was seeing didn't cause the locomotive. In fact, I was sure it didn't. There was definitely something else going on here.

I looked at Beth in the fading light. She was truly a beautiful woman and could easily have been a model, but she wanted to be a cop. And eventually, she became a homicide detective, which, I say with some modesty, is sort of the top of the heap. That was about the only thing that Beth and I had in common when we met—except for some internal organs, and not even all of those.

I recalled that working with Detective Penrose on the Plum Island case had been interesting, to use a nicer word than I'd used at the time. Beth Penrose had been tight-lipped and tight-assed, to be sure, and not fun to work with. But she was also sharp, and she knew when to think outside the box and when to stick to the book. This is a rare gift, and I admired her ability to shift gears on the curves.

There's not much I don't know about how to investigate a murder, but even I can learn a thing or two, and I recalled something she'd said that stuck with me: "When you hear hoofbeats, you think horse. But sometimes you have to think zebra."

I actually used that line in one of my classes at John Jay, and it so impressed a young female student that she wanted to discuss it over drinks. But that's another story.

It was dark now, and I excused myself to use the loo, but actually got my Glock. I'm not one of those guys who feels naked without his gun, but I never want to be a guy who's found shot dead without a gun in his hand.

Beth and I retired to the chaise longues and held hands, looking at the night sky. I didn't know what she was thinking about—maybe what caterer to use for the engagement party—but I was thinking about being at Security Solutions tomorrow, not mentioning Beth Penrose or Sharon Hite. I was also thinking about Beth sharing with me some of the police matters that she and Max had talked about. When you hear hoofbeats . . . something is coming at you.

Beth had a few unsolved cases she wanted my opin-

ion on, which was flattering or B.S. I think she was trying to play to my ego and show me that, despite my new
circumstances at a PI agency, I was still relevant. Which
means you're not. How the mighty are fallen. Well, my
new job—and my new living arrangement—came up for
renewal in September.

We decided to call it a night and went inside, checked
the doors and windows, and went to bed. We both slept
au naturel, and it was nice having warm flesh in the bed
and a Glock on each nightstand.

Beth wanted to make love and I wanted to have sex,
so that worked out. Afterwards I read Nero Wolfe, paying
special attention to the subtle clues. I love a good mystery, but I don't like being written out of one.

CHAPTER 16

Beth—now Detective Sergeant Penrose—was up with the sun, showered and dressed for work before I was fully awake.

She leaned down and gave me a kiss. "Good luck today. I'll call you later. We'll celebrate your new job and TGIF tonight. Coffee is made. Bye."

She left, and as the dawn came through the window, I got out of bed, put on my robe, went into the kitchen, and poured a mug of coffee.

There was a note on the counter, *Home about 6. Have a great day! Love, B.*

She also left a house key, which made it official: I lived here.

I took my coffee out to the patio. Everything was wet with morning dew, so I stood there listening to the birds who were greeting the new day with a song. Then they eat worms for breakfast.

Well . . . home alone with time to kill before I reported in at Security Solutions. I could make the bed and put some cut flowers in a vase. Or I could shoot birds in the backyard. That would shut them up. Or I could go for a run. I needed to think . . . something was definitely off here. Nero Wolfe thinks best when he's sitting on his ass; I think best when I'm running.

I got into my running shoes, shorts, and T-shirt, and stuck my Glock, creds, cell phone, and key in my belly band, then left the house. The sun was above the trees now and the air was damp. I remembered the neighborhood and headed south toward Cutchogue Harbor.

Running gets the blood flowing into my alcohol stream and fires up the neurons. So . . . Sharon Hite and Beth Penrose. And Beth and Max giving me plausible/ implausible reasons why I shouldn't mention either name at Security Solutions. Also, Beth's insistence that she and I not be seen together in public seemed disproportionate to her explanation. And then there was Beth texting someone at work to ask who from Security Solutions had come to Missing Persons in headquarters. I'd asked the question in an offhand way, but it wasn't that important for her to make the inquiry. And who at police headquarters would even remember a visit from former detective Sharon Hite? Conclusion: Beth hadn't texted anyone. She already knew about Sharon Hite and had taken the opportunity to tell me not to mention that name at Security Solutions. But why? And there was another thing to think about: Max and Beth talking about police matters that she would share with me—shortly. Was any of this actually connected?

If I were a patient man, I'd wait for Beth to fill me in. But I'm not patient, and I like to figure things out for myself so that if I'm listening to bullshit, I already have my own information programmed in my bullshit detector.

A police chaplain—an old rabbi—once said to me, "The mind is a great wanderer." So as I made my way toward the water, my mind wandered back to Beth Penrose's unexpected appearance on my back porch. My impression at the time was that there was something off about that—like Max asking her to deliver the secondhand message about Security Solutions wanting to hire me. That was not Max's M.O., and I'd interpreted Beth's visit as *her* idea because she wanted to see me, which is what any egotistical male would conclude. Then Max, at Claudio's, sort of confirmed that. So ... was it just a happy coincidence that Beth, who happened to be on the North Fork, had dinner with Max, and that Max happened to have a message for me, and that Beth, hearing I was at Uncle Harry's house, was hot to deliver the message in person so she could see me? Could be.

But what if the smoke didn't cause the locomotive? What if it was the other way around? When you hear hoofbeats, you think horse. But sometimes you have to think zebra. So what if it was *Beth* who wanted me to get a job at Security Solutions, and she was using Max as her cover? Did that make any sense? It didn't yesterday, or the day before, but today there were things that needed better explanations than I was getting.

So, was something more going on than my former lover wanting to see me employed? Specifically, employed at Security Solutions? If I wanted to be a PI, there were dozens of reputable firms that would want to hire me, and Beth and Max knew that and could have suggested that. Instead, they seemed excited about Security Solutions, who were not exactly the Pinkertons. Why would they do that? They knew me and knew what I'd think of Steve Landowski and his PI agency. So was this suspicious behavior? Or bad judgment on their part? Well, Max and Beth, for all their minor faults, had never displayed such bad judgment. So when you subtract one possibility from two, you're left with suspicious behavior.

If I put all this together in a certain way, I could conclude that I was going to become a police spy at Security Solutions for Detective Sergeant Penrose, what we call a CI—a Confidential Informant. Was that possible? Or was I having one of my boredom-induced fantasies?

I mean, was I flattering myself to think that Beth Penrose needed me to penetrate the inner workings of Security Solutions? Well . . . no. I'm a great detective. Ask anyone. Ask Max, who'd hired me at a hundred bucks a day to consult on the Gordon murders, which was maybe where Max and Beth had gotten this idea, and maybe that was the purpose of Max and Beth's dinner at Claudio's. This all made sense—but only if I picked and chose the facts that I liked. Which you can't do. Also, this presupposes that Security Solutions and/or Steve Landowski was into something that was not legal. Which, after my morning there, I could easily believe.

I picked up my pace on the downgrade toward the water, as though chasing an elusive truth. A little faster and I might tackle it.

Anyway, if all of the above was true, then the obvious question was: Why didn't Max and Beth just tell me what they were investigating and ask me to take a job at Security Solutions to work undercover for them? I probably would have jumped on it, to get off my ass and get the juices flowing. On the other hand, I'd gone into that interview with Landowski with an honestly bad attitude. No playacting there, as I'd have had to do if I'd been asked by Beth to get a job at Security Solutions so that I could help her on a case. Beth and Max are smart. But . . . I'm smarter.

I also thought about Max's role in my new scenario. His pitch at Claudio's had been good, but not good enough, as he'd undoubtedly reported to Beth. Also, Max told me it was Lou Santangelo who'd brought up my name at the retirement dinner, but that was unlikely. More likely it was Max who'd brought my name up to Lou Santangelo—at Beth's request. And Max had casually asked me not to mention Beth Penrose's name if I had an interview at Security Solutions. So then it was Beth's turn at bat, and she had a much better way of convincing me that I needed to take the job. But if I'd said no— postcoitally—then Beth would have had to come clean. Either way, I was going to work for Steve Landowski— and for Sergeant Penrose. So it was now time for Beth to tell me what this was all about. She was probably waiting until after my first day or two of work at Security Solutions.

Well . . . if any of my speculations were accurate, did that mean I had been seduced by Beth for reasons other than her longing to rekindle a romance with the man she once loved? That would make her a conniving woman, but a very dedicated detective. Must be a very important case.

Actually, it didn't have to be one or the other—it could be that Beth's feelings were real, but her motives for getting me working at Security Solutions were not what she said. I did, however, like her recruiting method.

I got to the end of the street and turned onto a street that followed the shore. A thick fog clung to the water and rolled out over the beach and into the road. When you run in this stuff, you get a feeling of disorientation and a sense of unreality. But nothing like the sense of unreality I was feeling now, after coming to some conclusions that even I found hard to believe.

I knew that if I ran all of this through my mind again, I might come up with just as much evidence that everything was as it seemed. Statistically, if you're in Kentucky, the hoofbeats you hear are horses. If you're in Uganda, they're probably zebras. You just have to know where you are.

They tell you in CIC—the Criminal Investigation Course—not to get fixated on a suspect or a theory. And this is good advice, as too many detectives who've botched a case can confirm. They also tell you, "The simplest explanation for what you see is usually the best explanation." Don't complicate things. If it looks like shit, smells like shit, and feels like shit, you don't have to taste it.

Well . . . in this case, everything looked and smelled like roses. But roses grow best when they're rooted in bullshit.

I turned onto a path that went down to the water, and I stopped at the shore, catching my breath. The blanket of fog made it hard to tell where land and water met. If you swim in something like this, you can get turned around, and you are just as likely to swim deeper into the water as you are to swim to the shore. At some point, your senses fail you, and you know you're in trouble. This could be a metaphor for life, or it could be practical swimming advice; in either case, don't swim in the fog.

Sometimes, though, you get thrown overboard, and you don't have much choice. You sink or you swim. And that's when you realize you should never have gotten into that boat with those people.

Final thought on my suspicions: This might not be the safe job that Beth said it was. That was the good news.

———

Back in the honeymoon cottage, I shaved and showered, then stood in front of my closet. If I'd had time, I could have gone into town and bought a Tony Soprano shirt so I'd look like Steve Landowski. But Steve might think I was mocking him. Amy would definitely think so. Maybe she'd like the pink pants, but it's best to be yourself, so I got into my khakis, polo shirt, and blue blazer. I also had my wallet, my phone, my new key, and my gun, and an extra mag in case I had to shoot my way out of there.

I left the house, got into my Jeep, and was on my way.

The sun was burning away the mist, and it looked like another nice day on the North Fork.

There were a few wineries along the route, and I thought about stopping to pick up a nice wine for Amy, to thank her for her . . . whatever. And if not for Beth in my life, I would have done that. Actually, if not for Beth, I wouldn't be on my way to Security Solutions.

On that subject, I've learned over the years that once you get an unprovable theory in your head, you have to stop playing with it or it will drive you crazy. If you leave it alone, it will sort itself out in your subconscious. More importantly, once you're aware that things are not as they seem—that there may be an alternate universe—you are prepped to interpret new information in a different way. And there is a lot of dark matter in that universe. You can't see it, but you can infer it.

I could see the American flag flying from a pole in front of the big farmhouse, and I slowed down.

So, if I was about to become a confidential informant— a mole at Security Solutions—that would be great, though it would also mean that Beth had manipulated me. But if I was just a consultant for a sleazy PI firm, that was not so great, though it would mean that Beth was just in love. Well, after work, when I saw Beth, I'd make sure I knew what I was celebrating.

Meanwhile, first day on the job. Could be interesting. Stay alert.

CHAPTER 17

I parked on the side of the farmhouse near Landowski's Escalade, got out of my Jeep, and locked it. I noted that there were five other vehicles in the lot: the three cars I'd seen last time, plus an old Mercedes sedan and a black Dodge Durango that had seen better days. The old Mercedes looked like something a disbarred lawyer had bought new, and the Durango had retired cop written all over it. Sort of like my Jeep.

If I was on a case, I'd photograph the license plates and have them run through DMV and NCIC—the National Crime Information Center—to begin a preliminary investigation. And maybe I *was* on a case. But I was also on camera, so I'd have to use my photographic memory on my way out. I love this shit.

I walked onto the porch to the front door, pushed the buzzer, and waited for the unlock buzz. If Landowski was smarter than he looked, everyone who worked here would have their own entry code for the keypad, which would be electronically recorded so that Landowski would know who entered and at what time. Meaning, if I was Beth's confidential informant, and if I came here at 3 A.M. to snoop, I'd leave evidence of my entry—even if I was driving another car and wearing Aunt June's cocktail dress for the surveillance cameras. Well, even the best security can be outwitted by a pro like me, but the very best security was a man with a gun who lived in the house, and that was Steve Landowski. This would be a challenge.

I was buzzed in and entered the farmhouse, a.k.a. Security Solutions, a.k.a. Animal House.

Before I could get to the reception area, Amy was in the foyer, looking like she wanted to hug me, which she did. "Welcome!" she said, holding the hug long enough for me to get a whiff of her nice floral scent. Very glad I had sex last night.

"Great to be here," I said, but only if I'm spying on you. Otherwise, this sucks.

She took my arm. "We'll sit in the storage room," meaning the classy office where they brought the clients. "Jack will be along shortly."

I guess Landowski told Amy to soften me up before Jack Berger got down to business. But after I signed on the dotted line, she'd drop me like a moldy yogurt.

As we walked down the hallway, Amy said, "I'm glad to see that someone around here knows how to dress."

"Well," I admitted, "I wanted to dress more casual—to fit in. But I don't know where Steve gets his shirts."

She laughed to show me that her loyalty to Steve was not unconditional. She observed, "You have a nice tan. You get to the beach?"

"Just a backyard tan."

"I know some secluded beaches where the tourists don't go."

"You'll have to tell me."

"I'll show you." Amy opened the door to the office. "Have a seat, Detective."

I sat at the round mahogany table, on which was a legal folder and a pen.

Amy closed the door and asked, "Can I make you a Scotch and soda?"

"Only if Jack Berger has two."

She smiled, obviously impressed with my quick wit. It occurred to me that flirting can work both ways; Amy Lang might be useful in my undercover role. But could I trust her? Maybe. If I seduced her. I was really getting into this. I should have brought the wine.

She asked, "How about a club soda with me?"

"Sure." Easy on the knockout drops, babe. I go under fast.

She moved to the bar cabinet. Amy was wearing a short gray skirt and a white knit top that may have shrunk in the wash. I now noticed that she was barefoot. Did they also know about my foot fetish? Who ratted?

She handed me my glass and raised hers. "I look forward to working with you."

"Same here."

We touched glasses and she sat across from me. "I have a few things to go over with you before I get Jack."

"I'm all yours."

She smiled.

I was fairly sure that this room was monitored—for quality assurance and other purposes. The hidden mic could probably be turned off in here so that Steve Landowski could have privacy when he didn't want to be recorded, or it could be turned on to record clients and visitors when it suited him. I mean, this is what you do if you're Steve Landowski, even if secret recordings are illegal. In fact, my meeting with Landowski in here may have been recorded, but I didn't think he'd share that conversation with anyone.

The question was: Did Amy know about a hidden mic? And if so, was she able to shut it off? And did she? Or was Landowski now in his upstairs office listening to every word? You can usually tell if you're being recorded by how the other person speaks and what they say or don't say. Also, there could be a video camera behind that mirror. And why wouldn't there be?

I asked, "Is Lou here today?"

"No, but he'll be here in time for our lunch."

"Have you ever actually seen him?"

She smiled. "He does a lot of our fieldwork." She added, "I'll bet you guys were an awesome team on Missing Persons."

Actually, Lou Santangelo couldn't find his own ass with both hands. I said, "We weren't partners, but all the Missing Persons detectives worked and played well together." I asked, "Does Lou do most of your missing persons cases?"

"He does."

"Anyone else do missing persons?"

She glanced at me. "No. That's Lou's specialty. Why do you ask?"

"Just wondering." Also wondering why she didn't mention Sharon Hite, who'd worked on the case of the missing prostitute, Tiffany Sanders. Wondering too if that case was still active here at Security Solutions, and who the client was. Who would pay a PI agency to find a missing prostitute? Usually, it's the family.

Amy changed the subject. "Steve says you're not starting here until after the Fourth."

"Correct."

"Are you going away?"

"My plans are up in the air."

"Would you be available to come in if we needed you here to pitch an important client?"

"If Lou Santangelo can find me, I'll be here."

She smiled but was not satisfied with the evasive answer. "Okay. So I also understand that this is a trial period, ending in September, and that you'll be a consultant."

"It was you who suggested a trial period."

"Whose idea was it to be a consultant?"

"Mine."

"What was your thinking on that?"

Because I didn't want a PI agency on my résumé. Especially this one. But I think my new girlfriend wants me to work here as her confidential informant. Not sure why, but I'll find out. I replied, "It's a good way for everyone to see if it's working out, and maybe for me to see if I can make constructive recommendations before I commit."

"That could work." She tapped the folder. "I read your résumé. *Very* impressive."

"Thank you."

"I see why Steve wanted you here."

"I hope I can contribute to the continued success of Security Solutions," I said loudly for the mic.

"I'm sure you can." She glanced at my résumé. "I know what the Anti-Terrorist Task Force is, but what is the Diplomatic Surveillance Group?"

"What is your security clearance?"

She smiled. "I can keep a secret."

I returned the smile. "Well . . . okay. The Diplomatic Surveillance Group, as the name implies, surveils foreign diplomats who represent nations that are considered unfriendly to U.S. interests."

"Sounds exciting."

"It has its moments." Like when Russian SVR agents, posing as diplomats, try to kill you. "But mostly routine surveillance."

"I'm sure you're being modest."

"I'm a very modest man."

She smiled. "Why did you leave?"

"I'm not at liberty to discuss that."

"Maybe someday you'll give me a redacted answer."

I didn't reply.

She said, "I'd like to have a career as successful and interesting as yours."

"I'm sure you will."

She looked at me. "I know you think that working here is a step down from what you've done."

"The money is a step up," I said, then added, "It's time for me to think of myself."

"I was going to say that."

"All work has dignity." Except maybe this job.

She suggested, "You can offer some good advice here in the next two months, then maybe decide to stay."

Beth made a similar point, but she was conning me so I'd show up for work. "I'll try to raise the already high standards here."

She let that bullshit slide and looked at my résumé again. "I see you're on three-quarter disability from the NYPD."

"I should have specified that's a mental disability."

She glanced at me to make sure I was joking. "You were wounded in the line of duty."

"Correct."

"Steve says he remembers that. It was in all the papers."

"I can show you my press clippings." And my bullet wounds. The one in the groin is particularly interesting.

She looked at me with those big blue eyes. "That must have been awful. Traumatic."

"It was a career-ender. But I moved on." To other dangerous shit, convinced that I was immortal. Or at least lucky.

She nodded. "Everything happens for a reason." She smiled again. "Now you're here."

"Fate," I agreed.

She returned to the business at hand and flipped through the papers in the folder. "There was no local address on your résumé—only your Manhattan address." She picked up the pen and said, "I'd like to add your local address to the consultant agreement."

I gave her Uncle Harry's address, which she wrote on the agreement.

"And that will be through the summer?"

"Until further notice."

"Okay." She asked, "Do you have any questions for me?"

"How was Thirsty Thursday?"

She smiled. "I told you, I'm not invited."

"That will be one of my first recommendations."

"Don't do me any favors."

"I'm sure the female PI who worked here was invited." Sorry, Beth.

She replied, "I don't know. Sharon wasn't here long."

I dropped the subject to show Amy—and whoever else was listening—that I had no further interest in the female PI who had worked here. In any case, if or when I spoke to former detective Sharon Hite, I'd find out why she left this job. I asked, "Any news on your appointment to the Academy?"

"No. But I'll let you know."

"You might want to get a PI license and stay here."

"Steve has said that. But my dream has always been NYPD."

"Then follow your dream."

"I will. You did." She asked, "Any regrets?"

"I don't know that word."

She smiled, then slid the folder toward me. "There's a company personnel form in there for you to fill out. Do the best you can." She put the pen down. "Okay. I'll let Jack know we're done." She stood. "See you at lunch." She walked toward the door, then looked back over her shoulder. "My cell number is in the folder. Call me if you need anything."

"Thank you, Ms. Lang."

She smiled and walked out, leaving a scent of lavender in the room and bare footprints on the carpet.

Well . . . I was already burrowing deep into this place, and Beth would be proud of me if I got Amy Lang into bed and recruited her. Deep undercover work is dangerous, but somebody has to do it. Or . . . even scarier, I'd come to some bad conclusions, and this was just the shitty job it appeared to be.

I pulled the folder toward me, opened it, and found Amy's cell number written on her business card, which showed her title as Receptionist, though there was more to her than met the eye. I put the card in my pocket, then looked at the Security Solutions personnel form, which asked for things like my driver's license info, pistol license number, types of pistols I had registered, and other professional information, some of which was on my résumé. Most of this didn't apply to me as a consultant, and it was more information than I wanted to give them, but so as not to seem arrogant or secretive, I filled out some of it, including my passport number, which I made up.

It also occurred to me that Security Solutions, a PI agency that did background checks for clients, could also do a background check on me. They wouldn't bother to vet my résumé, which they liked as is. But they might— for whatever reason—check into my personal life or even put a tail on me and discover that I was living with Detective Beth Penrose, whose name I wasn't supposed to mention here for some reason—and not the reason that Beth had given me. The real reason would be that if this PI agency was under investigation, and if Landowski knew or suspected that, then he shouldn't know that his new hire, John Corey, was sleeping with a Suffolk County Police detective.

But what if Steve Landowski, former Suffolk County detective—or someone else here—remembered the Plum Island case, a.k.a. the Gordon double homicide? Detective Penrose got most of the credit for cracking the case, and my role was behind the scenes, so there was no public connection between me and Detective Penrose, and the romance came later.

Though to be safe and proactive, I'd have to keep an eye out for freelance PIs hired by Security Solutions to surveil my off-duty movements. I'd have to tell Beth to do the same—if and when she told me that I was Secret Agent 001. Also I needed to ask Max if he thought Landowski could make a connection between me and Detective Penrose. Stupid stuff like this can blow your cover. And all my instincts and all my experience told me I was here undercover. In fact, I was so undercover that it was secret even to me.

Anyway, I signed and dated the personnel form, then got more club soda.

I looked out the window to see if any other cars had arrived, but there were still the same vehicles in the parking area.

Situational awareness. That's what you learn in the Academy, and what you need as a rookie on patrol or as a seasoned detective on a stakeout. You need to know where people, places, and things are, i.e., keep your head out of your ass.

If I was on camera, I couldn't look for a hidden mic. But I *could* check for a hidden video camera.

I moved toward the wall where Landowski had his framed photos and citations and read one of them. Then I looked at myself in the mounted mirror and finger-combed my hair with one hand while pressing a finger from my other hand against the mirror. So if there's no space or gap between your fingertip and the reflection of the fingertip, then it's a regular mirror. But if there's a small gap, it's a two-way mirror, and there is probably a video camera behind it. I glanced at my finger and saw a small gap between my fingertip and the reflection.

Okay. I moved away from the wall and studied the books on the shelves. Anyone watching this live, or on a video playback, would know what I'd just done. Good. I wouldn't want Steve Landowski to think he'd hired an idiot.

On the subject of situational awareness, I noticed that the old floorboards were laid in a typical staggered pattern, except there was a straight cut about four feet long close to the edge of the Oriental rug. This was obviously a trapdoor, mostly covered by the rug. The trapdoor would lead from this former storage room to the basement—probably a common feature in a farmhouse of this vintage. I should definitely go down there someday. I mean, the basement door in the kitchen had a padlock, which was an invite for someone like me to snoop.

I sipped my club soda. Well . . . as Max had blabbed to Beth, I'd really hit it off with Amy. But Amy was playing a game, and so were Max and Beth. And in their minds, I was the pawn. But in reality, I am and have always been the king.

I thought about why Beth had pressed for a vacation before I started working here. Maybe the vacation was going to include a briefing and a pitch to penetrate the inner workings of Security Solutions while the Suffolk

County PD continued the investigation before I started working here.

On the other hand, the simplest explanation for the Bermuda vacation was that it was a vacation, a romantic way for Beth and me to get reacquainted. I needed to stop overthinking. But underthinking is worse. Anyway, if there was nothing more to this than me getting talked into a shitty job, then my best hope for an exciting summer was the Russian assassins. Well . . . maybe Amy too. That could be exciting. Especially if Beth got wind of her. Anyway, one step at a time. Next step, Jack Berger, disbarred lawyer. We could use more of those.

CHAPTER 18

The door opened, and a man entered.

"Good morning, Detective Corey. I'm Jack Berger."

He had a can of Coke in one hand and a folder in his other, which he put on the table. We shook and he said, "Welcome to Security Solutions."

"Thank you."

"Please have a seat."

We both sat at the table, and he looked over my partially completed personnel form as he sipped his Coke.

Jack Berger was in his early sixties, with a full head of white hair and a blotchy complexion which could be high blood pressure or grain alcohol. He had a pleasant face and alert eyes, and he was well spoken. I guess I'd expected a sleazebag, but Jack Berger seemed like a gentleman, and as out of place here as I was. In fact, he was wearing a white dress shirt and expensive-looking slacks and shoes, and he lacked only a tie and jacket to make himself presentable in court. Well . . . a license to practice law would also help.

He seemed satisfied with the information I'd provided, then looked at me and asked, "What prompted you to apply for a position here?"

Meaning, "What's a guy like you doing in a place like this?"

I replied, "I was actually recruited, as you know."

"Yes. But—"

"Money." The best defense is a good offense, and I

like to be the one asking the questions. "How about you, Counselor?"

He replied, "To be very candid, employment opportunities for disbarred lawyers are limited." He added, "This gets me out of the house."

I saw he had a wedding ring, a rarity around here, and he dressed well, so the missus thought he was going to a nice office. How the mighty are fallen. Including, I guess, me. In my case, however, the fall had to do with me being pushed; in Jack Berger's case, he'd slipped on his own shit. And now he was Steve Landowski's consigliere. I asked, "How long have you been here?"

"About two years." He thought a moment, then said, "I was making over a million a year, but spending more. I figured out a way to make up the deficit." He added, "Ironic that I should think I could get away with what a lot of my clients went to jail for."

Right. I like a man who admits to a felony and takes personal responsibility.

He continued, without prompting, "My wife was very understanding and forgiving. We gave up our club memberships, sold our condo in the city and the house in Southampton, and my BMW and Rolex, and I made full restitution."

Which probably kept him out of jail. But I hoped Mrs. Berger got to keep some of her jewelry. I said, "A million dollars is not what it used to be."

"So I discovered." His mea culpa out of the way, he returned to the subject of John Corey. "I saw your city address on your résumé. I know the building. And I wondered why you'd own a place like that . . . and how you pay for it."

"Well, not the way you paid for yours, Jack. And your story makes me realize it's time to do some math."

"I would advise that. Or you can do very well here and pay for all the things you don't need."

"I guess that's why I'm here."

He thought about that, then said, "I understand why you're here from a financial standpoint. But not why you're here from a professional standpoint."

I could see why he would wonder about that. But Steve Landowski never gave it a second thought. And, unfortunately, neither did Max or Beth, who should have realized that me agreeing to work at Security Solutions might raise some eyebrows—and also some suspicions, if this PI agency was not completely legit.

"Mr. Corey?"

"I've thought about that myself, Jack, and aside from the money, my good friend Chief Sylvester Maxwell"— and my past and present lover, Beth Penrose—"pointed out to me that a PI firm would be the next best thing to police work, which, to be honest, I miss."

"Yes, I hear that from a number of our private investigators."

But that didn't answer the real question of why I was *here*, rather than a better PI agency in the city. I added, "Also, Chief Maxwell convinced me that I needed a lifestyle change. Less stress, and maybe a permanent move out of the city to this quiet piece of the world."

"I'm renting a small place out here. It's not so bad. Winters are . . . quiet."

"Right. And all the bugs die."

He smiled, then asked, "Are you renting this place in Mattituck?"

"I am there as a guest of my rich uncle."

"It's good to have one of those."

"A rich girlfriend would be better."

He changed the subject and said, "I had the impression from Steve that you weren't enthused about working here."

"His offer changed my mind."

"I see. But you came here for an interview without knowing that he would make you such a generous offer."

Landowski had told me that Jack Berger thought it was a good idea to hire John Corey, but this was starting to sound like an interrogation. And I had to remind myself that Jack Berger, former criminal defense attorney, knew how to ask innocent-sounding and very leading questions. Same with Robin when I came home late at night. Landowski hiring Berger may have been the smartest thing he ever did. Hiring me, not so smart. And on the subject of smart, I've been grilled on the witness stand a hundred times by smart lawyers like Jack Berger and Robin Paine, and even though they had the tactical advantage of me being under oath while they were not, I always sounded credible. Today, neither Jack Berger nor John Corey was under oath, but it's good to tell the truth, though not necessarily the whole truth, and I replied, "I agreed to meet Steve Landowski as a favor to Chief Maxwell." Also, I wanted to get Beth Penrose in bed.

He nodded. "That was good of you. And happily for all of us, you decided to consider Mr. Landowski's offer." He added, "Steve can be very convincing."

No. Me agreeing to work here was a postcoital decision, Jack. I said to him, "Truthfully, Steve Landowski couldn't convince me to wipe the snot off my nose." I hoped Landowski was listening.

Jack suppressed a smile. "Well, however you reached your decision to work at Security Solutions, we are all excited to welcome you here as a consultant and hope you will stay on as a private investigator."

"Thank you."

"Though . . . given your enthusiasm about the possibility of making three or four hundred thousand a year, you didn't ask for a detailed and binding hiring contract that would have spelled out what Steve said to you." He continued, "Instead, you wanted this—" He tapped the consulting agreement. "What was your thinking?"

Jack was pushing and pressing, but as a twice-married man, I'm used to that. I replied, "I've been exploring other opportunities, and I'll evaluate them as they materialize. Meanwhile, this is my summer job—and it will not be part of my otherwise impressive résumé. At some point you can draw up a hiring contract incorporating everything that Steve promised me verbally, and I'll have that looked at by counsel, and if it's acceptable, I may sign it in September." *Unless everyone here is in jail by that time.*

Jack looked at me and said, "Thank you for explaining."

"Maybe you'd like to explain why you're questioning my decision to work here."

"I just want to be sure that neither of us is making a mistake."

"That's why I want this temporary arrangement."

"I understand."

But he didn't seem convinced, so I said, "To give you more information than you need, Amy Lang has charmed me."

He smiled. "Ah, yes. She does that."

And that clinched it. Men think with their weenies. But . . . Jack Berger, in his former profession, had heard as much bullshit from his clients as I'd heard from my suspects. So if I had to score this exchange with Mr. Berger, I'd admit it was a draw. He was good, but I'm also good, though we were both a bit rusty since our days in court. More importantly, he either suspected something—which meant this place was not totally legit—or he was just doing his job. Or, more likely, he was honestly curious about why John Corey would want to work in this place. Hopefully, I'd convinced him.

You should stop chasing the bus when you've caught it, but I felt I needed to throw in something else and said, "Steve briefed me about Thirsty Thursday, which sounds like fun." I asked, "Will I see you there?"

He replied, "I've applied to the bar to have my license reinstated."

Which meant, "I know nothing about what goes on upstairs."

I said, "Well, good luck with that."

"Thank you." He changed the subject. "May I ask why you left your last job with the Federal government?"

"You can ask. But I'm not at liberty to say."

He nodded; unlike Amy, he knew that was the end of that. He got down to business. "Did you read and understand the agreement?"

"I did."

"Are you represented by counsel?"

"I just fired my attorney."

"May I ask why?"

"She wanted my parking space." If he'd had a hearing aid, he would have adjusted it. I explained, "My ex-wife—Robin Paine."

He smiled. "Ah. Yes."

Which said it all.

"A very good defense attorney," he said.

Sort of an oxymoron, but that's not my world.

He looked at me a moment, then informed me, "I had lunch with her a few times, and I should tell you, she spoke very highly of you."

Not around the house. But Robin and I had a postnuptial understanding not to speak badly of each other. I had respected her work—until she switched sides—and she respected mine. I said, "It was an amicable divorce."

"The best kind, unless you're a divorce lawyer. Though I'm sorry to hear that your present relationship with Ms. Paine is not so amicable. If that changes, I would be happy to work with her on your future hiring contract."

I was sure he would. They'd slip in a clause giving her my parking space.

"Let me know if you retain an attorney."

"I will."

"And I understand that you are currently in the process of . . . another divorce."

"Correct."

"I'm sorry to hear that."

"The first divorce with Robin worked really well." I added, "I got the condo."

"I hope you can keep it in this divorce."

Funny. Not funny.

He continued, "I have heard—I believe from Chief Maxwell—that Mrs. Corey is an FBI agent."

"Mrs. Corey is my mother. Ms. Mayfield is the FBI agent. Why do you ask?"

"Just verifying." He asked, "Any chance of a reconciliation?"

"Only if I won the lottery and got a frontal lobotomy."

He smiled, then tapped the folder he'd brought with him. "As a condition of your employment as a consultant, I need you to sign a nondisclosure statement. Meaning, anything you see or hear—"

"I know what that means, Jack."

"Good. Any problem with that?"

Well . . . if I signed a nondisclosure, how could I report on this place to my girlfriend, Sergeant Penrose?

"John?"

"I've signed and adhered to the most stringent confidentiality statements with the Feds. No problem."

"Good. And I'll also ask you to sign a noncompete letter, in effect for two years after you leave Security Solutions."

"You mean I can't start my own PI agency for two years?"

"That is correct."

"Well . . ." To give the impression that this was a real issue, I said, "I'll sign the noncompete only if I become an employee in September."

Jack suggested, "You can speak to Steve about that." He glanced at the agreement. "You've asked for a delayed hiring date, so your contract will start on July sixth and end on September sixth."

"Correct."

"You will be compensated as an outside consultant at one thousand dollars a week, regardless of hours worked."

"Correct."

"You will attend all scheduled meetings and meet with potential and existing clients as requested."

"Right."

"The use of your name in connection with Security Solutions will be by mutual consent, not to be unreasonably withheld."

"Jack, I read it."

"All right. I'll skip to the last point—you will, within fifteen days of your last day as a consultant, turn in a written report of no fewer than twenty typed pages, outlining your evaluation of the agency, its employees, policies, and practices, with your recommendations for improvements in all areas of the agency's operation."

"I only get twenty pages?"

Jack smiled. "No less than. But no more than a hundred, please."

I returned the smile to show we shared the joke about this place.

So, as it turned out, being a consultant gave me more access to the inner workings here than if I was a PI. And if there was something illegal going on here, I wouldn't have to write a report for Landowski. But I'd probably have to write a few for the DA.

"Are you ready to sign your consultation agreement and nondisclosure statement?"

"Sure."

He took three fresh copies of each out of his folder and slid them toward me along with a pen.

I signed on the dotted lines, noting that Steve Landowski had already countersigned for Security Solutions. Done deal.

So now I was a paid consultant for a private investigation agency. Which, I hoped, triggered my other job as a confidential informant for the police. But if Beth didn't confirm that soon, then . . . I really didn't think I could work here for two whole months. Even for Amy.

Jack stood and went to the bar, returning with two tumblers of ice and Scotch and handed one to me, saying, "I always like to seal a deal with a drink."

I stood. "Me too. I did that when I got my first job in junior high school delivering groceries."

He smiled, we clinked, and he said, "Welcome aboard."

That's what they said on the *Titanic*.

Jack glanced at his watch. "We'll go up to Steve's office in a few minutes."

"Good." We remained standing, sipping our Scotch, and I asked him, "You ever read Nero Wolfe?"

He smiled. "I think I've read most of them. Why?"

"Did you notice that he never has sex?"

He smiled again. "You shouldn't assume that, Detective."

"Good point. But . . . this guy weighs over three hundred pounds and can't even see his dick."

"Why is this troubling you?"

"I'm not sure . . . maybe I'm seeing my future."

"I would recommend exercise and a healthy diet."

"Right." On the subject of divorces and shaky finances, I said, "Steve tells me you're handling his divorce. And his tax grievance."

Jack smiled. Or was it a grimace? "I'm advising him." He had a grievance of his own, and added, "I advised him to get a divorce attorney and a tax attorney." But Jack understood what I was getting at and said, "Security Solutions is solvent and wholly in Mr. Landowski's name."

"Good. As long as I don't wind up working for Mrs. Landowski after their divorce." Though that wasn't why I'd asked the question. When you're looking for motives for criminal conduct, you look for financial distress—as Jack Berger would agree. There didn't seem to be any, but Jack might not be fully informed.

I changed the subject and said, "So Robin and my FBI wife are lawyers." I gave him the punch line. "I enjoyed screwing lawyers rather than vice versa."

He smiled good-naturedly.

I actually liked Jack Berger, but I was disappointed in him for working here, just as I was disappointed in Amy for the same reason. I've seen bad people in good organizations, and good people in bad organizations, which was harder to understand. In fact, Jack Berger had trouble understanding why *I* was here. But if I was actually here to help the police make a bust, then Jack would eventually know the real reason I wanted this job. I could almost picture him and Landowski in cuffs—maybe Amy too . . . I could see her looking at me with those big blue eyes as she was led into a squad car, sobbing: "We could have had it all, John. I still love you." Or maybe she'd say, "Fuck you, asshole."

"John?"

I came out of my reverie. "Yes?"

"Steve is expecting us. We can leave the paperwork here."

We finished our Scotch, and I followed him out of the classy office and up the staircase to the office where Steve Landowski has his bright ideas, and where maybe he'd heard everything I said. Jack turned left in the dark hallway and I followed.

Hopefully, this wasn't a surprise party for me in the party room. I hate surprise parties. Especially the kind where everyone pulls a gun and someone shouts, "Are you a cop?" Been there, done that.

CHAPTER 19

Landowski's office door was closed, and a sign on the door said: <u>MEAN BOSS—KNOCK. ENTER. DUCK.</u>

Jack knocked, opened the door, but didn't duck.

He motioned me to go in, and the first thing I saw was Steve Landowski standing behind his desk, wearing a green Tony Soprano shirt. I should've ducked, because something—probably a leather sap—connected with my head, and the lights went out.

When I came to, I was on the floor, and the room was spinning like a pole dancer in a strip joint. Amy Lang was standing over me, smoking a cigarette and holding my Glock, and I could hear words coming out of her sneering lips: "I told you there was more to this place than meets the eye, sucker." Landowski and Berger laughed, and Landowski shouted, "Who ya workin' for, chump?"

Well . . . that's not exactly what happened. But I know that this happens to a lot of other private dicks—as we PIs used to be called in old books and movies. You'd think those guys would get wise after the fifth or sixth knockout.

Landowski's voice boomed, "Hey, John! Come on in!"

Was that a gun in his hand? Yes. And why was he pointing it at me?

"C'mere, John. Look at this."

It was actually a remote control device for something. I went behind Landowski's desk and stood next to him as he pointed the remote out the open window, causing a quadcopter drone to lift off the back lawn.

"It's got a great video camera." He motioned toward his desk. "Take a look."

I looked back at his desk where the detached monitor sat, and I saw the aerial image of the farmhouse's backyard, including the brick patio. On the patio was a large round table with an umbrella, and also a picnic table, on which was what looked like catering trays covered with plastic wrap. I thought I spotted a roast beef on rye.

"You watching?"

"Yeah. Your lawn needs cutting."

He laughed. "I'm growing hay. Agriculture. Right, Jack?"

Jack had no reply.

Landowski moved the drone slowly to the left, then he walked quickly to the north-facing window in his corner office. "Take a look."

I looked out the window and saw that the drone was approaching what I'd thought was a hedgerow along his property, but which Landowski had told me was his neighbor's maze. I looked back at the monitor, and I could see the camera view from above as the drone gained altitude: about three or four acres of hedge maze—walls of tall green parallel hedges forming wide paths, most of which seemed to dead-end or circle back on themselves.

Landowski glanced at the maze on the monitor and said, "Some sick asshole designed that." He looked at me. "We're gonna try it someday. Right?"

I had no reply.

Landowski looked at his consigliere, who was standing patiently near the door. "Whaddaya say, Jack? You wanna pay five bucks to get your head fucked up in a maze?"

Jack replied in a dry tone that he'd probably perfected for his boss, "I get that here for free."

Funny. Also, interesting to see how Jack Berger spoke to his boss. That usually means that the employee has something on the boss.

As I looked at the monitor, Landowski maneuvered the drone over the hedges, and I could see the maze entrance set back from the farm road, but I couldn't see the maze's exit, which may have been the same as the entrance. Maybe you paid to get in, then had to pay double to get let out.

Landowski looked at the monitor as he hovered the drone over something in a cul-de-sac and said, "That looks like Frankenstein."

Actually, the dummy looked like Steve Landowski, complete with untucked shirt, but I kept that to myself.

Landowski got tired of his toy and flew it into his backyard and landed it, saying, "This thing is terrific for surveillance. It's got infrared for nighttime. I can control it up to about three miles." He looked at me. "You can follow a car, you can look into the backyards of these big Hampton estates that're surrounded by walls and hedgerows. Right?"

"Right," I agreed.

"It can do about forty-five miles an hour. You can record and show the client the tape of his wife driving to a hot-sheet motel or to some guy's house." He broke into a wide grin. "Hell, it's so quiet, you can hover at the window and see them screwing." He looked at me for affirmation.

"I'd sell the tape to the wife and boyfriend for fifty grand."

Steve smiled as though he'd been thinking the same thing.

Maybe I should ask for a raise.

Steve threw the remote on his desk. "Fucking thing cost me five grand. But . . . you gotta spend money to make money." He added, "I could get a moonlighting cop to use that thing. Cheaper than a freelance PI at a hundred an hour."

I asked, "You got an FAA license for that?"

He glanced at his disbarred lawyer. "Workin' on it."

I also asked, "What's the flight time?"

He looked at the spec manual. "Forty, forty-five minutes."

"I've been on a surveillance for forty-five hours, Steve, as I'm sure you have." I gave him some acquired wisdom. "Technology doesn't take the place of humans on the ground. Tech is a tool for smart operatives."

He looked at me like I'd told him his expensive new toy wasn't going to make him any smarter or richer. He nodded, though, and said, "You're earning your pay before you start."

"Please consult me before you buy anything." Including your next shirt.

Landowski said, "Yeah. If it flies, floats, or fucks, rent it."

Sounded like he was getting advice from Max. Interesting.

Anyway, we shook hands belatedly, and Landowski invited me to sit. I took a seat facing his desk, but Jack Berger said, "I'll be downstairs if you need me," meaning he didn't want to be a witness to anything his boss said to me. And vice versa.

Jack left, and while Landowski was perusing the drone instruction manual, I scoped out the room.

The office—once a corner bedroom—was as untidy as the former living room and dining room downstairs, the walls covered with bulletin boards and pinned papers, and the desk and side table stacked with folders. There were no personal photos or police memorabilia in this private office, not even Landowski's high school equivalency diploma.

On Landowski's desk, next to the drone monitor, was an open laptop that was displaying a succession of live images from his outside surveillance cameras and also his inside cameras—hidden and not hidden. In fact, I noticed an infrared eyeball on the ceiling which covered the room.

Also on his cluttered desk was a hip holster, from which protruded the butt of a Glock, probably the standard Glock 22, .40-caliber, which the Suffolk PD—including Beth—carried. I had the 9mm Glock 17, which held seventeen rounds, usually more than you needed if your aim—or the other guy's aim—was good enough to put a quick end to the shoot-out.

Landowski pushed aside the drone box and asked, "Everything go okay with Jack?"

"It did." How did it sound to you on the hidden mic? But maybe Steve wasn't allowed to listen in on his consigliere.

He asked, "How'd it go with Amy?"

"What did she tell you?" Or what did you hear?

He smiled. "I think she likes you." He let me know, "She spent three hundred bucks on a catered lunch for you." He laughed. "But we're gonna make some good money together."

"Right." To sound like I took my new career seriously, I said, "But I have an issue with the noncompete. Can't sign it until I'm an employee here in September."

I couldn't tell if he'd heard that already on his earphones, but he said, "No problem." He added, "You couldn't compete with me anyway."

I think he was serious.

He changed the subject. "I'm having business cards printed up for you. Jack says your title should be Consulting Detective." He handed me a computer mock-up of my business card, and I saw that it said, *NYPD, Homicide, Retired*, and also *Federal Anti-Terrorist Task Force* and *Diplomatic Surveillance Group*. The company logo was two S's intertwined, like snakes, which seemed appropriate. There was also the agency e-mail address and a phone number that wasn't mine. "What number is this?"

"You get a company cell phone."

Also known as a tracking device. There was no way I was going to carry a company phone, but I said, "Okay."

He informed me, "Everybody who works here has their own keypad code." He handed me a Post-it sticker. "Memorize it and burn it."

I looked at the six-digit number. "Easy to remember. It's the same number as my secret Swiss bank account."

"Yeah . . . ?"

"Just kidding."

He forced a smile.

Now that I was getting paid as a consultant, maybe I needed to stop jerking Landowski around. But I didn't want to give him the impression that I was suddenly, for some reason, more excited about being here than I was yesterday. While I was sure that Jack Berger had discussed some of his concerns about me with his boss, a man like Steve Landowski would dismiss wise counsel and trust his own judgment, which was colored by his belief that John Corey could make him money and give him and his agency some prestige—if I may be so immodest.

"The card okay?"

I handed the mock-up back to him. "Looks great."

"Good." He asked, "What did you think of Jack?"

"He thinks you're stupid," I wanted to say. But I said, "He's a smart guy."

"Yeah. And I don't have to pay him what lawyers charge."

"Best of both worlds," I agreed.

"He knows your ex-wife."

"He said. You said."

"Right. He said she was one of the best."

Did Jack fuck her too? I said with a smile, "If you ever get arrested, Steve, I'd highly recommend her." Could be an interesting trial, with me testifying for the prosecution. I could almost hear Robin cross-examining me.

Landowski didn't respond to my advice and asked, "So, you all squared away with Jack?"

"I am."

"And Amy?" He smiled.

"She's made me feel welcome."

"She might make you feel more welcome if you promise to sign on in September."

"Can I have that in writing?"

He thought that was funny, then said, "Hey, you missed a great Thirsty Thursday."

"Are you sure you want me there?"

"Yeah. Why not?"

"I'll have to put it in my final report."

He wasn't sure if I was joking or not and said sternly, "You signed a confidentiality agreement." He added, "What goes on upstairs, stays upstairs."

Which reminded me to say, "You didn't tell me you worked Vice."

He didn't ask where I'd heard that, but he smiled. "Somebody's got to do it." He changed the subject and asked, "Why can't you start right away?"

"I need a few days in the city to tie up loose ends, then I might go away for a few days."

"You're gonna miss my big July Fourth party."

"I'll be there in spirit."

"I need you there to show you off. Lots of important people are gonna be there."

"Tell them I was invited to the White House for the Fourth."

He smiled. "Yeah. I like that." He added, "You're a good bullshitter."

"I learned from the best."

He informed me, "You're gonna be on my website, starting today, as a consultant to the agency."

"Starting July sixth, the day you start paying me."

"That's not what it says in the agreement."

"I don't care what it says in the agreement."

We made eye contact. I didn't really give a shit, but I needed to let Steve Landowski know that John Corey made his own rules. If he hadn't figured that out by now.

Steve blinked and said, "Okay . . . so maybe a compromise. I give you a thousand for the time you're not here, and the website can say John Corey is joining the agency on July sixth. And I put your creds on the website."

Time for a bone again. "Okay. That's fair."

"Good. You got any questions for me?"

"Where's my check?"

He smiled. "You'll walk out of here with it. Anything else?"

Yeah. Like, why is the basement door padlocked? Why do you invite prominent men here to see strippers? Why am I not supposed to mention Detective Beth Penrose or your former PI Detective Sharon Hite? What are you up to, Steve? The usual crap? Bribery? Prostitution? Blackmail? All of the above? Or something else? Well, now that I was here again, I could sense that Security Solutions was more than met the eye, and I was sure that Beth would confirm that. And if she didn't . . . ? What if she said to me, "What the hell are you talking about?" Then I really needed a vacation. And an overseas job.

"John?"

"Sorry. I was just thinking that you should be going paperless here."

"I don't wanna hear that shit. You sound like Jack. This works for me. And if it ain't broke, don't fix it."

"I'll put my recommendation in my report."

Meanwhile, I was sure that Steve Landowski had made some good busts with paper evidence seized from bookies and escort service madams, most of whom kept records of their customers the old-fashioned way, with paper. So Landowski knew the danger of a paper trail. But I was fairly sure that Steve Landowski, in a perversely arrogant way, did the same as the people he busted, and that somewhere in this house—probably the padlocked basement—was paper evidence of something illegal. Right? And all I had to do was find it and take it.

Landowski asked, "What are you thinking about?"

"I'm thinking this job could be fun."

"We try to make it fun." He added, "We make good money, and we answer to nobody, and we take no shit from nobody." He smiled. "Except the clients sometimes." He had a rare insight. "The opposite of police work." He tapped the Glock on his desk. "And we still have our guns."

"It's a dream job," I said.

"That's what I've been telling you."

"I'm having an epiphany, Steve."

"I thought that came after Christmas."

"Right. Okay, I'm ready for lunch."

He glanced at his watch. "Not yet. I wanna show you around up here."

"Good."

He stood, and I stood. He took his gun, and I took a last look around his untidy office, committing it to memory for when I came back here with a flashlight and a self-issued midnight search warrant. Hopefully soon.

CHAPTER 20

Out in the hallway, Landowski motioned to a closed door opposite his office. "That's my bedroom."

"Short commute."

"Yeah. I eat, sleep, and work here."

Which would make it difficult for me to issue myself that midnight search warrant. "You need a vacation from this place."

"Yeah. I'm taking my kids for a week to the Jersey Shore."

"Good idea." Very good idea. I asked, "When are you leaving?"

"Second week in July. Unless that bitch gets a court order to stop me."

Well, let's hope that bitch—a.k.a. Mrs. Landowski, mother of his children—doesn't do that.

"The kids need a father," he said. "And I need a coupla days in Atlantic City."

"Right." You can make it an educational vacation. Okay, kids, remember, the slot machines favor the house. Poker is your best bet.

He moved down the hallway, and opposite the stair landing was an open door which revealed the communal bathroom. I glanced inside, noting the pink tiles and dingy white fixtures, solid clues that the bathroom had been modernized sometime during the Eisenhower administration.

Next to the bathroom was a narrow door that Landowski said led to the attic. I saw it had an old doorknob but also a newer dead bolt lock, which meant there was something in the attic that needed to be secured, as with the basement padlock. Landowski didn't say anything about the locked attic, and I wasn't going to ask him. I'd ask someone else. Amy came to mind.

We continued down the dimly lit hall, and Landowski pointed out two bedrooms. "You ever need a place to crash, or entertain a lady, either room is yours." He smiled. "Honeymoon suites."

I hoped his kids didn't sleep over. They'd be scratching for weeks.

He said, "You can keep overnight stuff here in your desk."

Right. Toothbrush and Trojans. Which led me to think Trojan horse. Which led me to the solution of how to get inside Security Solutions after hours without having to get past the security. "Thanks. I may need a room some night." While you're away.

He smiled, happy to see I was one of the boys.

We came to the last door, on which was a sign that said: RECREATION ROOM. Landowski threw open the door to reveal a very large room that obviously once was the master bedroom suite but had been converted to a bar and lounge. He went in and I followed.

The floor was covered with what was probably the last black shag carpet outside of New Jersey. The ceiling too was black, and the walls were painted bordello red. Along the left wall was a rolling bar with shelves of liquor and a floor-to-ceiling mirror behind it, and also a big refrigerator. Scattered around the room were five aptly named love seats where couples could cuddle and get to know each other. There were also ashtrays around the room, which signaled that maybe marijuana was smoked here. Or a more controlled substance—tobacco.

There were, of course, big floor speakers, and a rack of electronics for audio and video, and a flat-screen TV which I'm sure showed a full range of porn. Also, the windows were covered with thick drone-proof blackout curtains.

As for mood lighting, there were a few floor lamps, and also track lights in the middle of the ceiling so that the exotic dancers could be illuminated when they took the floor.

I didn't see a video camera, but the mirror behind the bar would be a good place for a hidden camera to record the show for posterity or blackmail.

Well, a recreation room like this at One Police Plaza would have improved morale and attendance. At 26 Fed, where boring is the order of the day, it would be an alcohol-free training facility to teach agents how to conduct a raid on a tax-delinquent establishment. Here at Security Solutions, it was a speakeasy, where prominent citizens and select politicians and police officials could relax, then go to a honeymoon suite and get laid.

Landowski asked, "Whaddaya think?"

"It's everything I imagined since you told me about it."

"Great. So I'll see you here the first Thursday you're back."

"I can't wait." Beth would understand.

He briefed me on the lounge's schedule. "First Thursday of the month—when you'll be back—is the exotic dancers. You're in luck. Second Thursday is usually date night. Real dates if you got one that likes fun. Third Thursday is poker night. No girls. We set up card tables. Fourth Thursday—last night—was the party girls."

"I hope that went well."

"You shoulda been here."

"I shoulda." I could see why Amy was not invited to Thirsty Thursdays. Though maybe I should ask her to date night.

Also, I wondered if Max was a frequent guest here. And if so, was he just collecting information and evidence? Or was he an enthusiastic participant? The lines get blurred when you're undercover.

Landowski informed me, "You can have your own party in this room if you clear it with me." He smiled. "And invite me."

"I was thinking of a karaoke night."

He thought that was funny, then continued his briefing. "There's a coupla massage tables in the closet there . . . and some toys. You know? I got a list of massage ladies. Real ones, like licensed, and also ones that'll give you a happy ending. Or you can bring your own." He added, "Nothing like a massage after a long day."

"Right. You got one hell of an H.R. Department here, Steve."

He laughed. "I'm the H.R. Department."

"Does your female staff get any perks?"

"Yeah. They get a job and a paycheck. And all the strawberries they can pick." He added, "I keep the kitchen stocked."

"I'd recommend male strippers on Tuesdays."

He laughed again. "I'm not paying you to cost me money."

Which brought up the question of how Security Solutions—or Steve Landowski—could afford all the entertainment. These girls weren't cheap—as I'd heard—and they didn't take checks or credit cards. They wanted cash, and I was sure Landowski didn't pass the hat around to his prominent guests to kick in. So it was cash out of his pocket every week, and if I did the math, it could be as much as sixty or seventy thousand a year, maybe more, including the Doritos. When I see this much cash going out, I have to think about how that cash came in. A few of the agency's clients might prefer to pay in cash, but . . . The real question was: What did Steve Landowski get in return for his generous hospitality? Answer: Favors. Protection. And blackmail opportunities.

Landowski looked at his watch. "We have time for a beer before lunch."

He sounded like he had something more to tell me, and I had something to tell him, so I said, "Okay."

He went to the refrigerator, got two cans of some local IPA, and handed one to me. We popped the tops, and he said, "Welcome to Security Solutions."

"Glad to be here."

Landowski looked around the lounge. "This has always been my dream."

And some dreams are attainable. Like living and working in a snake pit.

"I put in twenty years on the job. Ten in vice work. You know what I learned?"

I thought I did, but I said, "Tell me."

"I learned that gambling and prostitution is none of the government's f-ing business." He looked at me.

"Can't say I disagree."

"Yeah. Maybe it's the business of the church or the social workers. But it's a waste of police time and money. A waste of my fucking time when I was on the job."

"You didn't have to work vice."

"I didn't say I didn't enjoy it. No heavy lifting. Lots of laughs. Got to know some interesting people."

"Right."

He seemed to be thinking—if that were possible—and

he said, "In the old days, adultery was a crime. Cohabitation was a crime. Getting a blow job from your girlfriend—or even your wife—was a crime. A perversion."

"Holy shit . . . I'd be doing twenty to life."

He laughed. "Yeah. You and me both." He continued, "So now none of that is a crime. But guys did time for stuff that's now legal. The government makes the rules and changes the rules. You can gamble, but only in places where the government gets a cut. You can fuck your best friend's wife and adultery is not a crime anymore. But if you pay some hardworking girl a few hundred bucks for sex, then you both get busted."

"Right."

He was on a roll and continued, "Meantime, some rich asshole can have a mistress that he gives money to, and he's not breaking the law. But if some construction worker pays for a massage and a hand job after breaking his ass all day, he's a criminal and she's a criminal and I was supposed to make a collar."

Can you collar people who aren't wearing clothes?

"Gays used to go to jail, but now in some places they can get married. And you can live with anybody you want. You can go to a licensed strip joint and pay to see tits and ass, but if you take a stripper into a back room and I'm there undercover, I'm gonna bust you."

I suddenly realized I could have been on the Vice Squad, hanging around strip joints and massage parlors for all those years instead of looking at dead bodies. Well . . . but murder is murder. No moral ambiguities there. I asked, "Did you actually make those busts?"

He smiled. "You gotta make a few. Especially if the DA is up the chief's ass because of some civilian complaint. But my heart wasn't in it." He added, "It was mostly catch and release."

"Right. Well, it's good that you were able to transfer your police skills and experience to the private sector."

"Yeah . . ." He chugged his beer. "I got tired of being the fun police. People do what people do. Human nature. They fuck. They gamble. They watch porn. But when you make it a crime, then you get corruption. The police get corrupt. The politicians get corrupt. The judges get corrupt." He tapped his beer can. "It's like Prohibition. Right? You criminalize what normal people want, and you make everybody a criminal. And when everybody's a criminal, nobody's a criminal."

Well, apparently, Steve Landowski had thought long and hard about all this and had developed some vocabulary to express his thoughts—or someone else's thoughts—on this subject. I was impressed. But not convinced that his justification for Thirsty Thursdays—and whatever other corruption he was into—would sway a jury. Or his priest. And certainly not his wife. But . . . I and most guys I knew on the job and in civilian life would agree that vice was in the eye of the beholder and that the Vice Squad was a waste of taxpayer money, court time and police time, and also a hot spot for graft, bribery, and corruption. On the other hand, the law is the law. If you're a cop, you don't get to pick and choose which laws you like. But you could look the other way—and maybe make a few bucks instead of a few busts, as I'm sure Detective Landowski had done.

Landowski continued, "Anyways, what you see *here* is legit. The girls get paid to dance. They can show bush, but they can't show pink."

I wasn't actually familiar with the letter of the law on this subject, but I'd trust Landowski's professional judgment. And so to seem like a regular guy and a good hire,

I said, quoting Uncle Harry, "Whatever is not a crime is a business."

"Yeah. And if one of the girls wants to get romantic with one of my guests, she and him can use one of the guest rooms—but she can't ask for money or name a price."

"Right. It's just love or lust."

He smiled. "And that's not illegal."

I assumed the price was set ahead of time, and the money was offered to the girls as a gratuity in appreciation of a great dance routine, or for ten minutes of stimulating conversation on the love seat. Well, there is the letter of the law, and then there is the spirit of the law. Landowski had the first one covered. Not so sure about the second. But this was his police skill, not mine.

He said, "You see how fucked up the law is."

"You seem to have cleared up some of the contradictions."

"Yeah. Any moron could."

I give you Exhibit A, having a beer with me.

"There's some sex stuff that's not good. Fucking animals or underage girls."

Or underage animals. I thought there was more, but he seemed to have run out of taboo sex acts, then he remembered another. "If you don't pay the girls, it's rape." He smiled. "Or maybe theft of services."

"Check with Jack on that."

I wondered if Steve Landowski, like a lot of cops I knew, had started his career with good intentions to serve the public, and then gotten corrupted when he became a detective working on vice cases. I saw this in the NYPD, especially in Narcotics. Or was Landowski a bad apple from the beginning? I'm sure the seeds were there.

He seemed to be thinking about that himself and said,

"I knew guys I worked with who busted rich johns just to shake them down. Sometimes you busted a pimp, and you took his wad and made him pay you to stay in business. Same with the strip joints and the massage parlors. But we mostly left the madams alone—the ladies who ran the escort services. They usually ran a clean operation and looked after their girls—and looked after us."

Right. Vice Squad boners get serviced pro bono. Bottom line, it seemed that Detective Landowski had misinterpreted the meaning of vice work, not understanding that he was supposed to *fight* it, not participate ... well, he may have missed that class. More importantly, he'd just admitted to a number of on-the-job felonies. But I was sure he was clean now. Right?

Landowski took a pack of cigarettes from the bar, lit one, and continued, "The undercover women were more into the job. They loved to dress up and play hooker, busting johns, busting our balls." He smiled. "Pains in the ass. But now and then, you'd get one of them drunk and get them in a compromising situation, and if she was married or had a boyfriend, you could hold it over her and make her play the game." He went silent, then surprised me by saying, "It was a fucking cesspool."

Which was an insult to cesspools. I'm no Boy Scout, but ... jeez. Homicide was simple. Clean.

He asked me, "Wanna smoke?"

"No, thanks."

"You gotta die of something."

"I'd rather it be venereal disease."

He laughed. "You're a regular guy." He looked at me. "You're a cop. A cop's cop."

The Brotherhood. But sometimes your loyalty to the brotherhood was tested. I can't say I had a higher opinion of Steve Landowski than I'd had this morning, but I could understand how and why he got to this place. There are police jobs that serve the public, and there are police jobs that are thankless. And if you spend ten years in a thankless job, it's going to screw you up. You can talk to the PD shrink or the chaplain, or to your partner or your wife, but first you have to talk to yourself. And if Steve Landowski had ever had that conversation with himself, he'd decided that he was okay and that the perps were okay too, so it was an easy transition to become one of them.

"Whaddaya thinkin'?"

"I assume you're Catholic?"

"Yeah . . ."

"You remember in confraternity class when we had to raise our right hand and renounce all the pleasures of the flesh and the temptations of the Devil?"

He smiled. "Yeah."

"Did you have your fingers crossed? I did," I confessed.

He laughed, then said seriously, "They had me scared shitless. You know? If I committed a mortal sin, my flesh was gonna burn in hell forever and my soul was gonna belong to the Devil."

"You still believe that?"

"No. And I'll tell you why. Because they also said I'd go to hell if I ate meat on Friday or if I jerked off."

"I think they decriminalized the meat thing and reduced jerking off to a venial sin."

"Yeah. That's the point. You can't take that shit seriously, and you can't take this shit"—he motioned around the room—"seriously."

"Right. As long as you're not breaking New York State law here."

"I'm not stupid."

Well, you are. But you're also crafty and cunning. The Devil ain't got nothin' on you, Steve.

He looked at me. "You okay with all this?"

"No problem."

He stubbed out his cigarette and finished his beer. "Let's go to lunch."

Well, I'd had my company orientation and my initiation into the boys' club, so it was time to go, but I said, "I need a minute of your time."

He looked at me. "Okay. Shoot."

I finished my beer. "Okay, as you know, it's standard practice on the job to let people who you work with know if you're hot—if there have been credible threats made against you."

He nodded. "Right. Who wants to kill you?"

"My ex-wife and maybe my mother. But also I've been involved in operations against Islamic terrorists, and those operations have led to the deaths of a number of those terrorists."

"Hey! I like that."

"Me too. But the point is—"

"Yeah. I got it. Those assholes want payback."

"Correct."

"Bring 'em on. We'll send those ragheads to Paradise."

"I'm glad you're taking this well, Steve." I let him know, "A lot of people won't even sit next to me at lunch."

"Hey! I'll sit next to you anyplace, and we'll cap those camel fuckers—"

"Right. And there's a more serious threat. The Russians."

"No shit?"

"The SVR." I didn't see a glimmer of recognition, so I explained, "The old KGB with a new name."

"No shit? You kill some of them?"

"I can't confirm or deny, but—"

"How'd you get out of Russia?"

Actually, it happened not too far from here, but that was compartmentalized information, so I replied, "Night train to Warsaw, disguised as a Canadian hockey player."

"No shit?"

"So I'm just giving you a heads-up, as a required courtesy, and you can disseminate the information in any way you see fit."

He nodded. "Okay . . . that's good." He looked at me. "You were into some shit."

I didn't reply.

"John, the only thing you gotta worry about here is maybe some cheatin' husband we busted showing up with a baseball bat."

"I'm sure I can handle that."

He said, "Okay . . . thanks for the heads-up." He asked, "Anybody got your back?"

Meaning the police or the Feds, which could be uncomfortable for him if any law enforcement agency was keeping an eye on my workplace at Security Solutions. I replied, "My former colleagues have cut me loose, but I'm a big boy with a big gun, and I can take care of myself."

"Yeah. And we have your back. I'll let the boys know."

"Thanks." Ironically, I might be safer here than anyplace else. Unless I was outed as a police informant.

We left the den of iniquity, and I followed him into the hallway toward the stairs.

I had no real idea what went on here, but if it was just boys having fun—venial sins—then it didn't make sense for Beth to go through all that trouble to get me inside this place. Beth was Homicide, and whatever went on here was a case for Steve Landowski's former vice-buster colleagues—assuming they weren't part of the problem.

So it must be something more than suspected prostitution or gambling. It had to be corruption, bribery, and blackmail of public officials—and cops. And my role, as a confidential informant, would be to find enough evidence for the DA to get a judge to issue a search warrant. Then a search and seizure would prove or disprove the presence of major felonies—mortal sins—committed at Security Solutions. That sort of made sense.

We went down the staircase, into the hallway, and toward the kitchen.

And then it hit me. *A judge.* If the DA asked the wrong judge—a judge who had been a guest here—then that judge was just as likely to tip off Landowski as he was to issue a search warrant. Same with the wrong person in the DA's office. And even if the warrant was issued, the existence of that warrant could come to the attention of the wrong people at police headquarters, and before the warrant was executed by the police, Landowski could get the tip-off from a cop who'd been a satisfied guest here.

I glanced at the padlocked basement door as we moved into the kitchen.

Some of this made sense, but then other things didn't make sense. Like why was Beth Penrose of Homicide involved? If I stepped back from this . . . actually, if I was watching this on a drone monitor, I'd be looking down on a maze . . . twisting paths with lots of dead ends and Frankensteins along the way; a labyrinth of corruption and deception, ending in a cesspool.

And if there was widespread official corruption at various levels of government and law enforcement, then a confidential police informant—me—was not going to stay in business for long.

CHAPTER 21

Landowski and I went through the former mudroom, now used to store his expensive toys and guns, and stepped out on the sunny patio, where the buffet and beverages were set up on the picnic table. The round table with the umbrella sat empty while the small staff of Security Solutions stood and chatted with Solo cups in their hands. I saw Amy first, of course, and Jack Berger, and the two clerical ladies, Kim and Judy. There were also two men talking to each other who I IDed through ethnic profiling: the Italian-looking guy was Joseph Ferrara, and the Irish-looking guy was Chip Quinlan. Lou Santangelo was still MIA, but if I looked in the kitchen, I'd probably find his face on a milk carton.

Anyway, Landowski got everyone's attention and announced, "And here's our guest of honor, Detective John Corey, the newest member of our family!" He began clapping to demonstrate what everyone should be doing.

Solo cups got tabled and there was some faint applause. Amy clapped loudest.

I acknowledged the applause with a cheery wave and said, "Happy to be aboard." Can I have a roast beef sandwich to go?

Amy, acting as hostess, took my arm and began the intros. "John, this is Kim Horton from clerical, who I think you met briefly, and Judy Ortega, who is Steve's personal secretary when she's not doing important work."

The nice matronly ladies smiled and we shook hands. They both looked happy to be out in the sun and getting tipsy on the boss's wine and time.

I wondered which lady was in charge of shredding evidence. I also wondered if either of them had the key to the basement or the attic, or the combo to the company safe.

I said to the ladies, "I look forward to working with you both and learning what you do." I added, "Please don't hesitate to come to me with any problems or suggestions."

I was sure they'd never heard that before, and Judy said, "We need new desk chairs."

"You got it." I also told them, "One of my first recommendations here will be to have a Chippendale night. And I don't mean furniture."

Both ladies giggled, but Amy assured them, "He's just kidding."

"Maybe. Maybe not." I smiled, picturing Kim and Judy shoving dollar bills in a male stripper's jockstrap. As for Amy . . . well, she's probably seen more beef than a Costco butcher, and I knew she'd enjoy putting her money where her mouth wanted to be. Sorry.

Anyway, before I could decide which of the two ladies was more likely to succumb to my charms and betray their mean boss, Jack Berger stepped in and said to me, "I look forward to getting to know you better."

Hopefully not too much better. "Same here," I said.

"Did you tie up loose ends with Steve?"

"We're all set. I had a great tour of the second floor."

He did not respond.

"Not sure that the Rec Room or guest rooms meet the legal standards for public health or occupancy, Counselor."

He replied, "I'll look into that. Meanwhile, read your nondisclosure statement."

I liked sparring with Jack. He was bright and kept me on my toes, and I was sure he felt the same about me. He'd make a good lunch companion—or maybe a good witness for the prosecution in exchange for immunity. That's how cops think.

Amy seemed to want this conversation cut short, and she turned me around to face the two PIs. "This is Chip Quinlan," she said, confirming my profile.

Quinlan was in his early forties, so he was maybe twenty when he got his shield, then put twenty in and was out. He was a big boy with reddish hair, a ruddy complexion, and unblinking eyes.

Quinlan and I shook hands, and I was ready for a bone-crusher, but I got a limp squeeze instead, and no smile. "Good to meet you," he said in a monotone.

"Same here."

Amy continued, "And this is Joseph Ferrara."

Ferrara and I shook. "Good to meet you."

"Same." Ferrara was a slightly built man, maybe midsixties, balding and serious-looking. Recalling that Amy tried to match a client to a PI, I guessed that Ferrara got assigned to mature clients who would relate better to a man like Joseph Ferrara than to a bruiser like Quinlan or a jerk-off like Lou Santangelo.

Neither Quinlan nor Ferrara seemed to know what to say after "Good to meet you," and I wasn't getting a warm feeling, but that's how cops are until they trust you. If they like you, that's good too. But they're not going to like you until they trust you.

Anyway, both men wore black pants and untucked short-sleeve shirts, which easily hides a big Glock and also seemed to be the PI uniform here.

I recalled that Quinlan was NYPD, so we had something in common. I asked, "Where'd you work?"

"Fugitive."

Meaning chasing them, not being one. Interesting work, sort of like Missing Persons, except the missing person was a fugitive from justice—most often a bail-jumper who is usually found in another jurisdiction. And Chip Quinlan was built for escorting recaptured felons on planes, trains, and automobiles. Landowski probably also used him to collect overdue bills from his clients.

Ferrara, I remembered, had been a detective in Nassau County, the affluent suburban county west of here that bordered on the NYC borough of Queens. I asked Ferrara, "Where'd you work?"

"Organized Crime."

I tried a joke. "I meant on the job—not on your days off."

He didn't smile. Maybe he'd heard that one before.

Quinlan and Ferrara seemed to be men of few words—sort of like the old movie detectives who talk out of the side of their mouth. I could see why Landowski—who liked to hear himself talk—had hired them.

You get good at sizing up people and their relationships to each other if you do it for a living, and I wasn't sensing a big, happy family. Nor did I believe that Landowski had spoken to these two guys, as I'd asked him to do, and gotten a thumbs-up on hiring John Corey. Steve Landowski was a bullshit artist, and worse, he believed his own bullshit and insisted that everyone else believe it.

Amy, to fill in the silence, said, "John and Lou worked together, as you know, and Lou is looking forward to working with John again."

Meaning that Lou Santangelo vouched for John Corey, who was one of the best detectives he ever worked with—even though I once had a missing person poster made with his face on it and hung it in the squad room.

Anyway, before I could ask my new colleagues if they read Nero Wolfe, Amy said to me, "Let's get you a drink."

I excused myself, and Amy led me to the picnic table, where the catering and bar were set up. I ground-confirmed the platter of roast beef sandwiches I'd seen from the air.

She asked, "White or red?"

I didn't see any beer, so I said, "Red."

She took a bottle of a local Cab, poured it in a red Solo cup, and handed it to me.

"Thanks."

I noticed that Landowski was off to the side, talking with Jack Berger, probably discussing their separate conversations with me.

While Amy was pouring a red wine for herself, I noticed something that had escaped my attention: an outside stairwell that led down to the basement. I could see the door at the bottom of the concrete steps, and it looked like a steel security door with a keypad, and I was sure it had an alarm. So that made three entrances to the basement, and the trapdoor in Landowski's downstairs office seemed the easiest to breach—unless it was nailed shut. I could, of course, just tell Steve Landowski that I'd like to see the basement, but that would tip my hand, as I'd be asking to see his cards. Also, it could be that the only things in the basement were his wine cellar and the furnace, and maybe the hub of all the audio and visual electronics.

Amy broke into my thoughts. "Chip and Joseph will warm up."

"I'm sure they will after we share a night in the Rec Room."

She ignored that and said, "When you bring in business, you'll be their best friend."

"Right." I asked, "Where's Lost Louie?" As we used to call him.

She smiled. "On his way." She had a suggestion. "If you're around next week, we should have a drink, and I can fill you in on a few things here."

That could be useful. And interesting. But . . . "I'll probably be at my place in Manhattan for the week."

"I can meet you there."

I never get lucky when I'm looking. But when I'm not looking . . . "I may go away. I'll let you know what I'm doing."

"Okay."

Steve Landowski, without an announcement, launched his drone from the lawn, and everyone looked up toward the faint noise of the rotors.

I said to Amy, "Maybe he's looking for Lou."

She laughed.

Landowski put on a show for his staff, flying the drone in circles, then figure eights. He called out, "Trying to locate lunch," then flew the drone over the picnic table and hovered about five feet above the macaroni salad. "Lunch located!" he shouted. "Come and get it!"

A few obligatory laughs from the staff, who may have been thinking that the drone money could be better spent on their Christmas bonuses.

Landowski put the drone down on the lawn, and everyone drifted toward the picnic table.

Amy said to me, "You go sit. I'll get you a plate. What do you want?"

"You don't have to be nice to me. I signed the contract."

She laughed. "You're the guest of honor. What do you want?"

I want what you're offering, but I said, "Roast beef sandwich. Potato salad."

"I'll make you a nice plate. Take my wine and save me a seat."

"Thanks." I took her wine and went to the round table, removed my blazer and draped it over my chair, and sat by myself. I took a swig of wine and pictured myself out of here, hopefully soon.

Tonight I'd ask Beth if I was working for the Suffolk PD or for Security Solutions. If my suspicions weren't confirmed, there was no way I could work here for two months. Not even for Amy Lang, or for a thousand bucks a week, or for stripper night . . . Well . . . now that I put it that way . . . Anyway, thinking about the Rec Room, it was easy to see how quickly men can be corrupted. I've seen it too often on the job and in civilian life. Even the holier-than-thou Feds were susceptible to temptation. It's baked into the human condition. Find the right temptation—money, power, sex, fame, your coworker's wife, or whatever—and offer it to the person who craves it, and you have that person's soul. Steve Landowski learned more in religious instruction class than he realized.

Also, even if I wasn't a CI for the Suffolk PD, maybe I needed to be here to see what went on at Thirsty Thursdays. The job is what you make of it.

Amy, with a bottle of red wine tucked under her arm, put two paper plates of food on the table with plastic utensils and paper napkins, then set the wine down and sat to my right.

"Thanks," I said. "You are a good hostess."

"My pleasure." She poured red wine into my Solo cup and love into my heart.

I picked up my plastic fork and looked at the plate, piled with deli salad and a roast beef sandwich. I tried the potato salad. Too much mayo. I was missing New York delis. Actually, I was missing the whole city. Could I really live out here?

Amy, between bites, asked, "How did it go with Jack and Steve?"

"Good." I confessed, "I was pleasantly surprised by Jack."

She took a swig of wine. "He's very smart."

That was the problem. "I'm not sure he wanted me on board."

"To be discussed."

Maybe I did have time for a drink with Amy. Beth would want me to do that.

She glanced at the picnic table where people were loading up and coming toward our round table. "I meant to tell you, Chip dated Sharon."

I held my fork in midair. "Who?"

"Sharon Hite. The PI who used to work here."

"Oh . . ."

"So if you're talking to him—like about old cases or something—be sensitive to that."

"Okay." I asked, "Bad breakup?"

She looked at me. "No. I thought you knew."

"No."

"She committed suicide."

Whoa!

"Really tragic." She said again, "I thought you knew."

"How would I know?"

"I thought maybe Steve or Jack . . . or Max might have mentioned it to you."

I think I would have remembered if Max had told me that one of the PIs here—specifically Sharon Hite—had killed herself. Definitely didn't come up at dinner. And Beth, of course, knew. And neither of them had told me, so that I'd be genuinely shocked if I heard the news here. Well, I wouldn't be talking to Sharon Hite about why she left Security Solutions.

Amy said, "We don't like to talk about it here."

Apparently not. Anyway, before I could elicit more info on this tragic death, the bereaved boyfriend, Chip, sat down next to Amy, and Judy sat down next to me, followed by the rest of the gang who couldn't talk straight.

So everyone made conversation as they gobbled the free lunch—Steve, Jack, Judy, Kim, Joseph, Chip, Amy, and I. One big happy family. Amy went back for seconds. She must exercise a lot.

Landowski was sitting across from me, with Jack on his right and an empty chair to his left for our missing PI, though I thought there was a better chance of Sharon Hite showing up than Lou Santangelo.

Landowski called for everyone's attention, raised his Solo cup, and said, "A toast to our new private investigator, Detective John Corey, NYPD, medically retired in the line of duty, but still armed and dangerous." He added, "John worked for the Feds for a while, but now he's back with his brothers."

Everyone drank to that, and Amy gave me a poke in the ribs, meaning, "Say something nice."

I stood, looked around the table, and said, "One of you here killed Sharon Hite, and I'm going to find out who did it."

Well, no, that would have been premature—and maybe a little loony—so I said, "Thank you for the warm welcome, and thank you, Steve, for pulling me, kicking and screaming, out of retirement."

A few laughs.

"And thanks to Steve and Jack for their confidence in me, and special thanks to Amy"—I put my hand on her shoulder—"for her hospitality and her assurances that Lou Santangelo is alive and well . . . and on his way."

Some good laughs. They knew Lou.

"I look forward to working with you all."

I sat to scattered applause, and Amy said, "Very nice."

Judy, to my left, said, "I have a check for you before you leave."

"Hold it until I get back." I added, "We'll use it for ladies' night."

She sort of bounced in her seat.

Thank God, it was a mercifully short lunch, and just as it seemed ready to break up, who should arrive but Lou Santangelo, carrying two boxes of Dunkin' Donuts. *Shit.*

He called out, "Sorry I'm late. Got stuck on the Expressway." He set the boxes on the picnic table. "Long line at Dunkin' Donuts."

Don't forget "had to stop for gas."

"Had to stop for gas."

I mean, if I told him once, I told him a thousand times: More than one excuse is no excuse.

He saw me and hurried over. I stood and turned toward him, hoping he'd take my outstretched hand, but bracing myself for the manly Italian hug.

He brushed aside my hand, wrapped his arms around me, and squeezed. "John! This is great!"

My arms were free, and I could have grabbed his head and snapped his skinny neck, but there were witnesses, so I patted his back—sort of like I was beating dust out of his shirt.

He released his grip and stepped back. "You look great."

"You too." Do *not* kiss me.

"How many years has it been?"

Not enough.

He looked at his colleagues around the table. "This is the greatest detective I ever worked with."

Landowski called out, "I hope you learned something, Lou."

A few laughs.

Lou Santangelo was one of those guys who had a lean and hungry look, and he hadn't changed much since the last time I saw him. He still had his pencil mustache and swept-back black hair, a sallow complexion, and a long, thin nose. His eyes tended to stare, but now and then they'd dart around the room as though he was looking toward some sound of danger. In fact, he always reminded me of . . . well, a rat. And he had this annoying nasal voice. But, to be more kind to a former colleague, he had a permanent smile on his face. Like he'd just spotted cheese.

Lou was wearing the approved black pants and an untucked chartreuse short-sleeve shirt that people probably took pictures of.

Amy was standing now, and she suggested to Lou, "Go get some food and take my seat."

"Naw," he said, "I'm not hungry. But I'll sit next to John."

"Shit!" I hope I didn't say that out loud.

Lou urged everyone, "Go get some donuts. Still warm."

Not if he scrounged them from the discard bin as he used to do.

Judy and Kim were the first to stand, followed by everyone else, who seemed grateful for an excuse to leave the family table.

Lou, still standing, looked me up and down like he couldn't believe his eyes. "You look terrific. Life been good to you?"

"Pretty good. Aside from taking three bullets."

"Yeah . . . that was a shame."

"I think it was attempted murder."

"Yeah . . . hey, sorry I didn't get to see you in the hospital." He explained, "I was out of town on a case."

And?

"I picked up some kind of bug, and they wouldn't let me in your room."

"Don't worry about it."

"We got a lot of catch-up to do. We'll get some beers one night."

I had some questions for him about Security Solutions, so I said, "Sounds good."

"Yeah. You still married to that lawyer?"

"Which one?"

He thought that was funny, but it wasn't a joke. I said, "Divorced." I changed the subject. "Thanks for going to bat for me at that retirement party when Chief Maxwell pitched me to Steve."

"Hey, that was a no-brainer."

So it was as I suspected—it was Max who had brought up my name and made the pitch to Landowski. And he'd done that at Beth's suggestion, of course.

"To be honest," he said, "I was surprised to hear you were out of work and looking for a PI gig."

No more surprised than I am to hear that. "This has always been something I wanted to do."

"You're gonna love it. No brass up your ass here." He glanced over his shoulder, then moved closer and tilted his head toward the picnic table. "Whaddaya think?"

"About?"

"Amy."

"Nice girl."

"C'mon, John. You on that?"

"I thought she belonged to the boss."

"Naw. She's fair game." He let me know: "We got a pool. Me, Chip, Steve—not Joseph or Jack—and seven or eight freelance PIs. First guy who bops her gets a hundred bucks a man."

Did Jack put that in my contract? The perks never ended here.

"You could be a contender." *A contenda.*

"Does Amy know about the pool?"

He laughed. "She'd want half."

"Hell, I'd give it all to her."

Lou laughed again. We were bonding. And suddenly, I was back in the squad room, a long time ago. But I was not feeling nostalgic. Could it be that I was evolving? Holy shit...

Before I could get the rules of the pool straight, Amy returned with a plate piled with donuts which she set on the table, and said to me, "There's coffee inside. Can I get you a cup?"

I felt a poke in the ribs from Santangelo. Asshole. "No, thanks." I looked at my watch. "I have to meet my plumber at three. Barely make it."

Amy looked disappointed. "Okay...I'll walk you out."

"Thanks." I put on my blazer as she wrapped a donut in a paper napkin for my ride home.

I shook hands with Santangelo, who gave me a wink and a smile, meaning I was obviously a contenda. Eat your heart out, Lou.

I said my good-byes to everyone and thanked them all for a great welcome and a great lunch, and I extended my apologies for having to eat and run.

Landowski said he'd call me later or tomorrow, and Jack reminded me to pick up my paperwork. Chip Quinlan and Joseph Ferrara seemed as indifferent to my departure as they were to my arrival. Kim and Judy were eating donuts while looking at their cell phones, probably checking out websites for male strippers.

Amy and I went inside, and when we got to the hall-way, she ducked into the office and came back with my paperwork in a manila envelope and insisted on walking me to my car.

Outside, I saw that the small parking area was full, and one of the cars was a yellow vintage 'vette ragtop that I knew must belong to Lou Santangelo, even though there were no fuzzy dice hanging from the rearview.

Amy said, "I hope you enjoyed your lunch."

"Very nice. Thanks."

"I'm glad you got to see Lou."

"Me too." Should I tell her about the bop-Amy pool? Probably not. I said, "New chairs for the ladies."

She smiled and nodded. "You'd be a good boss."

"I want gender-equal access to the Recreation Room."

She smiled again. "Kim and Judy are excited."

This was not the time or place to ask Amy about Sha-ron Hite, and in any case, Detective Penrose, who I was sure knew about this, would fill me in shortly.

So we stood there, both aware that the security cam-eras were recording our reluctant parting. I smiled. "You've been terrific."

"I look forward to working with you." She handed me my envelope, and instead of a good-bye hug, she gave me my donut. "If you're around next week, call me."

"I will."

I got in my Jeep and headed back to the North Fork, munching on the stale donut, which, I was sure, had been destined for a soup kitchen. Lou Santangelo was a scam-mer, a schemer, a bullshit artist, and a slacker. He'd been a lousy cop, but I think he found his dream job.

As for everyone else at Security Solutions, they were either where they wanted to be, or they were where they had to be because they were all complicit in something. Including Amy Lang.

So, Sharon Hite . . . Suicide . . . Beth Penrose . . . Homicide. You didn't have to be Nero Wolfe to connect those dots.

CHAPTER 22

On the off chance that one of my new colleagues at Security Solutions had stuck a tracking device under my Jeep, I did not drive to Beth's house, but headed to Uncle Harry's house, my stated summer residence.

As I drove, I put my brain on fast replay and thought about my initiation into Landowski's big happy family. Nothing was unexpected or surprising, except for Jack Berger being a gentleman—and being too smart. And, of course, Amy telling me that Sharon Hite had committed suicide.

The only other surprise this afternoon was Lou Santangelo's appearance. But what was not a surprise was Santangelo confirming my suspicion that Max had pitched me to Landowski at that retirement party, and not the other way around—i.e., the smoke did not cause the locomotive.

Also, I was not particularly surprised or shocked by Landowski's Recreation Room. Boys will be boys—even in this enlightened age. And, as I say, it takes two to tango, and there was no shortage of girls to help the boys be boys. The question was: What was Steve Landowski actually up to? Just some clean dirty fun? Or maybe the Rec Room was Landowski's creative attempt at How to Make Friends and Influence Important People. Maybe a little subtle blackmail too. Or not so subtle.

Well, as we used to say in the detectives' squad room,

speculation is masturbation. What I had to think about now was my upcoming conversation with Beth Penrose.

Assuming I'm right about her and Max conning me into this job with Security Solutions for the purpose of me being a confidential informant, should I be angry? Well, I *am* angry, though I've done plenty of lying myself in pursuit of the truth. What makes me angry is that Beth and Max thought they could juke and jive *me*. You have to wake up real early to pull one over on John Corey.

So the best way for me to handle this would be for me to let them know—tonight—that I'd figured this out from the start. And then I'd blow them away with my brilliant deductive reasoning.

But . . . what if I was actually wrong? Well . . . I'd play it by ear.

About thirty minutes after I left the farmhouse, I was on Great Peconic Bay Boulevard. As I approached Harry's house, I slowed down and checked out the area, then doubled back and pulled into the circular driveway.

I was supposed to be living here, so it was best if my Jeep was here and not at Beth's house. I called a local car service and gave them my credit card info. Ten minutes for pickup.

I collected my stuff from the Jeep and stood on the front porch, dividing my attention between checking the road for any slow-moving vehicles and checking my phone messages. No texts or e-mails of interest, no one cruising past the house, and no drones overhead. Apparently, no one was interested in me except me.

The car arrived—a beat-up black Toyota sedan with tinted windows—and I got in. The driver, a young pimply-faced guy, asked, "Anyone else coming?"

"Just me and you."

He pulled onto Great Peconic Bay Boulevard and

headed east toward Cutchogue, saying, "Some place you got there."

"Thanks. I inherited it from my uncle."

"Lucky you."

"He wasn't so lucky."

"Yeah?"

"He committed suicide."

"Sorry."

"Cops thought I killed him."

No reply.

"You know. For his money. And his house."

No reply. But the car sped up. And within ten minutes I was in front of Beth's cottage. I would have given the driver a cash tip, but he sped away.

Anyway, I entered the cottage with my new house key and did due diligence, including a sweep of the bedrooms and closets. Sometimes you feel silly doing all this, but you'd feel even sillier if you plopped your ass on the couch, turned on the TV, and didn't hear the guys with guns and garrotes coming out of the bedroom. The leading cause of death in my world is cured paranoia.

I deposited my Security Solutions paperwork on Beth's desk in the guest bedroom, got a beer from the fridge, and went out to the patio.

I took off my blazer, sat on a chaise longue, and sipped my beer. Well, if I was an armchair detective, I'd now put all the pieces of the puzzle together, analyze the facts and clues, and name the suspects—Steve Landowski and a few of his shady staff. But what's the crime? Bribery, corruption, blackmail? Maybe. Murder? Yes, if the suicide was homicide.

The person who had more answers than I had questions was Beth Penrose, so I called her cell phone.

It rang once and she answered. "Hi, John. Everything okay?"

"All is well."

"Where are you?"

"I'm in our love nest."

"How did it go?"

"I am officially employed as a consulting detective."

"Good. We'll celebrate later." She informed me, "I've asked Max to have a drink with us at home. Is that okay?"

"Sounds good. I need to talk to Max."

"I thought you'd want to."

"Right. Look, the reason I'm calling is that I think you should come home now."

"Why?"

"There's a body floating in your hot tub."

"What . . . ?"

"Not dead. Just floating. That'll be me. And I need company."

"All right . . . I'll cut out. See you in about an hour."

"Can't wait." I added, "My Jeep is in the shop. But I'm here."

"Okay. See you soon."

I hung up, went to the hot tub, and turned on the heater and whirlpool. I put my Glock, cell phone, and beer on the ledge, stripped down, and climbed into the tub.

I sipped my beer and let the swirling water lift my body and soothe my mind, and I was once again confident that I was correct in believing I was about to go undercover and crack a big case—maybe murder—for the county police and for Beth Penrose; a case that they obviously couldn't solve themselves. Who you gonna call? John Corey. I was back in the game.

But this time I wouldn't slip into the shadows, as I'd

done with the Gordon murders. This time I'd take all the credit and all the media attention I deserved. The ATTF and the DSG would beg me to come back. And Robin would ask if I could help her on a tough case. And Tess would call to congratulate me and ask if we could have a drink next time she was in New York or I was in DC— which I would be, to kick Tom Walsh's ass. As for Kate, she'd realize she made a huge mistake, and she'd start drinking too much and wind up in a rehab clinic, staring at my photo on her cell phone.

Max was right: The best revenge is living well.

I finished my beer and floated on my back, my eyes closed and my mind wandering through a montage of payback fantasies, which, I realized, had been buried somewhere in my subconscious.

Well, this might not be all about me; it might be about bringing some perps to justice, and if doing that would get me some payback, then all the better.

The world doesn't try to screw you; the world is indifferent to you. But people try to screw you, and people need to know when they've picked the wrong guy to screw. And that's me.

CHAPTER 23

Beth came out of the house wearing a short kimono and carrying a tray on which was a bottle of Moët, two flutes, and her Glock. I don't actually like champagne, but I was sure she did, and at fifty bucks a bottle, it was a nice way to celebrate my new job and her successful con job.

She smiled. "You look relaxed."

"You look great in a kimono."

"Thank you."

She put the tray on the tub ledge next to my Glock, then dropped her kimono and climbed the tub steps, lowering herself into the swirling water. "Oooh . . . that feels so good."

We hugged and kissed, and it occurred to me that I was probably not the first sperm whale in this pool.

She asked, "Car problem?"

"No. I actually left it at Harry's."

"Why?"

"In case Landowski does a drive-by at Harry's."

"Okay . . . Good thinking."

"That's what I do."

"What do you do when you're not congratulating yourself?"

"I practice good tradecraft."

She didn't reply and leaned back against the tub, raised her legs, and floated.

I asked, "How was work?"

"Quiet day."

"Nobody killed nobody today?"

"Not yet. And I'm off-duty, burning up some vacation days until July sixth."

"Good." I couldn't remember a day when there wasn't at least one homicide in New York City. What we used to call job security. Out here, in this suburban and semi-rural county, weeks could pass without a murder, and when it happened, it was, as Beth had said, mostly unpremeditated acts of family, friends, and neighbors pissed off about something, or crimes of passion. Now and then, when something more complicated came along, the county Homicide Squad wasn't always . . . well, let's say trained or experienced enough to solve the crime. But that's just my perspective as former NYPD Homicide, and I wouldn't share that thought with Detective Sergeant Penrose if I ever wanted to get laid again. Bottom line, I was sure I was about to become an informant in a tough unsolved murder case. Probably the Sharon Hite so-called suicide.

On the subject of not much to do in the Homicide Squad, Beth said, "I booked our Bermuda flights. We depart JFK tomorrow night, JetBlue, arrive in Bermuda at ten-twenty-six. We return on the fifth."

"Great."

"I also booked our hotel. A place called Cambridge Beaches Resort and Spa." She added, "Looked very romantic on their website. Not cheap. But you deserve a great vacation."

"So will you after spending ten days with me."

She smiled, floated off, and stood. "Did you see your old colleague today? Lou?"

"I did." I added, "He had a different memory of who asked whom about hiring me at that retirement party."

Beth left that alone and handed me the champagne bottle. "Pop it."

I popped the cork and poured the bubbly into the flutes that Beth was holding. We touched glasses and she said, "Here's to your new job."

We sipped the champagne, which had a distinct musty aroma, like my Jeep upholstery.

Beth asked, "Did you see or hear anything interesting today?"

"Both."

"Like?"

The bop-Amy pool came immediately to mind, but I'd keep that to myself. I said, "I signed a confidentiality statement, so I'm not at liberty to say."

"Be serious."

I looked at her. "Okay, here's a simple yes-or-no question for you. Ready?"

She looked at me and nodded.

"Are you going to ask me to become a confidential informant at Security Solutions?"

She kept looking at me, and I couldn't tell if she was stunned by my brilliance, or shocked by my mental breakdown. And quite frankly, now that I'd said it out loud, it didn't sound as brilliant as it did in my head. In fact, I was about to say, "Just kidding. What's for dinner?"

But she said, "I told Max you'd figure it out."

Which, even if not the truth, was the right thing to say to pump up my ego and deflate my anger at being conned by her and bullshitted by Max. "And when were you going to reveal all this to me?"

She put her glass on the ledge and replied, "Max and I were going to talk to you tonight."

"Talk to me now."

"I hope you're not angry."

I didn't reply.

"We wanted you to go into that job interview clean and clueless. If we'd told you, you would have thought you had to put on some kind of act." She forced a smile. "Instead of being your arrogant self."

"I get all that. But what if I'd told you right off the bat that I had no interest in working for Security Solutions?"

"Then I'd have told you why I wanted you to work there."

"And then you wouldn't have had to have sex with me to con me into taking the job."

She stared at me, then said, "I had sex with you because I love you."

What clever reply do I have to *that*?

She kept staring at me. "Now let me ask *you* a simple yes-or-no question."

I was prepared to say, "Yes, I love you too," or, "Yes, I know the baby is mine," but that wasn't the question, thank God.

"Are you in?" she asked.

"I need to know more."

"You can't know more unless you're in."

Which was not the first time in my career that I'd been told I could not be given sensitive information until I said I was in. The Feds did this all the time.

"John?"

"Well . . . don't you want to hear how I figured this all out?"

"No. I'm sure I'd be impressed—and you'd be sure to tell me how much smarter you are than me and Max, and how we couldn't pull one over on you. What I want to know now is if you're in."

Of course I'm in. But why can't I brag a little? Maybe Max would listen to me explaining my dazzling deductive reasoning which led me to my brilliant conclusion that I was being recruited as a confidential informant.

"Let me help you, John. You're in."

"Right."

"But even if you said no, you'd still be my live-in lover."

"I wouldn't want to put that to the test."

She smiled and poured more bubbly in our glasses. We clinked again, and she said, "Welcome to the group."

I wasn't sure who else was in the group, or what the group was, but I was about to find out.

Beth said, "Let's sit on the patio, and I'll explain everything to you."

"We can talk here. But before we talk, I want you to assure me that you're not wearing a wire."

"I'm naked, John."

"Right. Let's keep it that way."

She sort of rolled her eyes, then shut off the whirlpool, finished her champagne, and said, "Okay. First, you need to understand that this investigation, which is of Steve Landowski and Security Solutions and some of his staff, is not officially sanctioned by the Suffolk County Police Department or the county DA's office. Or by any other law enforcement agency. In fact, they don't know about it."

That was a big surprise, and very unlike the Detective Penrose I once knew. But if my suspicions about official corruption were correct, then I could understand why this group—whoever they were—had gone underground.

She said, "Now that you know that, and understand that we could all be subject to disciplinary and even legal action, I'll give you the opportunity to change your mind and say you want no part of this."

"How would that affect my chances of getting laid tonight?"

She suppressed a smile. "I told you—one has nothing to do with the other."

Easy to say. "This may come as a surprise to you, but I've gone rogue myself a few times."

"I know that." She looked at me. "In fact, maybe it was your example that inspired me to do the same."

Nice to know I inspire people to bend the law. "Thank you."

"You should also know that my group has reached out to your favorite law enforcement agency—the FBI."

That's a bummer. I asked, "Who are you talking to there?"

"There's only one guy we talk to, and he's at Twenty-six Fed."

"Name?"

"Don't know. Code name. Don't ask."

I had code names for all of them. Well, this was obviously a big case if the FBI was interested—officially or unofficially. So my instincts and deductions had been correct, though I still wasn't sure what the alleged crime or crimes were. Sharon Hite's death? No. That wasn't big enough for FBI involvement.

Beth asked, "What are you thinking?"

"I'm thinking about you going rogue, and I'm thinking that you'll be easier to work with this time than you were on the Gordon case."

"I hope I can say the same about you." She smiled to show me she wasn't joking. "Okay, let's start with Sharon Hite."

"The late Sharon Hite."

Beth looked at me. "Who told you?"

"Amy."

"What else did she tell you?"

I wasn't sure I was making the right move by answering that question, but to be accurate in my reporting, I said, "She told me she wants to have sex with me. Though not in those exact words."

Beth seemed to be processing that, then said, "Well, that's not going to happen."

"I need to be free to recruit valuable assets."

"You need to keep your dick in your pants."

"Okay. I guess I'm now a private dick."

"Very private." She added, "Asshole."

"Maybe we should have Max try to seduce her."

She informed me, "He tried. Struck out."

"He never mentioned that."

"I don't know many men who brag about not scoring."

"Right. You found the right man for the job this time," I assured her. "I score."

"Let's move on to Sharon—"

"Do you know or suspect that Amy Lang has knowledge of or is herself involved in any criminal activity?"

"There is a strong presumption that she is."

Probably a weak presumption until I said she wanted to fuck me. "But no hard evidence?"

"No . . . but we checked on her status at the Police Academy and discovered that she has deferred twice. So, Amy Lang seems happier working as a receptionist at Security Solutions. Which, you will agree, seems odd."

And which was not what she'd told me. Well . . . there could be lots of explanations for that.

And Beth had one of them. "Your new friend is probably in cahoots with her boss." She advised me, "Do *not* attempt to charm her and expect her to reveal anything to you. She will go right to Landowski."

That was very disappointing. Or Beth was making

this up—so that I'd keep my pee-pee in the teepee. But if true . . . that left me with trying to seduce Kim or Judy. I'd need a couple of stiff drinks for that.

"Clear?"

I nodded.

"Okay," she said in her Detective Sergeant Penrose voice, "let's move on to Sharon Hite. What did Amy Lang tell you?"

"She told me that Sharon Hite had committed suicide."

"What was the context of that statement?"

Well, we were sitting cheek to cheek, sharing a bottle of red wine. She was wearing a lavender scent. "The context was that Chip Quinlan had been dating Sharon, and Ms. Lang said that I should know this so that I would be sensitive about mentioning Sharon's name if discussing old cases with Chip Quinlan."

She nodded. "So when Amy Lang told you that Sharon Hite had committed suicide, you were truly surprised."

"I was."

"So, I rest my case regarding keeping you in the dark."

"Case closed. But I'm still annoyed."

"You're actually gloating because you figured it out. Okay, so Sharon Hite's death. This happened about three weeks after she'd left Security Solutions, and—"

"Quit or fired?"

"Apparently, she'd quit."

"Can't imagine why."

"Just listen. Okay, because she died alone, an autopsy was required, and the M.E. ruled it suicide." Beth explained, "Sharon was found at home by her adult son, who'd come by because his mother had not answered his texts, e-mails, or phone calls for two days. This was on a Sunday afternoon. He'd last spoken to her on Friday afternoon—on December fifteenth, last year. Sharon was divorced and living alone in a garden apartment complex in Yaphank, not far from headquarters. Her son found her in her bed, wearing a nightgown, and on her nightstand was a nearly empty glass of what had been a gin and tonic, and an empty vial of Valium, for which she had a prescription. A high dose of Valium, when combined with alcohol, is potentially fatal, and she took enough Valium to kill her, according to Toxicology. The M.E. confirms that as the probable and proximate cause of death. Time of death was sometime Friday night or early Saturday A.M. There were no signs of foul play—no forced entry, no bruises on the body, no sexual assault, nothing of value missing, Glock service pistol in her nightstand, her off-duty revolver in a lockbox, car in her garage, no prints or DNA that couldn't be identified."

"Suicide note?"

"No."

"Why did the M.E. not think it could have been an accidental overdose?"

"She took about forty ten-milligram tablets, according to Toxicology. And that dose does not indicate a therapeutic accident."

I nodded. "Any prior suicide attempts?"

"No. And no expressed suicide thoughts to anyone we questioned."

"Shrink?"

"No. Family and friends say she was a happy lady. Happy about her recent divorce."

I can relate to that. "You check out the ex-husband?"

"He's clean. Retired UPS driver. Living in Florida. Equally happy about the divorce, which was amicable. Also, the son is clean. Good alibi. Devastated. Close to his mother."

"This happened in December. Holiday blues?"

"Her condo was decorated for Christmas. Presents wrapped. Cards ready to be mailed."

"Okay . . ." With murder, you look for motive. Similar with suicide. If there's no evident reason to kill yourself, and no prior attempts or signals, and no suicide note, then you have to question the appearance of suicide. I mean, if you've already written out all your Christmas cards, that's one less reason to kill yourself. And she was not working for Security Solutions at the time of her death, which was another reason not to kill yourself. I asked, "Why did she quit?"

"I'll get to that."

"Okay . . . was she still dating Chip Quinlan at the time of her death?"

"She'd told him she wanted to break it off."

"How do you know?"

"From friends and family."

"Was she depressed about that?"

"Not depressed."

"Fearful?"

"Maybe."

"Why?"

"We think Sharon confided something to Chip Quinlan that she realized she should not have confided."

"About what?"

"About the missing person case she had been working on. The missing prostitute. Tiffany Sanders."

"Okay . . . let's cut to the chase. Do you think Quinlan killed his girlfriend?"

"I do."

I nodded, picturing Chip Quinlan in my mind. He didn't look like a killer—but something told me he had it in him. I said, "So Quinlan's motive was to shut his girlfriend up about what she'd discovered regarding Tiffany Sanders's disappearance."

"That's my strong suspicion."

"Okay . . . I assume Chip Quinlan was questioned about his girlfriend's suicide."

"He was."

"And I assume he had an airtight alibi regarding his whereabouts during the two-day weekend that Sharon Hite had gone silent."

"He did. Quinlan said he was staying at the farmhouse, working through case files all weekend, and he had witnesses who could place him there day and night. Steve Landowski and Lou Santangelo."

I nodded. "So we have a possible conspiracy to commit murder."

"Correct. Retired police officers are credible and experienced witnesses, and there was no way to shake that alibi." She reiterated, "We're dealing with cops here—detectives who've seen it all and know how to do it."

"Right. Like how do you get forty tablets down a person's throat without leaving signs of a struggle? Answer, you don't use tablets."

"Correct. You use the liquid form of Valium in a drink—a gin and tonic—to make her sleepy, then you squirt more liquid Valium down her throat, or inject it, then flush the tablets and leave the vial on her nightstand. If this all happened in, say, the living room, and she was dressed to go out or to receive a visitor, then that visitor—who we believe was Chip Quinlan—spikes her drink with liquid Valium, and after she's comatose, he changes her location and changes her clothes and gets the lethal dose of Valium into her. Or something like that. And to all appearances, she went to bed alone and washed down about forty pills with a gin and tonic to end her life."

I nodded. Wrong conclusions are caused by good illusions. Chip Quinlan was not as stupid as he looked. In fact, as Beth pointed out, he was a detective who'd seen it all and knew how to do it. I asked, "Any indication that she had been moved or re-dressed?"

"Don't know, because the scene was not initially treated as a crime scene, and her death was not initially investigated as a possible murder." She added, "That was done a few days later, because some of my colleagues in Homicide found the suicide suspicious."

"Findings?"

"None. Because my boss, Lieutenant Charles Stuckley, was told to order his detectives—including me—to accept the M.E.'s findings and stop wasting time and resources on the Hite suicide."

"Told by whom?"

"By the Suffolk County Chief of Police, Edward Conners." She added, "Conners's order could be seen as surprising or suspicious—if for no other reason than Sharon had been one of us, and her unusual death should have been thoroughly investigated."

A real conspiracy theorist would be salivating about now. But there are sometimes good reasons for a boss to tell his overly imaginative and ambitious detectives to stick to the official findings and conclusions. "Do *you* think that Chief Conners's action—or inaction—is suspicious?"

"More on that later."

"Okay, so if Chip Quinlan did kill his girlfriend, he had easy access to her, and his DNA and fingerprints would legitimately be all over her house and disqualified as evidence. Plus, he has an airtight alibi for the time period involved, and I assume there are no witnesses who saw him or his vehicle near Sharon Hite's condo."

"Correct. We questioned everyone who lived in that

complex." She added before I could ask, "And no hits on Quinlan's cell phone, no calls between the parties for the previous twenty-four hours, and no mention by Sharon to anyone that Chip Quinlan was coming to her house. He probably showed up unannounced—maybe with a Christmas present—and wanted to talk, or whatever. Also, he may have had a key. And for sure he'd been dropped off a distance away by an accomplice—Landowski or Santangelo—and he walked in the cold, dark night, probably with a hoodie or a face scarf, to her garden apartment, where Sharon made the fatal mistake of letting him in." She informed me, "Women who are emotionally involved can be stupid."

"Present company excluded." Well, as I said and as I knew, Detective Penrose could rise to the challenge of a complicated and well-planned and -executed homicide, as she'd done with the Gordon murders. I had no doubt that if she'd been given a free hand on the Sharon Hite case, Chip Quinlan would by now be indicted for murder and awaiting trial, and his accomplices—Landowski and Santangelo—would be competing to rat him out in exchange for a plea deal. But that was a missed opportunity. The older the case, the colder the case.

I said, "So officially, Chip Quinlan is very clean. Except you say he had a motive to murder her. To shut her up about the missing prostitute, Tiffany Sanders. But why?"

"More on that later."

"Okay. And if I recall correctly, you said that Sharon Hite, when she was working for Security Solutions, had gone to Missing Persons to inquire about Tiffany Sanders."

"That's partly correct. Sharon had actually come to headquarters with some information and some suspicions having to do with Security Solutions."

"That's easy to believe." I said jokingly, "I almost did

the same after my lunch there. But I thought I'd speak to you first."

She looked at me. "If you'd actually gone to police headquarters and spoken to the wrong person or persons about Security Solutions, as I think Sharon Hite did, you too could have met with an untimely end."

I looked at her. She was serious.

"That's why we have an informal—unauthorized—group looking into this." She added, "People we can trust."

"Okay . . . and who did Sharon Hite speak to at headquarters?"

"She bypassed Missing Persons and also Homicide and went right to someone in the Commissioner's office who says—claims—that Sharon Hite was there to speak to him about employment opportunities for a civilian job at headquarters. Which is plausible, but probably a lie."

"Who did she speak to?"

"Apparently, she spoke to the wrong person." Beth advised me, "The fewer names you know, the better."

"Okay. So you're saying Sharon Hite had discovered that Security Solutions had something to do with the missing prostitute, Tiffany Sanders, and Sharon may have confided this to Chip Quinlan, then realized she shouldn't have done that. So she then went directly to the Commissioner's office with this information or suspicion and wound up speaking to someone who you believe was in cahoots with Landowski and/or Quinlan on some level, and that this person tipped off Landowski, which led to Quinlan killing Sharon Hite to shut her up."

"Correct." She added, "If anything was missing from Sharon's condo, it was her notes about the Tiffany Sanders missing person case that she'd worked on at Security Solutions."

"All right . . ." And I thought *I* was paranoid. Well . . .

conspiracy theorists love to string together odd facts and coincidences to prove something that's not true. Bad detectives do the same thing. But Beth Penrose was neither a conspiracy nut nor a bad detective. I said, "I assume that Tiffany Sanders is no longer missing."

"Correct."

Meaning dead. Which was no surprise.

Beth said, "I'll fill you in on that later."

"All right . . ." This case—if you could call it that—seemed to have lots of twists and turns with many beginnings, and no end in sight, except dead ends. Like a maze. "So Max is in your group?"

"He is. And that is the only name I'll give you."

"Okay . . . so you're talking about criminal conspiracy and collusion at a high level."

"At many levels. High and low."

And murder. And cover-up. And Security Solutions. And Steve Landowski, Chip Quinlan, and Lou Santangelo, and apparently, the Suffolk County Chief of Police, whose name, Edward Conners, I'd actually heard in some context—and not a good context. I asked, "Do you think your life is at risk?"

"It could be—if I or anyone in my group speaks to the wrong person. And maybe that's already happened—which is one reason Max asked you not to mention my name at Security Solutions. Another reason is that Landowski knows I wasn't satisfied with Quinlan's alibi, and that I'm on his case and Quinlan's case and Santangelo's case." She added, "I think they murdered Sharon Hite, and they may have murdered Tiffany Sanders, and they'd murder anyone who was a threat to them."

"All right . . . so if your life is in danger, and if I'm snooping around the bowels of Security Solutions for you, I'll bet mine would be too."

"Good deduction."

"Maybe you should have mentioned that earlier."

"I don't think that makes any difference to John Corey."

She really knew how to stroke a guy's ego. "You told me this would be a safe job. You'd sleep better at night."

"I lied."

"I see that."

"You look for danger, John. We both know that."

"Right. Am I getting paid for this?"

"You're getting laid."

"You said I'd get laid anyway."

"I lied about that too."

Funny. Or not a joke.

She asked, "How much is Security Solutions paying you?"

"A thousand a week."

"So, you're getting paid." She also informed me, "As a paid consultant to Security Solutions, you are a private citizen with no connection to the police. Whatever suspicious activity you see, hear, or discover there can be voluntarily and legally passed on to the police. But you'll actually pass this information to me. Your girlfriend. As of now the police can't question anyone at Security Solutions because we were told to drop the Hite investigation. We can't request a search warrant for the farmhouse for the same reason, and also because we have no probable cause. And even if we did, that request would get back to Landowski"—she looked at me—"because the corruption and collusion are present at every level. Police, DA's office, and the court."

I'd thought about that after seeing the Rec Room and hearing from Landowski about his high-profile guests. This is every cop's worst nightmare—society's worst nightmare—when the forces of law and order are themselves criminals.

I recalled a case that my ex, Robin, had worked on involving a police informant, and I said to Beth, "You seem to believe that my legal status as a civilian informant is clear. But if arrests are made, the defense attorney will argue at a challenge hearing that I was, in fact, an agent for the police, deliberately placed at Security Solutions as a police agent to gather evidence without probable cause. In other words, just a fishing expedition, which is illegal." I reminded her, "Any search or arrest warrant that is issued as a result of what I discover might seem valid up front, but the defense will argue that any evidence uncovered by that search warrant was illegally obtained and should be thrown out."

Beth looked at me, obviously impressed with my legal knowledge. I was tempted to say, "I'm not a lawyer, but I've slept with a few."

Beth said, "This is one reason we didn't tell you up front why we wanted you to get a job at Security Solutions. It was *your* idea."

"Really?"

"That's our story, and we're sticking to it. Also, as I said, you're not going to the police. You're going to me. And as for my group, it doesn't exist." She added, "A state court might have some problems with admitting evidence under these circumstances, but if we can make this a Federal case, we would get a better outcome."

"Right." Sometimes. But it seemed to me that this case could collapse because of those legal issues. Therefore, I might need to take more direct action against Landowski and company, as I did with the Plum Island case. And other cases where justice had to be delivered before trial.

Especially if the homicide victim was a cop—or retired cop, as in this case. I said, "Okay. Just mentioning the possible legal roadblocks."

"Which we can get around." She explained, "At some point, after you've been at Security Solutions awhile, you will go to your girlfriend—that's me again—and share with her your concerns and suspicions about Security Solutions. Pillow talk. But pillow talk from a former homicide detective and former Federal agent. To make this a Federal case, I will have to bypass my chain of command because of my suspicion—based partly on what you've told me—of possible corruption and conspiracy in my department, and I—and you—will go directly to the FBI, who will begin an investigation of Steve Landowski and Security Solutions, based on the knowledge and belief that local law enforcement is part of the problem and not the solution." She looked at me. "This is why you're working at Security Solutions. Clear?"

"Very. And I'm impressed with how you've thought this all out."

"I'm not as stupid as I look. Don't let the big tits fool you."

"Right. Also, good initiative and outstanding devotion to duty." I assured her, "You picked the right man to help you."

"I know that. And Max agrees."

"And does your group agree?"

"I told them I was recruiting a confidential informant. But I did not tell them your name."

"Why not?"

"For the same reason you don't know their names."

"Okay. But do you trust them?"

"I'm still alive."

"Right." I wondered if she'd told them *how* she recruited me. Probably not. Well, there seemed to be a lot of moving parts to this case, and what was not moving was missing. I thought a moment and said, "Tell me about Tiffany Sanders."

Beth looked at me. "Tiffany Sanders was one of the nine female bodies found dumped on Fire Island."

That took me by surprise. This unsolved and ongoing case of nine dead young women, apparently all prostitutes, was bizarre enough to have made national news, and I recalled that the case had a TV documentary made about it as well as a fictionalized TV movie. So all of a sudden I was involved in something much bigger than a suspicious suicide. This was mass murder, and a good example of the type of homicide investigation that the county police weren't experienced in handling. In fact, they had made no progress on this year-old case. So who you gonna call? Actually, when I'd seen and read some of the news coverage of the Fire Island case last summer and fall, I thought of my old friend Homicide detective Beth Penrose, whose jurisdiction included Fire Island, and I almost gave her a call. Or maybe I thought she'd call me. But . . . I said, "So you think there is a connection—Fire Island murders, Tiffany Sanders, Sharon Hite, and Security Solutions?"

"We know there is a connection."

"Okay." I said, "I recall that the FBI looked into these prostitute murders."

"They did. They were not invited by the County PD, but because the nine bodies were found in the Fire Island National Wilderness Area, which is covered by the U.S. Department of the Interior's National Park Service, their Investigative Services Branch was called in. When the ISB saw that this was potentially complicated, they called the FBI to work with them. And, of course, my Homicide

Squad got involved." She added, "Because of all these competing law enforcement agencies, the investigation soon became what we call, in police science terms, a clusterfuck."

I nodded. Been there. In one way, it was fortunate that the perp or perps dropped the bodies on Federal parkland, which got the FBI involved. That was stupid of them, though I was sure the perp or perps thought the bodies would never be found, or they didn't know they were on Federal land. In any case, there's nothing like a turf war to complicate a criminal investigation.

Beth continued, "Chief Conners was not happy with FBI and ISB involvement, and not cooperative. He stonewalled, withheld information, and ordered my Homicide Squad not to speak to the Federal agents. He characterized the ISB and FBI involvement as meddling in a local matter and said he was personally and professionally insulted by their intrusion and their arrogance."

"Right. I recall that now." I added, "Well, Chief Conners may be right about FBI arrogance. And he was protecting his turf."

"He's protecting himself."

I thought about that. Turf battles having to do with jurisdiction are common, and wounded egos are more common. But a police chief stonewalling the FBI and withholding information, especially in a major homicide case, is not so common—notwithstanding the FBI often keeping the local police in the dark and feeding them shit. What was also unusual here was that Chief Conners, according to Beth, had previously ordered his Homicide Squad to drop the Sharon Hite suicide investigation, which apparently was connected to the Fire Island murders by way of Tiffany Sanders. This maze was getting more twisted.

I looked at Beth. "So what you're saying is that the

Suffolk County Chief of Police, Edward Conners, knows more about these multiple murders than he's saying. In other words, he's involved in a conspiracy to cover up nine murders. Are you actually saying that?"

"Ten murders, if you count Sharon Hite."

"Okay . . . I think I might need a real drink to hear the rest of this."

"You might need two." She suggested, "Get dressed. Meet you inside."

She climbed out of the tub, put on her kimono, and went into the house.

So . . . apparently, I have walked into the perfect shitstorm. Again. Well, I was getting laid, getting paid, and my life was in danger. What more could I ask for? Maybe a Scotch and soda.

CHAPTER 24

Beth was sipping a vodka tonic, still in her kimono, sitting cross-legged on the couch. I was dressed, sitting in a chair across from her. On the cocktail table between us, Beth had set out an assortment of adult beverages.

Max was due at 6:30, according to Beth, which was enough time for her to complete my education. Now that I knew that this was about the Fire Island murders, I was focused and motivated. Big case. I made myself a Scotch and soda.

Beth said, "We need to conduct this unofficial and unauthorized investigation with the knowledge and belief that there is widespread official corruption, collusion, and conspiracy in this county at many levels—police, judiciary, politicians, and also the DA's office."

"Okay." This seemingly widespread corruption explained some of Beth's personality changes; she'd gone from good soldier to rogue when she realized that things were not as bright and clean in her world as she'd thought.

I remember when I too came to this realization. At that point you have your choice of playing the game, getting out of the game, or blowing the whistle to stop the game. And that could get you booted off the field or, now and then, killed. Which is allegedly what happened to former county detective Sharon Hite.

I asked, "How exactly do Steve Landowski and Security Solutions fit into all this?"

"The farmhouse, we believe, is the nexus of most, if not all, political and police corruption in this county."

"Okay . . . But if Landowski is the mastermind, then his co-conspirators must be mental midgets."

"Landowski is not the actual mastermind. Someone else is. He is the fixer—the guy who makes things go away and gets things done for crooked pols and bad cops. He is the guy with the guns and the guy with the muscle." She added, "His PI agency is a cover for a criminal enterprise."

"And," I informed her, "he's the guy who provides the entertainment."

I was going to fill her in on the Recreation Room, but Max had apparently already done that because she said, "I know about Thirsty Thursdays and the rooms upstairs. The prostitutes."

"Party girls. And exotic dancers."

"Prostitutes. And drugs."

"Landowski said there were no drugs."

"And if you asked him if Chip Quinlan was with him in the farmhouse on the night Sharon Hite died, he'd lie about that too. In fact, he already has. He's a liar. He corrupts and compromises people." She looked at me. "I'm sure Landowski is an accessory in the murder of Sharon Hite, and he may also be a murderer himself."

I couldn't wait to spend a night alone in the farmhouse, nosing around, looking for evidence. The basement would be the most fun. On the subject of real fun, I said, "I may need to attend one of Landowski's Thirsty Thursdays."

"You need to attend every Thirsty Thursday." She explained, "As you may have guessed, what goes on there is Landowski sexually compromising and corrupting public officials—and the police." She told me, "Max has been there a few times."

"I heard."

"To observe."

"That's why everyone is there."

She ignored that and said, "So Landowski thinks that Max is one of the boys—one of his compromised police officials. But Max hasn't been invited in a while." She added, "Apparently, there are more guests on the Thirsty Thursday list than there is room for."

Thursday at Steve's was a hot ticket with good reviews. I said, "I have a standing invitation. Actually, a work obligation to attend."

"Good. And you need to invite Max."

"Okay. So aside from corruption of police and public officials, what am I looking for?"

"We—my group—believe that some of those Thursday-night girls may have known some of the nine girls whose bodies were found on Fire Island. And some of those deceased girls, including Tiffany Sanders, may also have worked at the farmhouse as dancers or sex workers." She added, "You will get the contact info on these Thursday-night girls. Max will get the names of any of Landowski's prominent guests who he doesn't already know. My group will do the follow-up."

I nodded.

Beth seemed lost in thought, then said, "Okay, so how did all this begin? It began last April when a hiker in the Fire Island Wilderness Area discovered a decomposed body in the thick bramble off a hiking trail." She explained, "The hiker had his dog with him, so it was actually the dog—a German shepherd—that found the body."

It's always interesting how a homicide case begins, which is usually—but not always—with the discovery of a dead body. And from there it can go anywhere. Now and then the dead body that you see is sometimes just the tip of an iceberg, as happened with the Fire Island murders.

Beth continued, "The hiker notified the park rangers, who called the Investigative Services Branch of the Park Service. The ISB preserved the crime scene, and the body, which was nude, was handed over to the county medical examiner. All this was done before the Suffolk County Police were able to respond to the crime scene."

Meaning the Feds won round one of the turf war, and this all got off on the wrong foot.

Beth went on, "The autopsy could not determine the cause of death, but the time of death was about ten to twelve months earlier. The M.E. said the deceased was a Caucasian female in her mid-to-late twenties." She added, "The identity of the deceased could not be determined at the time, but was determined later." She added, "It was not Tiffany Sanders, who was IDed afterwards."

Beth filled me in on more details of the M.E.'s report, including evidence that death did not occur where the body was found, meaning it was dumped there. The body had been unclothed and with no wrapping of any kind. I actually remembered some of this from what I'd read and seen in the news when more bodies started turning up in the same Wilderness Area of Fire Island.

Beth continued, "The second body, also a female, was identified as East Asian by DNA and dental work and was also found by accident a month later by a park employee who'd been doing some sort of survey." She added, "The area off the hiking trails is almost impenetrable because of the thick brambles, thornbushes, and lots of poison ivy, so no one wanders too far from the trails, and all the bodies had been carried through the bramble and dumped about thirty or forty yards from the hiking trails where no one would normally be walking. So the second body, like the first, had lain undiscovered only about thirty yards off the trail since about spring or summer two years ago. So the two times of death were similar; both were females in their mid-to-late twenties, early thirties, unclothed, no jewelry, no discernible tattoos, no scars or deformities, and both victims had apparently died elsewhere and been dumped there."

"Right." When the body count rises to two, it becomes obvious to even the dullest detective that some person or persons were using this piece of terrain as a dumping site for his or their murder victims. But as I recalled, no search had been done after the first body was found, which I would have done on a hunch—or based on past experience.

Beth also knew this and said, "After the first body was found, we did do a search of the immediate area for evidence—but not for another body." She asked rhetorically, "Who would have thought there'd be more?"

Well, me.

"So," she continued, "after the second body was found in May, and after the Suffolk PD took the lead in the case, we used protective gear because of the poison ivy and ticks, and we had machetes for the bramble, and cadaver dogs with protective gear. We did an extensive search of the fourteen hundred acres of wilderness and found four more bodies in the next two months."

"That makes six."

She nodded. "The last three bodies were discovered in September and October last year. The first by another hiker with a dog, then the last two with our cadaver dog after we did a second sweep."

"There are probably more."

"Probably." She continued, "All nine bodies were female, as you know, and the three who were Caucasian were eventually IDed by name, through DNA and dental records supplied by families who'd read about this case and who were looking for a missing loved one. As you may recall, these three IDed women were known sex workers, so it was not a stretch to assume that the other six females were also prostitutes. So we reached out to Missing Persons in other law enforcement agencies, but we were not able to ID any of the other six bodies, all of whom were East Asian, which raised the possibility that none of those six women were here legally."

"Right." So if they disappeared, it wasn't noticed, because they had never appeared to begin with.

Beth said, "We IDed the third Caucasian body from DNA and dental records supplied by her mother. In fact, it was Tiffany Sanders whose body was the last found. In October." She added, "As supervisor, I made the phone notification to her family."

Beth made herself another drink.

Well, the life of a homicide detective is very glamorous if you don't count murder scenes, decomposing corpses, morgue visits, autopsies, and death notifications.

More of this was coming back to me. Obviously, these were not random murders, and the proximity of the dumped bodies was not a startling coincidence. The speculation and theories from the police, the news media, and a thousand amateur detectives was that there was a single person—like a Long Island Jack the Ripper—behind these murders. Or maybe a single entity—like the Mafia, who were known to re-use a safe dumping ground for their waste disposal program. But now . . . I think we were suspecting that Mr. Landowski might be providing a service not advertised on his website.

Beth was giving me a rundown of the autopsy findings,

but there wasn't much evidence of cause of death, except for one body that showed a blunt instrument trauma to the cranium. All the bodies were nude when dumped, and they were unwrapped, so there was no forensic evidence at the scene, except for the badly decomposed corpses. Any other crime scene evidence on or around the body had long since disappeared in the year between the spring and summer of two years ago—when the M.E. said they'd died—and the times that they were found last spring, summer, and fall.

Beth continued, "None of the other eight bodies showed trauma, but they were all so badly decomposed—and eaten and scattered by wildlife—that the M.E. couldn't determine cause of death, though Toxicology says that possibly a few were drug overdoses, which is how a lot of prostitutes die accidentally—or are murdered."

As I listened to the grisly details, I concluded that multiple dead bodies were not only a sanitation problem, they were also redundant: a case of too much evidence amounting to too little knowledge, the sum of the parts adding up to less than the whole of the known facts.

When this happens, you need to cut through the M.E. reports, forensics, toxicology, crime scene photographs, and so forth, and move on toward the goal line, meaning switching your attention away from the unfortunate victims and to begin thinking about the killer or killers. This is where knowledge, experience, and intelligence have to become wisdom. I said, "I assume you worked this case from the beginning."

"I did. In a fifty-person task force that included half the Homicide Bureau."

I nodded. Suffolk County had about twenty Homicide detectives, so half of that, plus forty other Suffolk PD, was a big commitment of local resources and personnel. But this weird and sensational case had drawn a lot of outside attention and media coverage, so when that happens, the Chief of Detectives or higher-ups assign more people than can be spared—to improve the optics, though not necessarily improving the outcome. I said, "I assume you're still working this case."

"No. I've been taken off the case." She added, "More on that later."

"Okay."

Beth switched from the gory details to the location of the grisly discoveries—Fire Island, which she described to her city boyfriend as a thirty-mile-long barrier island off the South Shore of Long Island, which I knew, though I'd been there only once, and only for a few hours. Fire Island had almost no roads, and in most areas no vehicles were allowed. People walked or biked, which gave it its pristine charm. The island was reached primarily by private boats or ferries which served the many small and isolated beach communities along the thin strip of land. There were, however, two access bridges at either end of the island. The east bridge, known as the Smith Point Bridge, was the access to the Wilderness Area where the nine bodies had been found.

Beth explained, "When you come off the bridge, if you go left, you enter the Smith Point County Park, where there is a parking lot. If you park there, you need to walk a few hundred yards west to the National Wilderness Area, where there is no parking allowed. There is a Wilderness Visitor Center there, manned by one or more park rangers until about four or five P.M. So after about five P.M., the entrance to the Wilderness Area is unsupervised."

"I assume this is not a well-visited place."

"The beach is visited by sunbathers and licensed fishermen who surf cast in the Atlantic. The woods—the

Wilderness Area—is not well visited. In fact, I didn't even know about the Wilderness Area until the first body showed up there." She further explained, "Most people who cross the bridge are going to the county park, which has amenities. The Wilderness Area has mosquitoes, ticks, poison ivy, and thornbushes."

Which is why it's called a wilderness. As I said, I'd been to the less wild Smith Point County Park once, for a ceremony at the TWA Flight 800 Memorial, which was erected near the beach to honor the victims who perished when their plane exploded—mysteriously?—in midair and fell into the Atlantic off the coast. So I must have been close to the Wilderness Area, and I could picture the terrain.

Beth continued, "The Visitor Center is a two-story structure built on pilings, and from the Visitor Center is an elevated boardwalk that runs for about three hundred yards through the wilderness. At the end of the boardwalk is a sandy trail that cuts through the brambles and goes down to the ocean beach. This is the most traveled part of the wilderness, so my team and I didn't expect to find any bodies along this route, and we didn't. We did, however, discover that this trail led to a part of the isolated beach used by nude sunbathers." She added, "Ten of them on the day I was there. Male and female."

Maybe I needed to see this crime scene. I asked, "Did you question the sunbathers?"

"We did. On the theory that the nude bodies that we'd found may have actually been nude sunbathers. This was after we'd found the second body and before we discovered that they had been prostitutes. So the proximity to the nude beach and the two nude bodies was worth exploring—according to my three male teammates."

"I would agree with that." I asked, "Did the sunbathers reveal anything more than their tans?"

"No. But they invited us to go skinny-dipping with them."

"I hope you accepted." I reminded her, "You have to win the trust and confidence of potential witnesses."

"That's exactly what my three male teammates said." She added, "All pigs oink alike."

Can't argue with that, but to sound enlightened and sensitive, I said, "I'm disappointed to hear that sexism is still rampant in your organization."

"It's not easy being a woman in a man's world, John."

"Life is not easy, Beth."

"Try life with a pretty face, big tits, and a vagina."

"Maybe in my next life. If I'm lucky."

"Easy for a man to say."

Apparently, there was a point to this tangent and she said, "Chief Conners has a low regard for women, and that sets a low standard on the job." She added, "He's married, but he has girlfriends, and he frequents prostitutes."

"I'll bet I know where he gets them."

She nodded. "Also, I should let you know that most of the detectives in my unauthorized group are female."

Holy shit. "Are you kidding?"

"No. I can trust them, and they're motivated. They hate Conners, and they want justice for the dead women."

"Okay . . . makes sense. I'd like to meet your group when this case is wrapped."

"Maybe. But for now it's just you, me, and Max as a team within the group."

"Who's the group leader?"

"Me."

"I'm impressed. Does your group have a name?"

"Just the Group." She added, "Not the Pussy Posse, as I'm sure you were thinking."

"Never crossed my mind."

She suggested, "Let's move on. So there are other trails through the wilderness, and that's where all nine bodies were eventually found—about thirty or forty yards off the trails." She further explained, "The bodies were found in different positions, and Forensics says that the broken vegetation under the bodies and the slight depressions in the ground are consistent with a body being thrown, probably by two people who took the body by the wrists and ankles and heaved it farther into the bramble, rather than laying it on the ground." She added, "So there were at least two people involved—probably fairly strong men—and that does not indicate a single serial murderer."

"Don't conflate the disposal of the bodies with the murderer."

"Correct. In fact, it could have been a single serial killer, but he had help disposing of the bodies."

"Right." Like . . . Well, two big guys like Steve Landowski and Chip Quinlan came to mind. The unadvertised specialty of the house: You bump them off and we dump them off. Was that possible?

Beth went on about the locations and positions of the bodies and so forth. Crime scene evidence is good and can solve a case. But too often the investigating detective gets lost in the weeds—literally and figuratively—and becomes process-oriented and not goal-oriented. The goal being: Who killed these women? And/or: Who dumped the bodies?

Anyway, whoever dumped them knew the area and knew how to dispose of bodies. And Beth had come to the right conclusion: This was a professional disposal job involving at least two people. But was one or both of them also the killer or killers?

Beth said, "We can assume that all these bodies were dumped after dark. As I said, the Visitor Center closes at five P.M., but the Wilderness Area—which the Park Service calls a hidden treasure—is open to the public twenty-four hours a day for surf fishing with a license and also overnight camping, most of which is done on the beach."

Leaving the tick- and mosquito-infested interior of this hidden treasure to people who needed to dump bodies. I asked, "Did you consider that the perps could have arrived at night by boat?"

"A boat would not have beached on the Atlantic side, because that's where people camp and fish. On the bay side, there are usually small boats anchored for night fishing and crabbing." She concluded, "The perps came by vehicle and used the Smith Point Bridge, which is toll-free. Unmanned and no cameras."

Well, Beth and her Homicide Squad had about a year head start on me and had thought long and hard on this and had walked the terrain and seen the bodies in situ, and smelled the evil smell of death. Despite Nero Wolfe's hundred percent success rate, armchair detective work had its limitations in the real world.

Beth said, "So, to reconstruct the disposal of the bodies, a vehicle crossed the Smith Point Bridge, probably in the early-morning hours, and there were probably two perps in the front and a dead body in the trunk of a car or the storage area of an SUV. They drove a few hundred yards west to the closed Visitor Center, which is as far as the bridge exit road goes, then got out of their vehicle and accessed a hiking trail, carrying the body with them— probably in a tent bag, which would not look suspicious in that setting. And they apparently weren't worried about running into a park ranger who might be passing through and who might be curious about their presence at that hour."

"Right. And I'm sure your two presumed perps were carrying good ID—maybe police ID—that they could show if they were being questioned. But more importantly, they had guns to end the questioning if necessary."

Beth nodded. "In fact, after the second body was found, we found a ranger who remembered two guys in an SUV who were parked near the Visitor Center two summers ago—in late August, at about one A.M. You can park on the beach if you have a fishing license, but no one is allowed to park anywhere else in the Wilderness Area, so the ranger questioned them. The guys said they had gone surf fishing, and they had fishing gear with them and a fishing license—and also four bluefish. They showed photo ID—driver's licenses—said the right things, and left, heading back to the bridge." She added, "No, the ranger couldn't remember their names or the type of SUV."

Probably an Escalade or Durango and probably two people I'd just had lunch with. The IDs were phony, of course, as were the fishing licenses, and the bluefish came from a fish market. And in the back of the SUV, along with the fishing gear, was a dead body in a tent bag—or the body had already been dumped. Also, I'd bet that was the last body dumped on Fire Island. Well, almost busted doesn't count. I asked, "Did you show this ranger a photo of Steve Landowski? Or Chip Quinlan? Lou Santangelo?"

"No, because I wasn't thinking of them in connection with the Fire Island murders at that time. But a few months later, I did do a photo array with this ranger, which included driver's license photos of Landowski,

Quinlan, and Santangelo. But it had been dark when the ranger saw these two guys, and too much time had passed for a positive ID."

"Right." So, to move toward the goal line, if Steve Landowski and a few of his PIs were the guys who procured the prostitutes and disposed of them—and maybe killed them—then who were the girls' customers? Thirsty Thursday guests? Maybe. But the M.E. said all these deaths occurred in summer, so I also thought of affluent city people who summer in the Hamptons and who have been known to use an escort service. Other possible customers of prostitutes were the people who lived or summered in the inhabited areas of Fire Island—people who had a well-deserved reputation of being strange: artists and writers, full-time nudists, trust fund dropouts, eccentrics, and locals who ranged from normal to nutty.

As for the Hamptons, which were not far from the east end of Fire Island, that summer playground is, as I said, populated with the rich and famous, a significant number of whom are weirdos. Wealth and an unlimited drug budget can do that to you. And as Beth could attest, there had been some almost unbelievable Hampton homicides committed by the privileged rich and the empowered nut jobs—including the murders of spouses, friends, lovers, neighbors, houseguests, and even household staff, including, I recalled, a chauffeur. And now and then a prostitute. In fact, the oversexed and under-loved gentlemen of the Hamptons imported more prostitutes than chardonnay every summer. And if most of these girls were illegal aliens, their disappearance would go unnoticed. Now and then, however, the girls were native-born with friends and family back in the Midwest or Appalachia, and when those girls disappeared—as Tiffany Sanders had done—someone would look for them.

In any case, the possible connection of these prostitute murders to summer residents of Fire Island or the Hamptons had become part of the story—part of the prurient fascination with this case. I mean, it's not usually a big or interesting case when a hooker disappears, but there were nine of them, and they kept turning up naked and dead in the same place, and that got everyone's attention, for starters. But human nature being what it is, for most people, the dead girls were the least interesting aspect of the mystery; the real interest—for the public, the press, and the police—was: Who killed the call girls? Hopefully, rich and famous men. A-listers. This was very juicy stuff, but mostly speculation and wishful thinking among the masses, who would love to see rich and famous men in handcuffs on the six o'clock news. Me too.

I freshened my drink and Beth's, and we sat in silence awhile, collecting and collating our thoughts.

So if you worked this backward, you started with the person or persons who procured the women and possibly delivered them to the customer or customers. Then the procurer—Steve Landowski, former Vice Squad detective, was a person of interest here—provided a hooker pickup service and took the girls away. Dead or alive. But why dead? Accidental OD? Murdered? The one bashed-in skull was a sure indication that murder was the cause of more than one of the deaths. I asked, "Regarding the perp or perps, what are the working theories?"

"Every theory known to police science. The first theory was a Jack the Ripper copycat, a guy who thought prostitutes were bad girls who deserved to die. But Jack would work alone and would probably carve up the bodies, and there was no evidence of that. And Jack would usually leave the bodies where he killed them. Because

Jack likes to make a statement and not hide his handiwork." She added, "The FBI confirms this."

"I agree with the FBI." Did I say that?

"But Chief Conners was pushing that theory, then when it didn't fly, he switched to the Mafia."

"Right. When in doubt, blame the Mafia." It's true that the Mafia always tries to hide the body for all the right reasons: no corpse, no crime. And when the Mob found a nice dumping ground, they tended to keep it on their GPS. And finally, a lot of high-end prostitution in New York was controlled by the Mafia. But the wiseguys weren't known to whack their girls who got out of line or held back their earnings; they just fired them or beat them up. I said, "There is nothing about these murders that follows any organized-crime M.O."

"I agree. But the county Organized Crime Task Force is actively investigating this possibility." She added, "At Chief Conners's directive."

Obviously, someone should be investigating Police Chief Conners. Or at least giving him an I.Q. test. But no one is *that* stupid. Therefore . . .

Beth continued, "So it appears that two or more people disposed of the bodies, but the actual murderer could be one guy, a customer, who is a sexual sadist, or whose sexual fantasies include the murder—usually by strangulation—of the woman he just had or was still having sex with. Or he killed them first and then had sex with them. Necrophilia." Beth went on to explain all this in case this was my first rodeo, which it wasn't.

The thing is, when you worked for over ten years in Homicide, there does come a time when you've seen it all and heard it all, and nothing surprises or shocks you. That's when you should ask for a transfer to the Art Forgery Squad or something. But it's not about you, it's about the victims, so you file all these cases in your brain so you can reference when a new case lands in your lap. And you compartmentalize—so you don't wind up on a shrink's couch or an autopsy table with a self-inflicted bullet wound to your head. The depths of human depravity are astounding, but the mind is resilient, though the soul is always in danger.

Beth went on, "Another possibility—theory—is that all or most of these deaths—except the blunt trauma case—may have been caused by drug overdoses—accidental or on purpose. If on purpose, it could be one very sick john killing his hookers. If accidental, that would be all too common. Sex, drugs, alcohol, and an overdose equal death. And that could indicate more than one john. And no premeditation. Just good times gone bad."

I nodded. "And that would mean that all these girls' customers had the same phone number to call to dispose of the body, because they all wound up in the same place."

"Correct. And we think that phone number belongs to Steve Landowski, who we believe was also the guy who procured and delivered the women to the customers, either at the customer's house or at a hotel or motel. Or possibly some of the deaths occurred in the farmhouse."

"Right. So let's go from abstract scenarios to Mr. Steve Landowski. First, he's a former Vice Squad detective who is running a honey trap in his farmhouse, compromising his guests who are local pols, judges, and law enforcement people. Most of these people have no real money, so he's not charging them for the girls, and he's not blackmailing them for money. But they have power, and they can protect him and his criminal activities, including his escort service. So Landowski blackmails them in that way— they all have each other by the balls." I asked, "Does that fit what you know?"

Beth nodded. "It fits one of a few theories and scenarios."

I continued, "As for Landowski's paying customers, they could be who everyone thinks they are—rich and maybe famous Hamptons guys. Specifically, clients of Security Solutions." Recalling my job interview with Steve Landowski, I said, "The link between the hookers and the johns and the dumped bodies could be Steve Landowski. He has access to the Hamptons crowd through his PI firm. He may have provided personal bodyguard services to them, or he may have done a marital case for them. Or just provided premises security for a house party. Whatever it was, he was making the acquaintance of these people and their friends. Next stop for the entrepreneurial Steve Landowski is to size up his rich customer, then hint that Security Solutions has another service that the customer may be interested in. And it's all safe and discreet, because Mr. Landowski is a former police officer, and his girls have all been vetted by him. And Landowski has assured his prospective customers that the girls will keep their mouths shut if they recognize the face or the name of the high-profile john—like an athlete, an actor, or a rock star."

Beth said, "We can't exclude the possibility that the girls were murdered—or killed accidentally—by one or more of the men who are guests at Thirsty Thursday." She added, "Don't get fixated on the Hamptons crowd."

"Right . . . but they as a group would more likely fit the profile of men who had a few screws loose and enjoyed sexual perversions, including strangling their hooker."

Beth had no comment, and I continued, "These are people with power and money. Presidents and presidential candidates who spend time in the Hamptons at the homes of their rich friends and donors, and who have been known to need female companionship. Also senators, congressmen, cabinet members, and British royalty. Then you have the Russian oligarchs, who don't need to be discreet or need to be talked into hiring a few prostitutes for a party, but who would like a package deal—hookers and armed guards for their parties."

Beth nodded and I continued, "I'm sure Landowski began his escort service with the intention of becoming the pimp to the rich and famous. Then maybe one of the girls died of an OD—or maybe the john got too rough with her or killed her as part of his sexual high—and Landowski saw an opportunity to make a lot of money by being a dead-hooker disposal service. I've seen this before. It's about the money. Pimping is good money, but disposing of dead bodies, as Steve Landowski may have discovered, is a gold mine. In fact, Landowski may have provided fentanyl-laced drugs to the girls when he realized they were worth more to him dead in some rich guy's bed than alive doing tricks for a thousand a night." I added, "I don't think we'll ever know if those girls ODed—accidentally or on purpose—or if a john killed them as part of his sexual high. But I think what the dead girls and the johns had in common was Steve Landowski, who delivered them to the john, then disposed of them for a lot of money—twenty, fifty thousand dollars, with maybe a follow-up blackmail demand." I added, "That's where he gets the cash to pay for those Thirsty Thursdays."

Beth said, "That's an interesting scenario."

I continued, "And Landowski may be using some of that money to pay off anyone who is getting close to figuring out that he had something to do with the bodies. Maybe someone like Edward Conners. Which would explain a lot of Conners's actions and inactions."

"It would," she agreed. "And what you're saying is what a lot of people are thinking but not saying."

"Right." I reminded her, "You need to be careful when you accuse the king of treason."

She stayed silent, then said, "There is another theory— a sort of unifying theory that fits most of the facts."

I asked, "What?"

"I'd like you to come to that conclusion yourself." She added, "Think about it."

"Okay . . . do I have all the facts to come to another conclusion?"

"You have most of what you need. More to come." She repeated, "Think about it."

I felt like a student in one of my classes. "Okay." I changed the subject. "It's my guess that Landowski has had a few other close calls and scares in the wilderness or elsewhere, and he may be out of that business—or he may be gearing up for another profitable summer."

Beth nodded, sipped her drink, then said, "The Fire Island murders are an f-ing public relations nightmare for the Suffolk PD."

Not to mention a public embarrassment. But she knew that.

"More importantly," she said, "nine young women are dead—maybe more—and these women, regardless of their life choices, deserve justice. And so do their families."

"That will happen."

She nodded, then said, "We started this group because we weren't satisfied with the official ruling on Sharon Hite's death. And we also weren't satisfied with how Chief Conners—and others—were proceeding with the Fire Island murders. And the more we looked and compared notes, the more we realized that there was a connection."

"Great detective work."

She continued, "What ties all this together is Chief Conners, who we believe is Landowski's boss—or partner—and who we also believe gets a cut from whatever criminal enterprises Landowski is into."

I had no reply.

She looked at me. "Conners has to go down. He's made us all look bad."

"Right. And as we say, no one hates a bad cop more than a good cop." Or Beth was having some boss issues. I mean, was the county Chief of Police really a criminal? Or was he just a convenient scapegoat? When I'd first started reading about the Fire Island case, it had seemed to me that the Suffolk County PD were stepping on their dicks with every step they took. But more to the point, it was the steps they hadn't taken that had left the Fire Island investigation at the starting point. I mean, unless I was forgetting something, the county police—specifically Beth's Homicide Squad—hadn't even taken enough steps to reach a dead end. So maybe it was a combination of a turf war with the Feds, bad detective work, *and* criminal interference from the top that had screwed up this investigation.

Beth said, "Conners made *me* look bad . . . in public. Took me off the case."

Well, it was easy to guess what was motivating Detective Sergeant Penrose.

"I want his balls in a jar above my fireplace."

I glanced at the fireplace mantel. Maybe a bit left of the clock.

There's nothing worse than a homicide investigation that's gone off the rails. Initially, everyone wants a piece of a high-profile case, until it becomes clear that there are no clues, no leads, no motives, no witnesses, no informants, no evidence, no suspects, and no imminent arrests—only dead bodies. At which point the case is not helping anyone's career. But in this case, Detective Sergeant Beth Penrose, along with some colleagues—mostly female—had decided to band together in an unofficial group to look further into Sharon Hite's death, which had led to their own investigation of the Fire Island murders and Security Solutions and also crooked cops and pols, all of which were apparently linked. This was above and beyond the call of duty, and very admirable. Also risky. Actually dangerous.

Beth seemed to be in deep thought—or emotionally drained—and she stayed silent for a few minutes, so I did too. Finally, she said, "We've made some mistakes."

"We all do. But then you solve the case."

"But we've also been sabotaged by a criminal cartel of public officials and police officials who are in collusion with Steve Landowski." She looked at me. "Do you believe that?"

"Since we're now being straight with each other, I'm not sure I believe all of that."

"Okay . . . I appreciate your honesty."

"But I can be convinced."

Beth stood. "I need some air and sunlight."

I stood, and we moved toward the patio door, carrying our drinks but leaving the resupply bottles behind.

Well, I've worked some multilayered cases before, but this one took the multilayered cake. With icing. I slid open the patio door and said, "There's a lot to digest here."

She looked at me. "I'm not done serving."

"I didn't think so."

In fact, the rest of this shit sandwich was going to be served al fresco, but that wouldn't make it taste better.

CHAPTER 25

Beth and I sat on the patio lounges in the late-afternoon sunlight. She said, "I haven't really talked this case out in a long time." She looked at me. "It's good to get your perspective."

"I'm shooting from the hip—as usual. I don't have all the facts or the case history that you do."

"But you have good instincts. And you're coming fresh to this." She added, "I've been working this case—on my own time—too long and too much."

"That's why you need to just go in for the kill."

"We need to develop the case."

Sharon Hite had been dead since December, and the first Fire Island murder victim had been discovered last April, but I said, "Okay. So aside from me attending Thirsty Thursdays, what exactly do you want me to do when I'm inside the farmhouse?"

"We can discuss that with Max. We have a few ideas—and we'd like to hear yours."

My idea was for me to snoop around, steal evidence from the farmhouse, and wrap this case up before Labor Day. Also maybe seduce and recruit Amy Lang. But Beth didn't want to hear that. I said, "Okay. What else?"

She put her drink on the side table and said, "All right . . . so a few local journalists have suggested that something is wrong in Chief Conners's office. And in the DA's office." She added, "When we get to Bermuda, I'll give you a few dozen links, and you can read what's been written about the Fire Island murders."

"So this is a working vacation."

"It is." She continued, "Very little of this local investigative reporting was picked up by the national media, but the TV movie about this case did raise these issues and raised awareness."

"I hope Chief Conners enjoyed the TV shows."

"I'm sure he didn't. The TV documentary—sort of an investigative report—was made without the cooperation of the Suffolk County PD, as per Chief Conners's directive to all police personnel."

"You missed a chance to be interviewed on TV."

She ignored that and said, "The two-hour documentary relied on interviews with victims' families and with a few retired police detectives who were willing to talk, as well as an assortment of colorful locals on Fire Island. Lots of heat but no light. Entertainment."

"Television journalism at its best."

She continued, "A local freelance investigative reporter, posing as a prospective client, actually went to Security Solutions last December, after Sharon Hite died. Then when this reporter was with Landowski in his office, he started grilling Landowski about Sharon Hite's death and about what goes on upstairs in the farmhouse. The reporter also asked Landowski if Sharon Hite had been looking into the disappearance of a prostitute, and if this could be connected to the Fire Island murders."

Apparently, Amy didn't do a good screening job that day.

"Landowski called someone in—I think Quinlan— and they physically threw the reporter out."

I didn't see that on their website. "How do you know this?"

"From my Missing Persons source who heard about this from another reporter."

"That's hearsay, twice removed. You need to go to the prime source. The reporter."

"He's not available."

I guess I knew what that meant.

"This reporter has gone missing. Just totally disappeared from the face of the earth."

"I assume the police are looking for him."

She nodded. "But maybe the wrong people from Missing Persons were assigned to the case." She added, "The reporter, Dan Perez, who was Hispanic, was also doing an investigative piece on the Salvadorian gang MS-13, and he'd actually penetrated the gang, so the Commissioner's office, the DA's office, and Chief Conners put out a joint statement implicating MS-13 in this man's disappearance." She added, "When we get to Bermuda, you can read all about it."

Hopefully by the pool. Well, if I was believing half of what Beth was saying, it would be easy to believe that this whole county of a million and a half mostly nice people was run by and policed by the most corrupt and murderous bunch of assholes this side of the Rio Grande. And maybe it was. And maybe we'd all wind up dead or missing. But, as they say, all it takes for evil to triumph is for good people to do nothing. And there was evil here—nine dead women, and probably more, dumped like garbage to be eaten by maggots and wild animals. And then there was former detective Sharon Hite, who, like Dan Perez, had apparently come too close to the truth and taken that truth to the grave.

I asked, "Anyone else missing or dead under suspicious circumstances?"

"We have no knowledge of that at this time."

"Good. And just to let you know, if something happens to me on this case, don't blame yourself."

She looked at me. "Did I make it clear to you that you will not go off on your own to do what you usually do? Which is to engage in unauthorized, high-risk, and harebrained activities."

Apparently, she mistook my personal initiatives for high-risk behavior. Not sure about harebrained.

"John?"

"I will defer to your judgment."

She kept looking at me. "I will not have a rogue within the rogue group."

Wouldn't two rogues make it right? "That would be counterproductive," I agreed.

"Don't push your luck, John. Because that endangers the people around you."

"I always try not to do that."

She reminded me, "You came into the Plum Island case like a bull in a china shop. You were arrogant and dismissive of Max's investigation, my investigation, and even dismissive of the FBI and the CIA."

"Who cracked the case?"

"You did. But you almost got yourself killed."

"*Almost* is sort of subjective."

"Not from where I was standing."

"Let me remind you that you too were not following orders. And *almost* got yourself killed." I further reminded her, "You too shouldn't have even been on Plum Island."

"I wouldn't have been there if I wasn't following you there. And you're lucky I *was* there."

Is this where I thank her for saving my life and ask her to marry me? I said, "I've learned since then that discretion is the better part of valor." I promised, "You can trust me to be a team player."

"All right . . . If we crack the Fire Island case and the Sharon Hite case, and maybe the Dan Perez case, you'll be rewarded with the knowledge that you were part of a team who did the right thing for the victims."

"How about some TV and print interviews?"

She ignored that and went on, "And if this unauthorized investigation goes sideways, I'll try to keep you out of legal trouble."

"I know a good criminal defense attorney." Who I just told to fuck off.

"What we're doing is not only unauthorized, it can also be dangerous." She reminded me, "These people are killers."

"Thank you for the opportunity."

She said, as if to herself, "I hope I'm not making a mistake bringing you into this."

"Your only mistake was not calling me a year ago."

"You're not a team player. You're an arrogant asshole."

"I think we've established that."

"And a loose cannon."

"You nailed it."

Beth seemed to agree and continued her briefing. "All right, if you're wondering who hired Security Solutions to find Tiffany Sanders, it was her mother, Lynne Sanders." She added, "Mrs. Sanders made a fictionalized appearance in the TV movie."

"Tell me about the real Mrs. Sanders."

"Widowed, supermarket cashier, two adult daughters, lives outside of Toledo, Ohio. Apparently, she'd read or seen something in the news about the bodies being found on Fire Island, and knowing that her daughter Carolyn, a.k.a. Tiffany, sometimes worked in this area—specifically the Hamptons—she called Suffolk County Police and filed a missing persons report."

"I assume by this time everyone knew that the missing girls were prostitutes."

"As per the missing persons report, which I've seen, Mrs. Sanders described her daughter as a model. And an actress."

"God bless mothers." Though my mother would agree with Beth's descriptions of me. Especially harebrained.

Beth continued, "According to my friend at Missing Persons, Mrs. Sanders spoke to another Suffolk County Missing Persons detective on the phone, and this detective—who I'll call Detective Smith—took the missing persons report over the phone."

"Why Detective Smith?"

"The fewer names you know, the better."

I felt I was back at 26 Fed, talking to Tom Walsh, who, as it turned out, had good reason to say that.

She continued, "According to Detective Smith's missing persons report, Carolyn Sanders had arrived in New York City about a year before she went missing."

And probably arrived at the Port Authority Bus Terminal, where the pimps waited for the buses and the fresh meat from the hinterlands. And the rest is history repeating itself.

Beth said, "There wasn't much useful info in Mrs. Sanders's missing persons report—not even her daughter's New York address. But I did learn from my reliable and trusted source at Missing Persons—who I'll call Detective Goodman—that Mrs. Sanders had decided to come to Long Island in August last year to look for her daughter. Her first stop was Suffolk County PD Missing Persons in Yaphank, where she met with Detective Smith." Beth added, "Mrs. Sanders supposedly gave Smith a written statement in the office."

"Why supposedly?"

"Because there is no written statement from Mrs. Sanders on file. Only Detective Smith's memo of her visit. I saw this memo, and it's basically a recap of the original missing persons report with no new information."

"How do you know that Mrs. Sanders gave Detective Smith a written statement?"

"Because my friend at Missing Persons, Detective Goodman, says he saw Lynne Sanders in an interview room by herself, handwriting a statement for over an hour."

"Okay . . . so should I conclude that there was something in Mrs. Sanders's statement that Detective Smith— or someone else—didn't want on record? And should I also conclude that Detective Smith is part of the conspiracy to cover up the facts of the Fire Island case? Or was this just sloppy record-keeping?"

"You know the answer to that."

"What does Detective Smith say about this?"

"He says that Mrs. Sanders never wrote out a statement in his presence, and if she did so in another room, the statement wasn't given to him."

"Plausible. And what do you think was in Mrs. Sanders's written statement?"

"I have no idea. But if it disappeared, it might have contained some references to what Tiffany had told her mother in phone conversations or e-mails about places she'd been and people she'd met. And maybe there was something in Mrs. Sanders's recollections of her daughter's calls and e-mails that caused Detective Smith some concern. In other words, incriminating evidence about people or places that Detective Smith didn't want on the record."

"Okay. Like, 'Hi, Mom, I met a wonderful man named

Steve who lives on a farm and offered me a modeling job.'"

"Something like that."

"So Detective Smith is Detective Badman."

"He is."

"Okay. I assume you spoke to Mrs. Sanders about all this."

"I called her in early December, about a month after my initial call to her about her daughter's body being found. By then I knew from my friend Detective Goodman about the written statement, and when I asked Mrs. Sanders if Detective Smith had seen her statement, she said yes, she had given it to him."

"So you got a live one on the line."

"I thought so. But then I asked her if she'd be willing to give me a statement on the phone, or come to my office—at my expense—or I could go to her. She then informed me that someone at police headquarters, whose name she wasn't allowed to give me, had told her there was an internal investigation of some detectives who'd mishandled the Fire Island case, and this person also told Mrs. Sanders not to speak to anyone about this case except the case officer—Detective Smith." Beth added, "And I wasn't Detective Smith."

I thought about all that and concluded that this was SOP—but only if an actual Internal Affairs investigation was underway.

Beth set that straight. "There was no such investigation."

"An investigation could have been contemplated. Or started in secret."

"I would know by now."

"Right. Well . . . this is a little suspicious." I asked,

"Who do you think it was who told Mrs. Sanders not to speak to anyone except Detective Smith?"

"Obviously, Police Chief Conners or someone in his office." She added, "But Mrs. Sanders would not confirm or deny."

"Would your source in Missing Persons, Detective Goodman, be willing to give a written statement about seeing Mrs. Sanders scribbling away in an interview room?"

"Not at this time." She explained, "There are a lot of ... let's say professional concerns and also mistrust around the Fire Island case."

"Sounds like some people in the Suffolk PD are frightened or intimidated. Or waiting to see how the wind blows."

"That's correct. Which is why we formed this group."

"Right."

She continued, "Edward Conners has put out a directive about the Fire Island case instructing all police personnel not to engage in interoffice rumors or speculation about the case, and not to speak directly to the news media, but to refer all requests for information to the Public Information Office with a copy to the Chief of Police's office."

"Interesting." But not unusual in a high-profile case, though it did sound a bit restrictive, especially the part about not engaging in rumor and speculation around the watercooler. That's the fun part of the job. "All trails seem to lead back to Chief Conners."

She nodded. "And in a separate, classified directive, Conners instructed all police personnel not to speak directly or indirectly to any other law enforcement agency—Federal, state, or local."

"He's trying to make sure the Suffolk PD speaks with one voice."

"Correct. His own."

"Not unusual."

"Are you playing devil's advocate? Or are you dense?"

"I'm offering alternate explanations for what you—and your group—see as conspiracy and cover-up."

"And what is that alternate explanation?"

"Ego and stupidity. I've seen more of that in law enforcement than conspiracy and cover-up." I put on my professor of criminal justice hat and advised her, "Don't get hung up on conspiracy and cover-up. Even if it exists here, it doesn't advance the case. That's another case. You and your group need to solve at least one of the murder cases you're working on—Sharon Hite, or the Fire Island murder victims, or the missing reporter. When you solve even one of those homicide cases, then the conspiracy and official cover-up will unravel very quickly."

"I see your point. But—"

"No buts. I've worked cases from both angles. It's easier to prove murder than it is to prove conspiracy to cover up a murder." I had another piece of advice. "When your boss is an asshole—and I've had my share of them—your inclination is to prove to yourself and to your colleagues that the boss is incompetent. Next step, you think the boss is on the take—because nobody can be that stupid or incompetent." I got down to specifics. "Apparently, Police Chief Conners is disliked by his subordinates—especially the female personnel. And, in addition to your group's suspicions of criminal activity, you also find Edward Conners to be a pig. And you'd all like to see him serving time with Bubba. I get it. So if you and your group can solve any of those murder cases, you'll have lots of people who'll want to be the first to testify about cover-up and corruption—including Detective Goodman and others who are now faint of heart and running scared. And once this house of cards starts to collapse, it will implicate Security Solutions. And Lou Santangelo will turn rat to save his ass, and he'll give up Chip Quinlan as Sharon Hite's killer and Steve Landowski as an accessory to the crime." I advised, "Prioritize the crimes. Murder is first. Conspiracy to cover up a murder is second. Bribery, corruption, human trafficking, and the piggishness of men—PIs, johns, and bosses—is a distant third."

She thought about that, then said, "I'll talk to my group."

"Tell them you're sleeping with a man whose intelligence and track record you admire."

She forced a smile. "I never advertise my man."

"Smart."

We both fell into silence, enjoying the early-summer sun and the soft sea breeze. Even the f-ing birds sounded good. Well, it had been a long winter and a rainy spring, but summer was here—though if you were dead and buried with no prospect of resurrection, none of that mattered. So when you're aboveground, you should get some sun. And do something you're good at. Like gardening. Or solving a murder mystery. Every life needs a purpose. Every death needs an explanation.

I sat up. "Okay. Back to Mrs. Sanders. You first spoke to her last October to notify her that her daughter had been found, apparently the victim of foul play, and that the ID was positive."

"Correct."

"And did you at that time bring up the subject of her August visit to Missing Persons?"

"No. Because so much information was being pigeonholed or suppressed, I didn't know about that visit when I made the notification call. And even if I did, it wasn't appropriate to question her at that time." Beth added,

"And she didn't bring it up. She was in shock. Devastated. Though she was not really surprised that her daughter had been one of the women found on Fire Island."

"Right." Mrs. Sanders knew that Carolyn had become Tiffany.

"But she was comforted to have closure. And have the body returned for burial."

I nodded. I've done too many of these notifications, and you need to be sensitive, but also stress that the perpetrator needs to be found and brought to justice before he—or she—strikes again, so you urge the bereaved family to work through their grief and try to cooperate in the investigation. In the case of Tiffany Sanders, her murderer could have been her customer or her pimp, or herself with the help of controlled substances, supplied by said customer or pimp—whose name could be Steve Landowski. In any case, one of the only possible leads in the Fire Island murders would have been what Tiffany had chatted about with, or e-mailed to, her mother—a name, a place—but Mrs. Sanders's statement had disappeared, and any follow-up questioning of her had been shut down by someone in the Suffolk County PD who had the power to do that. And that would be Chief Conners, who was either doing his duty or doing something else.

I asked, "How was it that Mrs. Sanders wound up hiring Security Solutions to find her daughter?"

"I'm not sure. Maybe she had a list of local PI agencies from the Internet. Or maybe when she was at headquarters, she asked for a recommendation for a PI agency." She added, "It's police policy not to recommend a PI agency, but maybe Detective Smith directed her to Security Solutions."

Which would be like a butcher directing a lamb to

the slaughterhouse. Assuming, of course, that Detective Smith was in on the cover-up. I asked, "How did Mrs. Sanders have the money to afford a PI agency?"

"I don't know. But a parent will mortgage the house to help their child."

Not my parents. They wouldn't even go on PayPal to pay a reasonable ransom. I said, "Maybe Tiffany sent money home to her widowed mother."

"Maybe. Which would be ironic if the money that Mrs. Sanders had to hire a PI agency to look for her daughter was the money that her daughter had made working for Steve Landowski as a hooker."

"Very ironic." Not to mention the hand of Fate. On that subject, I said, "It could be that Tiffany had been a Thirsty Thursday girl, and maybe she did mention to her mother the name Steve Landowski and/or Security Solutions in some context, and that's why Mrs. Sanders went there."

"Possible. In any case, Mrs. Sanders wound up hiring Security Solutions—and Sharon Hite. And after Sharon spoke to someone in the Commissioner's office about the Tiffany Sanders case—or about getting a job there, if you believe that story—Sharon reached out to my friend Detective Goodman in Missing Persons, who she also knew and trusted. They met for lunch, and Sharon shared some of her concerns and suspicions about Security Solutions with Detective Goodman." Beth reminded me, "At that point, in August, Tiffany was just a missing person, and any connection between Tiffany and the bodies that were being found on Fire Island was just speculation. But Mrs. Sanders, of course, suspected the worst, and this is what she told Sharon Hite, and what Sharon said to Detective Goodman, who later passed this on to me."

So, it seemed that a mother's instinct was correct, unfortunately. I asked, "But how was it that Sharon Hite—and not Lou Santangelo—got Mrs. Sanders as a client?"

Beth explained, "According to Detective Goodman, Sharon told him that Mrs. Sanders, who was staying in a local motel, had called Security Solutions after hours—about six o'clock—and the phone was answered by Sharon, who was presumably the only one in the office. Sharon, after speaking to Mrs. Sanders on the phone, invited her to come in and talk in person."

Amy, I'm sure, would have done the same thing after hearing from Mrs. Sanders what it was that she was calling about. But Amy would have had Lou Santangelo interview Mrs. Sanders—if Lou could be found. Or Landowski would have interviewed Mrs. Sanders himself. And if, during that interview, Mrs. Sanders had said that her missing daughter had in some way mentioned something about . . . let's say a nice man named Steve and a job offer in the Hamptons, then I don't think Mrs. Sanders would have made it back to Ohio. But Fate had Sharon Hite pick up Mrs. Sanders's phone call.

Beth continued, "Sharon also shared with Detective Goodman her suspicions that Steve Landowski may have known Tiffany professionally—her profession, not his—and that Steve Landowski's Thirsty Thursdays were more than boys drinking and playing cards. But Sharon didn't elaborate and just asked Goodman for a copy of the original missing persons report and also asked him to keep her apprised of any new information on the Tiffany Sanders case."

I thought about all that and concluded that Sharon Hite had been onto something, but she couldn't be sure if she was coming to the right conclusions. So she made the fatal decision to share her concerns with her lover— Chip Quinlan.

Beth confirmed that: "At some point, Sharon must have confided in—or confronted—her boyfriend. Maybe it was a confrontation about Thirsty Thursdays. Or concerns about Security Solutions in general. But sometime after Sharon met with Goodman at his house, the Sanders case was taken from her and given to Lou Santangelo. But apparently, Mrs. Sanders had bonded with Sharon and did not want to work with Santangelo, and Security Solutions dropped her as a client for nonpayment."

"Mrs. Sanders is lucky that Chip Quinlan didn't visit her in Toledo to collect on her bill."

Beth nodded. "I think she's lucky to be alive."

"Right." The thing about killing witnesses is that you never know where to stop. You can't kill everyone the witness spoke to. You have to be selective so you don't cause more problems than you think you're solving. Steve Landowski knew that.

Beth had another explanation for Mrs. Sanders's continued existence. "Landowski knows that he's covered— that Chief Conners controls all the information and that whatever information Mrs. Sanders gave to Missing Persons is dead and buried at headquarters."

"And whatever information Mrs. Sanders gave to Sharon Hite is also dead and buried."

Beth nodded. "As I said, we couldn't find Sharon's notes on the Tiffany Sanders missing person case. Sharon, I'm sure, stayed on the Tiffany Sanders case on her own time while she was still at Security Solutions. And we know from Goodman that even after Sharon was fired, she continued working on the Tiffany Sanders case. We have no idea who Sharon was speaking to, or what leads she was following, but we believe she was trying to make a connection between the Fire Island murders and Security Solutions. And had she stayed on at Security Solutions, she may have made that connection."

"Right. So am I now Sharon Hite?"

"You are."

"Just for the record, I don't take Valium."

"And you're also not sleeping with anyone who works at Security Solutions, as Sharon was. And let's keep it that way."

"Whatever you think is best." I added, "I didn't know Sharon Hite, but I admire her."

Beth nodded, but stayed silent, then said, as if to herself, "Sharon Hite should not have shared her suspicions or concerns with Chip Quinlan."

"Easy to say. But a romantic relationship is, by definition, intimate and trusting."

Beth looked at me, as if to say, "Where did you hear that?" But she said, "Women have to learn."

I wasn't sure what they had to learn, but the inference was that men shouldn't be trusted. Well, they shouldn't be trusted to keep their browser in their trousers. But Sharon Hite apparently thought she could trust her former NYPD boyfriend and confide in him her suspicion that their boss, Steve Landowski, was a pimp and maybe a murderer. Sharon Hite, a former cop herself, should have known better. But, blinded by love, she opened her heart, her mouth, and her door to the wrong guy. How many times have I seen that?

Beth said, "Chief Conners is playing whack-a-mole. When something pops up, he smashes it. But he can't do that forever."

"Sounds like he's doing a pretty good job of it."

"Which is why I thought of you."

"I thought you wanted to rekindle our romance."

"I did. When Max told me you were out here, my *first* thought was that I wanted to see you." She added, "It was only afterwards that I thought about you helping me with this investigation."

"How long afterwards?"

"About two minutes."

Funny. But not making me feel special.

Beth closed her eyes and took in the late-afternoon sun.

So I thought about all this and said to her, "If it's hate that's motivating you, nothing good will come of this, even if you succeed in getting Edward Conners behind bars."

She didn't reply.

"Same goes for Steve Landowski and his accomplices."

Again she didn't reply.

I said to her, "Don't become what you're fighting. If you do, even if you win, you lose."

"Correct me if I'm wrong, John, but I seem to recall you delivering justice with a knife on Plum Island."

"Heat of the moment. Not premeditated."

"Your filleted suspect would have been comforted to know that."

"Actually, it was self-defense."

"I'm going to take a nap."

"Max will be here in half an hour."

"I'll be ready."

I don't know what that means when a woman says it— but it doesn't mean "I'll be ready."

I stood and went into the house to get ready for cocktails, Part Two. I took a quick shower, found some clean clothes, then made myself a cup of coffee and sat in the living room. The Scotch bottle was nearly empty, and I hoped that Max remembered to bring the bottle he owed me for solving the Plum Island case for him. For solving this case, I wanted a whole case.

Well, I'd said what I had to say to Beth about the best way to approach this high-voltage and multilayered case, and more importantly, I'd said what needed to be said to save her soul.

I've seen too many good cops go bad, but what's even scarier is when a good cop loses faith in the system or thinks the wheels of justice grind too slowly and turns vigilante. I may have done this myself once or twice, back in my NYPD days—and maybe a few times when I worked for the Feds, whose methodical investigations ended only when the suspect died of old age. But as with everything in life, it's okay when I do it, though it was disturbing to see Beth—who I cared for—go down that road. But if that's the road she chose, I'd go down it with her. Though at a much quicker pace.

As for the case itself, not only was it multilayered, it also came with some danger of getting killed. It was, as I said, a maze of twists and turns, and also an odd but familiar collection of interlocking crimes and intertwined suspects. The crimes ranged from simple prostitution to the corruption of public officials and law enforcement people and went all the way up to every society's most heinous crime—murder. Thou shalt not kill. But if you do, odds are good that you will be visited by a homicide detective.

Hard to know where this maze started and where it went—but I knew where it was going to end.

CHAPTER 26

Beth was still getting ready when the doorbell rang at 6:40. Hit men don't usually ring the bell, so I assumed it was Max, but I looked through the peephole to be sure.

I opened the door, and Max extended his right hand for a shake, but I was more interested in the bottle of Dewar's in his left hand. We shook, and he entered, handing me the bottle. "I didn't forget what I owed you."

"Neither did I." I closed and bolted the door.

Max, wearing a nice sport jacket, followed me to the sitting area and plopped his ass on the couch, like he'd been here before. I asked, "What can I get you, Chief?"

He surveyed the cocktail table. "I'm ready for a TGIF drink. Vodka on the rocks."

I scooped some ice from the bucket, filled a glass with Grey Goose, and handed it to him, then made myself a Dewar's and soda. We clinked glasses and he said, "Cheers."

I sat in the armchair and we sipped in silence. I wanted to take this opportunity to talk to Max about a few things, but real men don't talk until they drink.

Well, I either trusted Max or I didn't. I mean, it was almost incomprehensible that Police Chief Sylvester Maxwell was in cahoots with Landowski—or with Police Chief Edward Conners. But once the seeds of distrust are sown . . .

Max asked, "Where's Beth?"

"Getting dressed."

"She brief you?"

"She did."

"This is some unbelievable shit."

"Shit for sure."

"You in?"

I was sure Beth texted him that I was in, and that's why he was here, but I confirmed, "I am."

"Good. I knew you would be." He added, "Sorry we had to con you."

Apparently, Beth had not told him how brilliant I was, so I did. "Max, the day you can con me is the day I take a security job at Home Depot."

He seemed skeptical, and I let it slide because he'd ask Beth.

He asked me, "Where's your Jeep?"

"My uncle's driveway." I explained, "I didn't want my Jeep in front of Beth's house while I'm in Bermuda."

"Right. I was going to tell you that."

"Beat you to it. I need you to talk to the renters when they arrive July first and tell them that the Jeep stays there. Comes with the rental or something."

"Okay. Good thinking."

I fished the keys out of my pocket and flipped them to him. I asked, "Do you think Landowski can make any connection between me and Beth?"

He replied as though he'd thought about it, "The only connection would be the Plum Island case. But you kept a low profile—especially after I fired you—and not many people know that you and Beth had become . . . intimate afterwards."

"As for getting fired, that's what motivates me." As it had motivated Sharon Hite at Security Solutions and Beth Penrose when Chief Conners took her off the Fire Island case. I asked, "But what if Beth was bragging around HQ that she was *intimate* with a famous NYPD Homicide detective, and Landowski, who worked there then, heard the gossip?"

"As long as she didn't use your name."

"Right." She doesn't advertise her men.

"Just ask her," he suggested.

"I will. But keep in mind that someone who Landowski knows on the job could recall the Plum Island case and bring it to his attention."

"It's more important that Landowski doesn't discover that you've reconnected. Because as you now know, Landowski knows—or suspects—that Detective Sergeant Beth Penrose is on his case."

"I thought you told me at dinner that you didn't know why I shouldn't mention her name to Landowski."

"John, don't bust my balls. Whatever I said at Claudio's about you getting a job at Security Solutions wasn't a lie. It just wasn't the full truth." He explained, "It was a strategy."

"It was a con."

He glanced at the hallway door, probably hoping that Beth would appear and save him from my ballbusting.

I said, "Amy Lang. You forgot to tell me she was a hot number."

He smiled. "I thought you'd like to be pleasantly surprised."

"I like to be forewarned and prepped. Like when you told me that Beth was interested in me."

"She asked me to tell you that."

"Glad you didn't forget. I could be shagging Amy now instead of Beth."

"It doesn't matter who you're shagging, as long as you're working for Security Solutions and for us."

"I'm not sure Beth would agree with that."

He shrugged.

"What a tangled web we weave, Max."

He remembered to warn me, "Amy Lang may be in cahoots with Landowski. So be careful."

"Obviously." I suggested, "You should try to seduce her."

"I actually did. Try. Struck out."

"At least you're honest about that."

He looked at me. "The minute you said you were in, the bullshit stopped."

Which was bullshit.

He added, "We—the group—expect the same from you."

"Is there a secret oath?"

"No. But this is a potentially deadly game." He added, "These people who you are now working with are killers."

"I've been briefed."

Max finished his drink and poured himself another.

I said, "On the subject of killers, my Southampton case could be shadowing me."

"Beth told me. Feds got you covered?"

"The Feds wouldn't tell me if my ass was on fire." But they could be using me as live bait to hook some SVR assassins. I hoped the FBI plan included killing the Russians before the Russians killed me.

"I don't know how you worked for them."

"It was never easy. But always interesting." I added, because it was apropos, "If nothing else, the Feds are incorruptible."

"So were the Gestapo. I'll order some drive-bys here—marked and unmarked." He assured me, "A cruiser will never be more than five minutes away."

"Thanks. But I don't think anyone could have tracked me here."

"If the Russians actually tracked you to Harry's place, and they know your car, then they tracked you here." He let me know, "I'm more concerned about Beth than you."

"I'm sure of that. But she's a big girl with a big gun." I suggested, "When you do your friendly-cop visit to Harry's renters, tell them not to hesitate to call the Southold PD if they see or hear anything suspicious."

"I'll leave my card. And order drive-bys." He smiled. "I'd love for my boys to bag some Ruskies."

"Be careful what you wish for."

Beth came into the room. "What are you boys talking about?"

Why do they always ask that? Do they think anyone is going to tell them?

I said to her, "Just some housekeeping." I stood and smiled. "You look great."

Beth was wearing a low-cut silky white top that a forensic accountant would say revealed two of her major assets. Also, she'd sprayed on a pair of shiny black pants.

Max stood, and Beth and Max did an XO. I'll bet he'd like to fuck her.

Beth suggested, "Take what you're drinking outside, and I'll bring out some snacks."

I was comfortable inside without the f-ing birds and bees, but I could use a few more minutes with Max, so he and I gathered up the cocktail stuff and took everything out to the patio table.

Max sat and asked, "How's it going here?"

I remained standing as I freshened my drink. "Great. Like old times."

"Good." He said, "So you're going to Bermuda."

Max probably knew that before I did. "Tomorrow. Returning July sixth."

"I wish I could get out of here for the Fourth."

"I thought you were a patriot, Max."

"I am. But this place goes crazy on the Fourth. Illegal fireworks, DWIs, and out-of-control parties."

I wondered if he was going to Landowski's party, but I didn't ask. "Sorry to miss seeing you have to work."

Max ignored that and asked, "So how did it go at Security Solutions?"

I took a seat at the table opposite him. "Amy made me feel very welcome."

Max smiled, then looked serious. "Did you get any bad vibes? Like they were onto you?"

"Maybe. From Jack Berger." I added, "Quinlan and Ferrara were not welcoming."

"Santangelo?"

"As Beth may have texted you before you got here, Santangelo told me it was you who brought up my name at that retirement party."

"Maybe that's how it happened. But more importantly, you didn't know you were working for us yet, so you didn't act sneaky or suspicious."

"Max, I knew. Because I'm smarter than you. That's why I asked Santangelo the question."

He seemed to accept that and asked, "What's your take on Amy Lang?"

I didn't need to share my thoughts with Chief Maxwell until I heard what he and Beth had to say—and maybe not even then. "Jury's out on her." I asked him, "When you and Beth were concocting this plan to get me inside Security Solutions, didn't it occur to you that Landowski— or somebody like Jack Berger or Chip Quinlan, Ferrara, or Santangelo—would wonder why John Corey would want this job? Also, why would Landowski want someone like me inside his shady organization?"

Again, Max replied as though he—and Beth—had

thought about that. "Landowski is trying to make Security Solutions and himself look legit. And maybe respected." He added, "Your name on Security Solutions' letterhead is good for business and also good cover. As for him thinking you might see something that's not legit, I'm sure any incriminating evidence is under lock and key or destroyed. As for hearing something, I'm also sure you won't be privy to anything he says to Quinlan or Santangelo, who we know are his co-conspirators. As for Ferrara, Berger, or Amy, we don't know if they're involved in any way." He advised me, "Just be careful."

I reminded him, "Sharon Hite was onto something." And look what happened to her. "So was that reporter."

He nodded. "Be careful."

I informed him, "I'll try to seduce Judy or Kim. Maybe both."

He smiled. "That's above and beyond." He said seriously, "You're just there to be there. Beth and I will explain later."

I didn't reply.

Max had another thought. "Also, maybe Landowski thinks he can suck you in, little by little." He reminded me, "He's had good luck with that, and he may be working on Joseph Ferrara, who we think is legit." He concluded, "Every man has a price."

"Right." I'd already thought about most of what Max was saying, and I'd add that Steve Landowski was a dangerous combination of stupid and cunning, sociopath and psycho, totally without a moral compass, and driven by ego, libido, and money. In fact, most of the criminals whose acquaintance I'd made over the years fit this description. In any case, I thought I had a handle on Steve Landowski, though psychopaths always surprise you.

I switched gears and asked him, "How many times have you been to Thirsty Thursday?"

"Well . . . let me think. Three times."

"Poker night? Or poke her night?"

He flashed a stupid smile. "Somebody has to do it. Now you have to do it." He let me know, "In addition to Thirsty Thursday, the farmhouse, a.k.a. Animal House, is active on other weeknights and also weekends, as you'll find out. There're two guest bedrooms that Landowski calls the honeymoon suites. I'm not sure how it works, but I guess you reserve the room and bring someone— or Landowski provides a date."

I nodded. Well, if you live alone, as Landowski does, it's good to have company in the evening. Maybe a judge. A police chief. A politician. A few hookers. And while I was sure that Steve Landowski didn't charge his prominent guests for room and broad, they'd pay for it afterwards, when he showed them a video of themselves doing bare-assed push-ups in bed. I hoped Max wasn't starring in any of those X-rated shows.

In any case, this was my good reason to book a honeymoon suite while Landowski was on vacation—the reason being I wanted a hooker, and Uncle Harry was coming out for the week and wouldn't allow that in his house. Actually, Harry would want a hooker for himself, but that's not what I'd tell Landowski.

Max informed me, "You gotta get down and dirty on Thirsty Thursday, John. The guy who doesn't looks like the undercover Vice Squad guy—or the police informant."

"I think I've done undercover before, Max."

"Good. Beth will understand. She's a cop."

Max was having too much fun with this, so I changed

the subject. "Who were the guys you saw on those Thirsty Thursdays?"

"Guys who mean nothing to you, but who are important people around here, or in Albany."

"Cops?"

"Some. Mostly politicians and public officials."

"Conners?"

He nodded.

"I hope you didn't wind up in a honeymoon suite."

He had no reply.

I moved on to a less touchy subject. "How did you get involved with Beth's unauthorized group? And why?"

He thought about that, then replied, "Beth asked."

I guess that covered the how and why. I asked, "You bored, Chief?"

"Sort of. But . . . I've spent thirty years as a cop. Never took a nickel from anybody. Maybe fixed a parking ticket a few times. Couple lunches on the cuff." He looked at me. "I don't like what I see now."

My instincts said that Max was straight and could be trusted. But I wouldn't bet my life on it. I said, "We all risk our lives on the job, Max. But don't risk your pension."

He smiled, then said, "Fuck it. Sometimes you gotta do something that makes you feel good about yourself."

Especially when a good-looking woman invites you to danger. In my case, I don't need an invite; I just need the address.

I asked, "Where do you stand in Steve Landowski's list of corrupted and compromised cops?"

He hesitated, then said, "You mean where does he *think* I stand."

"That's what I meant."

"Okay . . . good question. He thinks maybe I'll play ball if the time comes."

"You haven't done him any favors?"

"I just told you, John. My personal life may be a little messy, but my professional life is squeaky clean."

"They overlap, Max. You know that. Landowski's got you on a hidden video in a room full of titty jigglers. And if a search warrant turns up his video collection, you, me, Beth, and the Federal prosecutor can watch it together."

"I was there in the line of duty. Gathering evidence."

"Right. That was the first Thirsty Thursday. Second was to confirm what you saw on the first. Third . . . not so sure."

Max seemed to be getting pissed and said, "I don't need you to question my motives or my methods, Detective."

"Indulge me." I asked, "Did you take a prostitute into a bedroom?"

"I took a willing young lady into a bedroom." He reminded me, "I'm an unmarried man."

"And you're irresistible." I asked, "Do you think there was a hidden video camera in the bedroom?"

"I'm sure there was. Behind the vanity mirror. Which I covered with a blanket." He smiled. "Politicians, judges, and public officials are sometimes stupid and naïve. Cops are not."

"Right." I congratulated him: "Good countersurveillance."

He continued, "I wasn't at Thirsty Thursdays just to see evidence of vice—I was there mostly to see who among our distinguished citizens were participating in illegal and immoral activities."

"I like that. Remember it when the Feds interview you."

"I also don't need your legal advice."

"Well, it's not my legal advice. My ex was a great prosecutor and criminal defense attorney, and she taught me a lot about bullshit testimony."

"Nothing I don't already know." He informed me, "There's bullshit that flies and bullshit that stinks. And I know the difference."

"We all do. But we've gone off the reservation. And if the shit hits the fan on this case, the only cover we have from the shitstorm is each other."

"We have some legal cover . . . if we have knowledge and belief that the local police and politicians are in criminal collusion, we can act lawfully within the legal concept of posse comitatus to bring them to justice."

"I'm impressed with your Latin. But there's probably a Latin legal term for anything you want to justify. In fact, the courts may use another Latin word to describe your and Beth's group—vigilantes."

"Are you having second thoughts, or are you busting balls?"

I assured him, "I'm on board for all this. But just understand that it could go sideways and we could become the defendants." Or the deceased.

He looked at me. "Just don't go off on your own and do something stupid, and we'll be okay."

Apparently, he and Beth had spoken. And he remembered the Plum Island case. If the group assigned me a code name, it would definitely be "Loose Cannon." Better than "Arrogant Asshole," I guess.

Max glanced at the patio door, probably thinking, How long does it take to open a bag of Fritos? He said to me, "I haven't been invited to Thirsty Thursday in months. But you're going to get me invited." He added, "We'll keep an eye on each other."

Meaning Beth wanted him to keep an eye on me. I

asked him, "How did you get the initial invite to Landowski's Thirsty Thursday?"

He hesitated, then replied, "From my counterpart in
Riverhead—Larry Jenkins."

Recalling that the Security Solutions farmhouse was
located in Riverhead, I said, "So can I call Chief Jenkins if
I get into a situation and need backup?"

He looked at me. "I wouldn't advise that."

Sounded like everyone in the county worked for Steve
Landowski, maybe including the county police chief,
Edward Conners, the capo di tutti capi. I asked, "If I need
immediate assistance, who do I call?"

"Try your mother."

Funny. Not.

He said, "You call me. Or Beth. Do not call any police
emergency number in this county because there are some
desk sergeants and 9-1-1 operators who will flag any call
having to do with the Security Solutions premises. Calls
like that—from neighbors, or from Landowski's young
ladies in the house—are routed to the cell phone of the
local police chief, Larry Jenkins."

Who could respond very quickly if he was already at
the farmhouse having a beer and a blow job. I had to give
Steve Landowski credit for building this evil empire—
probably with the help of Chief Conners. It was amazing
how much protection you could buy with sex and money.
The flesh is weak. Boners are hard. Extra cash is good,
and drinks in the den of iniquity are always on the house.
But you pay for them later.

I asked Max, "Is Chief Jenkins a friend of yours?"

"He is."

And that was the other element to this. The Brotherhood. This is a good thing. But sometimes The Brotherhood puts you in a tough position. Thou shall not rat

out another cop. Max and I made eye contact. Finally, he said, "Jenkins has a wife and two kids in college. He runs a tight ship, and he's busted a lot of MS-13 members who were terrorizing the immigrant community. He is well liked and respected by his officers and by all segments of the civilian community."

A testament to the duality of man. I said, "If he's dirty, he's going to jail."

"Not if the bad guys win. Then it's us who have the problem." He added, "I'm less concerned about legal problems than I am about the kind of problem that Sharon Hite and Dan Perez had."

"Right." What I was hearing from Beth, and now from Max, was that this criminal enterprise was like an octopus with tentacles reaching into all aspects of public office and law enforcement. And murder was part of the enterprise. So my instincts said to go in quickly for the kill. The more you screw around and try to wrestle with the octopus, the more likely it is that you'll wind up being a high-protein meal.

Max said, "I've got eighty guys on the force, and I'm not sure how many of them moonlight as security guards or PIs for Landowski, or how many have had sex with one of his hookers. Or how many of them owe him a favor in return."

Well, that was scary. It also made me think that maybe I didn't want any of Max's people to do protective drive-bys here, where I lived with Detective Penrose—or at Harry's house, where I was supposed to be living. I'd have to weigh the pros and cons of that. And maybe discuss it with Beth.

Speaking of whom, she came out of the house, carrying a tray, and asked, "You boys having a good talk?"

I replied, "Not possible without you."

She had no comment and set down the tray, putting bowls of nuts, chips, dips, and other American hors d'oeuvres on the table.

Beth poured herself a white wine and sat between Max and me. She proposed a toast: "To good friends and good cops and good luck."

We all clinked and drank to that.

Beth said to Max, "I briefed John, as he probably told you. He knows the history of the Fire Island case, and our suspicion that Edward Conners has purposely hindered the investigation of that case, and also our suspicions about Sharon Hite's death, and about the connection we're trying to establish between all of this and Steve Landowski." She went on a bit, filling Max in.

I took the opportunity to pick the cashews out of the mixed nuts and scoop up the chunkier bits of the salsa with the biggest tortilla chips. And while I was doing that, I thought about the quickest way to cut through a year's worth of bullshit and failure and get to the cream filling of this multilayered case.

After Beth filled Max in, he asked me, "Do you see these connections? And do you see conspiracy at the highest levels to cover up these crimes? Or do you think we've talked ourselves into something?" He looked at me.

It was my turn to bullshit, so I said, "Doesn't matter what I think. You, Max, have seen, with your own trained eyes, illicit activity at the premises of Security Solutions. Or, at the least, you've seen activity that needs to be further investigated. Normally, you would alert your colleague Larry Jenkins, the Riverhead Chief of Police, about what you observed. But he has been the beneficiary of a few lap dances there. So he's out. And you believe that the county chief of police, Edward Conners, is similarly compromised or complicit. In a case like that, you should go directly to the county DA's office, but here again, both of you believe that the DA's office may also be compromised." I concluded, "There is no one you can safely speak to. So, based on what you've observed and heard, Chief, and also what I will see and hear at Security Solutions, we will, as you both said, turn this over to the FBI—or to the U.S. Attorney General's Office—for them to look for criminal conspiracy, and whatever other illegal activities in their jurisdiction that may turn up during the investigation—including the Fire Island murders." I added, "There is no reason to trouble the Feds with the knowledge that your rogue group of cops exists. That's irrelevant. The only things of relevance are two very credible witnesses—Max and me." I looked at Max and at Beth. "Keep it simple and keep it safe."

Max nodded, and so did Beth—though I think that Beth, who knew me too well, caught a whiff of bullshit.

I continued my bullshit. "I see our role as limited to submitting to the Feds sworn affidavits from me and from Max, then standing by as possible government witnesses in criminal proceedings." I asked, "How long would you want me to stay undercover at Security Solutions?"

Beth replied, "Until the end of the summer."

Max agreed. "Two months undercover as a confidential informant will weigh heavily when we go to the FBI and submit affidavits."

"Agreed." Of course, I had no intention of spending two months in that shithole. More like two weeks. Maybe two days. Which was enough time to go for the gold— meaning a midnight search warrant to seize every file in the farmhouse, including Landowski's Thirsty Thursday guest list and the honeymoon suite guest list, which I was sure he kept in electronic or written form on his secured premises. And I'd bet that those guest lists looked like a

Who's Who of this county. Similarly, Landowski would keep a list of his girls and their contact numbers, and though these girls all used professional names and burner phones, it would be interesting if one of those names was Tiffany. And it would be more interesting and incriminating if Landowski's hooker list included the names—real or professional—of the other two Fire Island victims who'd been IDed.

Also, Landowski would have to keep a cash ledger somewhere, and maybe a lot of unexplained cash, which would indicate tax evasion, the most heinous Federal crime—worse than murder.

And finally, you don't have a house full of hidden video cameras without having a house full of hidden videotapes somewhere. That should be interesting and entertaining evidence for the Federal prosecutors to analyze in front of a flat-screen.

Max had some suggestions for me regarding how to conduct my snooping without arousing suspicion. He said, "Do nothing for the first week or two. Just be a team player. Get to know your colleagues. Go to all the Thirsty Thursdays. Don't stay late after work to snoop around. Play the role of celebrity detective, pal around with Landowski and his PIs after hours. Win their confidence."

Beth reminded me, "You're not there to break the Fire Island case or solve the Sharon Hite case. You're there to open the door for the FBI to conduct a full Federal investigation and/or a raid and records seizure."

I assured her, "I've worked well with the FBI on the Anti-Terrorist Task Force." Despite what you may have heard.

Max pointed out, "Prostitution, which you'll see with your own eyes, is presumed to be interstate, and if the prostitutes also appear to be illegal aliens, then the

Feds can be involved on that level. Plus, there's presumed income tax evasion."

I said, "I get it. Let's just say that my role will evolve as the weeks pass, and I will look for and exploit any opportunities when I feel I'm accepted there. I won't endanger myself or others, or endanger the mission, and I will check with Beth before I pursue any line of investigation." I added, "You"—who have conned and bullshitted me—"have my word."

My teammates seemed happy with that, and we all drank to it. Meanwhile, I decided I needed a moving van to clean out every scrap of possible evidence in the farmhouse. And I needed to do that when Landowski took his vacation, meaning right after my Bermuda vacation.

We had another round of drinks, and Beth said she'd call for a pizza for us and a taxi for Max, who had a date and was running late, but couldn't walk a straight line. But Max called for a squad car instead. It's good to be the top cop.

I walked Max out front and said to him, "You understand that there are a lot of potential leaks in this kind of operation and people who can't be trusted."

"That's always an issue."

"As Sharon Hite found out the hard way."

"We know the problem, John. You got a solution?"

I did, which was to take Landowski down sooner than later—because as I'd seen with the Feds, the longer the investigation, the more likely it was that it would go bad, and someone would get killed. In this case, me. But I didn't want to share that with Max; I just wanted to raise the issue and prepare him for my quick solution to the problem. I said, "We all need to start compartmentalizing the info."

"We're doing that."

"Good." I asked, "You ever meet any of the group?"

"No. And I don't want to."

"Beth told me they're mostly female detectives. You know that?"

"I do."

"You comfortable with that?"

"In this case, I'm more likely to trust the sisterhood than the brotherhood."

"Good point." I changed the subject. "You or someone you trust should be surveilling the farmhouse while I'm gone, to see who's coming and going and to see if stuff is being moved out of there and where it's going."

He nodded. "We know."

"Okay. See you at Thirsty Thursday when I'm back."

"It's on my calendar."

The unmarked PD came, and Max wished me bon voyage and wove his way to the street.

So, now I knew what this was all about. And it wasn't about a safe job and an idyllic summer of love. But I always knew that.

CHAPTER 27

Beth was sleeping, so I got out of bed quietly, put on my robe, went into the kitchen, and made coffee, which I took outside with my cell phone and Glock.

It was still dark, but the birds had already started their bird-brained singing. The morning air felt good, and I sat at the patio table as the sky lightened.

So . . . what did I learn last night? I learned what everyone who lives in a shithole third-world country already knows: The police, the government, and the criminals can be more successful if they work together.

Beth came out on the patio wearing a robe and sat across from me with a mug of steaming coffee. "Good morning," she said. "How are you feeling?"

"Wonderful." Hungover.

She informed me, "We'll take a run, then a dip in the hot tub, then I'll make us a nice breakfast."

"Let's do that in reverse order."

She ignored my suggestion and asked, "Do you have any . . . issues about what we discussed last night?"

"No, it's all good."

"Okay. And you have no problem with me calling the shots?"

"This is your show, Sergeant."

She glanced at me, then said, "I've risked my career investigating the Sharon Hite suicide against orders, and also the Fire Island murders after I was taken off the case.

And I may be risking my life, and yours, and the lives and careers of everyone in this group." She looked at me. "We are up against something very powerful and dangerous."

"What's the bad news?"

She said in an annoyed tone, "This may seem like junior varsity to you after the work you did on the Anti-Terrorist Task Force, but even compared to NYPD Homicide, this is major-league stuff. And I want you to appreciate all of that."

"I'm actually in awe of what you're doing."

"Thank you. And I'm grateful to you for agreeing to voluntarily take on a dangerous job by going undercover at Security Solutions."

"No problem."

"And I'm feeling more confident with you on board."

"That's very flattering." What's for breakfast? "I will do my best."

"And if you feel at any time that your safety is at risk, you can back out. And I will not think any less of you."

I've heard that before. It's bullshit. "I'm all in." Women talk things to death. "End of discussion."

"You always have that option."

It was a bit early for all this, and I was about to go inside for another cup of coffee, but Beth said, "The only way you can spend two months at Security Solutions without arousing suspicion is if you become them."

"I refuse to wear those shirts."

"What shirts?"

"I'll e-mail you a photo."

She continued her thought. "Max told Landowski that you were in the midst of a divorce—which seems to be one of the qualifications for a PI there." She asked, "What did *you* tell Landowski?"

"Same."

She looked at me. "Okay. So Landowski and his PIs will expect you to act like an unattached man."

So I could bop Amy and win the pool. But I replied, "I'm not sure I want to—"

"Just listen. You will go to all the Thirsty Thursdays, as I said, and whatever else you do with the boys will be in the line of duty and will not affect our relationship."

John Corey knows a girlfriend trap when he hears one. I replied, "That's very open-minded of you, Beth, but—"

"Let me finish. If Landowski and his PIs see that you are not one of the boys, they will either suspect you're a plant, or they'll think that you think you're better than them, and they'll shut you out."

I'd already heard some of this from Max, who said that Beth would understand. Apparently, they'd discussed this. I replied, "It's not one or the other. In fact, I did mention to Landowski that I was laying low while my marital status was pending. Or I can manufacture a girlfriend so I don't have to participate in—"

"John, whether you were married, engaged, or had a girlfriend, it wouldn't matter to Landowski and company. Your new colleagues will expect you to wallow in the mud with them."

"Okay . . . I hear what you're saying about fitting into the pigsty, but I think if . . . well, I'm thinking that if I responded to Amy Lang's interest in me, that would be good cover and a good excuse not to participate in . . . whatever."

Beth thought about that, obviously conflicted. I mean, hookers and strippers were one thing, but the hot receptionist was something else. Should I offer to split the pool with her?

Finally, she said, "I don't micromanage people who work for me. Do what you have to do to fit in and not arouse suspicion."

"Thank you, Sergeant." That was a heavy conversation before the sun was even up. This could be a long day.

Actually, this was all moot, because I knew I was not staying at Security Solutions for two months. That would be too risky. So whatever I had to do to pass the pig test with the boys would be of short duration.

Regarding Amy, Beth said, "But remember, John, she's probably in bed—literally or figuratively—with Steve Landowski."

"Right. This could get complicated. Scratch Amy."

"Good idea."

"Right. So what's for breakfast?"

But she had more on her mind. "You okay with Max?"

"Not completely."

"You need to trust him."

"I don't need to confide in him. And neither do you." I explained, "He may have compromised himself. And he has no further role in this undercover operation that I can see."

She thought about that. "He did what he had to do at Thirsty Thursdays. Same as you'll do. As for his role, he's the one who's got your back if things go bad at the farmhouse."

"Okay. But put him on the back burner."

She could have reminded me that this was her show, not mine, but she said, "I'll think about that. Meanwhile, you'll both attend Thirsty Thursday when we get back from Bermuda."

"Right." Exotic-dancer night. I stood. "I need another coffee."

"You need a run." She stood, and we went into the house and changed into shorts and T-shirts. Beth, I saw, used her belly band for her Glock, as I did, though she'd never done that on a run the last time I lived here.

The sun was coming up, and the misty air was cool and damp as we began our run on the dark road down to the bay. I recalled my last run here when I came to the brilliant conclusion that I was being recruited as a confidential informant. But where was I when I agreed to accept the job? The hot tub. And that's the difference between thinking with your brain and thinking with your dick.

After about twenty minutes, we turned back and Beth called out, "Race you to the hot tub!" She put on a burst of speed on the upgrade and I kept up with her for a while, but last night caught up with me and I started to fall behind.

I became aware that a vehicle was behind us and I glanced back over my shoulder. The vehicle, an SUV with tinted windows and glaring headlights, drew closer. I veered off the road, positioning myself behind a tree, and plucked my gun out of the belly band and held it close to my side.

As the SUV drew abreast of me, the window went down and the driver, a uniformed cop, gave me a quick wave and the SUV kept going, past Beth and up the road. Apparently, Max didn't waste any time watching our backs. But thinking about what Max had said, any one of his people could mention to Landowski or his PIs that the Southold PD was doing protective drive-bys on the residence of Detective Sergeant Beth Penrose—where John Corey was living. And it would not be good if Steve Landowski knew that. Well, if I learned one thing working with the Anti-Terrorist Task Force, it was that security procedures were the leading cause of security breaches.

I resumed my sprint to the hot tub, but by the time I got to Beth's backyard, she was already in the water.

"You're out of shape, John. We'll work out every day in Bermuda."

"Great." I got into my birthday suit and joined her.

"Are there any nude beaches? I want to see some of those Bermuda triangles."

"Why was I worried that you wouldn't fit in at Security Solutions?"

Was that a compliment?

After a quick dip, Beth and I got out of the tub, and she said she'd bring breakfast out to the patio. I pulled on my shorts and T-shirt, sat at the table, and called Max, who answered, sounding like he was still in bed and probably not alone. "Can you talk?" I asked.

"Hold on."

I pictured him rolling bare-assed out of bed, trying to remember who was sleeping next to him.

"Whasup?"

"I saw one of your unmarkeds this morning."

"Good."

"Not. Listen, you have security issues. Follow?"

He was silent, then said, "Sorry if I gave you that impression."

"Sorry if I came away with the wrong impression when you said some of your guys could owe Landowski a favor."

No reply.

"I need you to call off the drive-bys." I added, "I don't know what you told your people, but I hope you didn't mention my name as an at-risk person residing at this address."

"I just told my guys it was the summer house of Detective Sergeant Beth Penrose, SCPD, and there was a credible threat from persons unknown."

"Okay. Whatever. Call it off."

"Your call."

"Do the drive-bys at Harry's house and tell your people I live there with houseguests, and I'm at risk from the

SVR. And talk to the renters when they get there about my Jeep in the driveway and about being vigilant. We'll revisit this when I get back."

"Okay. Anything else?"

I'm sure Max was regretting telling me that some of his people might be in Landowski's pocket. I should have figured that out myself, but the scope of this criminal enterprise was hard to comprehend. "I'll let you know." I hung up. And before I could think about this tangled web I'd stepped into, Beth, wearing her kimono, came out on the patio with a breakfast tray which held two bowls of granola and herbal tea that Beth said was good for hangovers.

I thought about sharing my concern about Max's people, but Max would tell her. They talked.

Beth went inside to dress for the day, and I called Uncle Harry, as promised.

Harry answered, "Hello, John. Good to hear from you."

"I just wanted to thank you for the use of the house."

"I'm happy when it gets used. So you've found new lodgings. And a new romance."

"I have."

"I wish I was young again."

"I'll trade you my dick for your bank account."

He laughed. "And you have a new job."

"A summer job. Private investigative work." I let him know, "I think I'll be back in the city after Labor Day." Hopefully sooner.

"Good. We'll have dinner. Bring your new lady."

"I will." I added, "You'll like her."

"I've liked all your many wives and girlfriends."

"I wish I could say the same. But I'll e-mail you their phone numbers."

He laughed again. I like Harry. We exchanged some

family news and he gave me a stock tip, which he always does. If I'd acted on any of those tips, I'd be living either on Park Avenue or in the park.

He said, "Sorry I rented the house, but it's a colleague, and he made me an unsolicited offer I couldn't refuse."

"Nothing to apologize for. But on that subject . . ." How do I say this? Well, blunt is always good. "I may be the target of an assassination attempt by Russian agents, and I'm concerned that they may have tracked me to your house and may kill your tenants. By mistake, of course." Or maybe blow your house up. I added, "I may also be the target of Islamic terrorists."

There was a silence on the phone. "Hello? Harry?"

"I . . . If that's a joke, it's not funny, John."

"Sorry. No joke."

Silence.

"I've alerted the Southold police, who will pay a courtesy visit to your renters—but without alarming them."

"All right . . ."

"Also, I need to leave my Jeep in your driveway while I'm on vacation." Actually, a bit longer than that. "Please let your renters know."

"All right . . ."

If Harry thought my Jeep would be something that my potential assassins would be looking for, he didn't say anything. I guess Wall Street guys don't think like cops.

I assured him, "I would classify this threat as low probability. But better safe than sorry. " I asked, "Does the husband look like me?"

Again, a silence, then, "What did you do to become the target—?"

"I'm not at liberty to say. But I leave it to you to decide if you want to call your renters and tell them what I've just told you." I hope he got the sixty thousand up front.

"I . . . don't know what to say, John." Harry sounded a bit distraught.

"I do apologize." The last refuge of a scoundrel is patriotism, and I guess I'm a scoundrel, so I said, "I'm sorry I've brought the war on terrorism and the new Cold War to your doorstep, Harry. That was not my intention when I was serving my country." Maybe I could move back in if his tenants backed out. Should I ask?

"I . . . I've always respected your service, John. To the city and to the country. Which is why I've offered the house . . ."

"And much appreciated. Well, sorry again if this has caused you any anxiety." I suggested, "Maybe offer your tenants a ten percent discount or an extra week."

He didn't respond to that and said, "Thank you for the call. You are an honest and forthright man."

"Dinner is on me. Caravaggio."

"Separate tables. Maybe separate restaurants."

Harry has a good sense of humor. But maybe he wasn't joking.

"Take care of yourself, John. Your parents worry about you."

"I'm about to call them."

"Send them my regards."

"I will. Let's think about a family reunion in the house after Labor Day." Or sooner, if your renters depart the house or depart this earth earlier than expected.

"That would be nice."

We hung up, and I went inside and got my laptop and webcam to set up a video call with M&D. Normally, I'd need two drinks before calling them, but a hangover would do as well.

Beth came into the living room, where I'd set the laptop on the cocktail table facing the couch.

"What are you doing?"

"We're going to video chat with my parents."

"I have to do my hair and makeup and change."

I looked at her. She looked fine. Nice tan, tight tank top that Dad would enjoy.

She left the room, and I texted my parents and arranged the video call.

Beth returned looking the same as when she left, except she was wearing a white cotton blouse and carrying one of my nice shirts that she insisted I put on over my grungy T-shirt. We sat apart in front of the laptop looking like we were on our way to Bible study.

I got the connection up and running, and there were M&D, sitting on what looked like their lanai—whatever that is—with a palm tree in the background. I said, "Hi, Mom. Hi, Dad. This is my friend Beth Penrose."

My father, who'd gone native with a floral shirt, waved. "Hi, John. Well, you're looking good." My mother, wearing a pink sweater, said, "It's good to see you, John." They were shouting, I guess because Florida is far away.

"Beth's a detective with the county police."

Beth waved. "It's nice to meet you."

My mother asked, "Where are you, John?"

"Beth's house. This is Beth."

"Why aren't you at Harry's house?" asked my father.

"He has—or may have—a renter. So Beth has offered me her guest bedroom."

My mother asked, "Why don't you go home?" Meaning my condo.

"I have a new job out here. Beth got me a job."

My father asked, "Where are you working?"

"A private investigative agency."

My mother said, "I hope it's safe."

"Beth says it is."

"Your face looks burned, John. Are you staying out of the sun? My friend's husband's brother has skin cancer."

"Beth makes sure I stay out of the sun and wear sunscreen."

Beth vouched for that. "I do, Mrs. Corey."

Well, the "Mrs. Corey" mention was all it took for my mother to ask me, "How is Kate?"

"She's terrific," I replied. "Still screwing her boyfriend in Washington. And how are you two doing?"

My mother adjusted her hearing aid, and my father changed the subject. "We were thinking of coming up to New York this summer."

"That would be wonderful. Let me know exactly when. And before I forget, I just spoke to Uncle Harry, who sends his regards and would love to have all the family at the summer house when his renters leave." Or get killed.

My father replied, "That would be nice."

I said, "Sorry, you're fading. Hello? Can you hear me?"

"I can hear you, John."

"Sorry, your voice is gone. I'll call you in a few days."

Beth waved. "Nice chatting with you."

I shut off the laptop and said, "You see what started me drinking."

"They seemed very nice. I can't wait to meet them."

"Let me know when you do." I stood. "What's on the agenda today?"

"Nothing. We need to pack and be at JFK at five-thirty for our seven-twenty-one flight to Bermuda."

"Okay. Let's go to the beach."

"We're going to the beach. In Bermuda." She reminded me, "We need to lay low around here."

"Right."

"But we can go to the city on weekends," she said.

Or I can wrap this case up the week after I get back and get on with . . . whatever. I asked her, "When we were together last time, did you tell anyone at work that you were dating the famous NYPD detective who'd recently been shot in the line of duty?"

"I don't discuss my personal life at work, and certainly not my love life."

"You could have at least bragged a little."

"Nothing to brag about."

We both got a laugh at that. Because she was kidding. Right?

Anyway, we did some preliminary packing, found our passports, had lunch—don't ask—and lay in the hammock, reading. Beth had a Frommer's guide to Bermuda and informed me, "There are no nude beaches in Bermuda."

"Gambling casinos?"

"No."

"Unsolved murders?"

"There may be after we're together for a week."

"Right." I got back into my Nero Wolfe book. The other thing that struck me about this reclusive private detective was that his life never seems to be in danger. He never once gets hit over the head or shot at. What kind of job is that?

My phone rang, and the caller ID said *Security Solutions*, which would be Landowski, who said he'd call, and I relayed that to Beth, then put the call on speaker and answered, "Hello."

"Hi."

Didn't sound like Steve.

"Hi," I replied.

Amy said, "I came in for a few hours this morning. Steve would like to talk to you."

I never thought I'd want to speak to Steve Landowski instead of Amy Lang. "Good. Put him on." I glanced at Beth, who was all ears.

Amy said, "I'm going to the beach this afternoon. Care to join me?"

I would love to, but, "I'm about to leave for the airport."

"Okay . . . where are you going?"

"Florida, visiting my parents."

"That's very nice. If anything comes up, can I call you?"

A suspect—and that's what Amy was—can call 24/7, as Beth knew, so I replied, "Of course."

"Steve's having his big barbecue for the Fourth. He rented the hedge maze next door for the day, and he has lots of fireworks. If you come back early, you're invited."

"Thanks." I glanced at Beth, who was now out of her hammock, standing beside me. I said to Amy, "I'm running late, so—"

"I'll put Steve on. Have a good trip."

"Thanks."

"Hold for Steve." She added, "Bye."

Beth said in a mocking tone, "If *anything* comes up, John, can I call you?"

Do I need this shit? "She's a *suspect*—"

"Hey, John!"

"Hey, Steve."

"Amy says you're flying out today."

"Right. Running—"

"You'll be back on the sixth. Right? I wanna make sure you're coming to Thirsty Thursday on the seventh. That's exotic-dancer night."

"Right."

"You don't want to miss that."

"Right."

"What's this about you giving Judy your paycheck to hire male strippers?"

"For the girls. Not for us, Steve."

He laughed. "Yeah. Don't go weird on us, John. And let me take care of the entertainment here. Okay?"

"Whatever you say, Steve."

"Amy says she told you about Sharon."

"Right." I glanced at Beth.

"Sharon had a lot of problems. Divorce. Booze. Chip tried to help her. He's still . . . like, he blames himself."

Well, he should if he killed her.

"So be sensitive to that."

"Of course."

"Amy said you're going to see your folks in Florida."

"That's right."

"Where do they live?"

"Orlando." I added, "They're character actors at Magic Kingdom. My old man is Goofy. Mom's a wicked witch."

He laughed. "You're pulling my leg."

"Steve, gotta run."

"Okay. Hey, gotta tell ya—Amy. Lou told you about the pool. You get laid, you get paid." He assured me, "You got this in the bag, John. She's hot to trot."

Was it getting warm in here? Is that why I was sweating?

"Thanks, Steve, but—"

"I'll let you go—but make sure you're here for Thirsty Thursday. Friday, me and you will go over some shit. I'm leaving that afternoon to pick up my kids for the Shore and Atlantic City."

"No problem."

"See ya."

I hung up. Asshole.

Beth asked, "How much is in the pool?"

"Don't know." I tried a smile. "I'll split it with you."

"Hell, I want it all."

Should I point out that I'd be doing all the work? Probably not. I said, "Okay, well, you see what I have to deal with." I added, "It's going to be a long summer."

No reply. But I detected a cold front moving in. I swung my legs out of the hammock and stood. The best defense is a good offense, so I said, "You—and Max— knew more about what I was getting into at Security Solutions than I did."

She nodded but said, "Amy was a bit of a surprise."

"Not to Max."

She nodded again. "Okay. Nothing more to be said."

Meaning I needed to say something, so I said, "I don't sleep with the enemy."

She gave me a kiss and went into the house.

We finished packing, showered, got dressed, and called a car service for the two-hour drive to JFK.

We made small talk in the car and held hands on our way to a romantic place where I could be further briefed about this case and also propose marriage.

As for my undercover job at Security Solutions, that was starting to look like it was on shaky ground before it got started.

But as I'd learned from twenty years of experience, if you abort every plan that's not perfect, you'll spend your life and your career waiting for perfect, which will never come. It's all about acceptable risk, ability to react, balls and brains. Who's smarter—me or Steve Landowski? Obviously me. But there's always the alligator factor. Sometimes the primitive tiny-brained reptile wins. You gotta watch that.

CHAPTER 28

The hotel brochure said: *Cambridge Beaches Resort &*
Spa, Bermuda's premier cottage resort . . .

Meaning this is going to cost you, sucker. Well, you
only live once. And maybe not long enough to even
see the Amex bill next month. So, as the brochure also
said, relax: *The resort's casually sophisticated environment*
encourages a sense of total relaxation, romance and renewal.

Right. Chill, get laid, and renew your relationship with
your bank.

Anyway, it was a nice resort, very British, and Beth
had booked a romantic cottage with an ocean view. A
good place, as per the brochure, to: *Reconnect, or simply*
do nothing at all, and do it well. Which is what I'd been
doing at Harry's house for free. The real issue, though,
was that I was not on American soil, so if the SVR were
tracking me, this would be a good place for them to settle
the score with John Corey. And, unfortunately, Bermuda
takes a dim view of American tourists bringing their guns
with them—even off-duty guns—so we had to leave ours
home. As I said, I don't feel naked without my gun, but it
becomes part of you after twenty years—sort of like your
dick—and being without it calls to mind the old saying,
"Better to have a gun and not need it than to need a gun
and not have it." Same with your dick.

Beth, however, was not troubled by this and said she

felt liberated being unarmed. Okay. We will see who we run into here.

Anyway, we'd gotten to the hotel after midnight, checked in, ordered a bottle of rum to be delivered, and were shown to our romantic cottage, which was a few hundred yards' walk from the main building, through dangerous tropical gardens.

By the time we'd unpacked, the rum setup had been delivered, and we took it out to our private patio. Beth poured two dark Bermuda rums over ice with lime and a splash of Coke. We clinked and drank.

I don't normally drink this stuff, but it goes well with palm trees and floral-scented breezes. A bright moon hung over the ocean and cast a silver beam on the calm sea. I felt like singing, but I asked, "Why are we here?"

"My group says I need a break."

"Okay."

"Also, there's a strategy here." She explained, "We didn't want you to seem too anxious to start work at Security Solutions. You're there reluctantly, as I'm sure you made clear to Landowski. Any suspicion that he—or anyone there—might have that you taking the job was too good to be true will be put to rest by your attitude and arrogance, and your insistence on a vacation before you start work."

"Okay. But don't overthink. And you might want to let me know what you're thinking from now on."

She nodded. "Also, my group is using this time to gather some intel, surveilling everyone there—Landowski, Santangelo, Ferrara, Quinlan, and Berger. Also Amy, Judy, and Kim."

Well, I give them credit for putting their own time into the unauthorized pursuit of truth and justice. I said, "Whoever is surveilling Amy needs to let me know if someone won the pool."

She ignored that and continued, "We're also keeping an eye on the farmhouse to see who visits and to see if there's any indication that they're moving stuff—evidence—out of the building."

I hoped not. That's what I was going to do after Landowski left for vacation.

She also let me know, "One member of my group—a female—will be at Landowski's July Fourth party."

"Good thinking."

"Also, you have some reading to do about the Fire Island murders, and news stories about Chief Edward Conners. Also, I brought my group's unofficial case file on Sharon Hite's death for you to read."

I was actually looking forward to finishing the Nero Wolfe book, and I had no intention of becoming an expert on the Fire Island murders, or reading press clippings about Chief Conners, or critiquing the work that was done—or not done—on Sharon Hite's suspicious death. Beth and her group, including Max, had been working this investigation for over a year. And now they wanted me to spend an additional two months this summer making careful notes of what Landowski ate for lunch. I was reminded of the Plum Island case, which would still be unsolved if I hadn't cut to the chase and sliced through the bullshit.

"John?"

"Right. Working vacation."

"Not all work . . . We're also here to reconnect. To renew."

She must have read the brochure.

We held hands and she said, "To fall in love again."

"That's easy."

Anyway, Beth had planned our time in paradise, of course, and we had spa appointments every morning in what was called the Couples Suite. I sort of enjoyed the couples massage, but wasn't sure about the couples manicure and pedicure. And I definitely didn't need the facial, though the facial lady was easy to look at.

Anyway, I think a lot of people must have recognized me, because after every spa treatment and every meal, they asked for my autograph. Ka-ching!

We spent most afternoons on the beach or at the pool, but afterwards Beth insisted we spend an hour in the Fitness Center, where I walked, ran, and rowed for miles without going anywhere. We also lifted weights that didn't need to be lifted.

One afternoon we rented mopeds and made a death-defying run to the other end of the island. I mean, they all drive on the wrong side of the road, and for a minute I thought I was in New Jersey.

On another afternoon, Beth wanted to go to something called high tea in the hotel, which sounded promising—Bermuda High. But when we got there, it was just tea—no high. And WTF are cucumber sandwiches?

In between all this, I did look at some of the online news stories about the Fire Island murders and read some stuff about Police Chief Edward Conners, which was not flattering, but also not suggestive of anything beyond incompetence. Beth gave me the case file on Sharon Hite, and I had to agree that her suicide looked suspicious and was probably murder—though there was no credible evidence that Chip Quinlan was the perpetrator.

I looked at the photos of Sharon Hite in the file and saw a nice-looking lady, bright and smiling with a look of maybe mischief in her eyes. I also looked at the police photo taken on her deathbed. Peaceful. But dead. And I wondered, for the thousandth time, how a person can kill another person who had been a lover, or a spouse, or a family member. It's always hard to believe, yet all too common, and usually easy to prove. Though not this time. Cops who kill don't make the same mistakes that most killers do.

A few news stories showed a photo of Carolyn Sanders, obviously supplied by her mother, and I saw a smiling young lady with long, straight blond hair, wearing a graduation cap and gown. Carolyn looked fresh and wholesome. There was no photo of Tiffany.

For lighter reading, I finished *The Rubber Band* and solved the case twenty pages before Nero Wolfe did. Wolfe is smart, but he needs to get off his fat ass and stop relying on other people for information. You gotta get into the belly of the beast yourself.

Anyway, the American guests at the hotel decided to celebrate the Fourth of July with a cocktail party on the restaurant terrace, and Beth and I were invited. Bermuda being a British colony, hotel management was not keen on American Independence Day, but being British, they were polite—until the patriots got a bit rowdy and some asshole set off a cherry bomb in a potted palm. But, all in all, I'd rather be here for the Fourth than at Landowski's party. On that subject, I hoped Max survived his working holiday. I hadn't heard from him, but I was sure Beth was getting a daily report.

On the subject of my constitutional right to bear arms, it appeared that Bermuda was a safe place, and crime was almost nonexistent—unless you counted highway robbery, which occurred every time I signed for something. More to the point, I was becoming relaxed and assured that no hit men had followed us to the island—no Russians, no Islamic terrorists, and no one from Security Solutions. The only way to die here was from brain atrophy.

On the plus side, the food was good, the people were nice, and the weather was perfect. All this place needed were nude beaches and casino gambling.

As for Beth and I, we did reconnect, emotionally and intellectually, which made the lovemaking even better. That's my story and I'm sticking to it.

As we sat in the fading sun on our patio the night before we were to fly home, Beth gave me a printout of a highly redacted e-mail, source unknown, that she said I needed to read. So I did.

The e-mail was written in journalistic style, as though it was a draft of a long newspaper or magazine article. The unknown author began by asking, *Who killed the nine women found on Fire Island?*

Good question. And it didn't take long for the author to give an answer: Chief of Police Edward Conners.

The author then made the case, describing Conners as a psychopath who had a history of abusing women, including a prostitute, name redacted, who said Conners tried to strangle her during sex. Also a former girlfriend, name redacted, who said that Eddie, as she called him, was into some strange sex, including sexual asphyxiation. She wasn't clear about who got the ligature around the neck—him or her—while having sex—maybe both—but my understanding of this act is that it produces an incredible high at the moment of climax. Or someone dies.

So, if you believed any of this, it seemed as though Edward Conners was into a type of sex that we call deviant and dangerous. But did that make him a serial killer?

No. But it made him a suspect. A person of interest.

Also of interest to me would be Mrs. Conners, who may have wondered why her husband wore a necktie to bed while making love to her—or why he wanted her to wear a choker. More likely, as per FBI profiles, Edward Conners at home was not as much fun in the sack as he was on the road.

Another interesting fact or speculation in the article was that Edward Conners's many misdeeds and apparent incompetence were covered up by someone very highly placed in the county District Attorney's office—maybe the DA himself, who was a longtime friend of Conners and who had mentored him as they both rose up the ranks of their respective organizations.

So, lots of circumstantial evidence here that would explain a lot of odd things about this case. But nothing you could actually take to the DA—who would not be happy to be asked to investigate himself.

Beth asked, "What do you think?"

I handed the e-mail pages back to her. "Another theory."

She looked at me. "I think Edward Conners is the prime suspect in the murder of all nine women."

I replied, "As the old saying goes, 'If you strike at the king, you must kill him.' "

She nodded.

———

On the JetBlue flight home, Beth said, "We needed that."

"Right." Not sure about the pedicure.

"What you're going to be doing is possibly dangerous."

"I think I've already thanked you for that."

"If something happened to you . . ."

"We'll always have Bermuda."

She didn't respond.

I squeezed her hand. "It's going to be all right."

She nodded, put her seat back, and closed her eyes.

We reached cruising altitude and the flight attendant,

Annie, approached with the beverage cart. "Would you like anything?"

"Can I have a cigarette?"

"No."

"I bought a whole carton at the airport, duty-free."

"Congratulations. You can step outside and light up."

Funny. "How about a Dewar's and soda?"

"Would you like a twist?"

"Sure. I'll meet you in the lavatory."

"Sir?"

"No twist."

She looked at Beth, who was sleeping. "Would the lady like anything?"

"Yes. A new boyfriend."

Annie thought that was funny. And probably agreed.

I said, "Vodka tonic for the lady, no twist."

She made the drinks, I paid, and she moved on to less interesting passengers.

So, I was fit and tan and ready to report in for my first day at Security Solutions. With luck, I'd have them all in jail by mid-July and I could take the rest of the summer off.

Of course, it could go the other way. Landowski was not as stupid as he looked. Chip Quinlan was probably a murderer. And Lou Santangelo . . . well, he always had an uncanny ability to smell danger. It takes a rat to smell a rat. As for Jack Berger, Joseph Ferrara, and Amy Lang . . . jury's still out. As for Police Chief Edward Conners, that was worth pursuing. But you get only one shot at killing the king.

Annie came by again with a basket of snacks. "Would you like something?"

"Do you have pigs in a blanket?"

"No, but I can get you a blanket and we can make one."

Everyone's a comedian. I took a bag of Fritos. I asked, "Do you like your job?"

"There are good days and bad days. A bad day is a double engine failure."

"That happen?"

"Once. Flight to San Juan."

"I guess it ended well."

"I'm here." She added, "Stuff happens."

Indeed it does. Odds were good that this flight was going to land safely. But not sure if the odds on the ground were as good. We will see.

CHAPTER 29

Great vacation but nice to be home. Beth went out to the patio to check her potted plants, and I texted Max: WE'RE BACK. As Beth has probably already told you. THIRSTY THURSDAY AT SEC SOL, 6:30.

He texted back: LOOK FORWARD TO TIT. Typo? Freudian slip?

Later, after Beth and I had unpacked and were having a cocktail on the patio, I asked her, "Any word from your group about the surveillance?"

"Nothing to report."

Meaning nothing to report to me, or they turned up nothing.

I asked, "You hear anything from your person who went to Landowski's July Fourth party?"

"My person said it was well attended by public officials and by retired and active-duty law enforcement people, including brass from HQ. She noted most of their names. Including Chief Conners."

More wheel-spinning. That's what you do when you can't pull the trigger. Beth didn't seem too communicative, and I could sense that she was keeping me out of the loop, maybe on the legal theory that the less I knew of the group's work, the better. Or she was practicing good tradecraft and compartmentalizing information so if I got busted by Landowski and company and they were putting my nuts through a wringer, I couldn't tell them what

I didn't know. In any case, she wasn't sharing. And neither was I.

Beth and I spent a quiet evening at home. We ordered Chinese takeout and watched a DVD of *Rosemary's Baby*. Not a good combination before bed.

———

The next day, Thursday, Beth was up bright and early, dressed for work. I didn't intend to drift into Security Solutions until about noon, but I got up and we had coffee on the patio.

Beth said, "I had a bad dream last night."

"Not surprised, after General Tso's spicy chicken and *Rosemary's Baby*."

"I dreamt that I was walking in the wilderness and I found your body."

What do you say to that at 7 A.M.? "Beth . . . I told you, it's going to be all right."

"You don't have to take this job."

How are we going to pay for Bermuda? "I can really take care of myself—"

"They've already killed Sharon Hite and the reporter, Dan Perez. And who knows how many of those girls were killed by them? Or by Conners himself?" She looked at me. "They're killers. Once you start killing—"

"Beth, murderers are our business. Homicide. Remember? If I was worried, I'd let you know."

"You wouldn't. And please understand that Steve Landowski is so well protected by Conners and people around him that he has what amounts to a license to kill. If something happened to you, it would be ruled a suicide, or an accident, or—"

"Beth—"

"And I'm not going to be responsible for—"

"I am responsible for me. I do me. You do you. Look, you just had a bad dream, and you're having a case of pre-game jitters—"

"I've thought it out. We don't need you."

Well, what had seemed like such a good idea to Beth and Max was now getting second thoughts from Beth. I mean, a good confidential informant is hard to find, but a potential husband is even harder to find and needs to be kept alive. But dangerous fucked-up jobs don't come along that often. I'd have to go overseas to get something this fucked up and dangerous. Plus, the media coverage when I cracked the case would be big. I said, "If I don't do this, the bad guys keep winning."

"Don't overestimate your importance."

I looked at her. "If Landowski and his friends know about you and your friends, they will come for you. Same with Chief Conners. So you better make sure you get them first."

She stayed silent awhile, then said, "We will . . . but not the way you want to do it."

"I told you—I'm a team player."

"You're not."

"Trust me." I reminded her, "You need to get to work."

She nodded and stood.

I also reminded her, "I'm going to Thirsty Thursday to-night. So I'll be a little late." I added, "Max will be with me."

Beth gave me a perfunctory kiss on the cheek and went in the house. A few minutes later, I heard her SUV starting in the driveway.

Well, it didn't take long for Detective Penrose to figure out that Detective Corey was going to do it his way. Hunting the beast can be a team effort. But killing the beast comes down to one person pulling the trigger. And it was long past the time when the trigger had to be pulled—before the beast spotted you and turned the game around.

CHAPTER 30

My Jeep was at Harry's so I took a taxi to Riverhead, where there was a U-Haul, and I rented a van big enough to Me-haul evidence out of the farmhouse. And I needed to make the heist before Detective Sergeant Penrose pulled me off the case, and while Landowski was on vacation—and also before Landowski sensed that he might be under the eye. It was possible that he knew about Beth's group and had already removed anything from the farmhouse that could be incriminating. But if Steve Landowski really believed he was protected by Conners and the power structure—and that he would at least be given a tip-off about a search warrant—then he'd feel safe keeping the evidence of his criminal enterprise under his control in the farmhouse. Well, we will see. Soon.

Anyway, the van came with a ramp and a dolly, but no burglar tools.

I was sure that Beth would ask me why I'd rented a moving van—instead of, say, a BMW convertible—and the reason I'd give her was that I was going to haul stuff from my condo to her cottage, including my La-Z-Boy recliner, which I missed more than my estranged wife.

Landowski or someone at Security Solutions would also ask why I was driving a van, and I'd give them a similar answer about my La-Z-Boy, though I'd substitute Harry's place for Beth's. The reason I was bringing the van to work today was so Landowski would associate the van with me, and if he saw the U-Haul at the farm-house on his laptop one night while he was on vacation, it wouldn't cause him any concern. He would, of course, be concerned if he saw me hauling his files out of the farmhouse—but he wasn't going to see that on his laptop.

I drove off in my rental van, and at 12:35 I pulled into the nearly empty parking area at Security Solutions. I didn't see Landowski's Escalade or Santangelo's Corvette. But I did see Amy's white Toyota.

I was dressed in khaki slacks, a blue blazer, and a crisp white shirt for my first day on the job—and for our dis-tinguished guests tonight and the exotic dancers. For Amy, I was wearing Dior Sauvage.

I walked jauntily onto the porch, making a good new-hire appearance for the surveillance cameras, and I punched in my new code and opened the door.

I expected Amy to run out of the reception room to greet me, but the hallway was empty, and so was her desk. Judy and Kim's office was also deserted. Lunchtime. So I walked down the hall into the kitchen, but it too was empty. I glanced at the door to the basement. The pad-lock was in place, which hopefully was an indicator that the basement was full of evidence, and not the cheap wine I'd had at my welcome lunch.

I could hear voices outside and looked out the kitchen window. Sitting around the patio table were Kim, Judy, and Amy, having lunch. Pizza, to be precise.

A voice behind me said, "How'd you get in here?"

I turned and looked at Chip Quinlan, wearing an un-tucked red shirt, beneath which would be his gun. We made eye contact, and in an NYPD instant, I knew we were not going to be job buddies. Especially if he'd killed another cop.

He kept staring at me, and my Neanderthal DNA lit

up and I stepped toward him and intruded on his personal space. "*What?*"

He hesitated—flinched—and said, "I was wondering how you got in."

"Through the door. Is there another way?"

"I guess you got a code."

I didn't reply and brushed past him, through the pantry, and into the former dining room where the PIs' desks sat. I sensed Quinlan behind me.

I found a desk that looked unused—no pizza box—took off my blazer, and draped it over the chair, revealing my pancake holster and Glock.

Quinlan, who was standing at the pantry door, now stepped into the office. He had the look of a frothing Doberman who'd just had his balls bitten by a pit bull. And Fido was looking for a rematch.

He said, "You can't use that desk. It's for our freelance PIs."

Still standing, I began going through the drawers and the hanging files, throwing stuff on the other desks. To further mark my territory I should piss on the rug.

I looked at Quinlan. "Don't you have something to do?"

"I'm doing it."

"If you don't have anything to work on, I'll find something for you."

"Who died and left you in charge?"

Time to make it clear who was top dog. I intruded again into his space—hoping he couldn't smell my Dior. "Look, pal, this can be easy, or it can be hard. Just like when we were on the job. And I can tell you right now, I've never lost a pissing match."

He kept eye contact. "Me neither."

I didn't know Sharon Hite, so I couldn't know what

she'd seen in this asshole, but I'd guess that Chip Quinlan could be a charming sociopath when it came to women. Though not so charming with another alpha male. I shifted gears to throw him off balance and said, "Hey, look, I know about Sharon. And if this was her desk, I'll move." I added, "Sorry for your loss."

He didn't exactly break down in tears and hug me, but he knew he was supposed to show an appropriate reaction of sadness—though, like a lot of killers I've comforted over their so-called loss, all he could manage was a bad imitation of grief that barely hid the look of guilt. We made eye contact, and in that second I knew he'd killed her. And he knew that I knew.

He said, "Steve tells me you got some enemies. Russians and ragheads. And you need protection." He smiled. "Yeah. We'll watch your back. Wouldn't want anything to happen to you."

Let me interpret that correctly. I think he was threatening to whack me. "Chip, I've killed more men than you've fired bullets at paper targets. And I've killed them for less reason than you're giving me now. Don't threaten me."

He thought about that and replied eloquently, "Fuck you." Then turned and left.

I called after him, "Get me a coffee. Black, no sugar."

My rule is not to stir the shit for at least twenty-four hours into a new assignment, but . . . I was provoked. A more mature man would have handled it better. I mean, all I had to reply to his first question was: "Oh, hi, Chip. Steve gave me my passcode. Sorry if you didn't know I'd be in today." But that's no fun. Anyway, the Sharon Hite death was now out there, and Chip Quinlan was thinking I needed to have an accident. This gig would definitely be over before Labor Day. Like, by Monday.

I went back into the kitchen, got a free beer from the

fridge, then went through the equipment room and out the security door to the patio.

Amy saw me first and stood. "John!"

"Amy!"

We hurried toward each other like we had bottle rockets up our asses. It was all an act, of course, at least on my part, but we hugged and she asked, "How was your vacation?"

"M and D get on my nerves, but good to see them."

"You got a great tan."

"You too." Wanna see my pedicure?

Kim and Judy were still sitting, watching the blossoming office romance between bites of pizza. Also, we were in view of the surveillance camera mounted on the back of the farmhouse.

Amy, who was wearing a tight white polo shirt and blue skirt, took my arm and steered me toward the table. I greeted Kim and Judy, and we took a seat.

Amy urged me to have a slice—pepperoni or plain—but Kim and Judy looked pizza-possessive, so I declined and stuck with my beer.

We all chatted for a few minutes, and Kim and Judy thanked me for the new desk chairs, and Judy reminded me that she had my paycheck. They also informed me that Steve had vetoed male-stripper night, and they hinted that I should push him on that. I promised the ladies I'd talk to Steve tonight between exotic-dance numbers.

Kim and Judy stood, took the pizza boxes, and returned to work.

Amy said, "I missed you."

I wished I could figure out what she was up to. "Me too."

"Did you have company?"

"Just Mom and Dad." I changed the subject and asked, "How was the July Fourth barbecue?"

"Steve does it up big."

"Cops tend to be patriotic."

She replied, "To tell you the truth, I don't think he knows why July Fourth is celebrated."

I did not find that hard to believe. More to the point, Amy was signaling that her boss was too dumb for her to sleep with, and her loyalty to him was conditional, and she'd found her confidant and soul mate in me. And because there was no hidden mic out here, we could both speak freely and lovingly. So I said, "We should have that drink soon, and you can fill me in on this place."

She smiled. "Sooner than later." She went on about the party: "There were maybe two hundred people here, coming and going. Steve rented a tent, tables, chairs. Band and caterer."

You gotta spend money to make money. But where did all that money come from? "Hope you had fun."

"I try to, but . . . I'm sort of the hostess."

"You're good at that."

She shrugged. "I can't bring a date, and Steve drags me around to meet and greet the big shots who show up."

"I'm sure he does. You are the pretty face of Security Solutions."

She smiled.

"Beauty and the beast."

She laughed.

I asked, "Who was here?"

"The usual. Lots of local politicians. And cops, of course. A group from Yaphank. Police Chief, Chief of Detectives, Chief of Patrol—the brass." She smiled again. "It's funny to see them in shorts—with half a load on."

I smiled in return. I wondered if Beth's boss, Lieutenant Stuckley, was here, but I didn't ask. I also wondered who from Beth's group was here. "They all hit on you?"

"What do you think?" She let me know, "Steve insists that I wear short shorts and a tight T-shirt."

Good marketing. "It's great that you had the Police Chief . . . what's his name . . . ?"

"Conners." She hesitated, then said, "A total pig." She shared a secret with me: "Someone—a cop—told me Conners has a bag full of snuff porn in his SUV." She added, "Bondage stuff. Like ropes and chains."

Well, that's interesting. I said, "Maybe it's seized evidence, placed in his custody."

She laughed. "You guys—cops—all cover for each other."

"Not always." I reminded her, "You'll be on the job someday. And there will come a day—more than once— when you'll have to make some decisions about your brothers and sisters."

She looked at me, then nodded. She let me know, "Your friend Chief Maxwell was here."

Max had not specifically mentioned that he'd be here. Did Beth know? "Was he here officially, on a neighbor's loud-party complaint?"

She laughed. "No. Max is Southold PD. Chief Jenkins is Riverhead, and he was here too, so no problem with any neighbor complaints." She added, "I need to introduce you to Chief Jenkins."

I can do that myself if I get him arrested. Or when he arrests me, if the bad guys win. Well, it sounded like all the right people were here, including Max, who'd whined to me about what a tough day July Fourth was, and I wondered again about his relationship with Landowski. Anyway, I had to give Steve Landowski a lot of credit for his networking skills. It's not everyone who can have cops and crooks at the same party. Well . . . I guess it's easier if they're the same people. I said, "Sorry I missed the fun."

"I'm sorry too. The fireworks were amazing. Steve gets them from . . . I think, confiscated police property."

Did Amy know she was describing a felony? Or was police misconduct just business as usual around here? Scary.

She said, "Steve rented the maze for the day."

I glanced at the tall wall of hedges across the side lawn. "I hope you didn't put the Porta Potties in there."

She laughed, but said, "The maze caused some problems. Like, drunks lost in there. One woman crying hysterically." She confided, "I think some people hooked up in there at night."

"Now I'm *really* sorry I missed the party."

She smiled, then asked, "How was your Fourth?"

"I had a fifth—of Scotch."

"You're funny."

I changed the subject and asked, "Where's everybody?"

"Steve is with clients in the city. Chip is around somewhere. Joseph is on a surveillance in the Hamptons. Jack doesn't come in on Thursdays or Fridays. Lou has a dentist appointment."

He used to have one a week when I worked with him. How many teeth does this guy have?

"They'll all be back later." She asked, "Are you going tonight?"

Meaning Thirsty Thursday. "Steve would like me there." Meaning I don't want you to think I'm looking forward to seeing naked women dancing.

She nodded, but had no comment.

I asked, "Any word from the Academy?"

"No. I think I'll call or write them."

"I have good contacts there. Let me call for you."

She hesitated, then smiled. "Are you trying to get rid of me?"

"I want to see you go where you belong."

"Thanks. But I'll make the call." She added, "I'll mention your name."

I switched gears and said, "I just bumped into Chip while I was looking for a desk to use. I think I picked Sharon's desk, and he seemed a bit . . . you know . . . maybe upset."

She processed that, then said, "He blames himself for not seeing the signs."

"Understandable. But he shouldn't feel guilty." Unless proven guilty.

She had no response.

So the question was: Did Amy Lang know or suspect that Chip Quinlan killed Sharon Hite? If so, she was up to her pretty blue eyes in what was going on here—murder, conspiracy to commit murder, prostitution, political corruption, police corruption, and on and on. I mean, how could she not know? But maybe she didn't. I very much doubted, for instance, that Kim or Judy knew what was going on here. The jury was still out on Joseph Ferrara, but Jack Berger had to know *something*. Lawyers pretend to see and hear nothing illegal. But they see and hear plenty.

Amy and I made eye contact. She smiled and I returned the smile. Well . . . my heart, my head, and my meat puppet were having a familiar argument. My heart belonged to Beth, my head said Amy Lang is trouble, but my meat puppet was screaming, "Let me at her!"

She asked, "Are you hungry?"

Only for your love. "I'm good." I finished my beer and stood. "I'm going to spend some time with Kim and Judy, go through some files, set up my desk, and get disorganized."

She smiled and stood. "If you need anything, or have any questions, I'm here."

"Thanks." Where's the key to the basement?

"I stay late today, to set up for . . ." She cocked her thumb toward the second-floor Rec Room. "Maybe I'll see you later."

Amy seemed to have a very broad job description. I pointed out, "And you're not even invited to stay around for the party."

She was silent, then confided, "Steve said I could stay if I joined the girls in a few dance numbers."

Well, Amy Lang seemed to be the most harassed female employee in the state. Made you wonder why she deferred twice for the Police Academy. And lied about it. Maybe Steve Landowski had made it clear to her that she knew too much and she wasn't going anywhere. She was a prisoner of the evil Lord of the Manor, and she was signaling that she needed a knight—me—to save her. Or she was full of shit. I said, flirtatiously, "All eyes would be on you."

She forced a smile, but said nothing.

"See you later," I said.

"Coffee break in the kitchen at three."

As I walked toward the farmhouse, I noticed again the stairwell that went from the patio down to the basement, where there was a steel security door with a keypad. I wondered if my entry code would open that door. Probably not.

I also noticed the electrical meter on the back of the house, and to the right of it was a brass barrel connector where the coaxial cable from the utility pole connected to the telephones and the Internet. If that connection was broken, the surveillance cameras could not send out live images to whoever was monitoring. That was a simple way to take down the surveillance system here, and if Landowski was monitoring on his laptop at the Jersey Shore, his screen would say something like: *Reconnecting* or *Service Down*. It wouldn't say: *John Corey Disconnected Your Service*. But Landowski might think that. Well, hopefully, if I did it at about 1 A.M., Steve Landowski would be sleeping while I was putting in overtime.

I went inside through the unlocked mudroom security door, and I took the opportunity to look around the equipment room, spotting Landowski's new drone. I checked out a few infrared night vision devices and the directional listening devices, all of which were state-of-the-art, comparable to the expensive toys that the Feds were able to buy with taxpayer money. Business must be good. I also noticed a toolbox which might come in handy when I ransacked this place.

I spotted four Kevlar vests, which you don't usually need in a PI agency, but better safe than sorry, I guess. I also saw four sets of top-quality handcuffs, which you also don't usually see in a private detective agency. Maybe Landowski used them for bedroom bondage. Along the same lines, I saw coils of rope and a box of zip ties. I would like to have found a tent bag big enough to stow a dead body. But anything that has body fluids or DNA on it gets burned. Everyone here knows that.

And finally, I discovered a box of disguises—mustaches, beards, eyeglasses, face paint, and wigs—which could be used on surveillances—or in the honeymoon suites to liven things up.

Anyway, Landowski had all the toys and tools of the trade, and in the context of a PI firm, most of it was what you'd expect to see. But in the context of a criminal enterprise, the tools and toys took on a more sinister appearance.

I looked at the washing machine and dryer, which must get a lot of use on Friday mornings. The machines took up space and belonged in the basement, but they were here, reinforcing my suspicion that the basement was off-limits to everyone except Steve Landowski. Right?

I checked out the gun safe, but it was locked, so I couldn't see Landowski's arsenal. I should, however, be able to get the safe in the van with the dolly and ramp. I doubted the Feds would find a gun connected to a crime, but you never leave guns with a suspect, even if they're all legal. Also, guns make a great photo op for the news media.

I had time to kill before quitting time, then the dance recital upstairs, so I made my way to Landowski's downstairs office, which was unlocked, and I entered. I looked at the books and photographs with feigned interest, aware that I was probably on a hidden camera behind the two-way mirror. I walked over to the bar, poured some Scotch, then stepped on what I suspected was the trapdoor under the rug. It did give a bit, but I couldn't tell if it was nailed shut, or locked from the basement, or if there was a pull ring under the rug to open it. In any case, when I booked a honeymoon suite upstairs for this weekend, I'd need to pack a pry bar in my overnight bag, along with my K-Y jelly.

I couldn't stay in this room too long, so I downed the Scotch and went to see Kim and Judy, who were hard at work, but always had time for me. Judy gave me my company cell phone and my new business cards with my cell number. She had my thousand-dollar check, and I again promised them I'd use it to finance girls' night in the Rec Room, which made the ladies smile. I said, "I don't have a local bank. Can Security Solutions cash this for me?"

Judy said, "No problem," and I countersigned the check while Judy opened the safe in the corner and counted out the money from a big stack of bills. I called out to her, "Keep some fives for you and Kim to stuff in the elastic piggy bank."

Kim said, "Make that twenties."

We all got a good laugh. Two more months in this place, and I'd be booking the entertainment for the Rec Room and wearing untucked shirts. I had to wrap this soon.

I spent a little time with Kim and Judy, asking dumb new-guy questions—and I would have asked some not so dumb questions if I didn't think the room was bugged. I noticed that the security monitor mounted on the wall displayed only the four exterior shots. The inside shots were probably displayed only in Landowski's upstairs office, or on a monitor in his bedroom, using an access code. And all the camera images would be available for live viewing on Landowski's laptop wherever he was. Unless the Internet was down.

I asked Judy, "Do you use a guard company?" Meaning a security firm that monitors your video cameras 24/7, or nights and weekends. Whatever you want to pay for.

She replied, "No. Steve is here most of the time, so that's not necessary." She added, "When he's gone, he can access the live feed on his laptop."

Well, no guard company was good news. I said, "I assume all the video camera shots are being recorded."

She nodded. "The VCRs are in the attic."

So that's why the attic was locked. The guts of a security system are usually in a basement, but this basement was off-limits, so whoever was tasked with changing the twenty-four-hour time-lapse tapes every day didn't need to go into the basement. I asked, "You use videocassettes?"

Again she nodded. "It's an old system. But Steve prefers tape over digital. Easier to label the daily tapes and find what he wants."

Right. And tapes burn well or can be chewed up in an industrial shredder if the law is banging on the door with a search warrant.

As a consultant to Security Solutions, I could ask questions, but I didn't want to ask too many questions, too soon. Especially if I was being recorded.

I thanked Judy and Kim for their time, then I got a cup of coffee from the kitchen and went back to my desk in the empty PI room, formerly the dining room of what had once been a farmhouse, filled with generations of hardworking Polish-American farm families. I could almost smell the sauerkraut and kielbasa. Now I smelled corruption and evil.

Hard to believe that a few weeks ago I was making up imaginary enemies, hoping for some real ones to come looking for me. Then along comes Beth Penrose, and I go from my playacting to hers. And from home alone to granola for breakfast. And from unemployed to working for Murder Inc. for a thousand bucks a week. And now here I was, in the nexus of evil. And Amy . . . well, I'd be lying if I said that wasn't titillating. Even Chip Quinlan gave me some pleasure in his own sick way—not to mention mine. And tonight there'd be some entertainment in the Recreation Room that you wouldn't see at Cambridge Beaches Resort & Spa.

I said to myself, "Enjoy the excitement while you can. By Monday it will all be over, one way or the other."

CHAPTER 31

I joined Amy, Kim, and Judy for coffee and donuts in the kitchen at three. Chip seemed to have disappeared, probably at the pistol range practicing for our shoot-out.

It was a beautiful day, so I suggested we bring our coffee and donuts out to the patio to enjoy the weather and also enjoy not having our conversation recorded, though I didn't say that.

The ladies chatted about summer being the busy season for Security Solutions, so assuming I was right about Landowski's side business, I wondered if he was going to get back into pimping now that his customers had returned to the Hamptons. Which was another reason for me to put him out of business sooner than later. In fact, if there are new victims during an active investigation—especially deaths—the investigators could be held partly to blame. So, time to shut this down.

Amy excused herself to get back to her desk for a phone call, and I asked Kim and Judy if my keypad code worked on the back door that led to the equipment room. Judy said it did.

I was sure it did, but the real question was: "So I guess it works on that outside door to the basement?"

They sort of glanced at each other, and Judy replied, "No. That's a separate code."

"Do I need that?"

Judy assured me I didn't. "There's nothing down there." She added, "Only Steve has that code."

And I was sure Landowski had the only key to the padlocked basement door in the kitchen. I smiled. "Is that where Steve hides his crazy aunt?"

The ladies forced a smile between bites of donut. Kim said, "He has expensive wine."

Right. Those gallon jugs of Manischewitz can get pricey. I could point out that there was expensive equipment in the old mudroom, accessible to anyone through the kitchen, but it was time to go light. "I've been thinking about ladies' night upstairs."

Kim and Judy were all ears.

"You and Amy can invite some friends. And as I said, I'll take care of the entertainment."

Kim said, "Thank you. We have a few phone numbers for that."

I sprang my surprise on them. "I'm the entertainment."

They looked at me, and I saw Kim undressing me with her eyes, and Judy was mentally shoving twenties in my jockstrap. Seriously.

Judy asked, "Are you joking?"

"I am," I confessed. "But I know a few young cops who do this." Which was actually true. They got laid a lot. Plus tips. I smiled. "I know you're disappointed. But you won't be if I can book Sean or Carlos."

Kim gave me a big smile. "We want *you*, John."

Judy laughed and said to Kim, "*Amy* wants him."

They both got a laugh at that and I blushed. I got back to the real business. "Do you know if anyone is staying overnight here this weekend?"

Judy replied, "Not that I know." She told me, "Steve will be out of town with his kids. Why?"

"Because I need a place for the weekend."

If she wondered why, she didn't ask but said, "Just check with Steve. It's not usually a problem."

"Okay. I know that sometimes the PIs work late and stay over."

Kim replied, "Sometimes they stay over, but it's not because they're working late."

Judy piped in, "They're *playing* late."

Or establishing an alibi for a murder. I got sheepish and confessed, "I'll also be playing." I explained, "My uncle's out here for the weekend with his uptight girlfriend, and they would not approve of the young lady I'll be with."

Kim and Judy, assuming I was talking about a paid escort, looked at me with mock disapproval but said nothing. I asked, "If I come here Saturday at about eight P.M., will our alarm sound?"

"No," Judy replied. "If you use your keypad code, then the alarms, including the interior motion sensors, are disarmed."

"Okay. So Central Station Monitoring won't call whoever is on their list. Like Steve. Or the cops."

"No," said Judy. "They only call if the alarm sounds. Steve first. Then Amy, if Steve doesn't answer, then me. If none of us answers, they call the police."

"So I'm okay here overnight . . . but Steve can monitor the surveillance cameras from wherever he is."

Judy, knowing what I was getting at, just nodded.

"Well . . . I understand the need for security . . . but sometimes privacy is what you want."

The ladies sipped their coffee.

"But I guess there aren't surveillance cameras in the guest bedrooms."

Again no response, because I was getting into company secrets. But I pressed on. "Is there any way I can have some privacy?"

Judy hesitated, obviously sensitive to my concerns about starring in a sex video, and replied, "You could go into the attic. Each camera has a labeled VCR. You can stop the tape recording for . . . any area where you'd like privacy for as long as you need." She seemed a bit embarrassed, but continued, "You won't be recorded—but you can still be seen live in real time—if anyone happens to be watching at that time."

Meaning Steve Landowski, who had the access code. Well, I wasn't going to have sex with any paid escort, but I did need to take her to the bedroom in case Landowski was watching from wherever he was in New Jersey. Then the low-tech solution to the hidden camera, as Max had suggested, was to put a blanket over the two-way mirror, which would annoy Landowski, but he'd understand that I didn't want to be part of his home movie collection.

As for the audio portion of the movie, my paid date and I could simulate screams of ecstasy while the TV was playing an episode of "Swamp People" or something.

In any case, what I really needed was about four or five hours to clean this place out after my date left here, and that meant shutting down *all* the surveillance cameras at about midnight.

I looked at the farmhouse and saw that the high-mounted surveillance cameras would not be able to see anything close to the house. So, after my date left, I'd be able to move along this dead zone, around to the rear, where the coaxial cable connection was mounted on the house. This was the weak link in the security system. And this was where the Internet connection would experience a technical problem.

I knew that the videocassettes had only a twenty-four-hour running time, so I asked, "Who replaces the tapes over the weekend?"

Judy replied, "Usually Steve. But when he's away, Kim or I or Amy come in and replace them."

I wanted to see the hub of the security and surveillance system in the attic before I decided the best way to get around it, and I also wanted to take all the videotapes with me when I cleaned this place out, so I offered, "I can do that."

Judy replied, "Okay . . . I guess that would be okay." She said, "The tapes are replaced every day at about five P.M. In the attic, you'll see the labeled VCRs and boxes of blank tapes."

"Okay. What do you do with the used tapes?"

Judy replied, "Just leave them there. Steve sometimes reviews them . . ."

I'm sure he does. Especially the ones from Thursday nights. And those tapes probably go to the basement for safekeeping and future blackmail.

Judy said, "Please don't forget to change the tapes. Steve gets annoyed if someone forgets." She added, "Steve will be leaving early Friday afternoon to pick up his kids and get on the road. So I'll replace the tapes Friday before I leave, and I can show you what I do. Then you'll do it Saturday at about five P.M. Then . . . will you be here Sunday at five?"

"I will." Not. But by that time, there won't be anything left in this house that needs a security system.

Bottom line on all this was that once the perimeter security had been breached or entered legitimately, then the Trojan horse was inside the walls and could take care of the internal security with a little tech savvy, a little luck, and big balls.

I finished my coffee and said to Kim and Judy, "Okay, back to work." I stood and smiled. "This is all a bit . . . embarrassing. But . . ." You probably won't be working here after I'm done with the place this weekend, and I hope you both find good jobs somewhere. And be prepared to talk to FBI agents. "But . . . well . . . all the hotels and motels were booked. I'll find someplace else next time."

Neither lady replied, and I said, "I'll ask Steve about the overnight room. And I'll let him know I can change the tapes." I looked at Judy. "Unless you'd rather come in Saturday and Sunday to do that."

Judy replied, "If you're here anyway, you can do it."

"No problem." I hesitated, as though trying to find the right words, then said, "I would appreciate it if you didn't mention this to Amy."

They nodded in unison, and I was sure this wasn't the first time they'd been asked—or ordered—by someone here to keep something like this to themselves. The question was: Would they? Yes, they would, if they wanted me to pay for male strippers upstairs.

I thanked them, left the patio, and went back inside to my desk.

Well, the first day on the job was going okay. Chip Quinlan wanted to kill me, Amy wanted to fuck me, and Kim and Judy wanted to see me in a jockstrap. And it wasn't even five yet. Exotic dancers later. Can't wait to get home and tell Beth about my first day with Security Solutions.

I spent the rest of the afternoon answering old e-mails and texts, checking out the case files piled in the pantry, and reading all the notes on the bulletin boards. I didn't think there would be any obvious evidence of criminal activity lying around this office, but everything would go in the van for the Feds to wade through.

As I killed time, I was hoping that Chip Quinlan would

show up and try to kill me. But no such luck. He seemed to have disappeared, but I knew I'd see him tonight. That should be interesting.

I texted Beth, but she didn't reply. She was probably still upset about her bad dream. Or maybe she was having second thoughts about urging me to be one of the boys on Thirsty Thursdays. But, as I said, this was her idea; not mine. But not a bad idea.

No texts or e-mails from Robin or Kate. And I suppose I could attribute that to the fact that they are both lawyers, and therefore knew to stop communication when asked to do so. Still, after so many years together, and to respect our past and present marriages, they could at least tell me to go fuck myself.

Anyway, on to more important and more immediate problems. If all went well with my Saturday-night search warrant, when everyone arrived on Monday morning, this place would look like it had been hit by a repo team.

I'd love to be here to see everyone's reactions to the heist—Quinlan, Ferrara, Santangelo (if he came to work), Judy, Kim, Jack Berger, and, of course, Amy. They'd know it was an inside job, and they didn't need to be John Corey to know that's who did it. I'd also like to be here to hear Jack Berger calling his vacationing boss: "Good news and bad news, Steve. The bad news is that all our files, records, and videotapes have been stolen. The good news is that it can't get any worse." Berger might add, "And by the way, Steve, Mr. Corey, whom I advised you not to hire, has not shown up for work."

And where was Mr. Corey? Well, on Sunday morning I should be at 26 Federal Plaza, helping the Feds go through my van full of Security Solutions' case files, records, ledgers, videotapes, audiotapes, laptops, weapons, and whatever else looked interesting. This heist would take lots of hard physical labor, but I was in great shape from lifting weights in Bermuda.

As for the stuff that I'd deliver to 26 Federal Plaza on Sunday morning, there were a few Special Agents on the Anti-Terrorist Task Force who I knew well, and who I respected, and the feeling was mutual. So I'd arrange to meet one or two of them at dawn on Sunday and turn over the contents of the van to them directly, and they would contact the FBI Organized Crime Task Force and hand off the evidence to them. They'd all be thrilled to get this stuff that could possibly solve the Fire Island murders—and advance their careers—and they'd find a way to make the evidence from my self-issued search warrant admissible in court.

Also, the Feds, if nothing else, were very good at IDing what looked like evidence of criminal activity. I mean, a cash ledger was like pornography to an FBI forensic accountant, and hard drives gave the tech guys hard-ons. God bless the nerds. They do the boring crap. Not everyone can be lucky enough to get shot at.

I had the thought, of course, that there might not be one scrap of criminal evidence in this whole farmhouse. And if that was the case, I'm sure Robin would represent me—pro bono—on a charge of burglary or misappropriation of property. So maybe I shouldn't have sent her that F/U text. What I knew for sure was that any legal troubles I'd have if the evidence was a bust would be nothing compared to the trouble I'd be in with Detective Sergeant Penrose—and her group.

On that subject, I'd keep Beth Penrose's name to myself when I spoke to the FBI agents, and I'd take the rap if there was no criminal evidence in my haul, or if the evidence was judged to be illegally obtained and therefore inadmissible. But if the evidence was good and admissible—and I was fairly sure the Feds would find a way to make it so—then Beth and I would be available for media interviews. She was going to thank me for this.

Well, sometimes you just have to roll the dice. No guts, no glory. Nothing ventured, nothing gained. And, finally, comes the hour, comes the man. I am the man, and this is the hour. Better than working here all summer.

CHAPTER 32

Five o'clock rolled around, and Kim and Judy poked their heads into the PIs' room to wish me a good night and a good time at my first Thirsty Thursday—which, if all went as planned this weekend, would be the last dance for everyone.

I left my new company cell phone in my desk because I was sure that Landowski had set it up as a tracking device, and I did not want to be located when I drove to Beth's house tonight after Thirsty Thursday. I went into the kitchen for a coffee and ran into Amy sitting at the table, talking on her cell phone while sipping a Diet Coke. She said into the phone, "Okay. See you about six," and hung up. She said to me, "I was just coming to look for you."

"You need help setting up for the party?"

"No, but thanks. I just got off with the deli guy. They'll set up the buffet."

I noticed a thick wad of cash on the kitchen table, and Amy said, "That's for the deli stuff."

"We having caviar?"

"And for the girls."

"Right. Steve is a very generous host."

She had no comment on that, but said, "Long day. Let's have that drink." She stood, picked up the cash, and said, "Follow me."

So I followed her into the hallway, then into Landowski's ground-floor office. But instead of heading for the bar cabinet, Amy went to the bookshelves, removed a few books, and hit two switches, saying to me, "This one is for the hidden camera behind the mirror, and this one is for the hidden mic. This overrides the system in this room. Okay?"

I nodded.

"If you ever need complete privacy in this place—audio and visual—this is where you can have it."

"Bathrooms?"

"Let's just say I wouldn't sing in the shower here."

Okay, so did Judy or Kim tell Amy about me booking a room here for Saturday night? And did Amy bring me here to tell me it was all over between us—before it even got started?

But she didn't mention any of that and walked to the bar and poured two tumblers of Scotch, saying, "Steve interviews clients here. And prospective employees, as you know. And sometimes he wants it recorded, and sometimes he doesn't." She handed me my drink, and we clinked and drank. She continued, "About once a week, he interviews a woman in here for a highly paid clerical position."

"Sounds like he can't find the right person."

She laughed, took another swig, and said, "So I greet these . . . professional women and escort them into this office." She thought a moment and said, "I'm pretty sure Steve tells them to dress like they're really here for a clerical job, but you should see how some of them show up."

I'm sure I will tonight.

"And he does this during business hours, when Kim and Judy are here."

Who were hoping Steve found the right person—even a hooker—to help them out.

Amy continued, "It's his stupid and sick fantasy. You

know? Girls coming here for a job interview, and I show them in, and he says, 'Thank you, Amy. We'll be about half an hour.' Then . . ." She walked to the door. "He locks the door . . ." Amy locked the door to show me how a door locks, then crossed the room and lowered the blinds, demonstrating Steve's careful preparation for the job interview.

Why did I think I knew where this was going? Maybe because I've been around too long.

Amy turned from the window and looked at me in the darkened room, then took another hit on her drink. She said, "My guess—based on whatever I know about male fantasies, which is not extensive, but also not insignificant—is that Steve tells the girl she's going to do the interview in the nude, and he tells her to take off her clothes, which, being a hooker or a stripper, she does before he can finish his sentence."

Amy had a good sense of humor. How do I get out of here?

"Or," Amy continued, "he's coached her on the script, and she's supposed to be a good girl, and she pleads with him not to make her take her clothes off. Right? Like, she says she's married or has a boyfriend or whatever. But she needs the job, so she takes off all her clothes, and Steve . . . he probably sits here with a drink, watching her strip."

Amy either had a good imagination or she had her eye to the keyhole. Or maybe Landowski sometimes forgot to turn off the camera and mic. In any case, Amy Lang was Steve Landowski's enabler, which made her complicit. This place was crazy.

Amy gulped another mouthful of Scotch and picked up the story. "Maybe he asks her a few questions, like about her sex life, how many lovers she's had, and when and how she lost her virginity."

And how many words a minute she can type. Short-hand? Well, I didn't think Steve Landowski was that sophisticated in his fantasy, Vice Squad notwithstanding. So maybe Amy was just projecting one of her own fantasies. Or that's how she got her job here. Or it was possible that the mic and camera were purposely left on so that Amy could watch. Nothing in this place would surprise me.

Amy looked at me again and our eyes met. She said, "So she's playacting at being very embarrassed answering these questions, standing there naked, and Steve is hot as a three-dollar pistol by now, and he tells her to kneel, and he pulls it out and tells her what she has to do." Amy added, in case I couldn't guess, "She has to give him oral sex."

Actually, the hooker or stripper wasn't going to get the clerical job, but she definitely nailed a job upstairs.

Amy put her glass on the cabinet, slipped out of her sandals, and came toward me, asking, "Did that turn you on?"

Actually . . . yes. But I didn't reply, and she took my glass from my hand and put it on the table. She said, "I'm ready for my job interview."

Before I could tell her I wasn't hiring, she put her hands on my shoulders, looked into my eyes, then kissed me. I tried to push her away, but my hands had somehow gotten on her ass and I was pushing the wrong way.

We held the kiss long enough for me to get a whiff of her lavender, and for her to get the full force of my Dior Sauvage. Then she stepped back, and in a swift motion she pulled off her polo shirt, then unhooked her bra and tossed it aside, freeing two tanned puppies. Just as quickly, she slipped out of her blue skirt and pink panties, revealing a heart-shaped bikini cut and a bottom-and-top color match.

We made eye contact for a second—she looked very goal-oriented—then she dropped to her knees.

Well, my chance to get out of here had long since passed, and even if I'd found the willpower to do so now, that would have left a very angry naked lady on her knees, and that probably would have jeopardized or ended my brief employment here. So I had to take one for the team—or the group. I think Beth said this was okay.

Nothing seemed to be happening down there, and I sensed that Ms. Lang required my participation in this consensual act, so I unbuckled my belt, but before I could unhook and unzip, she pulled down my pants and shorts, like she'd done this before.

Next thing I knew, her hands were on my butt, and my formerly private dick disappeared into Amy's mouth, and about ten seconds later Johnny Rocket blasted off. Holy . . . shit . . .

I had trouble focusing on what happened next, but I remember Amy standing and pushing a chair under my bare butt, then pressing on my shoulder and telling me to sit. She put my glass in my hand and said, "You need a drink."

She stood there naked for a few seconds, finishing her Scotch, then got dressed quicker than she'd gotten undressed, saying, "The deli guy will be here any minute."

Was she going to blow him too?

She went to the door, and as she opened it, she said sweetly, "I hope I got the job, Mr. Corey," and added not so sweetly, "Have a good time tonight." She left before I could say, "Thanks for coming." Actually, I was the one who came. Emission accomplished.

I noticed the drink in my hand and downed it. I also noticed that she'd taken the wad of cash off the table. She didn't even leave me a twenty. But I think I won the pool. Does this count?

My cell phone dinged, and I fished it out of my pants pocket, which was around my ankles. A text from Beth said: HOW WAS YOUR FIRST DAY?

Well . . . you won't believe this. So why mention it?

I sat there, drink in hand, pants down, heart beating fast, trying to remember what I said that would lead Amy to believe I wanted oral sex. True, I'd *thought* about it, but I never mentioned it in conversation. She must read minds. I wish I could read hers.

I stood, got my browser back in my trousers, and moved toward the door, but then turned and took the opportunity to check out the trapdoor.

I got down on one knee, pulled the Oriental carpet back, and exposed the trapdoor. There was a ring on it, which I pulled, and the heavy door lifted. I got my hands under the door and pushed it up into a vertical position, then peered down into the dark space below. There were no stairs or ladder, but it was only about a seven-foot drop to the basement floor. No problem.

I lowered the trapdoor, pulled the rug back, and stood, still a little unsteady.

Well, there's nothing like a surprise B.J. and a successful recon to turn your day around. Especially if it all happened in the boss's office with his receptionist and his whisky.

The downside to the abovementioned blow job was that I wasn't exactly fired up for the strippers now. Which, I guess, was just as well. I needed a clear head tonight.

I heard the doorbell ring, and I could hear voices and footsteps in the foyer, then on the stairs. The food had arrived. So I stayed in the office. I mean, I can make postcoital conversation in bed, but what do you say to a coworker who's occupied with a deli delivery right after giving you oral sex in the office? So I had another Scotch. Maybe she'd stick her head in to say good-bye. Then I could properly thank her.

Meanwhile, I texted Beth: I CAME IN ABOUT 12:30. Then came at about 5:30? No.

Well, I was feeling a wee bit guilty, but . . . I also texted: QUIET DAY, MOST PEOPLE OUT. I SNOOPED A LITTLE. TALK LATER.

I sipped my drink and tried to deconstruct what had just happened. And why. I'm smart, but not that smart. Only Amy Lang knew what that was about. But if I thought about it, maybe Amy thought she was getting back at the boss in some perverse way. Or, as I said, she wanted me to protect or rescue her. Or, as I'd been warned, she was loyal to Landowski and she suspected me of being a plant, so she'd established a sexual relationship to see if I'd try to recruit her. So, Amy Lang. Receptionist or deceptionist? Time would tell. But she wouldn't.

Anyway, tomorrow morning should be interesting. Should I bring flowers? Maybe lollipops.

I heard a car starting outside and I peered through the blinds. Amy's Toyota was pulling out—I wondered if she had a date—and I now saw Landowski's Escalade parked, and also Santangelo's yellow 'vette. Lou was never late for a party.

I also saw a passenger van arrive, and out of the van came seven—count 'em—seven young ladies, carrying big totes in which would be their work clothes, including glitter and props.

So, the food and entertainment had arrived, the hosts had arrived, and the guests would be arriving soon.

Business hours were over, and the monkey business was about to begin.

CHAPTER 33

I climbed the stairs, made a right in the hallway, and walked toward the Recreation Room.

On the way, I heard voices coming from one of the guest bedrooms. Sounded like tonight's entertainment, so I knocked and opened the door.

The seven ladies stopped talking and looked at me.

"Hi," I said, "I'm John." Not *a* john. Just John.

One of the ladies asked, "What's up?"

I explained to everyone, "I'm Steve's new partner. Just wanted to say hello before the show."

The lady smiled, happy this wasn't a bust. "Hi. I'm Chrystal."

Chrystal was a short, thin woman with a boob job and black curly hair, and she looked a bit past the time she should be doing this, so I IDed her as the house mother. And did I mention that Chrystal was wearing only a G-string?

In fact, all the young ladies—who usually referred to themselves as girls—were in various stages of undress, getting ready for the show. One girl was putting glitter on another girl's back, two girls were crowded around the vanity mirror applying makeup, and the other two girls were sitting up on the bed wearing nothing but smiles and tattoos, sharing a joint and watching an MTV show on the flat-screen. Just another Thursday night at Security Solutions Investigative Services.

The bedroom was lit with lamps, and I could see old mismatched furniture, a threadbare rug on the floor, faded wallpaper, and a few floral prints on the walls: the honeymoon suite—except there was no mirror on the ceiling. But there was definitely a hidden video camera behind the vanity mirror, and probably a mic to record the sounds of sexual ecstasy.

Chrystal closed the door behind me and said, "Girls, say hello to John." She pointed to a young Hispanic-looking woman putting on makeup and said to me, "That's Carmen."

Carmen looked up and waved. *"Hola."*

"Hola," I said, proud of my cultural inclusiveness.

Chrystal pointed to the blond lady sharing the vanity mirror with Carmen. "That's Honey."

Honey waved as she powdered her nose.

Chrystal intro'ed the two glitter ladies, both of whom were East Asian. "That's Jade, and that's Jasper."

Should I say they're real gems? Probably not. "Nice to meet you."

Jade said, "You cute." They giggled.

I'm magnetic tonight, and I wasn't even wearing the pink pants. Must be the Dior.

Chrystal drew my attention to the two naked pot smokers on the bed, who were blondes, but the drapes didn't match the carpets. "That's Stormy," said Chrystal, "and that's Destiny."

Normally, I would be Horny. But thanks to Amy, I was Mr. Softy.

On another subject, the pot was illegal, but not worth mentioning in this context. I should say here that not all exotic dancers are hookers, but the odds of finding one in this room were looking good, so I said to Chrystal in a quiet voice, "I'm looking for some company Saturday night."

Chrystal went into business mode and said, "That's a tough night. We're booked for a stag party."

"So you show up with six instead of seven."

"Yeah ... but ..."

"Security Solutions has always been a good customer. Right?"

"Yeah ... I guess ... I can call around ..."

"I want one of *your* girls. To meet me here. About nine. A few hours. How much?"

"Okay ... what are you looking for?"

"Good conversation. Loves dogs and loves to travel."

Chrystal smiled, then sized me up—nice clothes, partner in the firm, no swastika tattoos visible—and said, "For straight or half and half, I need five hundred." She rattled off the extras. "For, like, bondage, S and M, anal, enemas—"

"I'm Catholic. Let's stick to straight."

"Okay, you pay the girl before she leaves, plus carfare. If she's good to you or you want her longer, or something extra, you work it out with her." Chrystal added, "Cash."

Fortunately, I had a thousand bucks of Landowski's money in my pocket, which would pay for a hooker *and* the rental van, so the guy who was really getting fucked on Saturday night would be Steve Landowski.

Chrystal asked, "Who do you like?"

I looked at the girls. This was sort of the opposite of a blind date. "They all look great. But I like you."

She smiled—almost girlishly. "Thanks. But I need to run the show Saturday."

"Right." The girls seemed to sense that a deal was being made and that I was about to choose one of them for my sexual pleasure. I didn't want to hurt anyone's feelings, so I said, "You pick."

Chrystal thought a moment, probably considering who was her worst dancer and her best fucker. It didn't matter to me, because the hooker was just an excuse—honest, Beth—for me to spend an overnight in the farmhouse.

Chrystal didn't ask for volunteers to raise their hands, but Destiny, sitting on the bed with a J in her mouth, did raise both legs and spread them—which got a big laugh from the girls. It pays to advertise. But I thought they weren't supposed to show pink. Crazy kids. Probably all met in dance class at Vassar.

Chrystal called Destiny front and center, and she hopped off the bed and sort of skipped toward me and put out her hand, which I took. "Hi." I said, "So this is my Destiny." Sorry.

Chrystal said to me, "Destiny is one of my top girls. She'll be good to you."

I wonder what she looks like with her clothes on. "I'm easy to pleasure," I assured her.

Destiny—who was high as a kite on weed and who knew what else—asked me, "You a cop?"

"I was. Now I'm a private dick."

She thought that was funny, but didn't know why.

Chrystal said, "Tell Destiny what you need," then moved off to give us . . . privacy?

Destiny was about mid-twenties, a bit plump, to be honest, bottle-blond on top, nice brown eyes, a tattoo on each breast—flower petals around the nipples, if you're interested—long, sparkly red fingernails with toenails to match, and skin that looked spray-tanned. I'd say she needed a good spanking, but that was probably extra.

Anyway, I said to Destiny, "Saturday night. You meet

me here at nine P.M.—that's nighttime—and call my cell so I can open the door. I'll give Chrystal my number. How we doin'?"

"We're doin' great, Jack."

"Wonderful." Remembering this was business, I confirmed, "Five hundred. And maybe a nice tip. You'll be free to go before midnight." Unless you want to help me haul stuff out of here.

Destiny seemed indifferent to the details, but did ask me, "You like to see two girls getting it on?"

"Is this a marketing survey?"

"You know. I got a girlfriend. We'll give you a real good show. Two thousand."

There's always the upsell. I mean, you ask for a blow job and they want to sell you "Oh! Calcutta!" with a full cast and orchestra. "Let's get to know each other first. Okay. We have a date." I added, "Dress casually."

"Gimme a hug."

"Sure." I put out my arms, and Destiny put her arms under my blazer and around my back, which I don't like when I'm carrying, but she kept her hands high and hugged me tight, then stepped back, holding the lapels of my blazer apart. She looked at my shirt and laughed.

I looked down and saw two rouge-red nipple imprints on my crisp white shirt.

A few of the other girls laughed too. *Shit.* I could possibly explain lipstick on the collar to Beth, or even glitter, but two nipple imprints on the shirt looked incriminating.

Jasper asked me, "You marry man?" which got a laugh, and Jade had the punch line, "No anymore," which got another laugh. This seemed well rehearsed, and I was sure it was part of the show later, so I smiled and said, "My wife does the same thing to me after she works a party."

The girls laughed.

Well, it was time to leave before someone pulled down my pants to give me another blow job. I said, "See you later, girls."

They all said good-bye, and Chrystal walked me to the door and gave me her card. "Call me if you need anything."

And she meant *anything*. I gave her my new business card with my company cell phone number. "Have Destiny call me when she gets here Saturday at nine. I'll open the door."

Chrystal assured me, "We all know the routine here."

I was sure of that.

She looked at me. "So you're new here."

"Right."

"These are fun guys. Steve's got a good heart. Met him when he was on the job. Takes care of the working girls."

Apparently, he did, but not in the way Chrystal thought. I would have asked her to step into the hall to continue this conversation, but I had her card, and someone would be calling her from 26 Fed next week to talk about Steve Landowski and company. "Steve is all heart," I agreed.

"Lou is a pisser. Makes the girls laugh."

"Last of the big-time spenders."

She didn't second that and said, "The girls love Chip. He treats them right."

Right up until the time he kills them. Well, I was sure these girls didn't require much from the men who employed them—just some money, maybe drugs, a few drinks, and no beatings. I'd be lying if I said I never went to a cop-sponsored strip show, and the girls liked the cops because they knew we were safe. And, I think, that was the perception here. But things are not always as they appear.

I looked at Chrystal standing there in nothing but a

G-string, making her way in the world as best she could. And if Chrystal suspected that anything was wrong here—that some of the girls who'd worked here, and maybe some of her own girls, had gone missing—she wasn't putting two and two together because it wouldn't add up to anything in her world, where girls went missing all the time. Like the girls who were found on Fire Island. Too many psycho perv johns out there, as Chrystal knew too well. But, as Beth had said, it didn't matter what bad—or desperate—choices these women had made. They might not get any justice in life, but they deserved justice in death.

Chrystal said, "See you in the Rec Room." She smiled. "Give me a call sometime."

I nodded and left the room.

So, now for some good clean dirty fun.

CHAPTER 34

It was not yet 6:30 when I walked into the Recreation Room, which was empty except for Steve Landowski and Lou Santangelo at the bar, wearing untucked shirts— Steve in chartreuse and Lou in aquamarine, FYI.

Landowski called out, "Hey, John!"

"Hey, Steve! Hey, Lou!"

"Come on in," said Lou, "have a drink."

"Thought you'd never ask," I said, trying to sound like one of the boys.

I went to the bar as Lou got behind it and asked me, "What's your pleasure?"

Well . . . I already had a blow job and saw seven naked ladies, so I said, "I'll take a brew."

Santangelo smiled—to show me his new dental work?—then grabbed a can out of the fridge and even popped the top for me.

My two colleagues were also drinking canned beer, and we clinked and drank, and I said, "First one since the coffee break."

They both laughed and puffed their cigarettes while eating bar nuts and drinking cold beer. Does it get any better? I smiled for the video camera behind the two-way bar mirror.

I said to Landowski, "I invited Chief Maxwell to join us tonight."

He nodded. "Always room for one more," but he probably didn't like me extending invitations. I was sure that Landowski drew up carefully thought-out guest lists, taking into account the usual etiquette and protocols, like who mixed well with whom. But also taking into account more important things, like who's already done Steve a favor, and who needs to be corrupted and compromised so they'll do Steve a favor when the time comes. I didn't know which group Max was in, but I'd take him at his word: innocent until proven otherwise.

Landowski asked me, "How long d'ya know Max?"

"Since he tried to fuck a girl I was dating one summer."

Both men laughed. I was really getting into this, but I didn't want to overdo it. And I also didn't want Landowski to search his reptilian brain and maybe recall something Max had once said about the Plum Island case.

Anyway, I looked around the big red room. Against the far wall were three card tables piled with deli food for the boys. Everything else was as I'd seen it the first time, except now the blackout curtains were drawn, and the room was lit only by floor lamps. Also, there were about thirty folding chairs around the dance floor. All this prep had probably been done by Amy earlier. Maybe these two guys helped, but I doubted it—though I was sure Landowski had told Amy she could stay if she wanted to get naked with the exotic dancers. Steve Landowski was a pig and a sexual harasser, which was no surprise. What did surprise me was Amy Lang, John Jay grad. Maybe she got sexual enjoyment from being submissive. Or maybe she was waiting for a time to get revenge. Meanwhile, Ms. Lang was engaged in petty acts of rebellion, like blowing her boss's new hire. A shrink would have a field day in this place. But this place wasn't going to be here much longer.

Landowski said, "Chip and Joseph will be here soon." He looked at me. "You and Chip had some words today?"

"He didn't seem himself today." Actually, he did.

"He's a hothead," said Landowski. "Don't take it personally."

Actually, he's a psychotic asshole, and I always take it personally when someone threatens to kill me.

Santangelo said, "Redheads are all crazy. Especially the women. I dated one once who threatened to cut off my dick with a steak knife."

Does Beth's copper-colored hair count as red? I hope not.

Landowski informed me, "You and me and him are gonna have a talk later. You're both gonna shake hands."

I was sure Steve Landowski's peacemaking skills hadn't progressed much since the schoolyard, but I said, "Good with me," because I had other things in mind for Chip Quinlan.

Landowski dropped the subject and checked his watch. "People should be coming soon." He smiled. "Nobody wants to be first to get here. But nobody wants to be late for the show." He briefed me: "First show is at seven to warm up the crowd, then nine. No cameras allowed, and whatever happens here, stays here."

Except if it can be used for blackmail. Souvenir videos supplied by Security Solutions.

Landowski also let me know, "We got a good group of girls tonight."

"I know. I met them."

"Yeah? How?"

"I stopped by their dressing room."

"Yeah? Why?"

"To put them at ease. You know? In case they had stage fright."

Lou and Steve thought that was funny. Lou said, "Yeah, they get nervous."

They both laughed, and I joined in. This was fun.

I said, "I spoke to Chrystal. Nice girl."

Landowski nodded. "She keeps her girls in line. Keeps them clean. Makes them go for tests."

"I didn't know they had to take a test for exotic dancing."

Another big laugh. I was really on tonight. I said to Landowski, "I asked one of Chrystal's young ladies to keep me company Saturday night."

He looked at me. "Yeah? You do hookers?"

"I thought they were dancers."

Lou and Steve got a chuckle out of that. Steve asked, "Which one?"

"Destiny."

Landowski seemed to be trying to remember which girl that was, and Lou said, "That's the chubby one." He looked at me. "Right?"

"Pleasantly plump," I replied like a gentleman. "A little inhibited, but I think she'll come out of her shell."

Landowski smiled. "Yeah. Nice girl. Why'd you pick her?"

"She picked me." I unbuttoned my blazer and spread my lapels, revealing the red stamp of Destiny's nipples.

Steve and Lou got a big kick out of that and laughed hard. Lou and I did a high five. It's good to feel accepted, though I should not forget that Landowski and Santangelo were complicit in the murder of Quinlan's lover and their colleague, Sharon Hite. And probably in the murder of Dan Perez. Also, it was entirely possible that one or both of these clowns had something to do with the nine dead women found on Fire Island, including Tiffany Sanders. I mean, neither of them looked or acted like killers, and they seemed to have almost an affection for the working girls, but at the end of the day, the girls were no different to them than livestock or barnyard animals: good only as long as they were useful and productive. And when they weren't, or when they got out of line and caused problems for Landowski and company or his friends or clients . . . Then, good-bye, Animal House, and off to the slaughterhouse.

Landowski asked, "Whaddaya paying?"

"Five hundred."

"*Five hundred?* You paying by the pound?"

"By the day. Saturday night and Sunday morning," which was not quite true.

Lou came to my defense. "That ain't bad for an overnight. But then you gotta feed her." He smiled. "And take her to church Sunday morning."

Good one, Lou.

Landowski said to me, "You get the family discount. I'll talk to Chrystal."

"Thanks, Steve. But what I really need is a room." I explained, "My uncle's coming out for the weekend, and he'd get a little uptight with Destiny in the house." I added, "Every hotel and motel on the North Fork is booked," which was probably true.

Landowski had the perfect solution. "Get him a girl. Loosen him up."

Lou agreed. "Surprise him with a naked broad answering the door."

That actually didn't sound like a bad weekend, but to get where I needed to go, I said, "He's bringing his girlfriend. She's a tight-ass." I looked at Landowski. "So I'll take you up on your offer of a room here."

He smiled, happy to be part of my moral decline and maybe even record it. "Sure. Nobody's using the rooms. I'll be away."

"Thanks." I smiled. "I'll try to go easy on the bed."

"Hey, if those beds could talk."

Considering all the DNA they had in them, they probably could. In several languages.

Okay, so the stage was set. Easy. Too easy?

On a related subject, Steve asked me, "You know anything about that U-Haul out there?"

In fact, I do. That will haul u-ass to jail. I said, "I gotta haul some shit out here from my condo."

Lou nodded, but asked, "Why you drivin' it today?"

If I tell you, I have to kill you, but I replied, "My Jeep went dead while I was away."

Landowski said, "Not for nothing, John, but that thing should be in a junkyard."

I smiled. "Security Solutions is gonna put me in a new Escalade, Steve."

He returned my smile. "By Christmas, if you stay on."

Actually, maybe I could buy his Escalade if the Asset Forfeiture Squad seized it.

Landowski asked me, "How'd it go today?"

"Good. Spent time with Kim and Judy."

"I asked Amy to show you around. She do that?"

Is this a good time to claim the pool money? Probably not. "She made herself available."

"Good. She tell you about July Fourth?"

"She did. Sorry I missed it."

"Me too. That's the kind of thing I need you for, to mix with the big shots."

"That's why I'm here tonight, Steve."

"Yeah. But we had the top guns from Yaphank here. And all the local pols. Two hundred people. Some good-looking broads. Everybody wants to see and be seen. My July Fourth is a hot ticket."

"I heard." And couldn't help myself from asking, "What's the occasion?"

"Whaddaya mean?"

"July Fourth. Like . . . what's the celebration for?"

"July Fourth."

Amy wasn't kidding.

"Your friend Max was here."

Lou piped in, "He was chasing some broad through the maze."

"I hope he caught her."

Witty Steve said, "Can't run fast with your pants down."

That's for sure. As for Max, I remembered what he'd said at Claudio's: *Too many temptations on this job*. Right. And it's a thin line between posing as a corrupt cop and being one.

Landowski asked me, "How was your vacation?"

"Okay. Just visiting the old folks."

"You alone?"

"Yeah, that's why I need company Saturday."

He smiled. "Let me handle that for you next time. Eliminate the middle madam."

Meaning he was not only a customer of hookers but he also had a side business of procuring them. But I already knew that.

Landowski gave me some financial advice. "You can't be spending most of your paycheck every weekend on a hooker."

I remembered an old joke. "I spend most of my money on booze and broads, and I waste the rest of it."

Steve and Lou laughed, happy to see a different John Corey emerging before their eyes. Beth would be proud of my playacting. Actually, I could be regressing into old John Corey, NYPD.

Landowski got serious and said to me, "I told Lou, Joseph, and Chip about your problem with bad guys who wanna clip you."

Including Chip himself. "Thanks."

Lou said, "You shoulda stayed in Missing Persons." He expanded on that thought. "You went off to Homicide and got yourself shot, and then the Feds, and now you got ragheads and Russians gunning for you."

"I really fucked up," I admitted.

Landowski put in his two cents. "You shoulda transferred to Vice. Life was good in the pussy patrol."

"And look at you now," I said.

Landowski took that as a compliment and replied, "Yeah. Now guys like you work for me."

Asshole.

Lou assured me, "We got your back."

"Thanks." I'll put in a good word for you at your sentencing.

Lou said to me, "I need a hundred bucks from you."

"You charge to watch my back?"

He laughed. "For the bop-Amy pool. You're in."

Not only was I in, I'd already won. Depending on how you defined "bop."

Landowski said, "We got maybe ten freelance guys in. They don't got a chance. You might. So get in on this."

I asked, "Is there a time limit?"

Landowski assured me, "No. It's like . . . your bet is good until somebody claims the pool."

I wondered what kind of proof was needed. But maybe a gentleman's word was good enough.

Lou said, "C'mon, John. A hundred bucks."

Giving Lou Santangelo a hundred dollars to hold was like giving it to a junkie for safekeeping. But it wasn't my money, so I peeled off a hundred bucks from my unearned pay and put it on the bar, and before I could blink, it disappeared into Santangelo's pocket.

Lou said, "You get laid, you get paid. Sweet."

We all shook hands to seal the bet, then we popped another beer and I had a cigarette, because men who drink, gamble, smoke, and joke together are brothers.

I remembered my promise to Kim and Judy and said to Landowski, "I'm going to do a Chippendale night for the girls here while you're away." I added, "It's on me."

"Yeah? Why?"

"They deserve some fun."

"Amy has all the fun she can handle. For the other two, buy them a vibrator."

Santangelo laughed and I smiled. In any case, this wasn't about fun for the ladies while the boss was away; it was about creating the illusion that I and Security Solutions would be around next week.

Santangelo, who may have been thinking about a videotape of Chippendale night in the Rec Room, said to Landowski, "I think it's a good idea, boss. Maybe they'll blow the stripper."

Landowski said, "Yeah . . . Okay. Why not?"

We drank to that.

So, I think everything was checked off my list. Mission accomplished.

Joseph Ferrara came into the Rec Room and we chatted a bit. I got the impression he was the adult in the room, the benign face of Security Solutions and not a partner in crime. But as a former Organized Crime guy, he couldn't be entirely clueless about Security Solutions' other activities. I could see the Feds offering Ferrara and Jack Berger a deal. And maybe Amy—unless she was in this deeper than I knew. But whether she was a future witness for the government or a criminal defendant, my sincere hope was that Amy Lang, on the stand in open court, did not mention that she blew the star witness for the prosecution, Detective Corey.

Chip Quinlan arrived with his red head and red shirt, and greeted everyone else, but gave me a nasty look as he went behind the bar and got himself a beer.

I knew that Landowski wanted us to shake hands, but I wasn't going to let the insult pass, and I said to Quinlan, for all to hear, "If you look at me like that one more time, I'll rearrange your fucking face."

Quinlan spun toward me, and Landowski stepped in with his arms outstretched. "Hey! Hey!"

Quinlan shouted, "This *fuck*—"

I shouted, "Fuck you, punk!"

Lou shouted, "Hey! Hey!"

Then Ferrara surprised me by getting into Quinlan's face and said, very calmly, "That's enough. *Enough.*"

Quinlan and I were glaring at each other, and if we were Italians, the guns would have come out. Salvadorans would already be shooting.

Landowski said to Quinlan, "Take a break. Go greet the guests at the front door."

Lou suggested, "Go get a blow job."

That should put him in a better mood. It did wonders for me.

Quinlan looked at me and our eyes met. He wanted to say something, but knew to keep his mouth shut. He turned and stomped off.

Landowski said to me, "Sorry, John. He's not himself since his girlfriend's suicide."

"What the fuck does that have to do with me?"

"I dunno. Maybe you remind him of the Homicide guys who grilled him about the suicide. Like he was a fucking lowlife and not a retired cop. You know? Pissed him off. Can't get over it."

I assumed that Detective Sergeant Penrose was one of those Homicide guys. And I could imagine her easily pissing off a guy like Quinlan. I could also imagine him looking to eliminate another nosy woman someday. I said, "I don't need this shit, Steve."

"It's okay. I'll talk to him. Calm down."

"Fuck him."

Ferrara, who seemed to be a man of few words, said nothing, a skill he'd probably learned from his paisanos in organized crime. The quiet guys are the ones you need to watch.

Landowski suggested, "Let's have a real drink."

Santangelo set out four glasses.

So, whatever badmouthing Quinlan had done about me, Landowski would now put it down as two hard-asses who felt hate at first sight, which was partly true. Also, it was good for the boys to see that John Corey had psychotic episodes. They respect that. And finally, I enjoy going nuts now and then, and I'm happy for the opportunity to do it here for the boys and for the hidden video camera.

Lou was pouring a cheap cognac into the four glasses. We all took one and Landowski said, "Here's to us, and here's to a big-money summer." We clinked and drank.

Landowski and Ferrara moved off to talk about something—probably me—and Santangelo said to me, "You gotta be careful with Quinlan."

"Fuck him."

"A word to the wise, John."

I looked at Lou Santangelo, the guy who, with Landowski, had provided an alibi for Quinlan's whereabouts on the night Sharon Hite died. They weren't just covering for Quinlan—they were actually afraid of him. I've seen too many guys like Chip Quinlan, and I had no doubt that Quinlan would kill anyone who posed a threat to him, including his girlfriend and that reporter. And that certainly included me. And Beth. And anyone in her group who was sniffing around him.

That being the case, it was my professional opinion that Chip Quinlan had to be brought to quick justice before he was ever brought to court. I've done it before— as Beth had reminded me with the Plum Island case.

Santangelo said, "Give it time. You're gonna like it here."

"Hey, I'm liking it already."

CHAPTER 35

The distinguished guests began arriving, and Landowski wanted me with him near the Rec Room door to meet and greet, introducing me as the newest PI in his agency and making sure everyone knew I was famous—though famous for what wasn't made clear. More importantly, I looked professional and presentable, notwithstanding the nipple marks on my shirt. Actually, I kept my blazer buttoned.

A number of the cops to whom I was introduced did know who I was, and that made Steve Landowski happy he'd hired a good addition to the agency. The politicians, I noticed, greeted me with a big glad-hand and a smile, like I was a potential vote or a possible contributor to their next campaign. Interestingly, most of the pols were well dressed, in suits and ties, though the occasion was informal, and the entertainment would be naked.

Also, Landowski had invited four or five PIs who worked for him freelance. These guys were all retired police detectives, and Landowski employed dozens of them when he needed them for something like surveillance or a bodyguard job. Or maybe something off the books.

So Security Solutions was the tip of a much larger enterprise, part legit, part not so legit, part visible, part invisible. Sort of like Don Corleone's olive oil business. Except this criminal enterprise was run by ex-cops.

The question was: Who put all this together? Not Steve Landowski, whose organizational skills seemed limited.

Jack Berger? Maybe. Or maybe Joseph Ferrara, whose time on the Organized Crime Task Force would give him knowledge of how the underworld worked. But Ferrara was new here, though he may have started this job before his retirement. As for Police Chief Conners, he may be Landowski's capo—and he may also be the psycho serial killer. But Conners wasn't the brains running the show, because, as per Beth, he was stupid. Hard to figure out the chain of command of this successful criminal enterprise. If I let Beth's group continue their unofficial investigation, or if the investigation was turned over to the Feds, we'd have all the answers—though not for a year or two.

But all the evidence to crack this case quickly might be right under my feet. All I had to do was go and get it. And I had the plan, the balls, and the U-Haul to do it—before this thing got even bigger. And before someone else got killed. Like Beth. Or me.

Anyway, Santangelo or Ferrara had cranked up some music—sort of wedding reception stuff—and now they were at the bar, serving the incoming guests. It occurred to me that there would be no professional bartenders or a DJ tonight because neither Landowski nor his prominent guests wanted outsiders—witnesses—present for the show. Same with the deli buffet, which was self-serve. Amy could have helped out at the bar if she'd also agreed to strip naked on the dance floor. Not sure there was anything in that for her, but it might be a better career move than blowing the new hire.

Regarding Chrystal's girls, it was implicit in their verbal contract that they had never set foot in the farmhouse, and certainly didn't have sex with any police brass or politicians here. And somewhere in the back of their minds, the girls—and definitely Chrystal—knew there would be severe punishment awaiting them if they didn't keep their mouths shut, or if they tried to blackmail the distinguished guests whom they'd serviced in the honeymoon suites or elsewhere. In fact, they might wind up naked and dead on Fire Island, as had Tiffany Sanders and eight other girls.

I noticed that Landowski didn't always intro the arriving guests to me with their full names, or their titles—mostly, it was Bob, Bill, Tony, and so forth instead of "John, this is State Senator Bob Smith, and this is Town Tax Assessor Bill Jones, and this is Judge Tony Falanger."

But now and then one of the men would fill in the details of their public service. And some of the elected officials asked me to remember them at the polls in November. I certainly will. I mean, politicians are a breed apart.

As for the cops—and I could tell who they were at a glance—it was first names only, and no ranks or job descriptions, so I wouldn't know, for instance, if I was shaking hands with Suffolk County Police Chief Edward Conners, or Max's friend, Riverhead Police Chief Larry Jenkins, or Beth's Homicide boss, Lieutenant Stuckley.

I did, however, recognize Southold Police Chief Sylvester Maxwell. As Max and I were about to shake hands, Landowski said to me with a smile, "I think you know this guy." Max and I shook, and Landowski said to Max, "John tells me you tried to fuck his girlfriend."

Max was probably wondering if I meant Beth Penrose.

I said, "That's Max's M.O. He's not a buddy-fucker, but he *will* try to fuck his buddy's girlfriend."

We all got a laugh at that, and Max forced a smile and said to Landowski, "I can't believe you hired this guy."

More laughs, then Landowski said to Max, "Thanks for recommending him. I owe you one." He added, "He's on probation."

"Better than parole," I said, which is what you, Mr. Landowski, will be on after serving twenty to life.

Anyway, Max moved on and headed for the bar, where Lou and Joseph Ferrara were handing beers to the cops and pouring wine and hard stuff for the civilians. I called out, "Lou! The Chief wants his usual—a pink squirrel!"

More laughs. And to be honest, I was suddenly filled with a deep sense of nostalgia and good memories of the NYPD and NYC back in the day, when we had maybe too many stag nights. But as we used to say, whatever it takes to relieve the stress of the job.

And here I was, in what outwardly looked like what I was nostalgic for, but was actually a sinister imitation of clean dirty fun. It's all about context and subtext. NYPD stag nights had no agenda other than the obvious, i.e., pay two bits to see two tits and have a few laughs. Here . . . everybody had an agenda and a dirty secret.

I stayed with Landowski awhile, meeting and greeting, and earning my pay, and watching Max as he worked the room. He seemed to know everybody and vice versa, and he seemed to be well liked and well connected. But again, it's the context.

So, aside from the fact that almost everyone here was, to one degree or another, corrupt or corruptible, this was also an occasion to network and maybe even discuss some actual business. The lines were blurred, and that suited everyone here, especially Steve Landowski, who lived in a murky world of swamp water. And what amazed me here was the sheer number of upstanding citizens who were complicit in some sort of political or police corruption. As for moral corruption, that's not for me to judge.

Anyway, the arriving guests seemed to be dwindling, and I counted about thirty men in the room, maybe half of whom were cops and the others probably elected or appointed officials, including, I was sure, some judges and people from the DA's office—the power structure of this affluent county, which was populated with a high percentage of well-educated and enlightened citizens. I mean, this was not some rural county in the Old South where the sheriff and his deputies showed up at a Ku Klux Klan rally, not as law enforcers, but as Klan members. This was New York State, for God's sake, where the corruption was supposed to be more sophisticated and discreet. Right?

I'd been waiting for Chip Quinlan to return, but I guess he was still on a time-out. Or maybe he was in the equipment room, looking through the gun safe for an AR-15 to blow me away. I'd love an excuse to face off with this asshole, and if I was actually here all summer, only one of us would be celebrating Labor Day.

I said to Steve, "I'm going to mingle."

"Good. I want everybody to see you. Don't be shy about telling everybody who you are."

"Who am I?"

"You're John Corey. Ballbuster and wiseass. But that's not what you say. You say NYPD Homicide, Anti-Terrorist Task Force, top-secret clearance, wounded in the line of duty. That's what you say."

"My favorite subject is me."

"Yeah. And you don't ask them who they are or what they do. If they want to tell you, they'll tell you."

"Right." And I guess I shouldn't ask if they come here often.

"And you give out your card. I've done PI work for some of these guys. Some political shit. Some matrimonial. See if you can bring in more business tonight." He added, "You get four hundred an hour if they ask."

"I'm paying a hooker five just to get my dick wet."

He thought that was funny, which it was. He said, "You get four hundred by the *hour*. And you don't have to take your clothes off and suck strange dick."

"Right. Okay, see you later."

I stopped at the bar and got a Solo cup of ginger ale that could pass as a real drink and headed for Max, who was talking to two guys who looked like cops and were old enough to be bosses.

Max introduced me to them by first name, and we agreed we'd met at the door. In fact, the guy named Larry was obviously Larry Jenkins, Max's friend and Chief of Police for Riverhead. Chief Jenkins was here, I was sure, to enforce law and order in his bailiwick and ensure that there would be no trouble with the local police—who were under his command. The other guy, who was wearing dress slacks and a sport jacket, was named Ed. He hadn't stopped at the door to say hello when he arrived, but I recognized him from photos I'd seen online in Bermuda along with some unflattering news stories. It was, in fact, Suffolk County Chief of Police Edward Conners, the capo di tutti capi.

Conners was not tall, but he had a large build, a potbelly, and a pockmarked face. He didn't seem particularly friendly and said little, reminding me of a few of my former NYPD bosses who were smart enough to know they shouldn't say anything that would make them sound stupid—which was just about everything. I could easily see why Beth disliked him.

A few other guys drifted into the conversation and we all made small talk—mostly about summer plans, fishing, boating, and the city assholes who were arriving here for the summer—and I thought about what Beth and Amy had said regarding Chief Conners: total pig. And probably not the most faithful husband on the police force or the planet. What struck me about this guy was that everyone seemed to know he was either dirty or incompetent, and for sure an unpleasant asshole. And yet he was still the top cop in the county, making me believe he had his fingers around many political balls in this room. Which, if you get to the top, is how you stay on the top. In fact, nearly everyone here had their hands on someone's balls, and no one wanted their balls squeezed, twisted, or shaken, so they all played ball, so to speak.

I looked again at Edward Conners. Could this guy actually be the Fire Island serial killer? He certainly had opportunity and access, which were two boxes you checked off when you were looking for a murderer. The big box to check off was motive, and one motive for killing someone was to keep them quiet or end a blackmail. That fit. But you also look at past history, and Conners seemed to have a dark history of sexual abuse, not to mention a fondness for squeezing ladies' necks, which apparently gave him sexual gratification. And the sex toys he carried around in his car were a clue that Edward Conners needed more than a kiss and a hug in bed. He also needed a rope.

Anyway, remembering my instructions from Landowski, I handed out my new card and said, "If there's anything I can do for you gentlemen, please don't hesitate to call." I added conversationally, "In addition to NYPD Homicide, I did some work with NYPD Internal Affairs, busting a ring of dirty Vice cops who were moonlighting as pimps." Which wasn't true, but I was here to have fun, and I could see some frozen expressions and guessed that a few sphincters were tightening.

Max caught my eye and tilted his head toward the door. I nodded and we excused ourselves to get something to eat—which I, having skipped lunch, actually wanted to do and would have done earlier if I hadn't been getting my weenie eaten, followed by my detour into the girls' locker room.

I snagged a sandwich from the buffet and we went into the hallway, close to the door so the loud music would cover our voices if the hallway surveillance cameras had a mic.

Max asked, "Why did you say that?"

"What?" I took a bite. Corned beef. Not bad.

"You know what. Are you crazy?"

Eventually I'd have to answer that question.

Max said, "That was Chief Conners. And the other guy was Larry Jenkins—"

"Max, I don't give a shit who they are. Everyone here is either dirty or thinking about it."

"That's the fucking point. You are *not* supposed to brag that you busted dirty cops."

"I was just kidding. I never worked Internal Affairs. But did you see the expression on Conners's face?"

Max sensed, correctly, that he wasn't getting anywhere, so he said nothing.

I asked, "Did you speak to my uncle's renters?"

"Yes. Mr. and Mrs. Colby. I told them there'd been some burglaries in the area, and to be vigilant. I gave them my card."

Hopefully, the Colbys would be scared off and I'd get my free squat back after Beth kicked me out for burglarizing Security Solutions.

Max said, "If the Russians are stalking you, your Jeep in the driveway may be more than an inconvenience for the Colbys."

"Right . . . But as you said, it could be an opportunity for you to bag a few Russian assassins. You'll be a media star."

He had no response to that, but asked me, "What are you driving now?"

Well . . . stick to the story. "A van. I need to get some stuff from my condo. Then I'll get a convertible for the summer."

He looked at me, and I could see the wheels spinning in his head, but he had no response.

I changed the subject. "Amy told me you were at Landowski's July Fourth party instead of at work."

"That was work."

"Right. Just like tonight." I asked, "Learn anything new at the party?"

"Nothing I didn't already know." He asked, "What else did Amy tell you?"

"Nothing that relates to this case."

He advised me, "Stay away from her, John. She's poison."

Right. Just another reason to wrap this case up quickly—plus, it would be hard to keep up the pretense that I was living at my uncle's house. Also there was Landowski and Santangelo asking about my van, plus the psychotic Chip Quinlan, and the too-smart Jack Berger, and so forth. This whole operation was on shaky ground from day one—because I wasn't the one who planned it—and a loud voice in my head was shouting, "Abort! Abort!" but I ignored it.

I said, "I had a run-in with Chip Quinlan this afternoon, then up here a while ago."

"What happened?"

"If you think *I'm* crazy, just talk to him."

Max nodded. "We discovered that he had some issues on the job." He asked, "How did you leave it with him?"

"We'll work it out."

"I didn't see Quinlan in there."

"Landowski sent him to find his meds."

"You need to watch him."

"He needs to watch me."

Max had no comment and glanced at his watch. "Almost seven. We should go inside for the show."

"If we stand here, we can get an early peek at the talent."

Before he could respond, one of the bedroom doors swung open and out came the girls, dressed in sexy black negligees, wearing impossibly high heels.

Chrystal lined them up in single file, and they began clip-clopping toward us and the Rec Room, all smiles and full of youthful energy—and maybe a snort of Colombian marching powder.

Chrystal saw me and yelled, "Hi, John!"

"Hi, Chrystal!"

Max did a double take.

All the girls yelled, "Hi, John!" as they ran past me and Max, and Destiny playfully grabbed at my crotch on the run. I said to Max, "That's Destiny."

He looked at me. "How do you know—?"

I opened my blazer and flashed the two nipple marks. "I have a date with Destiny."

He had no reply.

I said, "I'll explain later."

We turned toward the Rec Room and entered just as the music got louder, and Chrystal led her girls onto the dance floor, where they all did cartwheels to the applause and whistles of about thirty men who appreciated modern dance, and who were now starring in a home movie that would bring them unwanted fame—if I could get my hands on the tapes. And I would. This weekend. Right?

CHAPTER 36

Chrystal's girls put on a good show. I mean, it wasn't *Swan Lake*, but it was certainly entertaining if your cultural tastes run more to tits and ass.

Max and I found folding chairs close to the dance floor. Most guys were seated, though a few stood near the bar or the buffet. Cigar and cigarette smoke hung in the air, which I hadn't seen or smelled indoors in a long time. The shag carpet added to the illusion of time marching backward here.

The speakers were blaring "Y.M.C.A." and the girls were really into it. I think they actually liked to dance, which I imagine is more liberating and less boring than having sex with a man they met ten minutes ago.

Most of the lights were off now, so I couldn't see all the faces in the audience, which I'm sure put the high-profile guests at ease, and the overhead track lights were shining on the girls, making them the center of attention, as they should be. Also, I was certain the hidden video camera and mics were recording the show and the guests for posterity and other purposes.

Assuming my Saturday-night search warrant was successful, the Feds would spend hours looking at these and other videotapes, IDing the distinguished guests, who, though not technically breaking the law, would nonetheless be upset when they were shown these tapes. I mean, there would be nothing on these tapes that a politician could justify as community outreach. Right? And nothing that the police brass would want to include in a public information film called *Your Police at Work*.

The U.S. Attorney's office has often been called the top blackmailers in the country, and I'd seen how quickly the Feds could get witness cooperation just by playing video- or audiotapes, or sharing surveillance photos with potential and reluctant witnesses. We live in an age of electronic surveillance. When I was a kid, my mother used to say to me, "God is watching you all the time, John." Well, maybe, but you didn't have to answer to God until Judgment Day. Now, every day is Judgment Day.

I turned my attention back to the show. The girls had kicked off their high heels and were dancing barefoot, which was a bummer for the shoe fetishists in the crowd, but a treat for the foot guys. The girls were still wearing their lacy peignoirs or whatever you call those things, and nothing was coming off, which is why it's called a strip-tease.

The speakers were now blaring "Do You Wanna Dance?" a nice oldie by the Beach Boys, and Chrystal got one of the younger cops on the floor, and the guy was good and really got into it, like he was auditioning for "Dancing with the Stars." The girls seemed to like him and were giving him booty bumps and titty taps. Good clean dirty fun—until he got home and had to explain the glitter. Or maybe he wasn't married. He danced like he wasn't.

I noticed that Quinlan had returned from the penalty box, and he was standing near the bar, talking to Landowski and Santangelo, and glance-glaring at me across the darkened room. Our eyes met, and if looks could kill, both of us would be DOA. And as I said, no matter how this all came down, Chip Quinlan had to go down, because my dance card was already filled with guys who wanted me to have my last dance with them.

Quinlan turned away, so I turned my attention to Police Chief Edward Conners, who was sitting across the room with a group of suits around him to show he had political power. More to the point, the unattractive Edward Conners had probably had his share of sexual rejection from women, and guys like that become women haters and hooker customers. And, as any vice cop will tell you, they sometimes take out their anger on the girls they have to pay for—assuming they have a screw loose to begin with. And Conners looked like he had several screws loose. Also, I had no doubt he was a big fan of hard-core misogynist pornography. And quite possibly, he acted out a few scenes he'd seen and liked in a porn film. Like tightening a rope around a woman's neck while he had sex with her.

Well, this was all speculation, though based on some circumstantial and anecdotal evidence. Also, Beth had prejudiced me to hate her boss. Chief Conners might be an incompetent, misogynist, stupid, ugly scumbag, but that didn't make him a murderer. It did, however, make him a suspect. I'd love to have an hour alone with this asshole in a locked room.

On another subject, this party, now that I was seeing it, must be costing Landowski and Security Solutions about three or four thousand, and he did one a week, though the Thirsty Thursdays without the exotic dancers would be less expensive. Bottom line, that was north of two hundred thousand a year for business entertainment, especially if Landowski picked up the tab for the after-party in the two honeymoon suites. So the payback to him must be big. And where did all this cash come from? The answer to that and other interesting questions lay somewhere in this farmhouse. And if I doubted that, I had only to look at Chief Conners and the other guests here, including the local police chief, Larry Jenkins. All of these guys had very good motives—along with the power—to ensure that this farmhouse was the last place on the planet subject to a police search and seizure. So that's where I come in.

The music stopped and so did the girls. And who should come out on center stage but former Vice Squad Detective Steve Landowski, looking like a proud papa hosting his son's First Holy Communion party.

Steve said, "On behalf of myself, Steve Landowski, and my terrific PI team, Joseph, Chip, and Lou, I welcome you all to Security Solutions' Thirsty Thursday."

He must have practiced that for an hour in front of a two-way mirror.

He referred to a note in his hand and continued, "And I want to introduce to you tonight the latest member of my team, a man who most of you know by reputation, a man who has earned many awards and citations from the NYPD and who was wounded in the line of duty while assigned to NYPD Homicide, and who went on to a second great career with the Federal Anti-Terrorist Task Force and the Diplomatic Surveillance Group."

And was fired by both. And don't forget two failed marriages. Also, I think Jack Berger wrote this for him.

The maestro continued, "And a man who has taught at John Jay College of Criminal Justice, and who holds a top-secret clearance with the United States government, and who has served his city and his country with great distinction, and who has also served on the NYPD with Lou Santangelo, who most of you know, and a man who is a great friend of our friend Police Chief Sylvester Maxwell."

Max leaned over and said to me, "Ask for a raise."

Landowski's voice got louder as he said, "And a man who is now serving the clients of Security Solutions and anyone here who can afford him."

A few laughs.

"May I now present to you the newest member of this agency's family and my latest superstar investigator, Detective John Corey."

Faint applause from the crowd, but the girls were really excited.

I stood, but before I could join my new boss on the dance floor, Chrystal and the six goblets swarmed me and showed their patriotic appreciation for my service and their continuing commitment to law and order.

I extricated myself from their embraces—but not their glitter and spray tan—and joined Steve, who smelled like cheap perfume. Or was that me? I think I might have to use the shower here before I go home.

"John, say a few words."

"You're all under arrest." Okay, I didn't say that. I said, "Thank you, Steve, for that very kind introduction." Steve acknowledged that, and I continued, "When I left Federal law enforcement and came out to this beautiful piece of paradise to relax, reflect, and connect with nature, I didn't know that I was just enjoying a short intermission between my second act and my third act, which promises to be the greatest act of my career—with Security Solutions."

No one seemed to believe that, me included, but I continued, "And when I look around this room, I see . . ." Love? No. "I see men who have devoted their lives to public service, and who take seriously the public trust that has been given them by the people they serve and protect. I see men—like Suffolk County Police Chief Edward Conners—who are committed to good, clean, and honest law enforcement. And I am humbled to be in your presence and honored to be at your Thursday social gathering. If there's *anything* I or Security Solutions can do for you—professionally or personally—just let us know."

I didn't look at Steve's face, but I was sure he was not smiling. I concluded, "Keep up the good work. Thank you."

The girls started clapping, but then realized that no one else was, so Chrystal led the girls out to the dance floor and someone hit the music—"Dancin' the Night Away"—and the girls came alive like Energizer Bunnies.

Steve stood motionless for a few seconds until Jade and Jasper grabbed his hands for a dance, but he shook them off.

I didn't go back to my seat but headed for the bar, where Santangelo was bartending and Quinlan was drinking and smoking.

I said to Santangelo, "Hey, Lou, I'll have a beer."

He nodded and got a cold one out of the fridge.

I was standing almost shoulder to shoulder with Quinlan, and he didn't move. This was one tough hombre, and I admire any man who walks the walk. I'd definitely make the time to go to his funeral.

Quinlan was obviously under orders to not say anything to me, but Santangelo said, "Your talk was maybe a little out of place here, John."

"Whaddaya mean?"

He didn't reply, because he'd have to be specific about what he meant.

Landowski came to the bar and ordered a Scotch, neat, which Santangelo poured into a Solo cup.

I said, "I think we drummed up some goodwill, Steve. Maybe some business."

He didn't respond, but downed the Scotch and ordered

another. Obviously, something was troubling him. Maybe me. He lit a cigarette and sort of forced himself to turn and look at his guests—maybe to see if anyone was leaving, or if the mood in the room had changed after my talk, which may have been misinterpreted as mocking.

I too turned toward the seated guests, and they all looked caught up in the show. There's nothing like semi-naked dancing women, booze, and music to make a man forget what it was that caused him some discomfort just a few minutes before. Men are primal.

Landowski didn't seem to have anything to say to me, but Max was making his way around the dance floor, and he headed for the bar, probably thinking my colleagues were upset with me.

Meanwhile, the girls had pulled one of the suit guys to his feet and gotten him on the dance floor to cha-cha with Destiny, who was now topless and who did her trademark nipple bump on his white shirt, which made everyone laugh. Me too, though I'd been the victim of her twin guns myself.

The girls were all topless now and would be bottom-less soon. And later, I was sure, when the show was over, some of the girls would accept the kind invitation of a guest to keep him company in one of the rooms here or elsewhere. I don't know where these girls get their energy. Maybe from Colombia.

Anyway, Max chatted with Steve and Lou for a minute, probably to get a feel for how they thought my remarks had been received.

Meanwhile, the girls were down to their G-strings and dancing to the tune of "La Bamba," and Carmen had a young Hispanic-looking guy on the dance floor, and the two of them showed the gringos how real dancing was done south of the border.

Honey now had some older pol on his hands and knees, and she was sitting on his back, riding him like Lady Godiva and swatting his ass to the laughter of the distinguished guests.

The music was loud enough to shake the room, and most of the men were now on their feet, clapping or wolf-whistling, imbibing alcohol and pushing a few of their colleagues onto the dance floor.

Chrystal was the first to take off her G-string, which she wrapped around the neck of a man who was wearing a tie that she took off and put around her neck. This set off an orgy of tie-stealing with the other girls, who swapped their G-strings for men's ties. The girls looked sexy in the ties. The men . . . not so good in the G-strings.

If I had to rate this show, I'd give it top marks for originality, improvisation, audience engagement, and costume design. I could see why it was well attended, and I gave Steve Landowski credit for bringing what he learned on the Vice Squad to a more selective audience. No, he wasn't as stupid as he looked or sounded. In fact, he had completely understood what the priests warned him against in confraternity class, and he clearly felt blessed to have gotten this intel at an early age about the temptations of the flesh and the weaknesses of men. And little Steve Landowski knew what he wanted to do when he grew up.

Max tapped me on the shoulder and said, "Let's take a break."

The speakers were now playing a tango, and the girls were doing a sensual girl-on-girl dance, to the delight of the men, who'd suddenly become quiet. Chrystal, like Steve Landowski, knew men.

"*John.* Let's take a break."

"Max, are you watching this?"

"I've seen the show. Come on."

"Okay . . ." So Max and I went out into the hall, and I followed him down the staircase, through the front door, and out to the parking area, where we could speak freely.

The air was cool and cleaner than in the Rec Room, and I saw that there were vehicles parked up and down Jacob's Path, as I'm sure there were every Thursday night.

Also, our movement had turned on the security lights, so I could see that Max was not happy. I already knew what he was going to say, but he said it anyway. "Why did you say that?"

"There's always a method to my madness, Max."

"Yeah? What?"

"Well . . ." Sometimes there isn't. But this time there was. "Look, if Landowski and his boys suspected that I was a plant who knew what was really going on here, the last thing they'd expect me to say to these guys was anything about good, clean, honest government and law enforcement . . . what else did I say?"

Max thought about that, probably trying to decide if I was a genius or an idiot.

I assured him, "I know how to go undercover and not arouse suspicion. That's why Beth recruited me."

He still seemed unhappy. "You should never have mentioned Chief Conners by name."

There was more method to my madness, and I said, "If we can ever get possession of the video- and audiotape of this Thirsty Thursday, the Feds will see me IDing Conners, and mocking everyone else here." I added, "Even the Feds will get a good laugh at that." And I'll be a hero, and the Feds would offer me a job on the Organized Crime Task Force, and I'd tell them to go fuck themselves.

Max processed my explanation, then nodded. "All right . . ." He asked me, "What's with you and Destiny?"

Could I trust Max? Beth and her group did, and my

instincts said that Max was an honest cop. Unless everything he'd said and done so far was an elaborate double-cross.

"John?"

"I have a date with Destiny. Here, Saturday night. Landowski will be out of town, leaving Friday, taking his kids to the Jersey Shore and A.C. He's offered me a room here for my date, so now I have a reason to be here after hours."

"Okay . . . and aside from fucking your date, what are you doing here Saturday night?"

"Snooping."

"Who authorized you to snoop?"

"Me."

"There's internal security here. Surveillance cameras, mics—"

"I know how to take care of that."

He shook his head. "No."

"Done deal, Max." I added, "A chance like this with Landowski out of the house overnight might not come along again this summer, and when opportunity knocks, you answer the door." I informed him, "We do this my way, or you can con another idiot to take this unpaid, unauthorized job."

He thought about that, then said, "I—and you—have to talk to Beth, and she has to talk to her group—"

"No. That is not one of your options. And not one of hers."

He tried another argument. "What will Beth think of you having a date with a hooker?"

"Destiny is cover, Max. Stop busting balls."

Max replied insincerely, "I'm sure Beth trusts you."

I didn't reply.

Max thought a moment and said, "I told her you were

not manageable." He looked at me. "I assume you've calculated all the risks."

"I have calculated all the risks, Max, and all the rewards."

He didn't ask me what the rewards were, but he—and Beth—would know what they were when I called Beth Sunday morning and told her I'd transferred all the files and videotapes of Security Solutions to 26 Federal Plaza.

I said, "Okay, let's not miss any more of the show."

"The show's over for you, John. Landowski thinks you should not interact with his guests any more than you already have."

"I was just getting started."

"Beth will be happy to see you home early."

But probably not happy to see my shirt. Not to mention Amy's lipstick on my dipstick. I said, "Enjoy the show. Take notes."

"Try to smooth things over with Landowski tomorrow."

"He wouldn't fire me after he gave me that great intro."

"He would," Max said, "if Chief Conners tells him to."

Interesting. "Okay, glad I had a chance to meet some of your and Landowski's friends and colleagues." I added, "I haven't seen police and political corruption like this since I was in Yemen."

Max had no reply.

We shook hands, and I let him get inside the house before I got in my van so he wouldn't see the van I was driving, which would get the wheels spinning again in his head. Max is not stupid, and he knew my M.O. from the Plum Island case. And he talks to Beth about me. Well, if they came to the right conclusion about why I'd rented a van, and confronted me with their suspicions, I'd just have to tell the truth: I needed my La-Z-Boy. Never swear to your story; just stick to it.

I opened the driver's door, and suddenly, a loud, echoing shot rang out, and as I spun around and drew my Glock, I saw a small explosion overhead. *Fireworks.* Left over from July Fourth—not Chip Quinlan on a search-and-destroy mission. Or Russians. Or Islamic terrorists. Or perps I'd put away. If I was ever found murdered, the answer to the question of "Who would want to kill him?" would be "Everybody."

I holstered my Glock, got in the van, drove onto the farm road, and headed home.

The last piece of my inspired plan was to tell Beth what I'd just told Max. And I saw no reason for her not to agree that my idea of spending Saturday night in the farmhouse with a prostitute was pure genius. Well . . . I might have to phrase it differently.

I checked my rearview and sideview, but no one seemed to be following. I wouldn't have minded a car chase and shoot-out with Chip Quinlan—to relieve the tension—but I had bigger things in mind for Security Solutions, so I did some SDR, surveillance detection route, which consisted of quick turns, sudden stops, and changing speeds and lanes. The only thing I was able to detect was pissed-off motorists.

As I drove toward Beth's house, I thought back on my first day as a PI and a CI, which, all things considered, was not a bad day's work.

But as every smart detective knows, you are not the only one who has plans for you.

CHAPTER 37

As I got closer to my love nest, I started feeling guilty about what had happened with Amy.

Well, in my defense, the flesh is weak, Scotch is strong, and none of this was my idea—not the job with Security Solutions and not the blow job. But that's no excuse for cheating, so if Beth ever asked about Amy, confession would be good for the soul. But outright denial is much better. Everyone wins.

I needed to call Beth, but first I needed to call Amy. I wasn't sure of the etiquette here. Maybe a text would do. Or, etiquette aside and deniability foremost, maybe it's best not to put anything in a text and not make a call that could be recorded.

But . . . despite my many shortcomings as a husband or a boyfriend, I am a gentleman. If you get oral sex, you say thanks. It's that simple. Just don't say, "Thanks for the oral sex." So I texted: THANKS FOR THE AFTER-WORK DRINK. I wasn't going to tell her I'd left T.T. early because she might ask me to stop by for a nightcap, which I'd do if I was unattached, but I wasn't, so I texted: SEE YOU TOMORROW.

Well, that was just the right balance of polite thank-you and cool guy.

Now for Beth. I dialed her cell.

She answered, "Hi, John. Where are you?"

"About ten minutes from home."

"Why so early?"

"Did Max call you?"

"No. Why did you leave early?"

"I'd rather be with you tonight, darling."

"You were supposed to stay and observe." She reminded me, "You will need to submit a sworn affidavit—"

"Max is still there. I'll copy his." I added, "I thought you'd be happy I left early."

"I'm not happy that you didn't follow through on this assignment."

"To tell you the truth, I was getting a little uncomfortable there." I explained, "The girls were sort of aggressive and I got manhandled—girl-handled—by a few of them, and—"

"Who is this? What have you done to John Corey? I want to speak to him right now."

Funny. "Okay, to tell you the real truth, I had some words with Chip Quinlan, so I thought it best to leave." I added, "Also, as Max will tell you, I made a few impromptu remarks to the guests that Max—and Landowski— thought may have caused the distinguished guests some discomfort."

Beth was silent, then asked, "Why do you do things like that?"

"Not sure. Dr. Wilkes—that's the FBI shrink—had a good insight into that. Let me check my notes and get back to you."

She didn't respond to that and said, "I'll unbolt the front door."

I was seriously considering a cleansing dip in the hot tub, so I said, "I'll come around back." But when I pulled into the driveway, Beth opened the front door. Busted.

So I got out of the van, buttoned my blazer, and went up the walk, wondering if the glitter sparkled in the moonlight. Actually, I'd prepared Beth for that. But what was not so easy to explain was the lovelock on my peacock, so I needed to hit the shower and wash away my sins. Or at least the evidence of them.

As I entered the cottage, Beth, wearing jeans and a white T-shirt, stepped aside as though I had a communicable disease, and commented, "You smell of cigarette smoke, beer, and cheap perfume."

Thank God she couldn't smell lipstick. I said, "I've worked with bloodhounds who couldn't do that."

"Bloodhounds are trained by wives and girlfriends."

Funny. But maybe true.

She asked, "Why do you have a van?"

"I'm going to haul my La-Z-Boy out here. And some other stuff I need." Before she could respond to that, I said, "I need a shower." I headed for the bathroom, and so she wouldn't follow, I said, "I could use a drink. Scotch and soda, please. I'll meet you on the patio."

"Don't get glitter on anything."

I got into the bathroom, locked the door, and stripped. The best place for my shirt and boxer shorts was out the window, and that's where I threw them.

I got in the shower and soaped up the barber pole first. It's called lipstick because it's supposed to stick to lips, but it *really* sticks to dicks.

I showered off the rest of the forensic evidence—makeup, perfume, and most of the glitter, while thinking about my imminent debriefing—interrogation—by Detective Sergeant Penrose. I dried off, slipped into a pair of shorts and an NYPD T-shirt, took my Glock, and went out on the patio.

Beth was sitting in a chair, sipping white wine. A Scotch and soda sat on the end table next to a citronella candle which flickered in the breeze, and her cell phone was playing "Sgt. Pepper's Lonely Hearts Club Band."

I sat beside her, and we listened to the music and looked out at the night sky. This is so much better than seven naked women doing the tango with one another. This is so much better than seven naked women doing the tango with one another. This is so much better—

"John?"

"Yes, dear?"

"How did it go tonight?"

"As I said, not all good. But I did start to bond with Landowski and Joseph Ferrara, and I reconnected with Lou Santangelo."

"Good. But what happened with Chip Quinlan?"

"He's crazy." I added, "I think he did kill Sharon Hite."

She stayed silent, then said, "Please be careful of him."

"He needs to be careful of me."

"No. You need to ratchet down your alpha male and be a team player for the next two months."

Well, that wasn't going to happen. And that was yet another reason for me to wrap it up this weekend.

I sipped my drink as Billy Joel was singing "New York State of Mind."

Beth said, "Brief me on your day at Security Solutions."

"Okay . . . I got in at about twelve-thirty. That's when I had my first run-in with Quinlan." I gave Beth a redacted version of that and a redacted version of my conversations with Kim and Judy, and also Amy. I got up to quitting time, and this is where the briefing would need very creative editing while still being accurate and truthful, in case the after-work drink came out in an FBI investigation or a court hearing, so I said, "Amy and I went into Steve's downstairs office and had a drink."

"Whose idea was that?"

"Not mine."

"Continue."

"She showed me how to shut off the hidden surveillance camera and the mic—"

"Why?"

Two reasons. But Beth needed only one. "Because she wanted privacy while she complained about her boss."

"Why was she complaining to *you*?"

"Maybe because I'm the new guy. Who else is she going to complain to?"

"Or she's using the old trick of playing the disgruntled employee to see if you're an undercover agent who's trying to recruit her."

"That crossed my mind."

"But don't forget the possibility that her interest in you may actually be romantic." She added, "As unlikely as that may be."

"Right. I'll keep you informed." On a need-to-know basis. "Can I get you another wine?"

"No." She asked, "Do you have any credible reason to believe that she or Landowski or Berger or anyone else there suspects that you're a CI?"

I did, but if I said so, I'd be unemployed before I finished my drink. I assured her, "Aside from my speech tonight, Landowski thinks he's made the best hire since Nero Wolfe hired Archie Goodwin. And that's all that counts." I added, "Let's not get paranoid."

"All right, how long were you with her?"

"Who . . . ? Oh . . . maybe thirty minutes. Then she had to go help set up for the party."

"What did you do after your drink with Amy?"

I pulled up my pants and answered your text. "I snooped around Landowski's office, of course, taking advantage of the surveillance camera and mic being off."

"Find anything?"

"A trapdoor to the basement which could be useful. Other than that, there was nothing of interest in that office, which is sort of a showcase for clients." And a good place for Landowski's weekly job interviews. I added, "More likely there'll be something of interest in Landowski's upstairs office. Or maybe something stored in the locked basement."

"Okay. But if I—or my group—decide that you should stay on this assignment, I don't want you to get caught snooping around." She reminded me, "You're there as a CI to listen, to observe—"

"Right." I let her know, "A lot of the power structure of this county was there tonight, so I'm fairly sure that no local police are going to ask the county DA to ask a local judge to issue a search warrant for that farmhouse. Or if they do, someone will tip off Landowski, and he knows that, so I'm equally sure he feels it's safe to keep incriminating evidence on the premises."

"We feel the same way." She added, "While we were in Bermuda, there was no indication that Landowski was moving anything out of the farmhouse."

"Good. So I would like to snoop around the farmhouse one night."

"I just said that would be too risky. Max says that Landowski has electronic security and surveillance cameras in every room."

"I've been trained on how to neutralize that. And it would be a shame to waste the opportunity."

"What opportunity?"

"I'm glad you asked. So, as it turns out, and as I've told Max, who will tell you, Landowski is going on vacation with his kids, leaving tomorrow afternoon. Jersey Shore and Atlantic City. And one of my job perks is the use of a guest room if I should need a place to stay. So I have booked a room for this Saturday night."

Beth processed that, then asked, "Why would you need a room there?"

"Because Uncle Harry is coming out this weekend with his girlfriend, who is a tight-ass, so I can't take the hooker to my room in Harry's house."

Beth said, "I think I missed something."

"All the hotels, motels, and B and Bs on the North Fork are booked this weekend."

"Something else." She gave me a hint. "The hooker."

"Oh. Right. Her name is Destiny. One of Chrystal's girls." I explained, "Chrystal is sort of the house mother for the exotic dancers. Some of whom supplement their artistic income as escorts."

"So you engaged the services of a prostitute."

"Destiny. Just for show, of course. I don't do hookers."

"That's good to hear. And you know that prostitution and soliciting prostitutes for paid sex is a crime."

"Is that still on the books?"

"I can't allow you to break the law, John, even to look for evidence of other criminal activity."

"As you know, an undercover cop posing as a john is only breaking the law if he actually engages in a sexual—"

"All right, let's assume you don't do that. What's the plan?"

"The plan is for me to go to the farmhouse Saturday night, and at nine P.M. Destiny arrives and we may have a drink on the patio, then we go to my room, and about midnight or earlier, Destiny calls a car service and leaves. Then I begin my snooping." Actually, my burglary of the farmhouse. But why mention that?

"But all this is being recorded on videotape, and this can be seen live by Landowski if he has a laptop with him and access to the Internet."

"I can make certain that he doesn't see anything."

"How?"

"There are a few ways to do that, but the easiest way is an Internet failure at about midnight."

"That would arouse his suspicion, knowing you were in the house."

True, but I replied, "I'm picturing Landowski either asleep at that hour, or at the gaming tables, or involved with his own hooker in his hotel room."

She thought of another problem, which she's good at, and said, "If there is a hidden camera in the guest bedroom, what do you do with *your* hooker in the room *before* midnight when the camera is still recording and still sending out signals in real time that Landowski can see?"

I was going to put a sheet over the two-way vanity mirror to block the hidden camera, and watch TV with Destiny, but I sensed the possibility of an entertaining conversation, so I said, "I hadn't really thought about that. What do you suggest?"

"I suggest you forget this idea and we go to your condo and have a nice weekend in the city." She added, "I'll help you load the La-Z-Boy into your van."

"We can do that next weekend. As for Destiny in my room . . . I guess we could watch TV while Landowski may be watching us. Then I fall asleep . . . maybe pretend I drank too much."

"Sounds like my last two boyfriends."

Not that funny.

"I have an idea," she said. "You can pretend you're an amateur photographer and you can take pictures of her posing in the nude." She assured me, "That's not illegal."

"Not a bad idea. Or I can be an artist. I'll buy an easel—"

"What are you paying her?"

"Half my paycheck. Five hundred."

"That's almost two hundred an hour. Maybe I should consider a career change."

"You'd easily get three hundred an hour."

"I think more."

"Didn't mean to insult you."

I thought it was time to put Beth's mind at ease about me being in a bedroom alone for three hours with a hooker. "The hidden camera is undoubtedly behind the two-way vanity mirror—as per Max, who seemed to know—and I can block it with a sheet, so Landowski will not see anything going out live, and nothing will be recorded in that room. So I don't have to spend three hours pretending to . . . do something with Destiny."

"Well, that's a relief, John. I feel much better." She pointed out, "And since Landowski can't see you live in the bedroom and you won't be videotaped, you can actually get your money's worth and fuck Destiny."

Did I detect a note of sarcasm? "You're going to have to trust me."

She looked at me. "I do trust you not to have sex with a hooker. But I don't trust this plan you've come up with, so this is not going to happen." She reiterated, "No snooping."

It was time to take charge of this. I sat at the edge of my chair, made eye contact, and said, "Here's the deal, Beth. It's either my way, or I'm out."

"I *want* you out. I told you that."

"Then this works for everyone." I stood. "I'll be packed and out of here in an hour."

She stood and took my hand. "I don't want you out of my life. I just want you out of Security Solutions." She added, "I have a bad feeling about this."

"I don't." Actually, I did. But that never stopped me before. I didn't want Beth consulting with her group on this because that would greatly increase the chances of a security leak, but that might be the only way to save this plan, so I said, "Take this idea to your group."

"My group doesn't know who you are, so they don't know what a reckless asshole you can be."

"I'll be happy to brief them on that."

She continued, "Max wants you on this case, and my group is thrilled that we have someone inside Security Solutions. But none of those people love you like I do, and they won't miss you like I would if something happened to you."

We looked at each other, and I knew she was speaking from the heart. The job always gets complicated when you're working a dangerous assignment with someone you have any kind of emotional or romantic tie to. Kate and I had that problem—until each of us wanted the other one dead. Just kidding.

I said to Beth, "I feel the same about you. But just let me do this snooping on Saturday—then I'll feel I've accomplished something for you and for your group and your investigation. Then, if you want, I'll turn in my resignation at Security Solutions and my resignation from this case." Which was true, because it would all be over, one way or the other, this weekend.

She thought about that, then looked at me. "If you promise me you won't take any unnecessary risks. And promise you'll ditch this plan if you think that anyone at Security Solutions is onto you. Really promise."

"I promise."

"And promise me that Destiny is just there for cover."
She smiled to show she trusted me.

I smiled in return. "We'll play board games for three
hours."

Beth seemed to be thinking, then said half-jokingly, "If
Amy gets wind of the hooker, John, she might think less
of you."

Or worse, she might see through my romantic evening
in the farmhouse with an exotic dancer and conclude that
I was up to something. Well . . . all bold plans have major
problems, but the risk was worth the reward. And the
reward was a total takedown of Security Solutions and
everyone there who was complicit in whatever criminal
activity they were involved in. Not to mention exposing a
lot of crooked politicians and dirty cops. And maybe solving the Fire Island murders and the murders of Sharon
Hite and Dan Perez. Very big rewards. Justice. National
media coverage. And the answer to a lot of people's questions about what I was doing with my life. The John Corey
legend continues. *That's* what I'm doing with my life.

"Hello? John?"

I said jokingly, "I'm sure Amy thinks I'm a saint compared to the pigs she works with."

She had no comment on that and said, "All right . . .
I'll take this up with my group." She added, "Against my
better judgment and because I trust you, I'll tell them I
recommend they approve of your plan to snoop around
the farmhouse on Saturday night."

"You won't regret your decision."

"I'll know soon enough."

You will. When I call you from 26 Federal Plaza.
So at this point, if Detective Penrose put two and two
together—the van and my Saturday night at Security

Solutions—she might deduce that reckless John was not in the farmhouse to snoop; reckless John was going to pull off a heist. And maybe it *had* passed through her mind, but she dismissed it as too crazy even for me. Hopefully, she—and Max and her group—wouldn't think too long or hard on this.

As for Amy Lang and my other colleagues at Security Solutions, they were all accustomed to overnight guests in the honeymoon suites, and it was hardly a subject of gossip or concern. So everything was in place—Landowski out of town, Saturday-night hooker, U-Haul van to move stuff out of there, and my knowledge of how to overcome the security system. Add to that a set of brass balls and a Glock, and everything was ready to go.

To get on a different topic, I said, "I'm starved."

"Don't they serve food at Thirsty Thursdays?"

"Deli buffet. But I was busy working the room."

"I'm sure you were feasting your eyes." She said, "I'll get you something," and went into the house.

I brought the citronella candle to the patio table and sat, sipping my Scotch and thinking about exotic dancers and prostitutes. And crooked politicians and dirty cops. And also about dedicated public servants and good, clean, honest cops, like Beth and her group. We all begin our journey in pretty much the same place, attached to an umbilical cord. Then somebody cuts us loose, and somebody gives us a name and a birth certificate. But the birth certificate doesn't say "policeman" or "prostitute" or "murderer" or "disbarred lawyer." There are many paths that can be taken on this journey from the womb to the tomb. Detective Sergeant Beth Penrose took one path, Chrystal took another. Detective John Corey and Detective Steve Landowski started on the same path, but he made a wrong turn.

Hard to know how or why this happens. If anyone should know, it should be a homicide cop, but I don't know.

Beth came out of the cottage carrying a tray which she set down on the table. I expected green salad and kombucha, but I saw pigs in a blanket and beer. I'm in love.

Beth sat, and we hoisted our beer bottles and clinked. She said, "Pigs for the piggy, because you had a long, hard day."

Now I was really feeling guilty about Amy—though not guilty enough to lose my appetite. Or confess.

But as though reading my mind, Beth said, "If something happened between you and Amy while you were drinking Scotch in Landowski's office with the electronic surveillance shut off, I will assume it was just a moment of passing lust and didn't mean anything. And/or you thought you could recruit her, and she thought she could get you to confide to her your true purpose at Security Solutions." She added, "It's part of the dirty job that I got you into, and it's okay."

Of course it is not. This interrogation trick—if you confess, you'll feel better and I'll forgive you—needed a carefully worded response. "Nothing happened."

"Okay. I won't mention it again."

Until next time. But if all went right Saturday night, there would be no next time with Amy Lang.

Beth said, "Brief me on exotic-dancer night."

"I'm not sure I can do justice to the evening."

"Try."

"Okay . . . there were seven young ladies who cartwheeled onto the dance floor—"

"I don't care about the ladies, John. I care about the men who were there."

"Right. Okay, so there were about thirty men, about

half of them cops, including, you'll be happy to know, Police Chief Conners. Also Police Chief Larry Jenkins, and some politicians—"

"Was my boss, Lieutenant Stuckley, there?"

"Don't know. Ask Max."

"Please continue."

So, as I dined on pigs and beer, I briefed Detective Sergeant Penrose on Landowski's guests, and because she would also be briefed by bigmouth Max, I shared with her my impromptu remarks that may have caused the guests some discomfort. And before she asked again, "Why do you do things like that?" I explained that someday— hopefully sooner than we thought—we would be getting possession of the videotape that recorded tonight's event, which would show me, the star government witness, being there and IDing Chief Conners. I added, "A video is worth a thousand-word affidavit."

She nodded, then said, "Smart."

"That's what I do."

She said, "Now that you've met Edward Conners, what do you think about him being a prime suspect in the Fire Island murders?"

"Well . . . he fits a lot of the psychological profiles of a serial killer who murders prostitutes."

She nodded. "And he's in a unique position to cover his crimes. Which explains why we've had no breaks in this case."

That could be true. And sabotage from within was a good explanation for the Homicide Division's many failures on this high-profile case. "Right. But not easy to prove." I reminded her, "The witnesses are all dead."

"The people who disposed of those nine bodies are alive and having a party with Conners right now." She added, "We'll need to get one of them to crack."

Which is how you crack a case when you have not one shred of forensic or documentary evidence, or even circumstantial evidence. But Chip Quinlan was not going to crack, because he'd committed an actual murder himself. And Landowski and Santangelo were accessories to that murder. It would not be in the best interest of any of those three assholes to admit they removed dead prostitutes from a honeymoon suite in the farmhouse, or from some other bedroom that Chief of Police Edward Conners had just used. Assuming Beth's theory or suspicion about Conners being the sole serial killer was correct.

"John?"

"The facts fit the theory, but the theory is a theory without facts."

"Thank you, Professor." She inquired, "Did people actually pay for your course?"

Funny. "I'd like to think I sent some good criminal investigators out into the world."

"I'm sure you did. And probably a few educated criminals."

"Could be."

"Think about Conners."

"Okay."

"Please continue."

So I continued my eyewitness report of the farmhouse follies.

Beth listened with no interruption as I described, with appropriate revulsion, the behavior of the distinguished guests on the dance floor—including Lady Godiva's horse. I concluded, "If—when—we get our hands on the tape that recorded all this, and tapes of other Thirsty Thursdays, you'll see faces you'll probably recognize: judges, police brass, and politicians, all giving in to their most primitive urges—with a little help from the booze, music, and naked ladies, and to be honest, it was a little shocking to watch these high-profile and successful men who have been sworn to public service, and who have a lot to lose, behaving like pigs in heat in front of each other." I added, "Then there are the tapes from the guest bedrooms."

She nodded. "Someday we will get those tapes and everything else in that farmhouse."

"I'm sure we will." Early Sunday morning.

So we dined al fresco, had another beer, then went inside to watch a movie. Beth chose a DVD of Hitchcock's *Psycho*—which may have been inspired by a subconscious thought about her boss. Afterwards, we went to bed, and Johnny, who had been pronounced dead at 5:30, had a miraculous recovery.

Interesting day. A death threat, oral sex, a date with a hooker, a strip show . . . This stuff doesn't happen in Bermuda. And yet, I'd rather be here than there. If the problem with doing nothing is not knowing when you're done, then the problem with doing something dangerous is not knowing when, where, and how it will end. And that's also the thrill. Sometimes you gotta get off your ass and make your own fun.

CHAPTER 38

Detective Penrose was up and out before I was awake, but she left me a note near the coffeepot: *Considering what happened with Quinlan, and also your remarks to the guests, you might want to call in sick today. Lay low.*

Well, that's a thought. But I actually wouldn't mind another run-in with Quinlan, though I didn't feel like listening to Landowski's crap about my impromptu remarks. And then there was—unbeknownst to Beth—my possibly awkward morning-after conversation with Amy Lang. Also, if Amy had heard about my Saturday-night hooker from Kim or Judy, she would, as Beth said, be disappointed in me. Probably pissed off. Hopefully, Kim and Judy would keep their mouths shut, as requested. Steve Landowski, however, would enjoy telling Amy that John Corey wasn't any better than the rest of the boys. Anyway, this thing with Amy was a complication that I hadn't foreseen. But maybe I had. And it had to be figured into my short-term plans. So, if I didn't go in today, Friday, I could avoid all this, because by Sunday morning there would be no Security Solutions.

But today Judy was going to show me the video surveillance setup in the attic. So I would go in and deal with whatever the day had in store for me. That's what makes life interesting.

There didn't seem to be any reason to get to work at nine, and I was sure that Santangelo, Quinlan, and Ferrara would be home nursing hangovers after Thirsty Thursday. Landowski, who lived there, would probably spend the morning reviewing videotapes from the night before—including replays of my speech and my psycho episode with Chip Quinlan. Also, assuming the two honeymoon suites had been used last night, then Landowski would be enjoying those tapes as well. *Is that Judge Falanger getting a spanking from Chrystal?*

Anyway, I killed some time with texts and e-mails, had leftover pigs for breakfast, then took a long shower to get the last of the glitter off. I put on my khakis and polo shirt, strapped on my pancake holster and Glock, then slipped on my blue blazer. For my Saturday-night caper, I'd want a few extra mags and also my off-duty piece, a Smith & Wesson Model 60 in an ankle holster. Not that I was anticipating any problems, but when it comes to guns and ammo, more is better. I didn't want Beth to see me taking extra hardware on Saturday night, so I threw the two mags and off-duty revolver in the glove compartment of the van and headed to work.

Before I got to the farmhouse, I needed a thank-you gift for Amy. Flowers are what you usually give or send the morning after, but flowers might cause some talk that neither of us wanted.

I saw a winery ahead—East Winds—and pulled into the gravel parking area of the large cedar-shingled building. I went into the wine shop, where a few tourists were wandering around, probably looking for the free cheese and wine that came in tiny tasting cups.

An elderly gentleman approached me. "Can I help you, sir?"

"Yes. I'm looking for a bottle of wine."

He glanced around at the hundreds of bottles of racked wine and replied, "I think you've come to the right place."

"Great."

"Is there anything in particular you're looking for?"

"Red."

"That narrows it down. And do you have a price range in mind?"

"The sky's the limit."

"Is it for you?"

"No. A gift."

"And what is the occasion?"

"It's a thank-you to a young lady for oral sex."

Without a flicker of expression, he said smoothly, "Then I would recommend our 2002 Cabernet Sauvignon." He added, "Not too fruity, a hint of oak, medium body."

I don't know wine from Kool-Aid, so I'd have to trust him to pair the wine with the sex act, and I said, "Sounds good. But she had a great body."

He smiled. "Is there anything else I can get you?"

I was curious about what wine went with the doggie position, but I replied, "That's it for now."

So he got the wine from a rack—forty-five bucks—slipped it in a Mylar sleeve with a ribbon, and said, "I hope she enjoys it as much as you enjoyed the occasion for giving it."

Funny.

Back on the road and a half hour later, I pulled into the parking area of Security Solutions and noted that Amy's car was there, as well as Judy's and Kim's. Landowski's Escalade was where he'd parked it last night, so he hadn't left yet to pick up his kids for vacation. As for Quinlan, Santangelo, and Ferrara, they were still sleeping it off or out on assignment. Jack Berger, who doesn't come to work on Thursdays or Fridays, wasn't here today either. I hope he shows up Monday to see how I'd tidied up his desk for him.

I grabbed the wine, got out of my van, locked it, and climbed the steps to the porch. I punched in my code and entered, striding purposely toward Amy's office, ready for any reception from the receptionist. But Amy's office was empty, so I put the wine on her chair. She'd know it was from me—assuming I was the last guy she'd seen last night.

I looked into Judy and Kim's office, which was also empty. Lunchtime. I glanced at their wall-mounted security monitor, confirming that the four outside cameras did not pick up anything within about six feet of the house. Also, I saw Kim, Judy, and Amy having lunch on the patio.

The house seemed deserted, but I could picture Landowski still in his pj's at noon, sitting in his bed, Hugh Hefner–style, watching reruns of last night on his laptop, and maybe making notes for future blackmail.

I went into the kitchen, which was also empty, and looked out the window. The three ladies were lunching on a platter of sandwiches, obviously scraps left over from the master's bacchanalia.

I watched them chatting, and for all I knew, Kim and Judy were right now telling Amy about my upcoming Saturday-night hooker date. And when Landowski made an appearance, Judy might tell him that I'd volunteered to change the videotapes on the security system this weekend, which might get him thinking—if that was possible. A wise man would have gotten back in his rental van and gone home, texting in sick. But my balls are bigger than my brain, so I went out to the patio to see what the weather was like.

I walked toward the table with an expression that conveyed pleasant surprise at seeing my three favorite women together.

All three ladies were dressed in summer-Friday casual: shorts and designer T-shirts. Amy did not jump up to greet me, but Judy and Kim stood and excused themselves, which was not a good sign.

Amy remained seated, so I sat across from her and asked, "Did you get my text?"

She nodded.

"There's a bottle of wine on your chair from your secret admirer."

She smiled, but it was forced. I think she knew about my Saturday-night date.

I asked, "Is something bothering you?"

"Why do you ask?"

"You don't seem yourself."

"I spent two hours cleaning the Rec Room."

"Why do you have to do that?"

"Because Steve doesn't want the cleaning lady to see what goes on."

Right. G-strings and glitter, pasties, perfume, and perspiration. I could speculate all day and not know why Amy Lang, a good-looking, educated young woman, would be so submissive to her Neanderthal boss. There was more to this than I or Sigmund Freud or even Sherlock Holmes could discover. I suggested, "Just say no."

She shrugged. "Kim and Judy helped with the laundry." She added, "We're a big, happy family."

"And the girls were rewarded with the boys' leftover food."

She had no reply to that and asked, "Did you enjoy Thirsty Thursday?"

"I'd be lying if I said no. But I did leave early."

"Why?"

"Well, as you'll hear if you haven't already, Steve asked me to say a few words to the guests, and I may have said the wrong words. Also, as you know, Chip and I had some words."

She looked at me. "If anyone can stand up to Chip Quinlan, it's you."

"I'm flattered."

"Don't be modest."

"I'm not." So when you've been intimate with someone, you can ask personal questions, and I asked, "Were you ever involved with Steve Landowski?"

She looked off into the distance. "It makes no difference."

"Okay."

We sat there in silence awhile, then she asked me, "What are you doing Saturday night?"

Was she asking me out? Or did Kim or Judy rat me out? Probably Landowski had told her—while she was disinfecting the Rec Room—that I'd booked a room and a hooker.

I replied, "I'm meeting one of the dancers here Saturday night. As you probably know."

She nodded, but I couldn't tell if she was disappointed in me, hurt, angry, or wondering why I'd do that.

I explained, "Seemed like a good idea at the time. You know—trying to fit in here. But in the clear light of day, maybe it's not a good idea."

"You can do whatever you want."

"Okay. Well . . . I might cancel my date. But I don't want to be at my uncle's house with his bitch of a girlfriend, so I'll sleep here this weekend."

I knew she wouldn't offer to keep me company, because she didn't want to be seen with me on the surveillance cameras. But, as with Landowski, I needed to create the illusion that I was thinking of our future after Saturday night—a future that would never come—so

I said, "My uncle and his girlfriend are leaving before noon on Sunday. Why don't you come to my house? We can have lunch, a swim in the bay, then a quiet dinner." Actually, I'd be at 26 Federal Plaza on Sunday, and Amy might be checking out the Internet failure at the farmhouse, stunned to see what that devious, lying bastard John Corey had really been doing in the house overnight. And I *was* feeling like a devious bastard, but . . . this was a criminal investigation, and the ends justified the means. Comes with the territory. I said, "We'll have a nice day."

"Thank you. But you may be too exhausted after your Saturday night."

I explained apologetically, "When I made this date, I wasn't factoring in . . . well, you."

Amy pointed out, "I was very nice to you in Steve's office *before* you went upstairs and asked Steve for a room and asked Chrystal for a woman."

So it *was* Landowski who'd told her. Asshole. I replied, "Guilty as charged. But I was still in the mind-set of showing off in front of the boys. And what happened with us in Steve's office was . . . unexpected. So I went ahead with—"

"All right. Enough said." She added, "I also have a date Saturday night. But I will come to your house on Sunday." She gave me a snide smile. "We can compare notes on our Saturday nights."

I returned her smile, but with some contriteness. "I guess I deserve some tit for tat." Was that the right expression to use? "Some payback for my stupid . . . whatever." I suggested, "On Sunday, let's pick up where we left off on Thursday." Which, if I recall, was her hasty exit to meet the deli guy after the blow job.

She wasn't through with this topic. "When you were

drinking with the boys last night, did you claim the pool money?"

"Excuse me? The . . . what?"

"The fuck-Amy pool, John. Someone must have told you."

"Well . . . let me think . . . as a matter of fact, Lou did say something—"

"So did you claim the pool?"

"I don't kiss and tell."

"But if you do, someone might object that oral sex doesn't count. So you can say you fucked me, and I'll back you up if you'll split the pool with me." She smiled.

I suggested, "Let's see if I can make a legitimate claim after Sunday."

"We'll see."

To make sure she understood this wasn't all about sex, I said, "I like you. And I enjoy your company." Which was true. Even if she *was* poison.

"I feel the same. You're interesting." We made eye contact. She asked, "What are you doing tonight?"

I was going to go home to my live-in girlfriend. But . . . I just had a better and brighter idea. I said, "I'm going to meet some friends—guys—for TGIF drinks." I added, "And rather than deal with Harry's bitch girlfriend, maybe I'll crash here. Steve will be out of town, so I won't be intruding on his plans."

"And if you get lucky tonight, you have a room." Amy smiled.

I returned the smile. "If I don't get lucky, I'll give you a call."

"I'll be sitting by the phone all night."

We both got a chuckle out of that. Well, I was liking Amy even more. She was too good to be true. In fact, she may have been playacting more than I was. I said, "So, we're on for Sunday."

"Look forward to it."

"Me too."

She stood. "I have to get back to my desk."

I stood, but we didn't kiss for the camera. "See you later."

She went back into the house, leaving the tray of sandwiches. I would have had one, but I knew where they came from.

More importantly, sometimes you need to change plans on the spot, and you need to be flexible. But always keep the goal in mind. So I wouldn't be here Saturday night with Destiny, or ransacking this place after she left. I also wouldn't be trying to win the fuck-Amy pool on Sunday. Or having drinks tonight with friends, or dinner with Beth. In fact, there was no reason why I shouldn't be here *tonight*, at Security Solutions, a day early, doing what I'd planned to do Saturday night. That's how you trick people and trick Fate—by breaking your date with Destiny. Usually works.

CHAPTER 39

Back in the farmhouse, I was ready for round three with Chip Quinlan, but Judy told me that he and Lou Santangelo were taking a long weekend and driving to Mohegan Sun, the Indian hotel and casino in Connecticut. Also, Joseph Ferrara was on assignment in the Hamptons. And Jack Berger didn't work Fridays. So I was the only cock in the roost, aside from Steve Landowski, who lived here, though the two ladies had not seen him yet. Hopefully, he was packing for his vacation.

I spent some time in Judy and Kim's office and was happy to learn that it was payday. Judy cashed my check again, which was good, because Security Solutions checks wouldn't be worth anything next week when the Feds froze all their assets.

To earn my pay as a consultant, I asked the two ladies to give me a tour of their file cabinets, which they did, showing me how they kept track of their cases and showing me the files on all their freelance PIs, past and present. I was sure that some of these freelancers did work for Steve Landowski, which was not noted in the files but maybe was stored elsewhere, like the basement. I was also sure the FBI would like to interview all these freelancers.

Judy showed me the files of all the moonlighting cops who Security Solutions had hired to do jobs like premises security, bodyguards, chauffeurs, and event security for, say, parties in the Hamptons. Guys like this, who blend into the background, see and hear more than people realize. Especially chauffeurs, who might be used to pick up and deliver hookers to the clients. So the moonlighting-cop files would go in my van tonight. This was exciting.

I asked to see the personnel files, which Kim said were confidential but which Judy said I could see because I was a consultant. Judy likes me.

I looked first at my own file, which consisted of my contract and nondisclosure statement, and the personnel form I'd filled out. There was no note in the file saying, *Possible informant—may need to whack him*, which was good.

On that subject, I looked for Sharon Hite's file, but it wasn't there and had probably gone through the shredder, along with Sharon's case file on Tiffany Sanders.

I saw the personnel files for Quinlan, Santangelo, Ferrara, and other PIs who once worked here, but there was no file for Jack Berger, who, I was sure, left as little evidence of his employment here as possible.

I asked Judy if they kept records of Thirsty Thursdays—guest lists, costs of food and entertainment, and so forth, and she replied, "Steve keeps those."

Right.

Kim showed me some of her computer files and programs, and I feigned lack of interest, like a larcenous overnight houseguest who was being shown around by his hostess as she pointed out all the valuable art that he intended to steal.

I wasn't sure what, if anything, was in the basement, and whatever was there wouldn't be obviously incriminating. But dark deeds leave shadow evidence if you know what you're looking for.

The world of private investigative services is mostly legit, but the opportunity and the temptation were there to enter the gray areas, and when you did that, the next shades of gray got darker, then turned black, and before you knew it, you were picking up dead hookers at some rich guy's house, or right here in the honeymoon suites, and dumping the bodies someplace. Security Solutions would not be the first PI agency that had gone to the dark side, but Steve Landowski had taken this to a whole new subterranean level.

On the subject of Chief of Police Edward Conners, there probably would not be one hint of evidence here to link him to the Fire Island murders, which could have occurred here, or somewhere like a hot-sheet motel or a rented safe house. On the other hand, if Steve Landowski wanted his hands firmly on Conners's balls, he'd have *something* hidden somewhere that Conners knew about and which made them blood partners in crime. Right?

Well, the FBI agents would have their work cut out for them when I delivered all this stuff to Federal Plaza tomorrow morning. And they had the resources to wade through all the files and go through the computers. And they were happiest when they were reading other people's files and e-mails.

In any case, the stuff that Judy and Kim were showing me was mostly the legitimate end of Security Solutions, though within those files were links to the criminal side of this business, evidence of which might be in Landowski's upstairs office or, more likely, in the so-called wine cellar, where I'd begin my heist tonight. Also in the basement or the attic would be the videotapes of all the Thirsty Thursdays and the tapes from the hidden cameras in the honeymoon suites. A picture is worth a thousand words. A videotape of prominent men fucking hookers is worth even more.

And finally, I'd empty the contents of Amy's desk. Maybe I'd leave her a note. And the note would say, *Sorry*.

I hoped, though, that Amy Lang was not mixed up in any of this, and she'd be free of this place and go on to the Police Academy and graduate, and get her rookie assignment in a nice precinct in Manhattan. Maybe someday I'd pull up next to a police car at a light and she'd be behind the wheel. We'd look at one another and smile. Maybe she'd call out, "Is that the famous John Corey?"

I'd give her a little salute and say, "Have a good day, Officer. And a good life."

She'd give me a wink, then move through the red light and leave me there, remembering our brief time together . . .

"John?"

I looked at Judy.

"I asked, how was last night?"

"Last night . . . ? Oh, it was okay. But I left early."

Judy had no response, but Kim asked, "Did you speak to Steve about ladies' night?"

"Yes. We're on." I smiled.

Kim and Judy broke into wide grins. I love to make people happy. I said, "We'll do it when Steve is gone. You pick the night."

"Monday," said Judy, and Kim agreed.

I said, "Check with Amy to see if she's free." She might be in jail. "And invite some friends. I'll book the entertainment." I added, "Order some food and wine and take it out of my next paycheck."

Kim and Judy seemed excited and Kim asked, "Will you be there?"

No. And neither will you. In fact, this place will be an FBI crime scene. But I said, "I'll make the intro to your dancer, then leave you ladies alone to enjoy the night."

Kim said, "You can stay. Have a drink with us."

"Let's see how it goes."

They both thanked me, and again I felt like a real prick. But when you're undercover and earning the trust and confidence of suspects and witnesses, you always leave a wake of destruction behind you. You betray people. You lie. Truth and justice is a bitch.

I changed the subject and said to Kim and Judy, "Amy seemed to know about my Saturday-night date."

Both ladies looked surprised. Kim said, "We didn't say anything."

I believed them, confirming that Steve Landowski was the rat. Asshole.

So, in the grand scheme of things, Amy finding out about my date wasn't so important, except that it had gotten me thinking about pulling off the heist tonight— which, all things considered, would be better and safer, because if Landowski suspected I was up to something, he'd think it was for Saturday or another night while he was gone, and he'd be glued to his laptop. Also, Beth's group—or Beth herself—might decide to veto my Saturday night here, out of an abundance of caution. There was also the possibility of a leak in Beth's group, which always has to be factored in. So if you think the enemy has intel about the time and place of your attack, and you can't change the place, then you change the time.

Or you abort. Which was still an option. When a man is not thinking with his dick, he should be able to think more clearly with his brain, except if he happens to have big balls. Then the balls take charge. And when that happens, the answer to the question "Are you crazy?" is Yes.

CHAPTER 40

It was time for the three o'clock coffee break, and I followed Kim and Judy into the hallway and glanced in Amy's office, but she wasn't there, and neither was she in the kitchen nor on the patio, though I'd seen her car on the monitor in Kim and Judy's office.

On the kitchen table was a platter of cookies from last night, and Kim and Judy dove in. I made myself a coffee and sat with the ladies, who asked me about my Florida vacation, which was actually in Bermuda. I'd shoveled a lot of bullshit here, including where I was living, and if I stayed at Security Solutions for the summer, as Beth had planned, it would be only a matter of time before the bullshit caught up with me, and before my new colleagues, Steve, Lou, and Chip, invited me to go night fishing with them on Fire Island. Well, the best defense is always a good offense. And the best offense is always a surprise attack.

If all went well tonight, the resulting criminal trials—maybe dozens of them—would be one hell of a show, and I couldn't wait to take the stand. With luck, the Federal prosecutor would show the jury the tape of last night's party, with my snide speech to the assembled guests. I'd be the golden boy of the media, the man who had the balls to mock these powerful men to their faces, and then, the very next night, pull a one-man raid on the secure premises and seize the evidence that led to the multiple indictments and trials of dozens of people—police brass, politicians, judges, government officials, and private investigators—on charges ranging from human trafficking to murder. If that's not worth a TV movie, I don't know what is. And, of course, justice would be done.

"John?"

I looked at Judy.

"I asked if you were sure you'd be here Saturday and Sunday at five to put in fresh tapes."

"No problem."

I was wondering where Amy had disappeared to, and just as I was about to ask, Landowski, wearing a black skintight T-shirt, strode into the kitchen and said to me, "You got a minute?"

There was no "Hey, John," and he didn't look happy.

I excused myself and followed Landowski into the hallway, noticing a suitcase and overnight bag at the foot of the stairs. He got right to the point. "I got some blowback from some of my guests last night."

"That's odd. I thought the girls were terrific."

"About *you*, John. About you telling some guys that you used to work Internal Affairs and you put some Vice cops away."

"You wanted me to brag about—"

"Not about *that*. And your speech was not very appreciated."

"My speech? I couldn't have been more complimentary to your guests."

He seemed frustrated—the way stupid people get who think they're talking to a stupid person. He said, "You need to read the room, pal. You need some lessons in . . . like, what you're saying and who you're saying it to."

"Okay. Tell me."

He hesitated, then said, "These are good guys, doing

a tough job, and they need to blow off steam once in a while."

"Couldn't agree more."

"Yeah, so you don't . . . like, tell them maybe they shouldn't be there."

"Never said that, Steve." Let's look at the tape.

He looked at me. "Chief Conners wasn't here. Understand?"

I guess it was time for my slow-witted awareness of what he was saying—before he fired me. "Okay . . . yeah. I get what you're saying. I guess I screwed up. Sorry." Asshole.

"We'll talk about this when I get back."

"Right." *Hasta la vista.* "Have a good time with your kids." Next time you see them, there'll be a sheet of Plexiglas between you, and your untucked shirt will be orange.

But he wasn't leaving just yet and said, "I told Chip to stay away from you while I'm gone. And you do the same. I don't want to hear about any shit."

"Right. We'll shake hands when you get back."

"And I hear you got ladies' night booked for Monday."

Good news travels fast. "Right."

"That's one and done. And don't be telling the girls they can buy shit for the office while I'm away. I got these girls trained." He suggested, "Don't fuck this place up while I'm gone."

You ain't seen nothing yet. "I'm here to help."

"We're a big, happy family. And while I'm gone, Ferrara is in charge. You listen to him, and you go to Jack if you got questions or problems."

"Will do."

"Judy says you'll change the tapes Saturday and Sunday night."

"Correct."

"Don't screw it up."

Steve was practically begging for my fist in his balls, but this was a time for delayed gratification. Tonight, I'd shove his world up his ass. "Judy is going to show me later."

"Yeah. " He asked, "You spending the whole weekend here with what's-her-name?"

"Destiny. I'll play it by ear."

"How many times can you fuck a fat hooker?"

Three? Actually, the question seemed rhetorical, but I replied, "I'll let you know."

He hadn't said anything about me going out on a bender tonight and sleeping it off here, so apparently, Amy hadn't mentioned it to him. And even if she had, Landowski wouldn't think anything of it—unless he was becoming suspicious about John Corey. But it sounded like he was more pissed off than suspicious. And if he *was* starting to get suspicious about why I was here, he'd think back to how I blew off his original job offer, then insisted on my terms, including a vacation. That didn't sound like a man who was trying to penetrate Security Solutions. Right?

I heard a sound at the top of the stairs and saw Amy coming down, carrying a beach bag. Hers? Landowski's? We made eye contact, and I had the feeling she'd heard some—maybe all—of this conversation.

Landowski said to me, so Amy could hear, "I banged Carmen once. That's the one you shoulda picked. Hot tamale."

I didn't reply.

"Second-best blow job I ever had." He tilted his head toward Amy on the stairs, smiled, and winked.

Now he was pissing *me* off. And I would have defended Amy's honor, but . . . the mission comes first.

Amy put the beach bag next to Landowski's luggage and said to him, "I think I got everything you need for the beach."

"Okay. Let's move." He grabbed his wheeled suitcase and headed for the front door, leaving Amy—or me—to carry his overnight bag and beach bag. Amy grabbed both, but I took the overnight bag from her, and we followed Landowski out to his Escalade.

He opened the hatch and threw in his suitcase, saying, "That bitch is gonna complain that I'm late. Every time I take the kids, she picks a fight."

Amy handed him his beach bag, and I tossed the overnight bag in the back as he closed the hatch. He said to Amy, "I hope the place you booked on the beach isn't a dump. Wednesday, I'll be checking in at Golden Nugget in A.C. Call only if there's something Jack or Joseph can't handle."

Amy nodded.

He got in his SUV, closed the door, lowered the window, and said to me, "Next Thursday is date night upstairs, and you'll be here. Bring your own if you got one. If you don't, Amy can call somebody from a list. Okay? I invited some guys from Yaphank. And you'll kiss ass to make up for last night. I wanna hear only good shit. Understand?"

Actually, by Thursday, Security Solutions would be re-named Secured Premises, and the invited guests would become persons of interest. But I replied, "I understand." Dickhead.

He said to Amy, "If you use my downstairs office this week, wash the glasses this time." He raised his window, pulled out, and got on the road, leaving us in the dust.

I looked at Amy, who seemed relieved to see the boss go, but also seemed angry and embarrassed. I moved closer to the side of the house where the surveillance camera couldn't see us having an intense conversation. She nodded in understanding and joined me.

I said, "I'll wash the glasses next time." Hell, I'll even shampoo the rug.

She didn't respond for a few seconds, then said, "He came down last night after the party, I think with one of the girls, and took her in his office. He saw that the mic and camera were turned off . . . and he saw the glasses with my lipstick, and he asked me about it this morning . . . so I said you and I had a drink after work."

"Right." Same as I said to Beth. "What's the problem?"

She looked at me. "He ran an ultraviolet light over my glass, and it revealed semen."

I wonder where that came from? I said, "That's sick. What did he say?"

"Doesn't matter."

"You're allowed a private life." I reminded her, "It was after five."

"This is his house."

"Excuse me, this house has more semen in it than a sperm bank."

She nodded. "It's . . . I don't know . . . he doesn't like it when he doesn't know everything that's going on here." She added, "He's a control freak."

And maybe a little jealous. Or sorry he couldn't see the blow job on videotape. "He doesn't own you. Or does he?"

She didn't reply.

So, apparently, Amy Lang and Steve Landowski had a past relationship, and for all I knew, Ms. Lang and her sociopathic boss still had something twisted going on. And maybe that was another reason he was pissed at me this morning. To be provocative, and because I truly wanted to know, I asked her, "How can you work here? *Why* do you work here?"

She looked at me. "I was going to ask you the same question."

Because I'm a confidential informant for the police. Why else would I be here? And I think she suspected something along those lines. And if Landowski did too, then he and Amy had scripted this whole unpleasant scene. But it could be real. In any case, she'd raised the question of why I was working here, which gave me the opening, so I said, "I'd like to talk to you about that. About working here."

We made eye contact.

"Sunday." I said, "When we're alone."

She nodded. "When you first walked in here . . . I knew that things were not going to be the same."

That's for sure. "Me too."

She took a deep breath. "Okay. Back to work."

"I'll be along shortly."

She started for the door, then turned, gave me a quick peck on the lips, bounded up to the porch, and disappeared through the front door.

Well, if they gave Academy Awards for bullshit, Amy and I would be nominees.

Or . . . my suspicious nature and my professional cynicism—which made me a great detective—were keeping me from believing that Amy Lang was who she seemed to be: a young woman with self-esteem issues, suffering from Stockholm syndrome—who also had a crush on me and was reaching out to me for help.

So, Amy Lang. Receptionist in distress? Or deceptionist out to entrap me?

Well, chivalry is not dead. But a lot of chivalrous guys are. You gotta be careful.

CHAPTER 41

I sat at my desk with a stack of case files, demonstrating to Kim and Judy my dedication to Security Solutions, while thinking about how I was going to bust this place tonight.

I understood that too much of my plan depended on too many people who had to keep their mouth shut, or tell the right lies to the right people at the right time, and/or believe my bullshit. And if your operational plan depends on all that, it has a shelf life of less than twenty-four hours—if that. So I had to move quickly. Or just bag it. The next few hours would give me the answer to that.

I got my company cell phone from my desk and went out to the patio with a beer and texted Chrystal, confirming Destiny for 9 P.M. Saturday. Destiny, unfortunately, would not find me here Saturday, but she would find the FBI Evidence Response Team here, searching and securing the premises. I could picture Destiny ringing the doorbell, telling the agents that she was here to fuck a guy named Jack, and she wasn't leaving until she fucked someone and got paid. FBI agents tend to be humorless, but they'd invite her in to chat. Maybe she'd offer to share a joint with them. Or offer to fuck one of them. Maybe both. I'd love to see how the FBI writes up that interview on their 302.

Anyway, it was important for me to confirm Saturday night so that if Landowski or his PIs happened to be in contact with Chrystal for any reason, it would appear that I'd be keeping my date with Destiny.

I took a sip of beer, then called Beth on my cell phone. I wasn't sure what I was going to say to her about my change of plans, but sometimes it's better to play it by ear than to rehearse a line of bullshit. You sound more truthful that way.

She answered, "Hi, John."

"Hi. You still at work?"

"Leaving soon. Where are you?" she asked.

"I decided to come to work and meet the beast."

"How'd it go?"

"Okay. Quinlan wasn't here. He and Santangelo are at Mohegan Sun. Berger is off today, and Landowski gave me his opinion of my behavior at Thirsty Thursday, then left for vacation."

"Okay . . . I'm glad you didn't have a run-in with Quinlan."

So is he. I continued, "I spent time with Kim and Judy, who showed me lots of files."

"Anything interesting?"

"Sort of. But I think the mother lode is in the basement. I'll check it out tomorrow night. Or maybe tonight."

"Tonight?"

"I'm thinking of jumping the gun on this and staying here for a while." Like until dawn.

"Why tonight?"

"Well . . ." Because they may be getting suspicious. "Because . . . Lou Santangelo has also booked a room and a hooker here for Saturday night." I explained, "He wants to bond with me. So that screws up my plan."

"Okay . . . but my group just voted to approve this for tomorrow night." She added, "They're cautiously excited."

"Great. Me too. But it has to be tonight. I'll beg off with Santangelo for tomorrow night." I added, "So, good news, I don't need to spend tomorrow night with Destiny."

"Okay . . . but what is your reason for staying there tonight?"

"I told Amy that I'm going drinking with some friends and will probably crash here instead of going home to Harry's bitch of a girlfriend." I added, "The farmhouse has a rep for hosting wasted PIs, so no problem."

"How do you know you'll be the only one there tonight?"

"Because Quinlan, Santangelo, and Landowski are out of town. And Berger and Ferrara aren't the kind of guys who'd show up here drunk or sober, or with a lady." But if they did, I'd have to sober them up with a Glock to their head and cuffs on their wrists. Because one way or the other, this heist was going down tonight. I assured her, "If I have unexpected company tonight, I'll come home. Landowski is gone for a week, so I can reschedule my snooping for another night while he's away."

"Okay . . . and where is Amy tonight?"

"How would I know?"

"Just make sure she's not working late tonight."

Was Beth's concern personal or professional? "She's about to go home."

"She's Landowski's eyes and ears, John."

And his brain. But not sure who owned her heart.

"Last night," said Beth, "you offered to terminate your assignment in exchange for permission to snoop while Landowski was on vacation."

"Right."

"I spoke to my group . . . and to Max. And we all agree that your personal safety may be at risk. So your CI status is going to be terminated."

"Okay. That's the deal."

"Good. I'm relieved."

And probably surprised that I wasn't arguing with her. "Okay, tonight I snoop, and when Landowski returns next week, I turn in my resignation."

"You'll e-mail him your resignation on Monday."

By Monday, he'd be out of business, but I agreed.

She reminded me, "Be careful tonight."

"Goes without saying."

"When do you think you'll be home?"

"Before dawn."

"All right. We'll stay in touch by text."

"We will. And let's limit this change of plans to you and me."

"I trust my people, John."

"Good. But this is strictly need-to-know. And that includes Max." I reminded her, "You're in charge. Take charge."

"Okay . . . I assume you're not going out drinking with friends. So what are you doing after work?"

"I'll hit a few bars, drink responsibly, and stagger back here to crash. At some point after midnight, I'll take care of the surveillance cameras, snoop around, and hopefully get into the basement. If I see anything interesting, I'll take photos or use the copy machine here." I threw in the sweetener: "I think I can locate the videotape of last night's Thirsty Thursday, and I can copy it, so you'll be able to see with your own eyes your police chief, Conners, in a roomful of naked women." Unless you'd rather watch *Psycho* again. I waited to see if all that passed the bullshit test.

There was a silence on the phone, then Detective Sergeant Penrose said, "Okay . . . It still sounds risky. But you won't be going back there again."

"Correct. Try to get some sleep."

"Be careful. I love you."

She hung up.

Well, my bullshit was piling up so high, it wouldn't take much for it to collapse and bury me. But so far, so good. Maybe I should run for office.

I stood, and as I moved toward the house, I looked at the black Internet cable that came from the telephone pole to the top of the house, then ran down the side of the house and ended a few feet to the right of the electric meter at about chest height. This was where the coaxial cable connected to the interior cable by means of a simple barrel connector, which could be unscrewed in about five seconds, and this was the Achilles' heel of an otherwise elaborate security system. You'd think the connection, which also served the TVs, telephones, and computers, would be mounted in a secure box at about twenty feet above the ground. But there it was, vulnerable to disconnection by a ten-year-old kid with curiosity—or an older kid, like me, with burglary on his mind.

As I headed toward the back door, Amy came out on the patio, carrying a tote bag from which protruded the neck of the well-earned bottle of wine.

She said, "I'm going home."

I glanced at my watch. It was a few minutes before five. Time to meet Judy.

Amy said, "Thanks for the wine. I'll bring it Sunday."

"Good. We'll enjoy it together."

"Do you know where you're going with your friends tonight?"

"No. I'm waiting for a call or text." Remembering that Amy had called me from work on a Saturday, I asked her, "Will anyone be coming in tomorrow?"

"The PIs sometimes stop by for something. Sometimes I come in if Steve asks." She looked at me. "Why do you ask?"

Because I'm wondering who will be the first person to see this place after I'm done cleaning it out tonight. But I said, "I just want to be sure I'm not in the kitchen in my underwear if Kim, Judy, or you show up."

She smiled, probably thinking, Been there, done that. She said, "I don't think anyone will stop by tomorrow, and Steve is on vacation, so you can have breakfast alone in your underwear."

Actually, I'd be on the road to Fed Plaza before dawn, but . . . for some reason that I couldn't explain, I wanted Amy Lang to be the first one here to see what I'd done. So I said, "If you're not busy tomorrow morning, come by for coffee about nine."

"All right . . . I'll bring bagels."

"Great. And I'll bring my pants."

She smiled. "You better. We'll be on camera."

"Right. I keep forgetting that." Not. Well, when Amy got here at nine, she'd quickly figure out that our Sunday date was canceled. It rarely bothers me to bullshit suspects—cons are part of the job—but now and then, like now, it does bother me. But that doesn't change what I have to do. I said, "Okay, see you tomorrow morning."

"I can only stay for a bit. I have Saturday errands."

"Me too." I suggested, "For Sunday, bring a bathing suit."

"Okay." She asked, "Do you have fishing poles?"

"I do."

"Sounds like a fun day," she said.

It sounded like the perfect summer Sunday-afternoon date. I almost wished it was real.

Amy turned and went into the house. And I would never see her again. Except maybe in court. Sometimes this job sucked.

CHAPTER 42

Judy was waiting for me in the kitchen, where she had a nice window view of my sweet parting with Amy. She probably couldn't understand why the charming John Corey would pay for a hooker when he could have Amy Lang for free. Well, Judy, you'll soon know the truth, and as my former CIA colleagues say, "The truth will set you free."

I said, "Sorry I kept you waiting."

"That's all right. But we should get up there so there won't be too long a gap in the tapes."

"Right. Lead the way."

I followed her to the top of the staircase, and as Judy walked down the hall toward the attic door, I glanced at Landowski's office. The door was closed, and I was sure it was locked. Same with his bedroom door. So I'd need a pry bar to open the doors or a sledgehammer to smash them in. I hadn't put any tools in the van today because I was supposed to do this tomorrow night, but there were tools in the equipment room. Or Mr. Glocksmith could easily open a lock.

"John?"

I looked at Judy, who had unlocked the attic door. "Coming."

I noticed the ceiling-mounted infrared camera that covered the length of the hallway. The VCRs should be out of tape about now, so I was not being recorded. I was, however, being transmitted live—but Landowski would still be on the road, away from Internet service, telling his kids to put the fucking cell phones away and look at the scenery.

The door to the Recreation Room was open, and I saw it was neat and clean, thanks to Amy, Judy, and Kim, who did double duty as the evidence eraser team. On that subject, I saw that the bedroom where I'd met Chrystal and her girls was also neat and clean, and so was the other bedroom. Assuming both these honeymoon suites had a hard workout last night, I also assumed that the three ladies had been tasked with the removal of bodily fluids, condoms, and lubricants—though Amy hadn't mentioned that. I wondered what Landowski paid his female staff. But it wasn't about the pay, it was about Steve Landowski needing to humiliate and dominate women. The strippers and hookers were easy; the clerical staff was a challenge, but somehow he'd shaken their self-confidence. Then he'd made the mistake of hiring Sharon Hite. And she'd made the mistake of not recognizing the snake pit she'd gotten into. Or recognizing it too late.

"John?"

I followed Judy up the dimly lit stairs into the attic. At the top of the stairs, she pulled on a hanging cord, and all the lightbulbs went on, revealing a large open attic and the high, sloping roof and rafters of the farmhouse. In the center of the attic, I could see a constellation of LED lights.

Judy stopped at the array of electronics and said, "So this is the hub—the brains of the audiovisual security system."

I surveyed the stacks of electronic equipment housed in tall metal units. There were five flat-screen monitors in their own shelving units, and each monitor was split into four images transmitted from the surveillance cameras. One split screen showed the four outside views, and I saw that all the vehicles were gone from the parking area except my van and Judy's Toyota. The other screens showed interior views of the farmhouse, including the images from the hidden cameras behind the mirrors in Landowski's downstairs office, the upstairs and downstairs bathrooms, and Landowski's bedroom, where he starred in his own "Funniest Home Videos" when he wasn't getting blow jobs in his showcase office. I was sure that Amy Lang was in a few of those tapes, which might explain why she was still here and not at the Police Academy.

The last four-image screen showed both guest bedrooms from behind the two-way vanity mirrors, and also two shots from the Rec Room—one from behind the bar mirror and one from a camera that must have been hidden or disguised near the wall-mounted flat-screen TV. So the big party room was well covered on Thirsty Thursdays. I pictured myself in a conference room at 26 Federal Plaza with case agents, watching the tapes of last night. It would be great if Beth and Max were there too. I didn't want Beth or her group to come to the attention of the FBI, but Beth and Max were the reason I was working at Security Solutions, and that would come out. So they'd be material witnesses, and they should be there, and Beth could see me talking to her boss, Conners, then giving my speech. She'd also see me going ballistic on Quinlan. Unfortunately, she'd also see and hear my bar banter with Landowski and Santangelo, talking about hookers and bopping Amy. Well . . . it was all an act. That's what you do when you're undercover. Beth would not give it a second thought. Or maybe I should edit the bar scene.

Judy noticed that I was looking at the hidden camera

screens, and she seemed embarrassed, but said nothing. I scanned the screens again and noted there was no image of this attic, so there was no camera here. Also, there was no image of the basement.

Judy thought it was time to draw my attention away from the monitors and said, "We use time-lapse video-tapes that run twenty-four hours. So you'll need to be here tomorrow about this time to change them."

"Right." I let her know, "Actually, I may also be here tonight to crash. I'm going out with some friends."

"Okay."

"Do you know if anyone else will be using the house tonight?"

"Only Lou and Chip use the house overnight, and they're away."

I smiled. "How about you and Kim?"

"No female staff allowed after hours, unless we've been asked to work late." She assured me, "You'll have the house to yourself tonight. And tomorrow night."

"Good." I informed her, "I booked Carlos for Monday night. He'll be here at six."

She smiled, then motioned me closer to the stacked VCRs and said, "All the tapes have run out, so there'll be a gap in the recordings. But the live images are going out, so Steve can monitor if he has Internet."

"And only Steve has the access code to monitor?"

"As far as I know." She continued, "Okay, so there are twenty VCRs, and each VCR is numbered from one to twenty, as you can see. When you remove the used tape, you label the tape with the number corresponding to the VCR. Steve has a list of which number corresponds to which camera. Then we put the tapes there, chrono-logically." She pointed to a row of steel shelves and said, "That's what you'll do."

I looked at the shelves crammed with videotapes, all of which needed to be taken to my van. I also noticed empty videotape cartons on the floor, which would make the task easier and quicker. "Okay."

So we popped out all the used tapes that had recorded from the unconcealed surveillance cameras, and she labeled them and put them on the shelf while I put blank tapes in the VCRs and put them on "Record." She said, "Steve keeps the surveillance tapes for a week or so, and maybe reviews a few of them if there's something he wants to see or something he wants to save, like the July Fourth party." She smiled. "I'm sure he'll keep the one of your welcome lunch. The others, he'll reuse."

I went to the VCRs that recorded from the hidden cameras and discovered there were no tapes in the recorders. *What the hell . . . ?*

Judy said, "Steve secured those tapes before he left."

Right. He wouldn't want Judy bringing the Thirsty Thursday tapes home over the weekend to watch with her friends. Especially the tapes of people fucking in the honeymoon suites.

I said, "I hope they're well secured." Like in the basement. "I wouldn't want anyone to see what I did last night on the dance floor."

Judy forced a smile, but seemed uncomfortable talking about hidden cameras and X-rated tapes, though she had obviously made peace with this place a long time ago. She and Kim, like Amy, were enablers for Steve Landowski, who, aside from giving them a paycheck, was also intimidating and well connected to the police and the political power structure. So whatever Steve Landowski did must be okay if it was okay with those in authority.

I looked at the VCRs and the stacks of tapes. There was a treasure trove of incriminating and embarrassing audio and video evidence in this farmhouse that would help bring down Steve Landowski and a lot of his friends and colleagues. And hopefully reveal some clues and links to the Fire Island murders. And all I had to do was make those tapes mine.

But first I had to get around the surveillance cameras, and as always, it's best to keep it simple. Meaning just disconnect the coaxial cable and kill the Internet service. The cable service out here on the East End of Long Island was not reliable, as I'd discovered over the years, so Landowski, if he was awake and watching at 1 A.M. in his beach house, would not be surprised to see the words *Service Interrupted* on his laptop, and he wouldn't get too upset because he'd know that whatever he couldn't see live, he'd be able to replay on videotape when he got home. Or so he thought.

Judy said, "Okay, we're done. Can you do this tomorrow at five?"

"No problem."

"I'll text your company cell phone at four-thirty tomorrow to remind you."

By that time, the FBI would have asked her and Kim to come to Security Solutions for a chat, but I replied, "Thanks."

Judy turned off the lights, and I led the way down the attic stairs to the hallway.

She locked the attic door, gave me the key, and said, "Call me if you're having any problems with this."

"Looks simple enough." Even Steve can do it.

We went downstairs to the foyer and she said, "Have fun tomorrow." She added, "And tonight, if you're here."

"I will." I walked her out to the front porch. "See you Monday morning. Have a great weekend."

"You too."

"And don't forget—Monday night is monkey night."

She smiled, walked to her car, and waved out the window as she drove past the porch.

I waved back and said, "And don't forget to apply for unemployment benefits Monday." But I don't think she heard me.

There were cars parked on the country road, and I could see families going into the hedge maze next door. The kids looked excited. So did some of the adults. I guess when your life is short on adventure and excitement, you have to pay a few bucks to buy some thrills. When there's real danger involved, they usually pay you. But you don't do it for the money; you do it for the thrills. And for justice.

I looked out at the American flag on the pole, and at the potato barn across the road, and out to the fields and the farms. A nice piece of Americana.

What pissed me off about a guy like Steve Landowski was that he had a legitimate thing going here, and he'd turned it into a criminal enterprise. It wasn't like he was stealing to feed his family; he was a sociopath and narcissist feeding his own ego. And he knew—instinctively or through on-the-job experience—how to exploit the weaknesses of people around him who were maybe too willing to take the ride to Hell with him.

And the scariest thing about all this was the level of corruption I was seeing and the fact that Landowski and everyone around him had gotten away with so much for so long. Including, I was now sure, multiple murders. I felt like a cowboy in the movies who rides into town and starts to suspect that the sheriff and the deputies, the mayor, the judge, and all the local pols are criminals and killers, and they're in charge. How did that happen?

Well, it happens. All over the world. But now and then

a few good people get together and form a posse—like Beth and her group—and fight back. And in the movies, a feisty, good-looking woman approaches the cowboy, who was once a legendary sheriff or gunslinger, but is now a drifter, and she says to him, "We need your help, mister."

The cowboy should keep riding. I mean, it's not his fight—and maybe he's on three-quarter disability—and what's in it for him? But maybe it *is* his fight. It's everyone's fight, she tells him. And maybe the cowboy hasn't been laid in so long, he can't think straight, and he agrees to help. Right?

Anyway, I was ready to wrap this up, and at sunrise I'd ride off to 26 Federal Plaza with a van full of incriminating evidence—the modern equivalent of the showdown and gunfight. Have evidence, will testify.

And, at the end, I get a kiss from the feisty lady—or I get yelled at for not following orders. And I ride off onto the Expressway, alone in my trusty Jeep Cherokee. Fade to black.

CHAPTER 43

When you're about to do something reckless and dangerous, it's easier when you've had a few drinks, but the end results may vary. So I got a Coke from the fridge, sat on the porch rocker, and watched the sun go down. I could hear kids screaming from the maze. Good training for when they get married, get a job, and have kids. No way out.

Beth and I exchanged texts, and I assured her that everything was going as planned and there was no sign of trouble. It would be good if trouble held up a sign, but it never does, and things always go according to plan when you're making it up as you go along.

I got in my van and went out to meet my imaginary friends for a few drinks. I had my Security Solutions cell phone with me so Landowski could track me if that was on his mind tonight. And if Judy—or, more likely, Amy—had called him about me barhopping and using the house as a crash pad, he wouldn't think it was odd—or suspicious—if he saw my cell phone signal moving around and stopping a few times, then returning here at about midnight. If he had Internet service at his rental beach house, he could see me returning here live on his laptop, staggering into the farmhouse, and maybe having a midnight snack before bed. Then at some point his Internet service would experience technical difficulties.

I was familiar with a few of the drinking establishments in this part of the world, and my first stop was a place called Wayne's, a dive bar in downtown Riverhead, crowded with old guys who looked like they'd been there since last Friday. It was a shot-and-a-beer kind of place, so I found a space at the bar and ordered a shot of cheap rye whisky and a draft beer for a chaser, and watched a boxing match on the TV. I sipped the beer and left the shot on the bar.

The old guy next to me said, "Do a depth charge."

I pushed the shot glass toward him. "On me."

His eyes lit up, and he dropped my shot glass into his beer. Depth charge.

So I spent an hour in Wayne's eating bar nuts, nursing a beer, and buying shots for the old guy and his friends, who dropped enough depth charges to sink a fleet of U-boats. Few people understand the shit a detective has to do on the job. At least I was still using Landowski's money.

My next stop was a sports bar in Aquebogue that I remembered called TR's, and the theme was Teddy Roosevelt, who'd been a Long Island native son and done well enough in life to have a bar named after him. The clientele here was younger and rowdier, including the women. I got a Rough Rider burger, fries, and Coke at the bar, and watched a Yankees/Chicago game on the flat-screen while conversing with a young lady who had her own opinion about the Yankees' starting lineup.

It wouldn't have surprised me to see Amy Lang walk into this place with a date or a few girlfriends. So I excused myself and left.

My next and hopefully last stop was more upscale: aMano in Mattituck, where I sat on the patio and ordered a wood-fired pizza and a bottle of East Winds Cabernet, in memory of my brief romance with Amy Lang. If I was honest with myself, I'd say that in some odd and perverse way I had become smitten with her—even before the blow job. Timing is everything.

I exchanged texts with Beth who said she'd stay up until I got home, which was not going to be anytime this weekend, so I texted: GET SOME ZZZS. I'LL CALL U LATER.

I gave the full bottle of wine to a young couple next to me and left aMano with a pizza to-go for breakfast; I wasn't going to have bagels with Amy, so cold pizza was something to look forward to on my way to Federal Plaza after a long night's work. You have to think ahead.

I made my way slowly back toward Riverhead, planning to arrive about midnight. If Landowski was following my route on his cell phone, he'd assume I was done drinking and heading back to the farmhouse to sleep it off.

Well, there are these rare moments when you've bet your future and your life on one throw of the dice— like Teddy Roosevelt's charge up San Juan Hill. Sometimes these things work. Sometimes—like with General Custer—they don't. And just like those two risk-takers, I'd seen an opportunity, put together a quick and bold plan, and was prepared to ride into history. No guts, no glory.

A few minutes past midnight, I turned into the empty parking lot of Security Solutions, weaving the van for the surveillance cameras as though I'd had a few. The maze had closed up shop, and everything looked dark and quiet as far as the eye could see.

I tucked the van in the blind spot close to the side of the house, then gathered my two extra mags and my Smith & Wesson revolver, which I strapped on my ankle. I left the pizza in the van and did a good imitation of a drunk as I walked toward the front door, which triggered the motion sensor spotlights and porch lights.

I climbed the porch steps, punched in my access code, and entered the farmhouse. A good drunk heads right for the kitchen, which I did, rummaging through the refrigerator for a midnight snack. I found a jar of pickles, a package of hot dogs, and a loaf of bread, which I brought to the table and made a hot dog and pickle sandwich. Not bad, actually.

I stood unsteadily, leaving a mess on the table, got a cold beer from the fridge, and made my way back to the front door and onto the porch. The eyeball camera above the front door could see about forty-five degrees in both directions, and I moved out of view to a chair near the end of the porch closest to the parking area.

I sat and sipped my beer. If Landowski had Internet service—and that was a big if—and if Judy or Amy had told him I was using the farmhouse tonight, and if he was monitoring his cameras on his laptop—and that was a bigger if—he would have seen all this. More likely, he was asleep at one in the morning. The only reason he'd be watching me was if he was suspicious—which was entirely possible—or if he was just curious to see if John Corey had picked up a woman in his travels. Well, I hadn't, so there was nothing to see in the honeymoon suites, and he'd go to sleep. But if it was suspicion that drove his insomnia, then he'd stay sleepless in New Jersey, and when his Internet service went down . . . hard to know what he'd think or what he'd do. Hopefully, the long ride and his two kids had tired him out, and he was now fast asleep in Scotchland.

I texted Beth: BACK AT THE RANCH. NO ONE HERE BUT THIS ROOSTER. Did that sound nonchalant enough? I continued: I'LL BEGIN SNOOPING

IN AN HOUR OR SO. HOPE YOU'RE IN DREAM-LAND.

She didn't reply immediately, so maybe she'd fallen asleep in front of the TV, watching PBS, which is the equivalent of a fatal dose of Valium.

So I sat there for an hour, keeping an eye on the dark country road to see if a vehicle passed by. I've been on dusk-to-dawn stakeouts and surveillances more times than I cared to remember, and you get good at doing nothing while all your senses are alert and awake—sort of like when I was sitting on Harry's porch, except this was real.

At half past one, the moon set and the night got darker. So with about four hours until dawn, and a lot of heavy lifting ahead of me, I put both my cell phones on mute and left my company phone on the porch so that when I headed out to 26 Fed at dawn, the phone location signal would stay here. I stood and vaulted over the side rail of the porch into the gravel parking area. I moved quickly along the side of the house, out of view of the overhead surveillance cameras and hopefully too close to the house for the security light sensors to pick up my movement.

I hugged the side of the house and squeezed between the house and my van, making my way in the dark toward the rear patio. I rounded the corner of the house and stepped onto the brick patio, still hugging the wall, like I was making a jailbreak.

I turned to face the rear wall of the house and crabbed sideways toward the coaxial cable connection, which was to the right of the electric meter.

I ran my hands over the clapboard siding until I felt the coaxial cable, then followed the cable up with my fingers until I felt the steel barrel connector.

So, this was the moment of truth. Unscrew it? Or

screw this and get out of here? There was really no hesitation—except to savor the moment. I love this shit.

I grasped the barrel connector with both hands and unscrewed it.

I pictured Landowski's laptop screen with the words: *WE'RE SORRY FOR THE SUDDEN INTERRUPTION OF SERVICE, MR. LANDOWSKI, BUT SOMEONE (PROBABLY JOHN COREY) JUST SEVERED THE CONNECTION.*

And service will not be restored soon, asshole.

I walked quickly to my U-Haul, got in, and drove the van onto the back patio, out of view of the road, and parked it between the door to the equipment room and the stairwell that led down to the basement door. This would be easy loading.

I got out, moved quickly to the back door, punched in my code, and entered the equipment room, which was dark. I could see the red light of the infrared camera, which was still powered and sending a signal to the VCR recorder in the attic, but no longer sending a live signal over the Internet. So, since I was still being recorded on tape, I waved at the camera for the Feds who would review the tapes I was about to steal and see John Corey pulling off the heist. This is how it's done, boys.

I turned on the overhead light in the equipment room and found a Maglite on the shelf, which I put in my pocket, then I opened the toolbox and helped myself to a short pry bar, which should be the only burglar tool I needed for this caper.

I went into the kitchen, which I'd left lit, and looked at the heavy padlock on the basement door. With a little effort, I should be able to rip off the hasp with the pry bar. But the trapdoor in Landowski's office might be a quicker and easier way into the basement.

So I left the padlocked door untouched and made my way down the hall to Landowski's downstairs office. The door was locked, but it was a cheap entry lock, and I used the claw end of the pry bar to rip the knob out of the door, exposing the mechanism and the latch bolt, which I slid out of the strike plate, and the door swung open. Burglary is easy, and you can leave a mess—as opposed to clandestine snooping, which is supposed to leave no trace of entry or theft, and which is what I'd told Beth I was doing tonight. But . . . I guess I just got carried away and started breaking and taking stuff.

I stuck the pry bar in my belt and walked into Landowski's showcase office, which was lit by a floor lamp, and I poured myself a short Scotch. I stood in front of the two-way mirror and said for the mic and camera, and for everyone at 26 Fed who would see this tape, including Landowski and his defense attorney, "Hey, Steve. Fuck you, and fuck all your dirty PIs who dishonored the badge." I drank the Scotch, then flung the heavy crystal glass at the two-way mirror, which shattered, exposing the lens of the video camera. I flashed my middle finger in case I hadn't made myself clear. Am I having fun yet? Yes, I am.

I moved quickly to the edge of the rug and pulled it back, revealing the large trapdoor. I grabbed the pull ring and lifted until the door locked into place, then I swung my legs into the opening and looked down into the dark basement.

Well . . . so far, so good.

I drew my Glock, slid my butt forward, and dropped feetfirst into the black abyss.

CHAPTER 44

I hit the floor, let my knees flex, and shoulder-rolled away from the shaft of light coming from the open trapdoor, then I came up into a crouched firing position and swept my Glock around the dark basement.

As my eyes adjusted to the darkness, I could make out the staircase coming down from the kitchen, and at the top of staircase, I could see light around the locked kitchen door. This oriented me, and I moved toward the rear of the basement and saw the outline of the steel security door that led to the patio stairs. I felt around on the wall and found two light switches. But before I turned them on, I ran my hand over the steel door and felt a push bar that would unlock the door. So with my back to the door in case I had to make an emergency exit, I flipped the two light switches while dropping into a firing position.

Fluorescent bulbs began flickering overhead, casting a harsh light into the darkness. I remained motionless, and as my eyes adjusted to the light, I scanned the large expanse of open basement.

There was nothing moving and no sound except my breathing. I stood and took in my surroundings.

The ceiling of the old basement was low, about seven feet, and the rafters were supported by what looked like tree trunks. The foundation walls were brick, and the floor was made of uneven paving stones, and the whole place smelled musty. They don't make them like this anymore.

I could see a workbench and wooden shelving units on the back wall, stacked with what looked like Mason jars which, in times past, must have held fruit and vegetable preserves before the Landowski farm switched from agriculture to evil.

I also noticed a blinking yellow light in the far corner, mounted close to the ceiling. A motion detector. Well ... according to Judy, my entry code should have disarmed the internal surveillance devices. But maybe not this one, which Landowski would want live 24/7. But the Internet was down, so the motion detector should not be sending a signal to Central Station Monitoring, or to Landowski, or to anyone. Right?

I continued my recon-by-eyeballs. Close to the kitchen staircase was a wooden wine rack, and I moved toward it. There were only about ten bottles in the rack, all with the same labels as the crap they'd served at my welcome lunch. If this was the Steve Landowski vintage wine collection, then the padlock was worth more. Obviously, there was something more valuable down here.

I turned my attention back to the large expanse of the basement. In the far-right corner were two wooden walls made of horizontal planks that, along with the foundation walls, once formed the coal bin. Next to the bin was an ancient coal furnace, and next to that was a modern oil furnace. Other than that twentieth-century upgrade, and the fluorescent lights, and the motion detector, this whole basement looked like it hadn't been visited since Grandma Landowski stored jars of pickled beets here. More importantly, there was no sign of any criminal evidence down here, unless you counted the bad wine.

So I stood there, Glock in hand, and stared into the

empty spaces. I'm not usually wrong about anything, and I wondered how I'd gotten this so wrong. I mean, when I first saw the padlock on the basement door, my instincts said there was something other than wine down here. Well . . . maybe the incriminating evidence I was looking for was in Landowski's second-floor office or in his bedroom. Or maybe it was in the potato barn across the road. Or hidden someplace else. Or maybe there was no evidence of anything anywhere, and maybe I needed to repair the lock, replace the mirror, reconnect the Internet, and go home.

No. Circumstantial evidence told me—and Beth—that Security Solutions was a criminal enterprise. And even criminal enterprises had to keep some sort of records. And, of course, there were also the incriminating videotapes and audio discs which Landowski stored somewhere so he could blackmail his prominent guests. But the tapes and discs were obviously not here. *Shit.*

So . . . on to Landowski's second-floor office and bedroom. I holstered my Glock, but left the strap unsnapped for a quick draw. I shut off the lights and walked toward the open trapdoor. I stood there a second, ready to pull myself back into Landowski's first-floor office, but an image flashed through my brain, and I moved quickly to the light switches, turned them on, and walked toward the coal bin in the far corner.

The two wood-planked walls were about six feet high, reaching almost to the ceiling, and were about twelve feet long, forming two sides of the square coal bin while the foundation walls formed the other two sides. On the wooden wall closest to the coal furnace was a crude door which, when opened, would give access to the mound of coal in the bin. Nothing unusual here except that the door had a padlock on it, and I knew I'd found what I was looking for.

I used my pry bar to rip the hasp off the wood and pulled the door open, revealing a small room lit by the overhead fluorescent bulbs. In the room were two file cabinets and metal shelves stacked with videotapes. Against one wall were two big industrial-grade shredders which could eat reams of paper and stacks of videocassettes as fast as they could be dumped in.

In my business this is what we call pay dirt. It wouldn't make me rich, but it would make me happy. And briefly famous. Now all I had to do was load this stuff in my van and get the truck out of here.

I looked around the room, which also held a small camp desk and chair, used no doubt by Steve Landowski when he was working after hours here on his X Files.

The room looked clean enough, with no trace of coal or coal dust on the stone floor, but I noticed an old coal shovel hanging by a short rope from a nail on the door I'd just broken into.

I went to one of the file cabinets and pulled on a drawer, but it was locked, so I pried it open with my bar.

Inside were hanging files with numbered tags. I pulled one out at random and looked at the legal pads inside, which were covered with handwritten numbers and what appeared to be people's initials, like *J.S.—1,500*, along with a date. So this was a ledger of either money paid or money collected.

All the files in the top drawer seemed to be cryptic ledgers, so I moved on to the second drawer, whose hanging files were filled with what appeared to be records of the entertainment side of Security Solutions: women's professional names—Nikki, Stormy, Ruby, and so forth—

and their cell numbers, along with the first names of men who were obviously customers—johns—and helpful notations, such as *Likes S&M* or *Likes Girl Show*. There were no cell numbers for the customers, but there were double digits next to each name which would correspond to a number on someone's speed dial.

Well, when it comes to encrypting and encoding, this wasn't exactly state-of-the-art, but it might present a few challenges to law enforcement—unless someone here like Lou Santangelo was cooperating with the Feds. And a rat like him would have no problem dumping his partners into the shredder to save his own worthless ass. Quinlan, a suspected murderer, would certainly not be cooperative and would get no deal offer. But if Amy was a partner in crime, and if the government was offering deals, and if she was willing to talk, I was sure I could get a sweetheart deal for her. I mean, I owed her something for her hospitality—if she was silent about that hospitality.

Anyway, I rummaged through the two file cabinets, finding a lot of legal pads and notebooks, all written in the same hand, which I was sure was Steve Landowski's. I wasn't sure what all these cryptic notes meant, but they weren't Grandma's recipes for stuffed cabbage.

What I didn't see was any reference to Fire Island, or to Chief Conners, or to Sharon Hite or Dan Perez, the missing reporter. And even after these legal pads and notebooks were deciphered, there would be no such references to any of those people or subjects. Even Steve Landowski is not that stupid. In fact, he was a high-functioning psychopath whose head was wired to get around his low intellect, like a cunning predator with a primitive brain and a big appetite. Also, he was once a cop, who had misused his training and his job experience.

But there must be *something* somewhere here that

Landowski had kept or saved and which he needed to blackmail his prominent guests, especially his boss, Police Chief Edward Conners—something beyond the X-rated videotapes. Some piece of physical or photographic evidence that linked Conners to at least one of the murdered women. Well . . . if I had time, I'd dig deeper. But for now, I had to skim the surface and get this stuff out of here.

I moved to the steel shelves and counted about a hundred labeled videotapes and maybe as many audio discs that had recorded from places like Landowski's office or wherever he'd placed hidden bugs. And when you record other people on audio or video, you also record yourself and your partners in crime. So I was sure there was enough audio and video evidence here to take down not only Steve Landowski but also his co-conspirators in this farmhouse, plus people like Chief Conners and other police and pols who'd been here for one unlawful purpose or another. I hoped that Max had not stepped over onto the dark side.

I looked at some of the videocassettes which had been labeled and dated, and I found last night's tapes—two from the Rec Room and one each from the two honeymoon suites. Hopefully, Chief Conners was featured in one of the love scenes. Not that I'd want to see that, but maybe Beth would enjoy seeing Conners bare-assed with one of Chrystal's girls.

Regarding that, I'd have to insist that Chrystal and her girls get a pass on anything that happened after the show. They'd suffered enough, having to fuck Conners and some of the other old fat guys. Especially the politicians.

Anyway, I'd advise the FBI to show these tapes from last night to a Federal judge as evidence of official corruption when they requested a search warrant for the farmhouse.

On that subject, before the FBI Evidence Response Team arrived tomorrow morning, there would be a few Special Agents here to keep an eye on the farmhouse while waiting for someone to bring them the search warrant to enter the premises. At about 9 A.M., they'd see Amy arrive with a bag of bagels. So maybe I should be here to show them and the ERT around when the search warrant arrived, and I could have that bagel with Amy and give her some good advice about not talking to Federal agents, and also give her Robin's phone number. But maybe not. Maybe I should just let Fate—and the legal process—run its course without my interference. Maybe I'd done enough with and for Amy Lang.

Anyway, next to the shelves were three big cardboard cartons stacked atop each other, and I ripped open the top one, expecting to find more tapes or files. But what I saw was fireworks—rockets, Roman candles, cherry bombs, and other pyrotechnics, obviously left over from the July Fourth party: an illegal gift from the police property clerk's office. But that was the least of Steve Landowski's problems and Chief Conners's problems.

So, having hit the mother lode, I needed to haul it out of here, and there was a hand truck in the van which would make things quicker and easier. I exited the coal bin and headed for the security door.

I'd empty the coal bin first and get this high-value stuff safely in the van, then I'd hit Landowski's upstairs office and bedroom, and if I still had time before the sun started to rise, I'd hit Kim and Judy's office, then Amy's. Whatever I didn't take, I'd leave for the Evidence Response Team. Sounded like a plan, and I am the man with the van. Score a big one for Detective John Corey.

As I passed under the open trapdoor, I stopped.

Why? Because something wasn't right in that coal bin.

I mean, *nothing* was right there, but something was out of place, and what was out of place was that coal shovel hanging from a rope on the door. Specifically, the rope.

Why would an old coal shovel even be in that repurposed coal bin, and why would anyone bother to hang it from a rope? Well . . . maybe because the rope—which did not look very old—was evidence hiding in plain sight. The rope was a ligature, and on that ligature would be DNA—and maybe blood—from the neck of a murder victim, and DNA from the hands of a person who twisted that rope around his victim's neck. And that DNA could belong to Edward Conners. And that could be Landowski's blackmail evidence that Edward Conners murdered at least one person. Right?

I stood there, thinking. That was the only thing that explained the hanging coal shovel. Or . . . I'd read one Nero Wolfe book too many.

Only one way to find out. Go get the rope.

As I was about to turn back to the coal bin, the floorboards overhead creaked. Old houses creak. Right? And sometimes you even hear voices in creepy old houses, like, "Hey, John! Whatcha doin' down there?"

Actually, that sounded just like Steve Landowski's voice.

In fact, it was. I guess he wasn't in New Jersey.

I looked up at the trapdoor opening, and I could see him now kneeling beside the opening, peering down at me. Was that a gun in his hand? Yes, it was. This was not part of the plan. Well, not *my* plan. But obviously his.

I think I need a new plan.

CHAPTER 45

Plan B often involves shooting Asshole A.

Landowski knew what I was thinking, so he advised me, "Don't even think about it."

My Glock was holstered in the small of my back, under my blazer, but I hadn't snapped the strap, so I could pull fast and take him out in about two seconds. But I knew that Steve Landowski would not be alone. In fact, a voice about ten feet behind me—Asshole B—said, "Just relax, John. I got ya covered, partner."

I replied, "Fuck you, Lou."

"Be nice. Keep your hands where I can see them. You know the drill."

I mean, this asshole never shows up on time for *anything*—and he shows up for *this*?

So what do I do? I drop and roll while pulling my Glock, take out Santangelo first, then empty my mag at the open trapdoor. Could work. And if you're dead anyway, there's nothing to lose now that you're not going to lose later. On five. One, two—

Landowski yelled down, "Put your hands on your head!"

Three—

The kitchen door at the top of the stairs swung open, and who should appear but Chip Quinlan, back from Mohegan Sun—or, like Santangelo, he'd never actually gone there, and I was feeling a bit . . . well, stupid.

Quinlan stopped about halfway down the stairs, and the gun in his hand was less of a concern to me than the smile on his face. Also of concern was that Quinlan and Landowski had the high ground and Santangelo was behind me, and I wasn't sure where he was, because he would have moved after he spoke if he remembered what he'd been taught. Shit Creek had gotten deeper and wider. To add insult to injury, Landowski and Quinlan were wearing puke-colored untucked shirts. I mean, is this the last thing I'm going to see on earth? Or better yet, I could paint those shirts red.

So where was I? Four?

Quinlan descended the stairs and stood about ten feet from me with his Glock pointed at my chest in a two-hand grip. Our eyes met, and I knew I was looking at my designated killer. And he knew I'd go for him first.

So we're all cops, and we all know the moves and the options and the possible scenarios, but no matter how many times you've been in these situations, everybody gets tense, and sometimes some asshole shoots first and asks questions later. In this case, that could be me. But Steve Landowski, I was sure, had lots of questions for me, so he was hoping I wouldn't do anything to get myself killed before he grilled.

In fact, he delivered the classic line: "If we wanted you dead, John, you'd already be dead."

Meaning we mean you no harm until we're ready to kill you.

Santangelo said, "With your left hand, John, pull out your gun, nice and slow, and let it fall to the floor."

He sounded farther away, more to my left now, but he'd move again. I replied, "Lou, if I pull my gun, I'm going to shove it up your ass and blow your brains out."

"Yeah? Fuck you."

I could spin, pull, and fire before he moved again, but if I could get off only one shot, I wanted it to be at Quinlan—who said tauntingly, "Go for it, hero."

So, we seemed to be at an impasse. I was still armed and dangerous and apparently noncompliant. On the other hand, my former colleagues held most of the cards—specifically, three Glocks to my one, which was not actually in my hand, and these clowns wanted it in their hands. I did have a Smith & Wesson in the hole, but it was hard to get at unless I asked permission to pull up my socks.

Landowski, without warning, suddenly dropped through the trapdoor and hit the floor not five feet from me, which triggered my reflex to go for my gun, but Landowski backpedaled fast and put ten feet between me and him, keeping his Glock pointed at me. We made eye contact and kept looking at each other.

He said to me, "Who's the stupid one, John?"

"Still you, Steve."

He laughed, which was his way of pointing out the obvious. I wasn't sure if Landowski had smelled a rat from the beginning, when Max pitched me to him, or if Jack Berger had alerted him to think rat. In any case, Landowski and/or Berger knew they had to check me out to see if I was legit and if they'd made a good score—or to see if they were under the eye. So next thing I knew, I was having dinner with Max and sex with Beth and a job interview in the office right above my head. And here I was. But how did Amy Lang fit into all this? Not sure. I could ask Landowski, but . . . maybe I didn't want to know.

Landowski said, "I'm not hearing anything smart coming out of your mouth, Professor."

I hate when people pressure me to live up to my wiseass reputation, but I'm always prepared, and I said,

"If you're so smart, Steve, why did you hire these two morons?"

Landowski didn't reply, but Santangelo took it personally and suggested that I shut the fuck up. He confessed, "I always hated you."

I reminded him, "No one hates a good cop more than a bad cop, Lou."

"Fuck you."

Chip Quinlan had a question. "Can I shoot him?"

Landowski answered honestly, "Not yet." He looked at me and asked, "Why you down here?"

Stupid questions deserve stupid answers. "Just looking for a bottle of wine."

"Help yourself, John. We're all family here."

That got a chuckle out of Quinlan.

Landowski asked, "You find anything interesting down here?"

Matching wits with a half-wit gets old fast, but I replied, "I found where Chip and Lou go to be alone together."

Landowski thought that was funny. Chip and Lou not so much. Landowski continued his mock interrogation: "You know anything about who broke into my office, smashed the mirror, and unscrewed the Internet cable?"

He was showing off for his boys, so I said, "No, but I can shove one end of the cable in your mouth and the other up your ass and restore service."

No one thought that was funny.

Landowski got back to business and asked me the important question: "Who ya working for, John?"

"I'm working for you, Steve."

"You're fired."

Bad word to use when nervous half-wits are holding guns.

Landowski, who was very concerned that his criminal enterprise was unraveling and that life as he knew it was coming to an end, asked, "Who sent you?"

"If I told you, I'd have to kill you."

"Yeah? Okay. Tell me."

"You tell me, smart guy."

He thought a second, then replied, "You think Max sent you. But Max is working for me."

If that was true, then Landowski would know about Beth and about the group, and obviously, he wouldn't be asking me these questions. I said, "If he's working for you, ask *him*."

"I'm asking *you*, asshole!"

Well, the good news was that Landowski didn't know about Beth. And if I got capped, she wouldn't rest until she brought these three assholes to justice. Or . . . she'd say to Max, "I told him not to do anything harebrained." Max would agree.

Landowski said to me, "I know you're not working for the county PD. We'd know that. So you're still with the Feds. Right?"

I could see that Landowski was worried about his future. I might be looking death in the eye, but Steve Landowski was looking at life in prison and no more Thirsty Thursdays forever if John Corey was working for the Feds. I was sensitive to his concern, but more importantly, I understood that Landowski's unanswered questions were what was keeping me alive.

He also understood that and said, "Maybe we can make a deal."

"I thought you'd never ask."

He looked at me and nodded. "Okay. Me, Lou, and Chip need four or five hours to clean this place out. Then, if you promise to keep your mouth shut, you can walk out of here like nothing happened." He added the kicker: "But first you tell me who you're working for and what they know."

I asked, "Do I stay on the payroll?"

Landowski got that I was smart-assing him and sort of went ballistic. "Listen, fuckhead! If you don't play ball, we cap you, put you through the wood chipper, and you fertilize the fucking strawberries!"

"Hold on. I have an organ donor card in my wallet."

Quinlan was practically frothing at the mouth. "Let me just shoot this fuck in the balls!"

Before Landowski got on board for that, I said what you say in these situations: "My people know I'm here, Steve." Which was true, but I'd also bullshitted Beth and her people, and I had no backup or scheduled check-ins. I promised myself I'd never do that again.

Landowski, former cop, knew that what I said had to be true, but he replied, "They know where you said you were going. But me, Lou, and Chip were playing cards here all night, and nobody saw you here."

Right. That alibi worked for them once. Could work again. But Landowski, for all his bluster, knew that he was standing on the slippery bank of Shit Creek. So I had to put Steve Landowski deep in the creek, where I was. "If I was Chip or Lou, I'd blow your ass away right now to get lenient treatment for saving my life." I glanced at Quinlan, then said to Landowski, "I'll go to bat for the guy who clips you and for the guy who lets it happen."

That made Steve Landowski a little more agitated, and he was now thinking that both his boys might take that offer.

But that didn't happen. What did happen was that Landowski came to the realization that he, the boss, was in a dangerous position because he'd put his men in a dangerous position and I'd given them a way out. There may or may not be honor among thieves, but for sure there is no loyalty among killers. The guy who is supposed to have your back is the same guy who has the best shot at you. So Landowski looked at me, and I knew he was going to take my deal off the table by taking me off the planet.

There was still a chance that Quinlan or Santangelo would plug the boss before he killed me and killed their deal, but the two dimwits said nothing and did nothing as Landowski steadied his Glock and said to me, but also for Santangelo and Quinlan, "You got so many Russians and ragheads who want you dead that when you disappear, this is the last place anybody's gonna look for you." He added, "*Das vadanya,* dickhead," which is Russian for "Good-bye, sir." He aimed for a chest shot.

I already had one of those, so I played my last card. "Okay, boys. Game's over. I've got a wire, and you're all on the air live and on tape. And this place is surrounded by FBI agents." I added, "That's who I work for."

Landowski sort of froze, then shouted at Quinlan, "Check it out!"

Quinlan turned to charge up the stairs, and Landowski made the mistake of glancing over his shoulder to make sure Quinlan was following his orders and not mine. I didn't know what Santangelo was looking at, but I knew he'd think twice before murdering a Federal agent who was wired for sound, and in that split second when Landowski took his eyes off me, and Quinlan was turned away, I jumped, grabbed the edge of the trapdoor opening, and kicked Landowski in the face as I did an adrenaline-fired pull-up and body twist that would impress an Olympic gymnast.

I rolled quickly and often over the floor in Landowski's

office, knowing that even these idiots would realize that my rapid exit must mean I was bullshitting about being wired and covered, so I expected to hear shots and see holes appearing in the floorboards and carpet. But I was out the door, in the hallway, and on my feet before the first shot was fired, followed by a fusillade of fire, and I could picture the three stooges shooting blindly into the ceiling instead of going off in hot pursuit, which is what you're supposed to do. Assholes. But assholes with Glocks.

Out in the hallway, I had to make a very quick decision: Stay here and shoot it out? Or get the fuck out the front door and keep going? Head said flight, balls said fight. Balls win.

I could hear running footsteps on the basement stairs and Quinlan would be charging into the kitchen in about three seconds, then into the hallway, where the last thing he'd see was the muzzle of my Glock. And that's what had to happen to Chip Quinlan.

As I reached for my Glock, I heard the unmistakable grunting sound of someone hoisting himself through the trapdoor opening. Whoever it was—Landowski or Santangelo—might beat Quinlan into the hallway for the honor of being the first man I'd killed since last year.

The only problem was, my Glock seemed to have fallen out of my unstrapped holster.

Holy shit.

CHAPTER 46

I still had my two magazines of 9 millimeter rounds, though they were now useless unless I could figure out how to shoot them out of my ass. Until then, I pulled my .38-caliber Smith & Wesson five-shot revolver from my ankle holster.

If any of those clowns had found my Glock, they might think I was now unarmed, so they wouldn't take the standard precautions you take in an armed pursuit—which would give me the advantage of surprise when I popped them.

On the other hand, just like you don't bring a knife to a gunfight, you don't want to go up against three Glock twenty-two-round automatics with a five-round pea-shooter in your hand.

So maybe it was time to call it a day and call home.

The front door was about twenty feet away, and as I moved quickly toward it, I pictured Quinlan coming out of the kitchen in a two-hand firing position with a big shit-eating grin on his face. I didn't want to offer him my back as a target, so I spun around, ready to face off with Quinlan or whoever showed up. But the hallway was still empty.

I backpedaled to the front door, and in one motion I pulled it open, then pulled it shut behind me as I sprinted across the porch and down the steps, which triggered the security lights, making me a good target.

As I ran, my mind registered that there were no vehicles in the parking area or anywhere in sight, so maybe the three stooges had been dropped off. But by who?

I got to the road, spun around, and aimed at the front door, which was about fifty feet away and still closed. If you have only five rounds in the cylinder and none in your pocket—because you couldn't conceive of a situation where you'd actually need to use the peashooter—you have to consider each trigger pull. But the best defense is an aggressive offense that keeps the other guys' heads down and their sphincters tight. So, it was time to announce my status as armed and dangerous, and without waiting for the door to open, I fired one round—twenty percent of my available munitions—at the center of the door, which hopefully passed through the steel and hit somebody in the balls. But if not, they were hitting the deck, and the sound of the loud discharge might draw some attention from the sleeping neighbors if they could hear it. Or the gunshot could be mistaken for fireworks. *Shit.*

Also, the perps, all ex-cops, knew that if the house was really surrounded by my backup, I wouldn't be shooting at them. So maybe I should have controlled my aggressive impulse. Double shit.

By now, the three assholes were probably running out the back door and heading around both sides of the house to outflank me. Shit sandwich.

So, time to go. Still facing the house in a firing stance, I swiveled my head like the kid in *The Exorcist* as I scoped out the terrain: farm road and open fields to my right, potato barn and fields across the road, and farm road to my left, then the hedge maze. Lots of exposed terrain. Except for the maze. If I could get in there without them seeing me, I could make a phone call and get some reinforcements here.

I made a dash for the hedge maze, about fifty yards away. But as I ran, I caught movement out of the corner of my right eye and saw a flash of red light on the back lawn, followed by the sound of a gunshot and the buzz of a bullet over my head. I've never been shot at without returning fire, but I'd let this one go on my to-do list.

I reached the edge of the hedge maze as another shot came from the backyard. I'd been spotted, so if I went into the maze, I'd have company. But continuing down the road was not a good option unless I could outrun bullets. Therefore, the maze was now my only option.

I could barely see the entrance to the hedge maze in the darkness, but as I reached it, I saw that the entrance was blocked by a stockade gate, about six feet high, which I assumed was locked. But with three killers on my ass and no place else to go, I charged toward the gate, shoved my gun in my pocket, and grabbed for the pickets at the top, then vaulted up and over, coming down hard on the other side, my ass and elbows slamming into the packed-down earth, which knocked the wind out of me. I checked to be sure I hadn't lost another gun, then stood and made a dash along the path between the towering hedge walls.

Just as the path made a left turn, I heard the Keystone Cops kicking at the gate and the sound of splintering wood. If I'd had my Glock I would have put a dozen rounds through the gate and demonstrated to them the fatal error of standing behind an inch of wood when pursuing an armed, trained, and dangerous man. But I could still make my point and I turned toward the entrance about fifty or sixty feet away, aimed, and fired one round into the splintering wood.

As the sound of the gunshot died away, I heard what sounded like someone in pain—or maybe just crapping his pants. I ducked around the corner of the path just as three shots came through the gate.

These assholes didn't know what I was carrying, but they could figure out I was conserving ammo. So if they guessed I had only the ammo in my gun, they'd be right. And sometimes you can tell the difference between the sound of an automatic and a revolver. So if they concluded that John Corey's second gun was a five-or-six-shot revolver with a short barrel for easy concealment—and maximum inaccuracy—they'd also be correct. Bottom line, I was still armed and dangerous, but only three bullets away from being totally fucked.

With that in mind, I had to put some distance between me and them and make an important phone call at my earliest convenience. As I moved quickly down the path into the three-acre maze, I heard four more shots fired through the gate, then more kicking and splintering wood.

The path between the hedges came to a T-intersection. I could go right. Or I could go left. I couldn't do both, but the assholes behind me could if they split up.

I listened to the stillness around me. There was no more kicking at the gate, so they were inside the maze. In fact, I heard Landowski's voice call out, "Hey, John! We gotta talk! We can work this out!" He assured me, "We don't wanna hurt you."

Could have fooled me. Anyway, the night was dark, but there was some starlight and my night vision seemed to be getting better, though I knew that some disorientation would set in after half an hour or so—if I lived that long.

The FBI Escape and Evasion course I'd taken at Quantico had stressed observation, experience, and terrain knowledge over instinct when you were lost in the woods and bad guys were trying to find and kill you. I recalled that moss grows on the north side of a tree, the sun and moon rise in the east and set in the west, bears shit in the woods, and people tend to bear right when they're lost and they wind up going in circles. All good stuff, but maybe not useful in a hedge maze purposely designed to give you no visual clues, especially on a moonless night. The only similarity between the E&E course and this maze was the bad guys trying to kill me—except that the E&E bad guys were just playacting. These guys were not.

I knelt on the path at the intersection and examined the ground with my Maglite. The earth was packed hard by the countless shoes and sneakers of clueless kids and their direction-deficient parents, so the path didn't leave much evidence of fresh footprints. There were, however, a few patches of boggy soil that would take a footprint, and a few patches of raked gravel that would make a crunching sound—at the wrong time, of course. I took a handful of the moist earth and rubbed it on my face to kill the shine. I also kicked off my docksiders, which were not made for running for your life.

I stood and listened again, but there was no sound of footsteps, or even knuckles dragging along the ground. Now that they knew I was armed, they were taking it very slow.

So, right or left? The goal wasn't to find the exit; the goal was to put distance between me and the flaming assholes and make a cell call to Beth—or maybe Max—and get them to call out the cavalry—but not Chief Conners or Chief Jenkins.

I would have called Beth right then and there, but I sensed that the A-holes were close.

I looked down the path to the left, but it was too dark to see how far it ran and where it turned. The shorter path to the right seemed to T-intersect again, which would give me—and them—two more paths to choose.

I moved quickly down the right-hand path to where it T'ed, but when I got to the intersection, I discovered that the right and left paths dead-ended after a few feet, so I was actually in a cul-de-sac, which is French for "You're fucked." *Shit.*

I spun around and ran back to the first T-intersection, knowing that I might intersect with the three dickheads, who should be very close by now.

I put on a burst of speed, and as I came to the T-intersection, I glanced to my left and there was Landowski and Quinlan, not ten feet away, and even in the dim light I could see the look of surprise on their faces, like "WTF was that?" as I streaked past them. And where the hell was Santangelo? Maybe I took him out. Or maybe he was in the farmhouse basement shredding stuff. Shit.

Before my passing image registered in their small brains, I was twenty yards down the path and approaching a crossroad intersection—left, right, or straight? I cut right and, after a few seconds, slowed up so I wouldn't miss my next bad choice of paths. I heard four shots behind me, and one of them ripped through the thick hedges to my right, reminding me that concealment—such as hedges—is not cover. Cover is a solid object that can stop a bullet, and there wasn't much of that around here except me. And them. I could hear running footsteps behind me now, so I picked up my pace.

The path I was on turned at a right angle with no choice, then turned left and ended at a T. I knew which way to go because I suddenly had a total recall of the three-acre maze as I'd seen it from the drone monitor in Landowski's office. I knew that the path to the left ended in a cul-de-sac, so I ran to the right. That's all bullshit, of course; I had no fucking idea where I was or where I was going, but I was making really good time.

I had a sense that I was somewhere toward the center of the maze now, because the paths were shorter, and there were more of them branching off at right and left angles. So I just chose paths at random, hoping I didn't get into another cul-de-sac or come around a corner and bump into my former brothers in blue who didn't want to hurt me.

I slowed down and listened. There was no way Landowski and Quinlan could have taken the same random paths that I had, but in a maze, there is a random chance that your paths will cross. The question was: Did the dickheads split up? If so, I had a good chance of popping one of them, taking his gun, and repeating the process, so that when Beth—or Max—arrived with reinforcements, all they'd have to do was call the meat wagon.

But where was Santangelo? Hopefully, I'd hit him at the gate and he was now at air temperature.

I came to a crossroad intersection which gave me four escape options as I made my phone call. I knelt and took my cell phone out, thinking about what to say to Beth, like: "Hey, you remember that time on Plum Island when I got my ass in a little jam? Well, you won't believe this, but . . ."

As I dialed, it occurred to me that she might be fast asleep and not even hear the phone. Same if I called Max. And if I dialed 9-1-1, that might not get the cops I wanted if Landowski had already called Chief Jenkins or Chief Conners. But I had other call options, like the fire department, which would get men and equipment here quickly and spook the A-holes.

But as I dialed, there seemed to be something wrong. The screen was saying, *Calling*, but then it said, *Failed*.

Bad reception? No. Someone was using a handheld cell jammer. This was not good. *Shit.*

I checked my GPS to see if I had a connection, and it was also jammed, so I couldn't use the compass to help navigate the maze. Well, neither could the cell phone–jamming assholes who were tracking me.

Thinking about Santangelo's absence and about the cell phone jammer, I concluded that Santangelo was alive and that Landowski had sent him to the equipment room to grab some stuff like the jammer and, I was sure, the AR-15 with a nightscope and maybe the night vision binoculars. Hopefully, I'd come to some wrong conclusions. But I didn't think so. Double shit.

One way out of this shit sandwich was to find where I'd come in—or maybe there was another exit—and get the hell out of here. I don't like to cut and run, but I wasn't having any fun, and I'd sort of accomplished my mission. But if Landowski had half a brain, and if Santangelo was alive, then Landowski would have posted him at the exit, and I pictured Santangelo there with the AR-15, waiting to kill the best detective he'd ever worked with.

If there was any good news, it was that the three oyster brains had also jammed their own cell phones and couldn't be in contact with each other. But then I heard the unmistakable squelch and crackle of a two-way radio, which confirmed my conclusion that Santangelo had raided the equipment room. So apparently, there was no good news. It was that kind of night.

Okay . . . so I had two, maybe three very desperate and homicidal ex-cops stalking me, and they each had semi-automatic Glocks with high-capacity magazines, and maybe they had a rifle and night vision devices, and they were in communication via handheld radios.

Meanwhile, I had a jammed cell phone, three rounds

left in my revolver, and no reinforcements on the horizon. How did that happen? Well . . . that's what happens when you let your cojones do your thinking. I'll remember this for next time.

I took one of my Glock mags out of my pocket and flung it as high and as far as I could toward the sound of the radio I was hearing.

Oldest trick in the book, but it worked and I heard a fusillade of shots, sounding like a string of firecrackers, coming from two Glocks only about twenty or thirty feet away. Apparently, they had ammo to spare.

I had to put some distance between me and the Glocks or I'd be in the strawberry field forever.

I moved quickly, but didn't run because it was pitch black and I had to get a sense of this claustrophobic labyrinth and try to figure out if there was any recurring pattern to this maze. It seemed to me that the longer paths—which most people would instinctively take—mostly led to cul-de-sacs or turned back on themselves.

I also noticed that the shorter paths with more twists and turns were less likely to take you into a cul-de-sac. If you were doing this for cheap thrills, a cul-de-sac was part of the fun. But if you somehow wound up in here to escape three killers, and you got trapped in a cul-de-sac with them right behind you, then you were going to pay the price of admission.

I kept walking and listening, gun in hand, finger on the trigger. Along the way, I ran into a vampire, a mummy, and a gorilla.

On that subject, three monkeys with three Glocks, moving at random on paths that gave an infinite number of turn options, would eventually intersect with another dumb monkey who should have thought this out before he jumped the gate. Landowski and company may have been stupid, but they were also trained and experienced.

So, if you're a predator being stalked by other predators, the best way to get predators off your ass is to kill them. And that meant ambush them.

In the daylight, the hokey mannequin monsters wouldn't make any kid pee his pants, but in the dark, they did stop me in my tracks. Also, these creep-show props were becoming landmarks when I saw them the second or third time around, and I knew there was an ogre or something nearby.

I turned a corner and came face-to-face with the Steve Landowski look-alike. The green-faced mannequin was about six feet tall, dressed in rags, and mounted on a wooden stand which kept it erect. I dragged it around the corner I'd just turned and put its back toward the direction of the shots I'd heard, then quickly took off my blazer and draped it over the back of the ogre and tied the sleeves around its chest. I saw a patch of boggy soil and freshened my makeup, then rolled on the ground so that my khakis and white shirt were sort of camouflaged.

I moved about ten feet back to the next intersecting path—my escape route—and got down into a prone firing position, which is the steadiest position for accuracy. Hopefully, this was the way they would come, but to help them to the right path, I shined my Maglite in the direction where I'd heard the firing, then swung the beam left and right as though I was either stupid or desperate to find a way out.

I turned off the light, drew my revolver, and held it in front of me with both hands, my elbows planted firmly on the path for a steady aim. I waited.

I could now hear my heartbeat, which I shouldn't take for granted. Also my stomach was growling, and I pictured that pizza box sitting on the front seat of my van. That was my goal.

I waited and listened. It was very quiet, but now and then I could hear the sound of a locust or cricket chirping somewhere. The night birds had long ago figured out that this was a place to avoid.

Lying in ambush has some psychological and tactical pros and cons. Psychologically, you feel you have the upper hand. But you need to stay laser-focused and definitely not go to sleep. Also, you need to visualize success, and not start imagining that there are any assholes behind you—other than your own.

And the most important thing is to hold your fire until they get close. Then let them get closer.

So I lay prone, both hands holding my Smith & Wesson to my front, and I watched and listened. I could take out two guys quickly, but if Santangelo was with them, that would be a problem. The narrow path was almost completely dark, and the towering hedges were like black walls, but I thought I should be able to distinguish movement. Also, my hearing had gotten attuned to the silence, and in fact, I heard the unmistakable sound of crunching gravel very close by. Then, not thirty feet away, I saw the black, shadowy outlines of two figures moving toward me on the path. I steadied my aim at the figure to my left, which was closer, and I began squeezing the trigger, waiting for them to spot the decoy and begin firing, which would cover the sound of my peashooter popping off two rounds, so if I missed, they wouldn't even know they'd been shot at, and I could safely withdraw. If both shots found their mark, they'd never know what hit them.

They were about twenty feet away now, and I was tempted to go for it, but the snub-nosed .38 is not known for accuracy, and if I didn't take them both out, I'd get rapid return fire from anyone still standing, and I'd have only one round left for a do-over.

I held my fire as the two figures moved very slowly toward me. The guy on the right was very big, so that had to be Landowski. The guy to my left was bigger than Santangelo, so it had to be Quinlan. Then, suddenly, two green glowing circles appeared, and I knew that Quinlan had just raised a pair of night vision binoculars, which were pointed toward me. *Shit.* I squeezed the trigger, using the green glow as an aiming point, but Quinlan obviously hadn't seen me, because he swung his binoculars away, toward the decoy, and all of a sudden he made a sound of surprise, and both Glocks opened up on the dummy, so now it was the turn of the real dummies to go down. I fired center mass at Quinlan, who was closest to me, and as I swung my aim to Landowski, I saw Quinlan going down and I fired at Landowski and he too went down. Two for two. Yes, I am very good.

I held my position for a few seconds, waiting to see if there were any signs of life coming from either armed asshole before I went over to them and rearmed myself with their Glocks. If one or both were still alive, I'd have to decide if I was taking prisoners tonight or not.

As I started to rise, Quinlan also started to rise, followed by Landowski, then both of them dropped into a prone firing position, and I could see the two green lenses again. *What the . . . ?* Well, either those untucked shirts were bulletproof or the two dickheads were wearing Kevlar vests.

Shit!

The green lenses seemed to be focused on me, so I did a double roll toward the intersecting path, sprang up into a crouch, and ran, motivated by the sound of gunfire and bullets ripping through the hedges around me. Even trained shooters fire too high in the dark, and too wide when they try to estimate the location of a running target, and that's what these assholes were doing. Not that I felt safe and happy, but as long as they were firing blindly, the odds of me and a bullet intersecting were slim. It was when the firing stopped—meaning they were in hot pursuit—that I had to worry.

The firing stopped. So they were up and running.

I had the sense that I was heading in the general direction of where I'd entered the maze, and I kept that thought as I navigated the twists and turns, trusting my instincts and my recently acquired knowledge of the labyrinth to keep me out of a cul-de-sac. A little luck would help too. But maybe all the great luck I'd been having tonight was running out. A man doesn't deserve so much good luck.

A happy thought was that Landowski and Quinlan were both shaken up and maybe hurt. Kevlar will stop a speeding bullet, but a .38 round at close range will not only knock you down, it will shake up your insides and maybe break a few ribs. For sure, it will fuck up your head.

I slowed up and listened, but I couldn't hear anything— no footsteps, no heavy breathing, and no crackling radios. Just silence. I looked over my shoulder, and through a row of thinner hedges, I could see the green glow of the binocular lenses.

Obviously, they were still in a kill-John mind-set. Maybe more so after being punched by a .38. I know I'd be pissed.

Time for the oldest trick in the book again, and I took my second mag out of my pocket and flung it up and over the hedges. I didn't hear it hit, but they did and fired toward the sound. That should keep them prone for a while, and hopefully send them off in the opposite direction.

I kept moving, and I was pretty sure I was close to the exit because I could see that the path was more packed down, which meant that most of the paying guests who entered or exited the maze had come this way. Or I was making this up in my head.

In any case, finding the exit might also mean finding Santangelo guarding it, but I might be able to reason with my old buddy because Lou Santangelo was a man who made the best deal for Lou Santangelo. Or I could use my last bullet to blow his shit-for-brains out.

As I was moving quickly and thinking ahead, I realized I'd walked into a cul-de-sac. *Shit.* I turned to retrace my steps, but I heard footsteps coming toward me in the dark. *Shit, shit, shit.*

I returned quickly to the cul-de-sac and put my back to the wall of hedges a few feet to the left of the path. Whoever came in first would enter slowly and scan to his front with the night vision binocs, and he'd see that it was a cul-de-sac, about ten feet square, and that no one was there, and off he'd go. But if he glanced to his left, he'd see the muzzle of my gun a few inches from his forehead, and then his brains would magically exit the back of his head.

The obvious problem with that trick was the second guy, who hadn't had his brains blown out. But only I would know that I'd fired my last bullet, so the second guy would dive for cover, and I should be able to retrieve the dead guy's gun and continue the engagement. In fact, I should look at this problem as an opportunity to wrap this up. Right. I could taste the cold pizza.

I pushed my back deeper into the hedge, trying not to rustle the branches, and waited. Sweat ran down my dirty face and forehead and into my eyes.

I could hear the faint sound of footsteps, and even the sound of breathing, so whoever it was, he was very close.

I was expecting Quinlan, but I'd be just as happy with Landowski.

I took a deep breath and used my handkerchief to wipe my eyes, then raised my gun and pointed it where Asshole A or B would step into the cul-de-sac. I waited, but whoever was coming up the path was taking his sweet time. And whoever was backing him up would be looking the other way to cover their rear. So, I reassured myself, after I whacked the guy who stepped into the cul-de-sac, I could quickly retrieve the dead guy's gun and blast away at the backup guy before he knew what was happening. Kevlar vest or not, he'd go down, and I'd go in fast for a close-up head shot.

I heard the unmistakable sound of someone alligator-crawling along the path, which I didn't expect. I looked down at where the path entered the cul-de-sac, and I could now see the glow of the binoculars and a hand gripping them. I could also see a piece of the crawler's head and face just three or four feet from me, and I recognized Chip Quinlan's red hair, which was about to become redder. I pointed my gun down at his head. It would be an easy kill—almost an execution—but the tricky part would be getting that Glock from his right hand into my right hand.

I stood very still, looking down at the binoculars that were now sweeping the cul-de-sac, right to left, toward me. He'd see my legs first, three feet from him, and he'd know in a heartbeat that this was the last thing he was ever going to see.

He swiveled his head and binoculars farther to the left to make sure that what he was seeing was a cul-de-sac with no exit and no one there.

As I was squeezing on the trigger, I heard footsteps,

and Landowski's voice only a few feet away whispered, "Whaddaya see?"

Quinlan replied, "Nothing. It's a dead end."

"Okay. Let's go."

Quinlan got up on one knee, his binoculars hanging from the strap. I mean, we were within smelling distance of each other, and he could have heard my breathing if I wasn't holding my breath. As much as I wanted to splatter Quinlan's brains out the side of his head, Landowski was too close now, and I could not possibly get to Quinlan's gun before Landowski emptied his mag into me.

As Quinlan stood, he disappeared from my view.

I stood there motionless except for a few deep breaths.

I had no idea which way they'd gone, but they were still together and not likely to split up, which would have increased their odds of finding me, but obviously, neither of them wanted to run into John Corey by themselves. And I don't blame them. But that made it impossible for me to pick them off one at a time and get a better gun. Also, the fact that they were still looking for me in the maze meant they knew I hadn't gotten out, which meant that Santangelo—or someone else—was at the exit, armed and waiting. And if it wasn't Santangelo, it could be Joseph Ferrara. Or maybe Landowski had called one or two of his contract PIs to help him out, which would be a game changer. But maybe the exit was unguarded. Well, one way to find out.

I moved quickly away from the cul-de-sac to the T-intersection where I'd made the wrong turn. I looked both ways on the path, but couldn't see any sign of green lenses or flaming assholes. I turned right, toward what I believed was west and the direction of the farm road and the exit out of here.

Sometimes it's good to put yourself in the place of the bad guys. In this case, that would mean thinking like a dimwit. But a desperate dimwit. Landowski and Quinlan knew they had only about two hours before the sun came up and the surrounding farms started to come to life. They also knew that their night vision device wouldn't give them a tactical advantage in the daylight. So time was on my side.

On the other hand, two hours was a long time for me to play hide-and-seek. It was possible—but maybe I shouldn't bet my life on it. So I had to either get out of here now, or kill them soon.

Killing them was my first choice, but the E&E course instructor had been clear that "E&E" meant "escape and evasion," not "encounter and engage." Sometimes you gotta run. I had given it my best shot—four of them, to be exact, and one left. And I might need that when I got to the exit.

I continued on the paths that I thought would take me toward the exit, keeping an eye out for the green-eyed monster and listening for the sound of a two-way radio.

I approached a T-intersection and slowed down. This looked like where I'd first taken a wrong turn and wound up in a cul-de-sac, then had to turn and run past Landowski and Quinlan, who'd popped off a few rounds at me. I knelt, and sure enough, I saw two spent 9mm cartridges on the ground, then I saw my docksiders. So now I knew where I was, and I knew the way out. But you're not out of the woods until you're out of the maze.

I stood and moved quickly down the path to where it turned right and continued toward the exit.

When I got to the turn, I dropped to one knee and stuck my head around the corner. I couldn't see all the way to the end of the wide entrance path, but I did see a break in the hedges silhouetted against the night sky, which would be where the gate was, maybe fifty or sixty feet away. There was nothing between me and the exit, but there could be someone concealed there. So . . . alligator-crawl? Mad dash? Or maybe a crab-walk with my back against the hedgerow for minimum visibility. This was a really important decision.

Well . . . I could do a fifty- or sixty-foot sprint from a crouch in about three or four seconds, which seems fast, but if someone at the gate was watching the path, then that was more than enough time for him to aim and fire multiple rounds at the approaching target. But if it was Loopy Lou at the gate, maybe he was not being fully attentive to his stakeout duties.

Speed, shock, and surprise are how you overcome bad odds. Teddy Roosevelt didn't crawl up San Juan Hill. I turned the corner in a crouch and got into a sprinter's stance.

Okay . . . on three. One, two . . .

I heard a strange but familiar sound close by and I froze. The sound got louder and I knew what it was: the drone.

I glanced up at the sky, and to my left I saw the glow of the drone's infrared camera about a hundred feet above me—a good height for the operator to see most of the maze from a hover. *Holy shit.*

I stayed frozen so that whoever was operating the drone and looking at the monitor would not detect movement. But I did crane my neck and head to follow the drone, which was now making a sweep of the whole hedge maze. Steve Landowski's investment may pay off after all.

I wondered who was operating the drone. If it was Santangelo, whose hand-eye coordination I once saw chal-

lenged by an ATM machine, then the drone would crash
and burn in a minute or two. But this operator seemed to
know what he was doing, because the drone completed
its hundred-foot wide-angled sweep, then dropped to
about fifty feet and repeated the sweep pattern. Meanwhile, I stayed in a crouch, trying to look like a giant por-
celain toad.

I pictured the drone operator standing somewhere
outside the maze, or maybe in Landowski's second-floor
office, holding the controls and monitor in both hands
and wearing a two-way radio headset, talking to Landowski and Quinlan, and also to Santangelo if he was alive
and still in the game.

Well . . . when the going gets tough, the tough get
pissed. And that's what I was. Pissed off. I mean, I'd just
spent the last frickin' hour beating the odds, and now
here comes this flying eye that I'd made fun of.

The drone was making its way toward me, and every
now and then it would hover, then drop to about twenty
feet as though it was checking out something that appeared
to be moving, or some irregularity in the maze—like
a mannequin or giant toad—which was how I hoped I
appeared on the infrared camera, crouched against the
hedgerow. *Shit.*

I could now hear the crackle of a radio nearby, and
I guessed that the drone operator was talking to Landowski and Quinlan, maybe directing them away from cul-
de-sacs as they moved along with the drone—or maybe
directing them toward me.

If I were to analyze this situation, I was now super-
fucked in three dimensions. And I was down to one bullet
and one option, which was a desperate dash to the exit.

Just as I was about to start my run, the drone suddenly
slid toward me, then hovered about twenty feet above

me, and I could see the infrared camera pointing at me. If the drone could speak, it would say, "Gotcha!"

I heard the nearby radios crackling, and I knew the boys were on the way. And so was I.

But first—I pulled out my Maglite, put it on narrow beam, and shined it directly at the infrared camera, which should cause the monitor to white-out for five or six seconds.

So with the drone overhead and two armed assholes closing in on me, I turned toward the gate, pulled out my gun, took a deep breath, and began my run toward the exit and into the gunsights of anyone waiting there for me.

I was about halfway to the exit, expecting to see muzzle flashes, which would be the last thing I'd see. And that was okay. Better than a bullet in the back.

I was less than twenty feet from the exit and starting to think no one was there and that I really was going to sail through the gate and out into open terrain, where I had a better chance of shaking off the galloping assholes.

Then, suddenly, I was blinded by two bright lights that lit up the path and the hedges and lit me up like that deer caught in the headlights. In fact, they *were* headlights, and I could hear an engine starting and the deep throaty sound of . . . a Corvette.

I stopped in midstride as the 'vette moved slowly down the path toward me, and I heard Lou Santangelo call out, "Hop in, John! I'll give you a ride!" followed by a laugh, which I think meant he was just kidding.

Apparently, they wanted to take me alive to continue the interrogation—or put me alive into the wood chipper. So, assholes to the rear of me, asshole to the front of me, and an asshole hovering a drone over me.

The 'vette stopped, and Santangelo stood on his seat

and leaned over his windshield. I could barely see him because of the headlights, but I could see the green glow of a nightscope probably mounted on an AR-15, which I was positively sure was aimed at me. Also, he'd be wearing Kevlar.

He shouted, "You move one fucking inch and you're dead! Drop your gun and put your hands up or I'll blow your balls off! Now!"

He meant now, so I tossed my gun toward him, but it somehow stuck to my hand and went off, sending my last bullet through his windshield, where it hit either his Kevlar or his unprotected groin. He was knocked back, and as he slipped down into his seat, I was on him in a heartbeat and smashed the butt of my revolver against his head, then did it again for fun.

By the glow of the dashboard lights, I could see that he wasn't gushing blood from his groin, so he'd been hit in the Kevlar and he was alive but not feeling as well as he had been a few seconds ago.

His AR-15 rifle was laying across his lap, and I reached in and took it. The tactical situation was looking better. And to make it even better, I swung the rifle up and around, looked through the nightscope, and drew a bead on the hovering drone. But the intelligent being operating it reacted quickly to the threat and slid the drone to the left, then right, but made the mistake of leaving the infrared on, which gave me a good aiming point. I fired at the drone just as it slid right to avoid death, and I fired again before it could change directions, but it suddenly dropped and I missed.

This was sort of fun, but I didn't want to be standing here all night trying to whack a drone with Landowski and Quinlan right around the corner. I looked down the path, which was illuminated by the Corvette's headlights, and I didn't see anyone. But now that I was feeling fat and flush with a twenty-round magazine, I fired two recon-by-fire rounds into the hedgerow where it turned the corner, but no one fired back and I pictured Landowski and Quinlan hugging the ground and listening to the drone operator trying to explain how the situation had turned to shit so fast.

Well, boys, shit happens. And before it was my turn again, I had to come up with an anti-shit plan. The logical thing to do now was get out of here. But I didn't know who—aside from the drone operator—was outside the hedge maze.

As I was thinking ahead, I heard the beat of the drone's four props, which got suddenly louder, and when I looked up, I saw the f-ing drone coming right at my head on a kamikaze mission. *What the . . . ?* Before I got a bad haircut, I ducked as the drone whizzed inches over my head, then I spun and fired at the retreating drone. If it had an ass, that's where I'd hit it, and it flipped over and went down outside the hedge maze.

Whoever was operating the drone had apparently made a radio call to Assholes A and B before the kamikaze mission, telling them that Superman would be momentarily distracted, because gunfire erupted from the end of the path, and I heard two or three rounds hit the 'vette as I dived for cover behind it. These assholes didn't give up, but their Glocks, which had been very lethal and effective weapons at close range in the maze, were not so accurate at this distance. But for my newly acquired scope-mounted AR-15 rifle, fifty feet was an easy shot—if the A-holes gave me a shot. But they were now quiet.

I could take cover here behind the Corvette until dawn—Option A—or, Option B, I could make a tactical withdrawal and put some distance between me and the maze and get beyond the range of their cell phone jammer, and also look for the drone operator before he fled the scene. Or, C, I could remove the immediate threat, meaning go find Landowski and Quinlan. But why would I do something that crazy?

I got up on one knee, moved to the driver's side door of the 'vette, and opened it. Santangelo was slumped over the wheel, but he seemed to be regaining whatever consciousness he'd had before I bashed his head, which was oozing blood.

I dragged him out of the car, keeping low behind the open door, and laid him on the ground. He had a Glock in his side holster, which I stuck in my belt, and when I pulled off his Kevlar vest, I saw another Glock stuck in his belt that looked very much like mine. In fact, it *was* mine, and I slid it into my empty holster.

Santangelo's eyes were now half open, and we made eye contact. He could have killed me, but he didn't, so I resisted the temptation. I told him, "You would have had more fun at Mohegan Sun."

He seemed to nod in agreement.

Nothing more to do here, so I got quickly into his Kevlar vest and prepared to make a mad dash for the exit. But a voice in my head said, "Wouldn't you like to drive a Corvette tonight?" Well, yes . . . but maybe I'd like to drive it into—and not out of—the maze. I mean, I was flying high on adrenaline now, pumped up and pissed off, and literally looking for blood.

Rearmed and armored, I slid behind the wheel of the Corvette, holding the AR-15 in my left hand, leaving the door open in case I needed to do a quick roll out.

I looked through the cracked windshield at the fifty-foot path ahead of me, illuminated by the headlights, which I left on to blind Quinlan's binoculars.

I put my hand on the gearshift and another voice in my head said, "Put it in reverse and get the fuck out of here," but it sounded like the voice of reason, so I ignored it.

It was an automatic transmission and I put it in Drive and pressed on the gas pedal. The engine roared, the mufflers rumbled, and off I went, holding the AR-15 by its pistol grip, its barrel sticking out between the windshield and the open doorframe with my itchy finger on the trigger.

I covered the fifty or sixty feet of the path in a few seconds, then cut hard left, and the 'vette's headlights illuminated the path where I expected to see Landowski and Quinlan either waiting for me or running away. But there was no one on the path and I hit the brakes.

The enemy seemed to have disappeared, which left me sitting in an open sports car with its headlights on in hostile territory.

I'm crazy, but I'm not stupid, and I knew that the tactical situation was starting to shift. I needed to get out of here and out of the range of the cell phone jammer and call for reinforcements, and also find the drone operator—if he'd stuck around to see how this played out. Landowski and Quinlan were trapped in the maze and could be dealt with later.

As I was backing out, keeping an eye on the illuminated path, I heard a voice—not in my head, but from above—and the voice said, "What's happening?"

I turned quickly toward the voice, which had come from a radio, and above the hedge to my left was the head and shoulders of Chip Quinlan, who was not ten feet tall, so he must be standing or sitting on the shoulders of the other asshole. Quinlan, holding his AR-15, was not quite in a firing position, and he had forgotten to silence his radio, which was as stupid a mistake as him using Alley Oop's shoulders for a firing perch.

Quinlan went for a one-handed shot, his other hand waving in the breeze for balance, but before he was able to pull the trigger, I raised my AR-15 with my left hand on the pistol grip and popped off three rounds through the hedges right below his head and shoulders.

Quinlan disappeared like a pop-up target, but if his vest had taken the hits, he was still an active shooter. Just as I killed the headlights, four shots came through the hedges, which would be Landowski firing blindly, and I returned the fire, emptying the rest of the twenty-round magazine in a left-right, up-down pattern. I then drew my Glock, rolled out of the 'vette, and lay prone on the path with my Glock stuck into the hedges. We were only about three or four feet apart, but concealed by the darkness and the green wall, and I had no way of knowing if any of my bullets had hit flesh and bone outside the Kevlar.

Sometimes what you can't see, you can hear, and I listened for sounds of movement—thrashing, crawling—or the sounds of a man in pain. Sometimes you can actually smell the blood or the gas from the guts. But I didn't hear anything except my heart or smell anything except my sweat.

I rolled away from the spot, got up, and ran toward the end of the path and turned to the left.

It took me a few minutes to find the parallel path, but when I did, I spotted Quinlan and Landowski on the ground. I approached cautiously, then stopped, gun to my front in a two-handed grip, looking for signs of life.

I gave it a full minute, then moved closer to the two bodies and turned on my Maglite. I could see that Chip

Quinlan had caught one in what must have been his femoral artery because there was a big pool of blood around his legs, and he would be feeling his head pounding as the blood gushed out of him, and his body temperature dropping, and he knew he was going to bleed out and die. I remember that feeling myself.

You should never speak ill of the dead, but sometimes it's okay to get in a last fuck-you to the dying and I said to him, "That's for Sharon Hite, you son of a bitch."

He had no reply.

I shined my light on Landowski's face. You can tell when a man is dead or close to death, but Steve Landowski seemed to be on this side of the thin line.

I crouched and ran my light over him, seeing one entry wound in his shin bone, which must have hurt, and a grazing wound along his jaw, which had taken some flesh and bone with it and probably some teeth. Ugly wound. Whatever other rounds he'd caught from my AR-15 had hit his vest, and the trauma had put him in a sort of shock.

I ran my light over him again, then around him, looking for his Glock. I noticed that he was lying on his right arm, and I holstered my gun, knelt, and grabbed his arm to pull it out from under him. He wasn't as near death as he looked, and he suddenly sat up, like Frankenstein's monster on the lab table, and turned his mutilated face toward me. I could see jawbone fragments and teeth clinging to the bloody flesh and frayed muscle tissue along the side of his face.

I was momentarily frozen as we made eye contact, and he tried to say something that sounded like "eye," but I think he was saying "die," and as I felt his arm pull away from my grip, I knew I'd hear the shot from his Glock before I saw it. I came down hard with both knees and pinned his arm to the ground as he got off a shot, which went wild. I then came around with a left hook that connected with the tip of his shattered jaw and he fell back. I pulled his Glock out of his hand and stood.

Amazingly, he sat up again, and sort of looked around, then looked at me and raised his arms—not in surrender, but straight out to his sides, like someone who'd just done something great on the stage, and was about to shout "Ta-da!" This guy didn't die easily. I stood there watching him, but then I looked away, off into the distance, and listened to the silence.

Well . . . This crime scene would be a nightmare to write up in a report. Even I, who was here, would have trouble reconstructing what happened. And, through experience, I knew that whatever I said and wrote would be contradicted or reinterpreted by someone else who'd been here. I hate when that happens. So sometimes— most of the time—a single narrative is the best way to get at the truth and to get justice.

I looked at Landowski, who was still sitting up, but now his hands were feeling around his face like he was trying to figure out why his jaw wasn't working right. He turned his head toward me, spit up some blood, and said distinctly, "Bus," which is cop slang for an ambulance. Apparently, he'd evaluated the situation and concluded correctly that I'd won, he'd lost, he needed medical attention, and he'd rather take his chance in court than die here.

I, however, had come to another conclusion. I aimed Landowski's gun at his forehead and pulled the trigger, then wiped the gun with my handkerchief and dropped it on the ground.

Quinlan was in his death throes, breathing rapidly. I found the cell phone jammer in his pocket and shut it off just as he died.

I glanced again at the bodies, then turned, and as I

walked away, I heard the radio crackle. "Steve? Chip? Lou? What's happening?"

I knew that voice.

I left the Corvette there and made my way to the exit path. Lou Santangelo was lying where I'd left him, his face caked in blood, moaning and groaning. I drew his Glock from my belt and pointed it at his heart. He opened his eyes and looked at me. We stared at each other for a while, then he closed his eyes, waiting for the verdict. He deserved to die, but . . . he would be more useful to the Feds alive, and maybe I'd delivered enough pretrial justice tonight.

I stuck the gun back in my belt and gave him a bare-foot kick. "You owe me, Lou." I added, for the record, "Asshole."

I walked through the splintered gate, out into the open countryside, and took a deep breath.

I turned left toward the farmhouse, then stopped and looked at the house, trying to register what I was see-ing . . . The big farmhouse was all lit up, and it took me a second to realize I was seeing flames—fire—through the windows. *What the . . . ?*

As I watched, flames burst through the bottom-floor windows and curled up the sides of the house, lighting up the lawn and driveway, and I could see a white car parked on the road.

I pulled my cell phone from my pocket. The protocol was to call for backup first, if needed, and ask for an ambu-lance, if needed. Last priority was saving property—or evidence. A call to Beth would accomplish all this, but I didn't need backup, and Landowski and Quinlan didn't need an ambulance. Lou did, but fuck him. So I decided to call the fire department. Maybe some evidence could be saved.

Before I could dial, there was a loud explosion from the burning house, followed by another, and a few seconds later a flaming rocket sailed into the sky from the collapsing roof, then a few more rockets, followed by balls of fire from a Roman candle. One of the rockets made a loud whistling sound, then exploded in the air, illuminating the American flag on the front lawn.

I stood there, sort of mesmerized by the show, wondering who'd been playing with matches.

Well . . . so much for the files and videotapes. As I watched the flames and the pyrotechnics, there was another huge explosion that rocked the ground, collapsing some of the house, and I knew that the flames had reached my van on the patio and ignited the fuel tank. So much for my pizza.

The shit just never stopped around here. And on that subject, just as I was about to call Beth, a voice behind me said, "Don't turn around."

Meaning "I have a gun on you."

"Hands where I can see them."

I held my arms out to both sides.

"Drop the phone."

I dropped it.

"Where are Steve, Chip, and Lou?"

I replied, "You're supposed to move after you talk." I explained, "So if I spun around and drew my gun—"

"Shut up."

"Yes, ma'am."

Amy Lang repeated the question. "Where are they?"

"Where do you think?"

There was no response, but she'd taken my advice about moving because I felt my Glock snatched out of my pancake holster, and when I turned around, I saw her backpedaling with my Glock in her left hand and her little Smith & Wesson Bodyguard in her right, pointed at me.

She was wearing what she'd worn when I'd seen her at quitting time—shorts and a designer T-shirt—as though she, like me and Landowski, Quinlan, and Santangelo, had been on duty all night. Apparently, no one here believed I was staying overnight to sleep off a drunk. Well, maybe Judy believed me.

Amy and I looked at each other in the dancing flames of the burning house. It may have been the harsh, fiery light, but it seemed that her face had changed and that I was seeing *her* for the first time, crazy eyes and all.

I guess we had a lot to catch up on, but she wasn't talking, and she seemed on the verge of a very bad decision, so to talk her down and also remind her that we were good friends, I asked, "Did you bring the bagels?"

No response. Not good. So I asked, "Was that you operating the drone?"

She nodded.

"Great flying. Except when you tried to take my head off—"

"Just shut up."

I knew she didn't mean that. She was distraught and had gotten herself worked up about something—like maybe me killing her coworkers and putting Security Solutions out of business. Also, the Police Academy didn't seem to be an option any longer. So of course she'd be upset that her life, like the farmhouse, was going up in flames. I asked, "Who lit the match?"

She looked at me. "You did." She added, "I tried to stop you."

She seemed to be making a future case for why she had to whack me. Well, given the confusing circumstances of what had happened here tonight, and that the local police were up to their asses in all this, and also that the files and records of Security Solutions were turning to ash, she might have a good case if she was the only one talking.

She asked again, "Where are Steve, Chip, and Lou?"

"Not able to come to the phone."

She stared at me and I could see she was wavering, caught between walking away or blowing me away. If I could come up with the right words, I was sure she'd drop the guns and run into my open arms and have a good cry.

"You ruined everything," she said. "I hate you."

Maybe not.

She noticed the Glock—Santangelo's gun—stuck in my belt and said tauntingly, "Go for it."

She was really around the bend, and sometimes you have to play along, so I said, "I'm wearing a vest and you're not. So you need to go for a head shot at twenty feet with your little purse gun, and I just need to draw and fire center mass." I asked, "You still wanna go for it?"

"You go first."

Was this suicide-by-cop? Or was she looking for a justifiable excuse to blow me away? I was fairly confident that she'd miss and I wouldn't. But . . . you never know. In fact, quick as a cat, she switched gun hands and she now had my big Glock in her right hand and her little gun in her left, and she was aiming the Glock at my chest. The first round would knock me back. The second would be up close to my head. I think she meant business.

She said, "Go for it, John."

I asked, "Does this mean our Sunday date is off?"

"You're not funny."

"Hold on. You thought I was—?"

"You're not even as smart as you think you are. We all knew what you were up to. And if I couldn't get you to confide in me, then Steve and Chip were going to take you into the basement and beat the truth out of you." She looked at me. "Which would have happened anyway, if you'd confided in me." She added, "Steve knows how to handle people like you. He's smart."

Talk about delusional. This whole place made a psych ward look like a think tank. Well, you're not supposed to confront delusional people with the truth, which might send them over the edge, but I was a little pissed off and said, "Steve is—was—stupid. Which is why he's dead. And I'm not."

She brought the Glock up in a steady one-hand grip, like she was about to end the conversation, so I tried a softer approach. "I just want you to know that I was . . . very taken with you." Which was true, but maybe that proved her point about me being stupid. Love is blind, but lust can be fatal. Meanwhile, we both knew that someone would be arriving soon, and I hoped it was the fire department and not the local PD. In the meantime, I needed to buy some time and said, "I know you had real feelings for me."

"I did. And I still do." She explained, "I hate you."

"You know you don't mean that." Even though you keep saying it. I was reasonably sure I could draw, crouch, and fire before she could pull the trigger, but . . . I'm just a softie sometimes, so I said, nicely but firmly, "You need to drop the guns, Amy." I pointed out the obvious: "It's over."

"You have to pay for what you've done."

"No. *You* have to pay," I said in my best voice-of-God tone. "Steve and Chip have paid for killing Sharon Hite, Dan Perez, and all those women found on Fire Island. Lou will go to jail if he lives, and so will you." I looked at her to see if I'd played this wrong. But you have to be straight with the perps. They know when you're bullshitting and they stop listening, and if they're crazy, they go off into crazy land again, which increases the chances of them doing something crazy. Like pulling the trigger. "If you voluntarily surrender, I'll note that in my report."

"And if I kill you, there won't be any report."

"Good point." Time to give her a better card to play. "Here's the deal. You don't mention what happened between us, and I'll do what I can for you."

She seemed to be thinking about that, probably wondering why I didn't want her to mention our sexual encounter in any future judicial proceedings, so I confessed, "I'm in a serious relationship with someone."

"So was I. And you killed him."

Ah. I should have figured that out. Steve Landowski had a face that only a sight-impaired mother could love, but love is truly blind. I said, "Steve pimped you out to me. For his own purposes."

She looked at me. "Not Steve. Chip."

What? Did I miss an episode of this sitcom? Well, I guess I now knew why Chip Quinlan hated me. But is it my fault that Steve Landowski ordered Amy to seduce me? Chip should have been pissed at his boss—and his girlfriend. Not *me.* Right? All I did was . . . unbuckle. I said, sincerely, "You're lucky you didn't wind up like Sharon Hite."

Amy replied almost automatically, "Sharon committed suicide."

"Her boyfriend—your boyfriend—killed her." I pushed the point and said, "And you're lucky you didn't wind up naked and dead on Fire Island."

"That has nothing to do with anyone here."

She knew it did, but she liked all the lies she'd been told. And most of the proof of those crimes would be buried with Landowski and Quinlan, and any evidence that Security Solutions was a criminal enterprise was now up in smoke. But maybe Santangelo would sing for a lighter sentence. As for Amy . . . maybe she could enter a plea of insanity.

On that subject, Amy said, "You killed Chip. You killed Steve. I have to kill you."

I looked at her and actually felt sorry for her. I said, "You're free now. You have a long life ahead of you."

"My life is over. And so is yours." She looked at me. "First you, then me."

Sounded like she'd come to a final decision. So . . . I had to pull and fire before she did. But a second before I did, I saw headlight beams on the farm road coming from behind me. I didn't glance over my shoulder, but Amy looked at the headlights coming toward her, and in that second I could have put two rounds in her before she turned back to me. But I didn't. And I might regret that.

I could hear the vehicle now and saw the headlight beams on the lawn as it turned toward us. I had no idea who this was, but the intrusion had broken into our intimate conversation, and we both stood there, waiting to see if this was friend, foe, or clueless civilian.

The vehicle—an SUV—kept coming across the lawn and stopped about thirty feet away, its high beams illuminating us.

The SUV door opened quickly, and the driver took up a two-hand pistol grip behind the open door and called out, "Police! Drop your gun!"

It was Detective Sergeant Beth Penrose, who I was sure had come here not knowing what she'd find, but worried and pissed off because she hadn't heard from me.

I said to Amy, "Drop both guns or you're going to get killed."

But she just stood there, aiming my Glock at me. I was a trigger pull away from taking a bullet, and she was going to die when Beth opened up on her. So to make her understand the situation better, I said, "You're not a killer. And don't make that lady a killer. You need to drop the guns. Now."

But she didn't, and she stood frozen, staring at me as though Beth didn't exist.

Sergeant Penrose, still behind the car door, yelled, "Drop it or I shoot! Now!"

I said to Amy, "I don't want you to die." I added, "Please."

Amy seemed to come out of her trance, looked at me, hesitated, then dropped my Glock and let her gun fall to the ground.

As Beth approached, I said to Amy, "Whatever you do, don't mention the blow job." No. I actually said, "I wish this had turned out differently."

She had no response, but I could see tears running down her face. She looked at me and said, "I wish I'd met you sooner."

"Me too."

Beth, wearing jeans and a black T-shirt, was a few feet away now and maybe she heard that, but she said to me, "Cover," and I drew the Glock from my belt as she put her gun in her side holster. Then, instead of pulling out her cuffs, she hauled off and clocked Amy, who went down like a tenpin. *Jeez.* Is that in the manual?

Beth collected Amy's arsenal, which she tossed at my feet. I put my Glock in my holster and Amy's gun in my pocket and retrieved my cell phone as Beth patted Amy down for concealed weapons and removed her wallet and cell phone, which she put in her pockets. I had the disturbing thought that Amy had recorded some of our past conversations on her cell phone—including the worrisome blow job. Well, every criminal investigation is a Pandora's box of secrets and surprises. That overseas job was looking better.

Beth stood and looked at me, noting my bare feet, dirty face, and disheveled appearance. "What the hell is going on here?"

"I'm fine. Thank you for asking."

"I called and texted you about ten times."

"They had a cell phone jammer."

"Who?"

"Landowski and Quinlan."

"Where are they?"

"In the maze."

She glanced toward the maze. "Active?"

"Dead."

She looked at me, but had no comment.

I continued, "Santangelo is injured, unconscious, and unarmed, also in the maze." I concluded my report: "Unsecured firearms at the scene."

"Okay . . ." She looked at Amy and asked, "What's with her?"

"I think she fainted and hit her chin on the ground."

Beth said, "I didn't bring cuffs."

That explained the right hook to the jaw. But not completely.

She asked me, "Why was she holding a gun on you?"

"She could answer that better than I could."

"Did she threaten your life?"

Detective Sergeant Penrose was trying to determine if she'd saved my life a second time, which would mean I owed her a favor or something. I said, "I was about to draw and fire. So you saved somebody's life."

She thought about that and replied, "The Homicide Squad—that's me—will need to talk to you today."

I didn't reply.

Detective Penrose took a break and Beth asked, belatedly but sincerely, "Are you all right?"

"I'm feeling pretty good about myself."

"Tough guy." She asked, "Did they catch you snooping?"

"They did."

"And you thought they were all out of town."

"That was pretty stupid of me."

"It was," she agreed. She also asked, "Were you snooping, or were you loading your U-Haul?"

"I was about to do that."

She nodded, but had no comment except, "You lied to me."

"You knew I was lying."

No comment on that, but she looked at Amy on the ground and asked, "Anything you want to tell me about that?"

I searched my brain, but couldn't think of anything she needed to know. "Just what I told you."

"Okay. I'm sure she'll have a lot to say during interrogation if she wants to mitigate her role in all of this."

This was my last chance to confess, but I said, "Amy Lang seems to have some issues with reality." Like making up stories about oral sex.

Beth looked at me, but had no reply.

I changed the subject by confessing to a lesser crime. "Sorry if I lied to you about tonight, and sorry that I went rogue on you and your group."

"I never should have brought you into this." She looked at the burning house. "This did not end well." She added, "You tend to leave a path of destruction behind you. Do you see a pattern?"

"Now that you mention it." But I added, "If we'd done

this your way, this investigation would have gone on past your retirement. So I did it my way. And you knew I was going to do that."

Beth did not confirm or deny and stared at the burning farmhouse, which was now almost consumed by flames. A solitary rocket rose into the air and exploded in a red starburst.

She asked, "How did that happen?"

"Not sure." I was actually pretty sure Amy did it. But maybe it was Jack Berger or Joseph Ferrara, or for all I knew, it was Chief Jenkins or Chief Conners or any one of a few dozen other people who'd be happy to see that farmhouse and everything in it go up in smoke. I said to Beth, "What you see here is not the end of this case—it's just the beginning."

"I know that." She asked, "How did you wind up in the maze?"

Well . . . I took the first step into the maze when Beth Penrose showed up on my porch. But I said, "I was being pursued. Seemed like a good idea at the time." I let her know, "According to Amy, they were suspicious of me before I even got here. And they wanted me to work here to check me out."

She had no comment.

I asked, "Didn't it occur to you—and Max—that sending John Corey to Security Solutions as a confidential informant would arouse some suspicions here?"

"It did occur to me. And to Max. But I think we talked ourselves into this brilliant idea." She asked, "Didn't it occur to you?"

"It did."

"Then you should have said so."

"I guess I was . . . bored, restless, and looking to be relevant." I added, "Also, I was thinking with my little brain."

"You need to stop blaming that guy for your bad decisions."

I looked at her. "Okay, so my big brain thinks that you and Max actually had two objectives in sending me here. The first was the one you told me—to be a CI and gather evidence. But if Landowski, Berger, or anyone else here was suspicious of me applying for the job, then they'd be spooked and they'd do something desperate, like take me into the basement and beat the truth out of me. Then I would disappear and the county Homicide Squad—that's you—would have probable cause to investigate Security Solutions and investigate my disappearance."

She looked at me. "I can't believe you would think I'd send you into a dangerous situation to . . . become a victim."

"I'm thinking sacrificial lamb. I'm also thinking you have a ruthless streak, Beth, and you believe the ends justify the means."

"John, stop this."

"And while I'm at it, your motives had as much to do with you getting even with your boss, Chief Conners, who embarrassed you personally and professionally, as they did with getting justice for those murdered women."

She turned and looked again at the burning farmhouse, and as with Amy, I saw Beth Penrose in a different light. Finally, she said, "It's not so black-and-white. It's not one or the other . . . it's a little of what you said, and what I said . . ."

As I used to teach in my class, never interrupt a confession, so I didn't.

She went on, "In the abstract . . . the idea of sending John Corey—who, by the way, dumped me—into the lion's den to see what would happen sounded like a good idea. But . . . when I saw you . . . when we were together, I realized I couldn't go through with it." She reminded me, "Didn't I tell you that you were off the case?"

"Yes. You did yell into the lion's den that I could come out now."

She turned away from the fire and looked at me. "I love you."

Thank God she didn't hate me. "Okay. Is that it?"

"I could say I'm sorry. And I am. But I want you to know that my motives were pure even if my methods weren't. I wanted justice for those murdered girls. And yes, I wanted revenge against Conners. And yes, I was angry at you for leaving me. And yes, I can sometimes be ruthless. But I risked my career and maybe my life to get justice. Not fame or glory. Justice. But I had no right to risk your life. So for that, I apologize." She added, "You should ask yourself how much of a willing participant you were."

"We both know I'm a danger junkie."

She nodded. "I shouldn't have put the temptation in front of you. You don't resist any temptation very well."

"Right." Sex, danger, canned chili. Hard to resist.

She looked at me again. "If we . . . stay together, we both need to understand that we lied to each other for a good reason, and we lied to ourselves for the same reason. Justice." She reminded me, "We're cops. That's what we do. That's what Sharon Hite did. And sometimes there's collateral damage. And I hope that doesn't include us."

She seemed sincere, and truly sorry she'd conned me, and happy that I was alive. Me too. There were still a few twists and turns left in this maze before the exit. But not now. I asked, "Am I free to go, Detective?"

"Where are you going?"

"Home."

Before she could ask which home I was referring to, I

heard the sound of sirens—fire trucks, not police—then saw the flashing lights on the farm road coming toward us. These rural volunteer firemen were always enthusiastic about smashing windows, but the farmhouse was now mostly glowing charcoal, so they couldn't do much more damage. But it was good that they were here before the police.

Beth said, as though the previous conversation had not taken place, "I called Max on my way here, and he said he'd call the County PD. They should be here in a few minutes. I'd like you to wait for them."

"Okay."

She told me, "This was all my idea. Not Max's."

"There's enough blame and enough glory to go around. See how it plays out."

She ignored that and said, "Chief Jenkins and the Township Police will be here soon. That could be a problem if they get here before my people do. So be aware. And don't talk to them."

"I'm barely talking to you."

She looked at me and said, "Please keep an eye on the suspect," then moved away to make a phone call. I went over to Amy, who was now sitting up cross-legged on the grass, looking a little better. She should have been formally placed under arrest, of course, cuffed and read her rights, but I'm not a cop anymore, and Beth seemed to have her hands full. More importantly, I needed to talk to her before someone reminded her of her right to remain silent.

I crouched beside Amy, and in the light of the headbeams, I saw that her left jaw was bruised and puffy. Hard to believe that Detective Sergeant Penrose had hauled off on an unarmed suspect, but I guess Beth was venting all her frustrations of this case on poor Amy.

We looked at each other. I asked, "How are you feeling?"

"Fuck you."

"I don't think we have time for that." But since I'd been taking shots in the dark all night, I took another one. "Tell me about your relationship with Max."

She stared at me, then turned away.

"I'm the only person on this planet who can help you. Tell me about Max."

"That's for me to know and for you to find out, Detective."

"Okay. So Steve told you to fuck Max, which you did, and you and Max had a lot of pillow talk, and he told you things that you passed on to Steve." I asked, "Where am I going wrong?"

She had no reply, so I wasn't going wrong. I continued, "So you were sharing Chip with Sharon Hite, and when it looked like Sharon was getting suspicious about Security Solutions' involvement in the Tiffany Sanders case and the Fire Island murders, you volunteered to pay a call on Sharon and have a drink with her." Thereby removing a rival and a threat, all in one night. I added, "Sharon would not have opened her door to Chip, but she would to you."

"Sharon committed suicide."

Amy wasn't admitting to murder, and maybe I was wrong. She did, however, tell me, "You should ask your friend Max about his relationship with your new girlfriend."

I didn't see that coming. Well . . . maybe I did. Sounded like there was a game of musical beds going on long before I got here. Not much else to do around here in the winter.

I looked at Amy. I've come across my share of sociopaths, femmes fatales, amazing actresses and bullshit artists in my years on the job, but Amy Lang was in a league of her own. I asked her, "Why did you do this?"

She thought a moment, then replied, "The money. Steve gave me four or five thousand in cash every few months." She forced a smile. "I might use the money to go to law school."

"You'd make a great lawyer." You could study for the law boards in the prison library. I asked again, "Why did you do this?"

She looked off into the distance and said, "I . . . don't know . . . I got sucked into the cesspool. It started slowly, then before I knew it, I was in it up to my eyes and couldn't get out."

"And it was exciting."

She nodded.

I certainly understood all that. And understood why a good-looking, intelligent, and educated woman who once wanted to be a cop would get herself involved in this snake pit. And as I've seen on the job, there's a certain allure to the bad side of town. Just like you have cop groupies, you have mob groupies. And they're often the same people. Maybe that explained it. Maybe it wasn't my problem.

I asked her, "Did you really like me?"

She smiled, though I could see it hurt to do that. She said, "I did. Still do."

And I believed her.

I stood and watched the firefighters, who, like me, had arrived here after the damage was done.

As for Detective Penrose, I'm sure her motives were pure—justice—but her methods were a good example of the warning that if you're fighting monsters, be careful you don't become one.

Police Chief Larry Jenkins, whose jurisdiction this

was, arrived with about a dozen uniformed officers and a few detectives.

Police Chief Maxwell, who was off his turf but who had been summoned by Beth, arrived alone. Max and his friend Chief Jenkins spotted each other and got into an intense conversation.

What a lot of these men had in common—aside from their jobs—was a secret sense of relief on seeing the farmhouse in ashes, and learning that their friends and Thursday-night hosts, Steve Landowski and Chip Quinlan, were dead. And I was sure they were all praying for Lou Santangelo's injuries to be fatal, and for Amy Lang to have traumatic amnesia.

The county police arrived in force, including a crime scene unit. A county detective came over to me, we exchanged a few words, and he took charge of the suspect, helping her to her feet and cuffing her.

Amy and I looked at each other. I reminded her, "You have the right to remain silent. But a full confession is what will save your soul."

She kept staring at me, then said, "Promise you'll help me."

"I'll do what I can."

The detective led her away and Beth's boss, Lieutenant Stuckley, came over to me. He wanted to talk to me in his car, but I did something I've never done before and told him I wouldn't make a statement until I retained a lawyer. I mean, I whacked two guys tonight, and self-defense is a legal term, not an opinion. I did give him Santangelo's Glock and Amy's purse gun and IDed the purported owners, but that was the extent of my cooperation.

However, I did suggest to Lieutenant Stuckley that he talk to Jack Berger sooner than later. Same with Joseph Ferrara, Kim Horton, and Judy Ortega, because some of what went up in smoke here was burned into the memories of Landowski's deaf, dumb, and blind employees.

Amy had been put in one ambulance and Lou Santangelo in another so they'd have no contact before they were questioned. Steve Landowski and Chip Quinlan would be able to share a ride after the medical examiner pronounced them dead.

By now, neighbors and curiosity seekers were lining the farm road on the other side of the crime scene tape, and there was a News 12 helicopter hovering overhead, soon to be joined by news vans and more helicopters from the city. A female TV reporter had gotten past the tape and past the uniformed cops, and she was going around with her camera guy and a microphone, asking questions of anyone who looked like they wanted to be famous for five minutes, but she wasn't having any luck getting answers.

She spotted me, dirty and barefoot, hesitated, then approached without holding up the mic, and asked, "Are you . . . ? *Who* are you?"

"I'm unemployed."

She hesitated, but put the mic under my nose, then told the camera guy to roll, and asked, "What happened here?"

This was my chance to kick off my media tour. I replied, "I think it was a faulty toaster oven."

I turned and walked away, looking for Chief Maxwell.

I found him standing on the patio near my burned-out U-Haul and the totally incinerated farmhouse. The firemen were standing around the smoking ruin, maybe looking for a window to smash.

Max glanced at me as I approached, checked out my appearance, then said, "Beth said you were okay."

I had no reply and stared down into the basement

of the house, which looked like a charcoal pit. Nothing could have survived the heat and flames.

Max asked, "What happened?"

"The less you know, the better."

He didn't respond to that and said, "Beth told me that when she got here, Amy had a gun on you."

"Whatever I have to say, Max, I'll say it on advice of counsel."

He looked at me. "We're all in this together, John. This is off the record."

"Let's change the subject. Why didn't you tell me that you had a sexual relationship with Amy Lang?"

He didn't reply for a few seconds, then said, "I was trying to get information out of her."

"She probably got more information out of you than you got out of her."

"Not true." He added, "I was doing my job."

"Right." Somebody's got to do it. "Did Beth know about that?"

He stayed silent, then replied, "No."

"Why not?"

"Because . . . I had nothing to report."

"Actually, you did report to her that you tried to seduce Amy Lang, but you'd struck out."

"Right . . . I did say that."

"Why would you lie to her?"

"I think you know why."

"Right. She would have been jealous."

He stayed silent again, then said, "My relationship with Beth was not exclusive, and she knew that. In fact, she was the one who thought I should take a run at Amy Lang."

"Then you should have reported mission accomplished."

"It got complicated."

"It always does."

He assured me, "Beth and I haven't been together since you stepped into the picture."

I had no reply.

"I'm out of the picture. Permanently."

Apparently, Max and I had more in common than a badge and a gun. Max and Amy and John. Beth and John and Max. I think that's two overlapping triangles. More if you count Amy and Chip, Chip and Sharon, and Amy and Steve Landowski. I might have to diagram this on a poster board.

Max said, "She really loves you."

And Max probably knew that before I did. As I said, I'd entered this long-running play in the third act. And before the curtain came down, I needed to exit stage left. But before I did, I said to him, "I don't know if you compromised yourself with Landowski, but be happy that he's dead, and that his files and videotapes are gone. And when the time comes for you to make a sworn statement, you don't owe any loyalty to dirty cops, including your friend Larry Jenkins." I looked at him and he nodded.

I turned away from Max and walked toward the road and ducked under the police tape. You're not supposed to leave a crime scene without logging out, but I'd never logged in, so I was never here. Also, now that I was outside the tape, I had to conceal my Glock, so I pulled my shirt out of my pants and let the shirttails hang. The untucked look. I knew those bastards would eventually get me to do this.

The sun was up, and I could see a line of vehicles parked on both sides of the road, along with knots of people who'd gotten word through the rural grapevine that there were big happenings on Jacob's Path.

I walked past the strawberry field, which I could have

been fertilizing had things gone the other way. I made a mental note to tell Suffolk PD to have it dug up. You never know where the bodies are buried unless you dig.

As for the Fire Island murders, that case was still unsolved, but if I was Police Chief Edward Conners—who was conspicuous here by his absence—I'd be more than a little nervous this morning, thinking about Lou Santangelo and Amy Lang, who had nothing left to lose and lots to gain by ratting out the big cheese.

There could be justice for those nine women, and I'd already delivered some of it from the muzzle of my gun.

I was about to call a car service to take me to Manhattan, when who should get out of an old Mercedes up the road but Jack Berger, who started walking toward me. He was wearing shorts, T-shirt, and sandals, as though he'd dressed quickly in response to an early-morning phone call.

He didn't seem surprised to see me or the smoldering farmhouse, so he'd obviously been briefed by someone— probably Chief Jenkins, or maybe Chief Conners. The cover-your-ass alarm around here was big, wide, and deep.

Jack didn't seem sure what facial expression was appropriate to this scene of destruction, but he settled on shocked and saddened.

We stopped a few feet from each other and he said, "This is awful. Terrible."

I agreed, "All the client billing is up in smoke."

He ignored that and said, "I've been briefed," though he didn't say by whom, and I didn't bother to ask. He looked at me. "So . . . Steve and Chip . . ."

"Are no longer with us," I confirmed. "Dead as doornails."

He nodded and ran his hand over his face, maybe to hide the smile. If anyone could walk away from this unscathed, it was Jack Berger, who, I was sure, had left few, if any, footprints or fingerprints at Security Solutions. He, like Beth, asked belatedly, "Are you all right?"

"Couldn't be better."

"Good." He hesitated, then asked, "And Amy?"

"I believe she's been taken in for questioning."

He had no response to that and asked, "Lou?"

"I'm kind of done answering questions, Jack." I advised him, "Go talk to a detective named Beth Penrose. She'll be the case officer."

I started to walk away, but he said, "I'm very impressed with you, John. And I'm thinking that we should talk about doing something together."

I didn't see that coming, but I guess it made sense to Jack, who, like me, was now unemployed. I reminded him, "I just signed a two-year non-compete, Jack. With your pen."

He forced a smile, then gave me his legal opinion. "The agreement, I'm sure, was destroyed in the fire. And so is the PI agency."

"Good point. Also, I killed the president of the company."

He didn't react to my explicit statement and returned to his subject. "There's a lot of money to be made—legitimately—in private investigative work."

"Good luck with that."

"Think about it. Kim, Judy, and Amy could be our first hires."

"Amy may not be available for a while, Counselor." I added, "And neither may you."

He didn't flinch—in fact, he looked me in the eye and said, "I'm not sure what you're talking about, John. But if you're suggesting that Steve, Chip, and Lou were involved in something illicit, I'm available as a cooperating witness for the government."

"Me too. Okay—"

"How does Corey, Berger, Ferrara, and Lang sound to you?"

Sounded like the start of a beautiful friendship, but I said, "Sounds like I might be the only partner who doesn't need a defense attorney."

He looked at me and shook his head. "You put too much faith in the system, my friend."

"Sometimes. And other times I *am* the system." I added, "If the dead could talk, they'd agree."

Jack's a cool customer, but that left him speechless, so I said, to lighten the moment, "I gotta go work on my consulting report."

He recovered his cool, forced a smile, and said, "Keep it short." He added, "The less you say, the better."

"You'll get what you paid for." As I walked past him, I suggested, "Give my ex a call. She'll give you a professional courtesy." Which may include a roll in the hay if you say you know me. Two lawyers fucking each other. I love it.

I left Jack Berger contemplating his future without me. As I walked, I called a local car service, and within fifteen minutes I was in a familiar beat-up Toyota with the pimply-faced driver who'd taken me from Harry's house to Beth's cottage. He recognized me, despite my appearance, and he didn't seem happy to have a murder suspect in his car, but he asked politely, "Where to?"

That was the question that I now had to answer as we headed for the crossroads that would take me to Beth's cottage or my condo in Manhattan.

"Home," I said.

"Where's that?"

"Home is where the heart is."

"Where's that?"

"That is the question." We approached the crossroads, and I fished Beth's key out of my pocket and lowered my window.

"Where to?"

I put the key back in my pocket and gave him Beth's address.

I settled back in my seat and looked out at the new day and the passing scenery.

Well . . . this time I was following my heart. And that felt good.

THE END

ACKNOWLEDGMENTS

Writing is a solitary occupation, but no writer knows everything about everything, so as with all my novels, I've reached out to friends and acquaintances in various professions to assist me with facts, details, and inside information that a writer needs but can't find in books or on the Internet.

As always, here is my disclaimer: Any errors of fact regarding the professions and procedures represented in this novel are either a result of my misunderstanding of the information given to me, or a result of my decision to take literary license and dramatic liberties.

First and foremost among the people who've assisted me is my good friend Kenny Hieb, a.k.a. John Corey. Kenny, like Corey, is a retired NYPD detective who had a second career with the Federal Joint Terrorism Task Force. Also like Corey, Kenny continued his Federal service with a special surveillance group and is now happily retired, not fired, as John Corey was. Thanks, Kenny, for your good info and, more importantly, for your work in keeping us safe on the home front.

Thanks once again to my good friend John Kennedy, labor arbitrator and former Deputy Police Commissioner, Nassau County (NY), and member of the New York State Bar. John has been an invaluable source of information to me regarding police procedures and the law, and has also shared with me his knowledge of the

Gilgo Beach murders, which are fictionalized in this book.

You can never have enough inside information about how the police speak, act, and think, so for my John Corey books, I've gone to Matty Travaglia, NYPD, Retired, whenever I needed some jargon or expression that Corey would use, or some insight into how a cop would think or react in a given situation. Thanks, Matty, for sharing your knowledge and experience, and for some very funny stories of life on the job.

Also, my gratitude to Vin Lanuto, president of AVAS Systems, Deer Park, NY, for sharing with me his extensive knowledge of premises security systems, which I shared with John Corey. Thanks, Vin, for your time, expertise, and patience.

Not all the assistance that I need to write a novel is of a technical nature; I also reach out to trusted friends and family for their editorial and critical opinion and their proofreading skills.

First among those who were early readers of *The Maze* is my son Alex, who co-authored *The Deserter* with me. Alex brings to the table not only his skills as a bestselling novelist but also his award-winning skills as a screenwriter, which translates well to contemporary fiction writing. His in-depth analysis of scenes and characters in *The Maze* was invaluable and spot-on. Add to that the energy of youth and his generation's easy familiarity with Internet research, and Alex fills in the gaps and lapses experienced by many technically challenged writers.

I'd also like to thank two other early readers of *The Maze* for their excellent suggestions. The first is Dr. Tina Funt. When people tell me they want to write a novel, I advise them to take two aspirin, lie down in a dark room, and wait for the feeling to pass, which is what I advised Dr. Funt. But she ignored my advice and wrote a novel titled *The Doctor's Secret*, which I've read, greatly enjoyed, and highly recommend. I gave Tina the manuscript of *The Maze*, and she gave me a good and honest reading and made invaluable editorial suggestions, especially regarding my female characters. Thanks also, Tina, for your professional care and your friendship.

If you consult a medical doctor about your manuscript, you should also consult a lawyer. So I gave the early manuscript to Dee Jae Diliberto, a good friend and a very good attorney. Dee Jae takes grammar, punctuation, and spelling very seriously, and she red-penciled my errors and lapses, and also straightened out some of the legal jargon for me. Thanks, Dee Jae, for doing this pro bono publico.

I get a lot of fan mail from my readers, which is very gratifying. I also get a lot of fan mail for Scott Brick, who is the award-winning narrator for many of the audio versions of my books, including the entire John Corey series. Scott has done an incredible job of bringing the written word to audio, and he's become the voice of John Corey. He says it's easy because he loves my books. Thanks, Scott, for the compliment and for bringing your golden voice to each recording session.

Anyone who reads and recalls my many past acknowledgments might be surprised to see that after over two decades my two assistants have still not quit. First, my heartfelt thanks and gratitude to Dianne Francis, who organizes my personal and professional life and has done it well for twenty-seven years. And many thanks to Patricia Chichester, the only person on earth who can read my handwritten hieroglyphic manuscript and has done so for twenty-two years. This book and past books would not have seen the light of day without the hard work and dedication of Dianne and Patricia.

When I started writing in 1974, the words "social media" probably meant the social pages or the gossip column of a newspaper. Now this means the Internet, and that means you need someone half your age to help you navigate Facebook, Twitter, Instagram, and all that, so I retained the services of Katy Tatzel, CEO and founder of Greene Digital Marketing, who has added a new and creative dimension to my reader outreach efforts. Thanks, Katy, for all your good advice and your patience.

I have acquired a new editor, Colin Harrison, Vice President and Editor-in-Chief at Scribner, whose list of authors was impressive even before he added me to that list. Colin gave *The Maze* a fresh read and made invaluable and original suggestions, which I incorporated into the manuscript and which have made the plot, characters, and story line even stronger. There's nothing as good as a fresh eye and an open mind from a veteran editor to see and understand what needs to be done before the manuscript goes off to the printer. Colin, I look forward to working with you on the next one.

I also want to take this opportunity to thank Jon Karp, President and CEO of Simon & Schuster, for his early read of the manuscript and his encouragement. But most of all, I want to thank Jon for his devotion to the world of book publishing. In this time of cancel culture, Jon has stood fast in his duty to publish diverse opinions.

On a sadder note, I want to acknowledge the late and great Carolyn Reidy, President and CEO of Simon & Schuster, who passed away suddenly in 2020. Carolyn was a good friend and a fan of my books long before I signed on with Simon & Schuster, and she made me an offer I'm glad I didn't refuse. May she rest in peace.

One of the toughest jobs in the world of book publishing is that of literary agent. Anyone who has to deal with authors every day needs infinite patience, a good sense of humor, and/or good meds. Jennifer Joel and Sloan Harris of ICM Partners have an abundance of the first two and hopefully an unlimited refill prescription for the meds. Jenn and Sloan are there when I need them—and not there when I don't. You can't ask for anything more. Thanks to you both for your encouragement, good counsel, and your friendship.

As many of you know, I lost my wife, Sandy, over four years ago to lung cancer, and I found myself widowed with a twelve-year-old son to raise and a household to run, which I couldn't do alone while still working long hours. Into the breach stepped four people who I'd like to thank publicly. The first is my brother Lance, who took over many of the responsibilities of house and garden and who became a super uncle to my son James, now sixteen. I'd also like to thank Lance's wife, Dory Anne, who is James's godmother and who took the responsibilities of a godparent seriously and was always there for James. Thank you both for all you've done and continue to do.

Also, I want to thank Monika Chelchowski, who Sandy hired fifteen years ago to help with household chores and who has stayed with us during good times and hard times, and who has been like a second mother to James. Many thanks for your loyalty and your caring, and for teaching James naughty words in Polish.

Finally, my thanks and eternal gratitude to James's nanny, Paola Watson, who could give lessons to Mary Poppins on how to raise, educate, and comfort a child. Paola was sent to me three years ago by the Nanny League, but really was sent by God, as were Lance, Dory Anne, and Monika. I am a lucky man.

Last but not least are my adult children, Lauren and Alex, and their respective spouses, Gabor and Dagmar, who have made my life as a writer and a father and a grandfather much brighter and easier than it would have been without their love and care.

Writing is a solitary profession, but life is a shared journey.

————

The following people or their families have made generous contributions to charities in return for having their name used as a character in this novel:

Sharon (Mrs. Larry) Dolch Hite—MedShare Atlanta; **Joseph Ferrara**—Boys & Girls Club of Oyster Bay–East Norwich; **Dr. Richard Shlofmitz**—who not only put himself in harm's way battling Covid-19 but also raised money for critically needed medical supplies and equipment in the dark, early days of the pandemic. Thanks too to Dr. Shlofmitz's staff and colleagues at St. Francis Hospital. You are all heroes.

Last but not least, **David Katz**, who supported the Crohn's & Colitis Foundation of America back in 2015. I could not do you justice with a good character named after you in this novel—but your name will appear in *Blood Lines* (tentative title), which my son Alex and I are now working on.

I hope all these individuals enjoy their fictitious alter egos and that they continue their good work for worthy causes.

ABOUT THE AUTHOR

NELSON DeMILLE is the author of twenty-three novels, six of which were #1 *New York Times* bestsellers. His novels include *Blood Lines* and *The Deserter* (written with Alex DeMille), *The Cuban Affair*, *Word of Honor*, *Plum Island*, *The Charm School*, *The Gold Coast*, and *The General's Daughter*, which was made into a major motion picture starring John Travolta. Nelson DeMille is a combat-decorated U.S. Army veteran; a member of Mensa, Poets & Writers, and the Authors Guild; and a past president of the Mystery Writers of America. He is also a member of the International Thriller Writers, who honored him as 2015 ThrillerMaster of the Year. He lives on Long Island with his family.

Learn more at www.nelsondemille.net
X: @nelsondemille
Instagram: @nelsondemilleauthor
Facebook: NelsonDeMilleAuthor

Read on for a preview of Nelson DeMille's
next book with Alex DeMille,

BLOOD
LINES

Available now from Scribner

CHAPTER 1

Harry Vance finished getting dressed in the dark bedroom, using his cell phone to find a pair of matching
socks. It was past two in the morning and he was trying to
leave without waking Anna, so he shouldn't have been so
particular. But at the age of fifty-three, Vance had learned
to accept and embrace his own bullshit. And he knew his
steps felt a little less sure when his socks didn't match.

He walked to the tall window and parted the curtains. The dark streets below were lined with turn-of-the-
century apartment buildings and shuttered storefronts,
and the day's rain had turned the curbside snowbanks
into rivers of gray slush. The sidewalks were barren on
this cold January night, but the bars and clubs tucked
away in this trendy corner of Berlin were still open, their
music and laughter echoing down the dark street.

Vance turned and looked at Anna, asleep under a thick
blanket. A space heater hummed at the far end of the
room. These old buildings were nice to look at, but they
weren't insulated, and nothing worked. Anna thought the
building had "character," a word that made Vance want
to step into traffic. Well, that's what he got for becoming
involved with a younger woman.

He approached the bed and took a closer look at her
by the dim light coming through the window. She didn't
look like herself when she slept. Her face was relaxed,
soft. So different from who she was.

Vance reached his hand out to . . . What? Touch her? Try to wake her? Tell her where he was going? Why would he do something like that? *Because you're an idiot.* Which is another way of saying you're in love.

He withdrew his hand. The point was to not tell her anything. She didn't like that, of course. And neither did the brass back at headquarters when he froze them out of his investigations until it was time to make arrests. But this was how Army CID Agent Harry Vance had always approached his job. Just do it. Only amateurs and cowards needed outside opinions before the job was done.

So, he hadn't told her about tonight's rendezvous, and he'd be back in bed before sunrise. They'd wake up together, maybe a morning roll in the sack, then fried eggs with black bread and coffee, watch the news. Sunday stuff.

Anna rolled over, muttering something in German that he couldn't make out. Her arm flopped onto the empty side of the mattress, which still contained his impression in the cheap memory foam.

He pictured her waking up in the night to use the bathroom or get some water and see that he was gone. She'd freak out.

He took out his phone and typed her a text: *Couldn't sleep. Went for a walk. Back by dawn.* He hesitated, then added: *I love you.*

Every word of that was true, though he may have left a few things out. He hit Send and heard her phone vibrate on the bedside table.

He walked to the foyer where he put on his scarf and wool cap. He eyed a small table piled with yesterday's mail, then slid open a drawer to reveal his Beretta M9 inside a pancake holster.

He stared at the pistol. He wasn't doing anything dangerous. Unless, of course, he was closer to the truth than he realized. And you never know you're there until you're there.

He clipped the holster to his belt, then put on his camel-hair topcoat. He unbolted the heavy door and stepped onto the dimly lit landing, closing the door quietly behind him.

He descended three flights of stairs, then stepped out into the winter night and felt the sharp snap of cold air on his face. He lit a cigarette and walked north to the Prenzlauer Allee S-Bahn train station, a handsome turn-of-the-century brick building that—like Anna's street and much of the neighborhood of Prenzlauer Berg—appeared to have somehow survived the war intact. Though in Berlin you didn't always know what was original and what got pieced back together from the rubble.

He walked down a set of icy stairs to the tracks, which ran along a trench below street level. He checked his watch as he waited on the platform: 2:27 A.M. It was the weekend, so the S-Bahn ran all night. He watched a young couple huddled inside a glass-paneled shelter as a cold north wind whipped down the platform.

On a typical case, he'd have his partner, Mark Jenkins, with him. But this wasn't a typical case. In fact, it wasn't a CID case at all. He was moonlighting here in Berlin, hundreds of miles from the headquarters of the U.S. Army's 5th Military Police Battalion in Kaiserslautern, a small city near Frankfurt where Vance lived and worked. His colleagues knew he came to Berlin whenever he had time off. They assumed it was for a woman, and they made their jokes. But they were only half right.

He thought about his wife, Julie, back in Kaiserslautern, soon-to-be ex if the papers ever went through. German efficiency, he'd found out, did not extend to divorce proceedings. She was a good woman and didn't deserve half the crap he put her through. Then again, she chose to stay in the marriage. We all make our own prisons.

Vance spotted the train approaching and took a last drag on his cigarette. He flicked the butt onto the tracks, then took out his cell and texted: *Ich bin unterwegs.* I'm on my way.

After a few seconds he received a reply: *Ich werde da sein.* I'll be there.

The train eased into the station and Vance boarded. He took a seat and looked around as the train pulled out. His car was mostly empty, as was the entire train, the length of which he could see due to the open gangway. He spotted a group of hyperactive twentysomethings at the far end, probably club-hopping until dawn. He'd done that once with Anna, which was one time too many. She thought she was keeping him young, but she was actually just reminding him of the age gulf between them.

The city slid by out the grimy window. He was heading southeast to Neukölln, a neighborhood with a large Turkish and Arab immigrant population, made larger in the last few years thanks to Germany's generous asylum policy toward Syrian refugees. It was a policy that made many Germans proud—and enraged and frightened just as many.

Vance tried to stay out of his host country's internal politics, though as a Chief Warrant Officer in the CID's Terrorism and Criminal Investigation Unit, or TCIU, this rapid influx of refugees had affected his caseload. There were dozens of U.S. Army installations across Europe, and Vance and his colleagues in the TCIU were responsible for investigating perceived terrorist threats against all of them, as well as threats against any U.S. Army personnel located on the European continent or North Africa, which was his command's area of responsibility.

In truth, most of the flood of refugees arriving in Germany came here to escape the ravages of war and create a better life, and even the criminal element among them largely restricted their activities to nonpolitical felonies. But it was the potential ISIS or al-Qaeda operatives who managed to slip through, and also the jobless and isolated young men who became radicalized once in Germany, that kept Vance and his colleagues busy. As they say in counterterrorism, the good guys need to succeed every time; the bad guys need to succeed only once.

Vance looked out the window as the train crossed over the Spree River, and then passed from the former East Berlin into the West. What had once been a fortified wall of concrete, razor wire, dogs, soldiers, and searchlights was now a phantom border crisscrossed by twenty-four-hour train lines and rejoined streets, and you'd have to have a sightseeing guide to find the few shards of the wall still standing. Vance figured that was probably a good thing. Berlin, more than most places, had to navigate remembering the past without becoming a shrine to its horrors.

He remembered watching the wall come down on TV. The cheering crowds as people took sledgehammers to the hated structure. East German police and soldiers standing impotent as Germans from the east and west defiantly held hands atop the wall, one people again.

He had been in his first semester of his senior year at Georgetown, thinking about a military career and what his role might be in helping to contain the Soviet menace. And then, in the blink of an eye, the forty-year Cold War was over. The Iron Curtain parted. The nuclear threat lifted. A new world had dawned overnight, and no one knew what to do about it. It turned out the new world was more complicated than the old, and thirty years later Vance was still trying to figure it out.

In a few minutes the train arrived at the Neukölln station and Vance got out. He walked along the elevated train platform, which was covered in graffiti and smelled vaguely of urine. He descended the stairs and exited onto Karl-Marx-Straße, a street that mocked its namesake with a McDonald's.

He walked north along Karl-Marx, passing a number of closed halal groceries, Turkish coffee shops, and Middle Eastern restaurants. Up ahead an Arab teenager in a winter parka leaned against a lamp pole, watching him. Vance wondered if he was a dealer or maybe a corner boy for one of the Arab crime syndicates that operated in this area. Vance—with his barrel chest and a healthy paunch due to his love affair with dark German lagers—didn't fit the profile of a heroin junkie looking for a fix. In fact, he probably looked to this kid to be exactly what he was— a plainclothes cop. As Vance got closer the boy averted his eyes.

After a couple of blocks, he found the place he was looking for—a five-story apartment building with a hookah lounge on the ground floor called Ember Berlin. There were only a few customers sitting in the dim smoky lounge amid Turkish tapestries, garish blue lighting, and thumping Arabic pop music.

Vance entered through the glass doors and looked around the lounge. A group of Turkish thirtysomething guys were in one corner smoking and laughing, and a couple of old Arab men in tracksuits were sitting near the front door quietly sharing a hookah. The tracksuits scanned him and one of them let out a huge puff of apple-scented smoke.

Vance walked to the back, where upholstered vinyl seating ran along the rear wall behind small tables and chairs. He took a seat facing the door and placed his hat on the table. He kept his coat on to make sure no one caught sight of his holstered M9.

A young Turkish waiter walked over and dropped a menu on the table. "*Guten Abend. Huka? Kaffee?*"

"*Türkischer Kaffee bitte.*"

The young man nodded and walked off.

Vance checked his watch. 3:05 A.M. He pulled his phone out and looked at the text thread he'd exchanged with the man he was there to meet, Abbas al Hamdani. He'd received the man's number from a local guy with connections. Hamdani wasn't known to CID, and Vance hadn't done much to verify al Hamdani's identity other than to request the man send a current photo of himself. Vance looked at the picture. Hamdani was a heavyset man in his seventies with a bushy gray mustache and large, sad eyes.

He looked at Hamdani's last message: *Ich werde da sein.* I'll be there.

The waiter returned with his coffee and he sipped it as he watched the door. The street outside was empty except for an occasional car or Vespa. After a few more minutes, he sent a text: *Ich bin da.* I'm here.

No response. Vance drank his coffee and began to wonder why he'd left a hot woman and a warm bed for this crap. Then again, the woman—Anna—was the reason he was here in the first place.

His wife used to tell him he had a savior complex. He became overly involved in other people's problems instead of keeping his own house in order. She was right, of course. It was probably why he was a good investigator and a bad husband. After twenty-five years together, he and Julie had each other pretty well figured out. Which was the problem. Marriages, like criminal investigations, tend to be over when there's no more mystery.

His phone vibrated. He checked it and saw a message that said in German: *I can no longer meet there.*

Vance tapped out a reply: *We had an arrangement.*

The reply came quickly: *I cannot be seen with you.*

Vance wrote: *No one knows who I am.*

No response for a moment. Then: *Come to Thomashöhe Park. Up the road. Inside the park by the eastern entrance. This is better security for us both.*

Vance waited to reply. He eyed the two old Arab guys in tracksuits and wondered if they knew Hamdani. Like a lot of immigrant and refugee communities, this place was insular, with complex alliances and resentments that dated back to their native lands, and probably to the beginning of time. Maybe Hamdani got tipped to these guys' presence and didn't want to be seen talking to a white guy at three in the morning. Too many questions.

Vance had insisted on a public place, and Hamdani could have picked anywhere, in any neighborhood. Why here, in his own backyard, if he was concerned about being seen? Something wasn't adding up.

He looked at the map on his phone and saw that Thomashöhe Park was only a few blocks away. His CID training told him that meeting an unknown informant in a park in the middle of the night was a bad idea, but his ego and his Beretta assured him it would be fine. He decided to split the difference and practice some minimal operational security. He spotted another park due south of Thomashöhe, called Körnerpark, and wrote back: *Meet me in Körnerpark. Near the northern entrance off Jonasstraße. Fifteen minutes.* He'd enter the park at the southern entrance and be there in five. If Hamdani balked, Vance would abort.

After a moment he received a response: *Okay. See you there.*

Vance knocked back the rest of the sludgy, sweet Turkish coffee, put on his hat, then dropped some euros on the table and left.

He continued north along Karl-Marx-Straße and after a few blocks made a left onto a side street. He walked a block and then saw the entrance to Körnerpark, which was sunk about twenty feet below street level and ringed with stone balustrades. A staircase led down into the park, with a chain stretched across it to indicate it was closed.

Vance walked up to one of the balustrades and looked into the park, which was lit by scattered lampposts. Gridded paths, manicured hedges, and white stone statues gave the impression of a palace garden. The place was nice to look at but turned out to be a bad tactical choice—a lot of open spaces, and anyone observing him from a distance could easily have the high ground.

He walked to the stairway and paused. A chill wind shook the bare branches of the trees around him, and the fat crescent moon cast a spectral pall over the frozen stone figures in the park.

I want to tell you what happened to my father.

He remembered just how Anna had said it, in her crisp German accent, and how she'd looked at the time—her stark features barely revealed through the dim light of the nightclub where she had taken him on one of their first dates, some trendy spot located in a former East Berlin brick factory. It was a real Anna kind of place—cool and hip but also heavy with the weight of history, where in the gloom beyond the dancers and club lights you could almost imagine the poor bastards in the sweltering brickworks, laboring toward a new world that would never come.

"He was betrayed," Anna had said between blasts of industrial techno. "And then he was murdered."

That's when it had truly begun, this obsession of his. And it was why Vance was standing here now, knee-deep in an investigation of a cold case he had no jurisdiction over, and which had occurred in a country that no longer existed. Leaving his wife for a younger woman might have seemed like the obvious sign of a midlife crisis. But maybe the real crisis was here, in the freezing night, looking for justice in all the wrong places.

He slid his M9 out of the pancake holster and held it inside the pocket of his topcoat, then ducked under the chain and descended the stairs into the park.

CHAPTER 2

Chief Warrant Officer Scott Brodie drove his Army-issued Chevy Impala down the narrow back road. Thick growths of Virginia pine crowded the shoulders between dirt driveways leading to dilapidated houses and shanties. It was a bright and frigid day in the middle of January, and yesterday's snow still clung to the pine needles and patchy lawns.

Nick Evans sat in the passenger seat. He cracked his window and lit a cigarette. "Hate these off-base busts."

Brodie did not reply.

"A soldier won't resist arrest in the barracks. But once he's got his own roof over his head, even one of these little shitboxes . . . his thinking is different. It's instinct. A man defends his castle."

Brodie preferred his partner in the morning, when he was hungover and didn't talk much. But it was 4 P.M., and by now Evans had had his Irish coffee for lunch, followed by two or three more, and he was all jaw.

Brodie, age thirty-nine, was a Special Agent in the United States Army Criminal Investigation Division, more commonly known as CID, which was responsible for investigating major felony crimes and violations of the Uniform Code of Military Justice within the Army. Nick Evans was his partner and, like many of Brodie's partners over the course of his thirteen-year career, Evans was an asshole.

Evans continued talking between drags. "These new

enlisteds think they can get away with anything. Remember that jerkoff in Norfolk? Growing enough weed to smoke out a brigade? Just heard they docked his pay, no reduction in rank, no confinement. Bullshit. What the hell kind of message ... ?"

Brodie let Evans ramble and focused on the road. Brodie and Evans shared an office at CID Headquarters, which was within Marine Corps Base Quantico, a large complex in northeast Virginia that also housed the Marine Officer Candidates School and the Basic School, as well as the Marine Corps University, the FBI Academy, the Drug Enforcement Administration training academy, and the Naval Criminal Investigative Service (NCIS), which was the Navy equivalent of Army CID, but with bigger egos thanks to the hit TV show.

Brodie lived in a rented house close to base, though until recently he'd been a nomad, traveling the country and the world on challenging assignments. But that was back when his life was interesting. Before his wings got clipped. Now he could actually spend time in his office. He even got around to checking his mail and doing paperwork, the ultimate indignity.

He eyed the rearview, where the Virginia state trooper was following close behind. Since they were conducting a search outside a military installation, civilian law enforcement had to ride along. Brodie also had to get the search warrant from a civilian judge. The military had its own ways of doing things, of course, and its own parallel justice system. But in America the civilians still ruled the realm, and intruded when they felt like it, which Brodie guessed meant it was still a free country. But it didn't make his job any easier.

Brodie glanced at his partner as the man kept smoking and yammering. Although CID was full of motivated professionals, Scott Brodie seemed to get stuck with the duds. He'd chosen to not read too much into this, despite his commanding officer Colonel Stanley Dombroski telling him on more than one occasion: "If everyone you work with is an asshole, the asshole is you."

Dombroski was a commissioned officer. Brodie and Evans were officers of a different stripe—Warrant Officers, which put them above all enlisted soldiers in the Army chain of command, including NCOs, but below the lowest-ranked commissioned officer, meaning a rookie lieutenant just out of OCS, ROTC, or The Point. Within the Warrant Officer rank there were five grades. Brodie was a CW-4. Evans was five years older than Brodie and had served longer, but was still a CW-3, which said a few things about Mr. Evans.

Scott Brodie, despite his time in service and his time in grade, was fairly sure he'd never get that final promotion to CW-5. And the reason for that was his tendency to buck authority when the authority was being stupid. But Brodie could close tough cases, and at the end of the day that's what the brass wanted to see—points on the board. Brodie had a lot of points, which partly made up for his bad attitude and other personality defects. He recalled another Dombroski-ism directed his way: "The only thing worse than a useless idiot you can't work with is an effective pain in the ass you can't fire." Brodie wondered how much of this wisdom the colonel had picked up at Officer Candidate School.

Warrant Officers, while technically considered commissioned officers, differed from regular commissioned officers in a few ways that made sense only to the Army. They didn't have formal officer titles and were simply referred to as Mr. or Ms.—or occasionally, the gender-neutral "Chief"—and as CID Agents they usually wore civilian clothing and drove unmarked civilian cars. Today, Brodie and Evans were both dressed in slacks, dress shirts, and dark blue windbreakers with "CID FEDERAL AGENT" emblazoned on the front and back in big yellow letters. When you're smashing down a suspect's door, you don't want any confusion. And in case there was, Brodie and Evans were packing their M9s.

Evans flicked his cigarette butt out the window and punched the power on the car radio. A rock song came on, something awful that Brodie half remembered from his college days. Evans started tapping the glove box along with the riffs. "These guys rock. Saw them last summer at the Birchmere. They still got it."

Brodie suggested, "Keep an eye out for the turn."

"Shoulda let the State cracker lead."

"Not when you're with me, Mr. Evans."

This should be a simple bust. But sometimes the cases that looked straightforward ended up going sideways and screwing up your whole day. Still, it beat parking your ass behind a desk all day like some of Brodie's colleagues at Quantico.

Within the CID were experts in a host of fields such as cybercrime, procurement fraud, forensic analysis, polygraph administration, criminal records processing—the desk jockeys—as well as specialists in counterterrorism, protective services, and, in special circumstances, war crimes and treason.

Brodie and Evans were not in a specialized unit, but general criminal investigators—the equivalent of a police detective—working felonies that fell outside the skills and purview of the specialists. They spent much of their day out on the beat gathering evidence, conducting interviews, and—on a good day—locating and arresting the bad guys. Lately, the bad guys seemed to be getting stupider and easier to catch, though in reality it was Brodie's cases that were getting stupider, and smaller. And this afternoon's assignment was a perfect example: searching for stolen goods at the home of Private First Class Eric Hinckley, who was suspected of involvement in a larceny ring operating out of Fort A.P. Hill, an Army base near Fredericksburg. Someone was stealing MREs—Meals Ready to Eat—the canned and dehydrated rations that kept America's fighting men and women satiated and constipated while deployed in the field. Private Hinckley worked as a guard at a warehouse that stored MREs, and he was suspected of supplying a third party who was running an online store that had so far done about sixty thousand dollars' worth of business. That was more than enough for a felony charge, though not generally enough to get Scott Brodie out of bed in the morning.

He used to work big cases. Homicides, narcotics, weapons theft. High-stakes stuff. Often overseas. Evans had, too, before he sabotaged his career with an assist from Johnnie Walker. Scott Brodie, on the other hand, hadn't drank himself into career oblivion. In fact, he'd done his job *too* well on his last major assignment, investigating beyond his mandate, pissing off several Intel agencies and learning a few things that were well above his pay grade. So, he got saddled with a deadbeat partner and a bullshit caseload not befitting his experience or skills. Brodie wasn't sure if this was temporary punishment, or an attempt to drive him into early retirement. Either way, the Army's aggression toward its maverick officers was often passive but never subtle.

The case that had gotten him on everyone's shit list was from five months back, and had involved tracking down an infamous deserter, Captain Kyle Mercer of the Army's elite Delta Force, who had apparently abandoned his remote post in Afghanistan and been captured by the Taliban. Captain Mercer eventually escaped his captors and turned up in—of all places—Caracas, Venezuela. It would have been more pleasant for everyone if Kyle Mercer had instead decamped to, say, Tahiti, or the Côte d'Azur, but he had chosen the armpit of the Western Hemisphere for very specific reasons that dated back to some wet stuff he'd gotten into while commanding a Black Ops team in Afghanistan. It was a complicated, messy, sensitive, and ultimately sad case, and more than one person who should have stood in front of a court-martial instead came home in a body bag. And people like Brodie and his former partner Maggie Taylor, and their boss Colonel Dombroski, should have gotten a promotion—but got a ton of shit instead. Shit happens.

Evans pointed to a roadside mailbox. "Two five six. Right here."

Brodie turned off the road onto a dirt driveway that led to an aluminum-sided ranch house. He parked his car fifty yards from the house and the Virginia state trooper pulled in behind them.

Brodie noticed a Toyota compact parked in front of the detached garage. Brodie, Evans, and the trooper got out without slamming their doors shut.

The Virginia trooper, a pale and lanky redhead in his late twenties named Dave Finley, walked up to them with a crowbar in his hands. Brodie had interacted with Finley before in executing a search warrant, and the guy was a straight arrow. Trooper Finley nodded to the door. "How do you want to do it?"

Brodie looked at the house. The front bay window had heavy curtains drawn. He said to Evans, "Cover the back."

"Copy."

Evans headed around back as Brodie and Finley approached the front door. Brodie noticed there was no doorbell. He could hear something playing loudly on the TV—explosions, gunfire, demonic screams. Probably a video game.

Brodie waited a moment to give Evans time to get to the back door, then he knocked loudly and dialed up his Virginia accent. "Delivery! Need ya'll to sign."

They waited. After a few moments the sound from the TV cut out. They heard footsteps approaching the door. Brodie put his thumb over the door's peephole as he pulled his M9 from his holster and held it at his side.

The footsteps stopped.

Brodie said, "Need a signature or I can't leave it."

All was quiet for a moment, then a face peeked out from behind the curtains, then disappeared.

Finley shoved the crowbar into the doorjamb and began to pry it open.

The door splintered and Brodie kicked it open as he raised his M9 and caught sight of a male figure running toward the back of the house.

"CID! Halt!" Which is military for "Stop, asshole."

But the asshole kept running.

As Brodie took off after him, the guy ran into a small kitchen, kicked open a metal storm door, and sprinted through the doorway where he collided with Nick Evans, who didn't seem ready for what was coming and got knocked on his ass.

The guy bolted across the backyard and Brodie chased after him, past a scrawny black Lab that was barking and howling and pulling on the end of a chain.

Brodie cut wide of the dog and headed for the man, who he assumed was PFC Hinckley, a pasty young guy with a military buzz cut in a tank top and jeans running barefoot. Hinckley was a few yards from a high chain-link fence that marked the edge of his property. Brodie yelled, "Halt or I shoot!"

The guy knew that was bullshit and jumped onto the fence and started to scramble up. Brodie holstered his pistol as he caught up to him, grabbed him by his belt, and threw him facedown onto the lawn. Hinckley, possibly recalling his basic training hand-to-hand combat class, tried to flip, but Brodie jumped on the guy's back and pressed his face into a patch of snow. "Say uncle, asshole!" Hinckley didn't, but he stopped resisting. Brodie grabbed the man's wrists and cuffed his hands behind his back.

"Private Eric Hinckley, I presume?"

"Fuck you."

"I will take that as an affirmative response."

Evans had recovered from his knockdown and was rushing toward them. "Guy came out of nowhere."

"Actually he came out of the house. Get in there and check for other occupants."

Evans muttered something as he jogged toward the open storm door, gun at his side.

Brodie pulled Hinckley to his feet and spun him around. He flashed his badge and said, "I'm Warrant Officer Scott Brodie, a Special Agent in the U.S. Army Criminal Investigation Division. I am investigating the alleged offense of larceny, of which you are suspected. I advise you that under the provisions of Article 31 of the Uniform Code of Military Justice, you have the right to remain silent."

Hinckley looked at Brodie, and they made eye contact.

"Yes, sir, I was—"

"Shut up."

Hinckley shut up.

Brodie continued, "Any statements you make, oral or written, may be used as evidence against you in a trial by court-martial or in other judicial or administrative proceedings." He continued to inform Hinckley of his Article 31 rights, essentially the military version of Miranda rights. Brodie had rattled this off hundreds of times over the course of his career, and most suspects were too scared, stupid, or belligerent to absorb what you were saying. But the inevitable lawyers sure as hell wanted to know that you said the magic words.

Brodie wrapped up his spiel with, "Do you understand your rights?"

"Yes, sir."

"Good. Now listen closely and answer yes or no. Do you want a lawyer? Do you want to see my search warrant? Do you want a kick in the balls?"

"No."

"Good." Brodie pushed Hinckley against the chain-link fence, patted him down, then pushed him toward the house. "Let's see how much trouble you're in."

They walked past the black Lab. Brodie now noticed the dog's rib cage pushing through its mangy black hair. The dog was barking at Hinckley, and not at the guy who had just tackled and cuffed its owner.

Hinckley said, "It's all right, girl."

The dog growled at him.

"I don't think she likes you much, Private."

Hinckley didn't respond. Brodie led him through the open door and into a small, filthy kitchen. About two dozen cardboard crates labeled "MEALS READY TO EAT," featuring the Department of Defense seal, were stacked against one wall. Brodie said to Hinckley, "Don't they feed you enough in the mess hall, soldier?"

No reply.

"You want to tell me where the rest is before I turn this place inside out?"

Hinckley stared at the floor, silent. Brodie wondered if the guy understood that his Army days were over, except for the time he'd spend in a military prison.

Brodie led him into the living room, where Officer Finley was taking photos with his cell phone. Finley said, "Did a sweep. No one else here."

"Copy."

Brodie pushed Hinckley onto the couch. "Don't move."

Brodie heard Evans rummaging around in a room off the living room and entered a small, cluttered bedroom. Evans, wearing latex gloves, was closing a dresser drawer and slipping a small baggie of white powder into his jacket pocket.

Evans looked up at him. "About six cases under the bed." He gestured to the open closet. "Few more in there. And you saw the ones in the kitchen."

Brodie stared at his partner for a moment. "Check the garage. Then circle back for a thorough search of the house."

Evans nodded and walked out. Brodie reopened the drawer, which was full of civilian and Army socks, along with a wad of cash.

Brodie walked back into the living room and sat down on the coffee table opposite the handcuffed Hinckley, who was staring at the pause screen of his video game on the big flat-screen across the room. A voluptuous woman in a Nazi uniform with bloody chain saws for hands was standing in some sort of bunker.

Brodie asked, "Why did you run?"

Hinckley shrugged, looked down at the floor. "I freaked."

"I didn't need the cardio, Private."

He looked at Brodie. "I'm sorry, sir."

"And you knocked down my partner. That's assault of a law enforcement officer, plus evading arrest in addition to the larceny charge. But maybe those additional charges won't show up in my report."

Hinckley looked at Brodie and nodded. "I certainly would appreciate that, sir."

"Is my partner going to find anything in the garage?"

Hinckley nodded.

"How much?"

"Fifty, sixty cases."

"You've got about ninety grand in stolen government property here, Private. And that's not counting what you've already moved. Who's helping you?"

Hinckley didn't reply.

"Someone at the base? Who's running the shop? They military?"

No reply. Brodie could still hear the dog barking in the backyard.

"We're going to call Animal Control about your dog."

Hinckley looked at him. "I don't want her to go to a pound."

"What do you care?"

He was silent for a moment. "My sister can take her. She lives in Charlottesville."

"Maybe." Brodie asked, "Whose bright idea was this?"

Hinckley hesitated. "The seller. I don't know his name. He's not active duty, maybe retired. Some kinda prepper dude. He heard from . . . someone that we had a big stash that had been ordered by DOD but wasn't going nowhere because of the drawdowns in Afghanistan. So, easy pickings. And demand's through the roof for this shit. Everyone's getting ready. You know?"

"Ready for what?"

Hinckley shrugged. "Things to go from bad to worse, I guess."

"I'd say it's already headed that way for you. Who linked you with the seller?"

Hinckley didn't reply.

"I might be able to keep you out of prison."

Hinckley looked at Brodie, maybe trying to read if this was bullshit.

CID Agents had a reputation for playing the good cop to a T, empathizing with the suspect and promising the moon for cooperation, when half the time they were just giving the perp the rope to hang himself. There was no rule that you couldn't lie through your teeth when trying to extract information from a bad soldier. Brodie had no idea what kind of deal PFC Hinckley could get, nor did he care. But over the years he'd learned to promise what he couldn't deliver.

Hinckley said, "I think . . . I need to talk to a lawyer."

Well, when the suspect said that, you were supposed to stop asking questions, but Brodie said, "Speak up, Private. I can't hear you."

Hinckley didn't respond and stared at the flat-screen.

Brodie regarded PFC Eric Hinckley. He knew from the man's file that he was nineteen years old, though he looked even younger. Probably a low-achieving student who got recruited in his high school on Career Day. Promised a steady paycheck, three hots and a cot, maybe some adventure, plus brotherhood and a meaningful career to boot. And that's not a lie. The Army can provide all those things if you're getting in for the right reasons.

Some guys, however, lost their way and went crooked, like Nick Evans, who was bored, burned out, and looking to start trouble if it didn't naturally present itself. But nineteen-year-old Private Hinckley hadn't lost his way. He never knew where he was going to begin with.

Well, the kid had asked for a lawyer, so the questions needed to stop. But Brodie still had something to say.

"Look at me, soldier."

Hinckley turned to him.

"You are a disgrace to your uniform and your country. You took an oath."

Hinckley averted his eyes.

"You made a bad choice, and you will face the consequences. And you better figure out why you made that bad choice, to prevent yourself from screwing up even more of your life. Do you understand me, Private?"

Hinckley looked back at him. "Yes, sir. I . . . wasn't thinking."

"This is a good time to start, Eric."

"Yes sir."

Brodie got up and noticed Officer Finley was looking at him and had probably listened to that interaction with some interest. There was no analog in the civilian world for what had just transpired. Cops don't usually dress down the perps they're arresting. But the Army was one big semi-functional family, and a criminal act within that family was a violation of something beyond and perhaps greater than the law.

Brodie went to the kitchen and opened the fridge. It was mostly bare except for a bottle of ketchup, a few cans of beer, and a couple of hot dogs.

He grabbed the hot dogs and walked out to the backyard. The dog was lying in the grass, lethargic. Her ears perked up as Brodie approached and tossed the hot dogs to her.

His cell rang. It was his boss, Colonel Dombroski. He picked up. "Brodie."

"Mr. Brodie. Where are you?"

Brodie watched as the Lab inhaled both hot dogs. "Executing an off-base search warrant."

"We need to meet."

"Is this business or pleasure?"

"I occasionally enjoy your company, Scott, but it's always business."

"Yes, sir. O Club?"

The Officers Club was an on-base bar and restaurant that, as the name suggested, was restricted to military officers and their guests. Dombroski liked the place and often held his meetings there. At the age of fifty-five, he was on the old end of colonel, and he had something of a chip on his shoulder about the general's star he might never get pinned on that shoulder. The O Club reminded the Colonel that he was still in the exclusive fraternity that is the military officers corps. Also, the place had a decent twelve-dollar sirloin.

Dombroski replied, "A little farther afield this time. Annie's Junction. Sports bar just off Ninety-Five, past the Lowe's."

"Is it ten-cent wing night?"

"Can you be there in twenty?"

"I'm working outside of Fredericksburg, Colonel. The Hinckley larceny case."

"Evans can handle that."

"Can I get that in writing?"

"It's urgent, Scott. Thirty minutes."

"Yes, sir."

Dombroski hung up.

Brodie put his phone back in his pocket as he saw Evans exit the detached garage and walk across the lawn toward him. "The mother lode's in there."

Brodie nodded.

"Chili mac 'n' cheese. Beef brisket. Doesn't sound bad. You eat that shit in Iraq?"

Brodie had served as an infantry sergeant in Iraq in 2003 and 2004. He didn't like to talk about it much, but Evans, who had never seen combat, was always asking him stupid questions. "I ate snakes."

Evans laughed. "Hard-core." He stopped walking and stared at the black Lab looking up at Brodie, tail wagging. "You feed it?"

"Someone had to."

"This guy's a real prick."

"I need to head out. Call the evidence team and catch a ride back with them to HQ once they wrap up. Have the MPs send a patrol car to collect Hinckley and let him call his sister to collect the dog."

"Where you going?"

"Something came up."

Evans didn't seem sure what to make of that, but he nodded. "Okay." He walked past Brodie toward the house.

Brodie watched him walk away for a moment, then said, "And don't remove any more evidence."

Evans turned around. "What?"

"You heard me."

"I don't know what you're talking about."

Brodie stared into the man's eyes for a moment. "How does it feel to be everyone's hardship duty?"

Evans glared at him. "You think you're better than me?"

Brodie didn't reply.

"It was less than an eight ball."

"Great."

"A nice Saturday night for me and the boys, or a year in prison for our young private on top of everything else he's facing. What do you think?"

"You're a saint, Evans. A real class act."

"If I go back in there and find a kilo in the toilet tank, we got possession with intent to distribute. Until then, let's keep it in the family."

"Get out of my face."

"No one told me you were a fucking narc."

"Everyone told me you were a useless burnout."

"Eat shit." Evans walked back into the house.

Well, that went well. Brodie had been looking for the right excuse to terminate this particular relationship. He wasn't going to rat the guy out to Dombroski, but this gave him all the justification he needed in his own mind to demand a new partner and maybe reassignment. Evans would second the motion.

Brodie looked down at the dog, who was whining for more food. He crouched down and scratched behind her ears.

He'd never had a dog, or a cat, or any pet higher on the food chain than a goldfish. He also couldn't imagine himself with kids and had never stayed in a relationship longer than six months. He told himself that he needed the freedom to do his job and live his life the way he wanted.

But what good was that freedom now? He was tooling around the Eastern Seaboard arresting petty crooks and wife beaters and solving blockbuster crimes like the curious case of the missing chili. And for the first time in his career, he had a partner who was even more screwed up than he was. This didn't work for him. This sucked in a whole new way.

Brodie walked around the house to his parked Impala. He climbed in, pulled out of the driveway, and navigated the narrow roads that led back to the highway.

It was past five and dusk was settling in. He noticed string lights and other holiday decorations on a few of the houses he passed.

Christmas was three weeks ago. Brodie was supposed to have gone back to his folk's place in upstate New York, but he didn't. He wasn't sure why. He lied and said he was spending the holidays with a friend, which he allowed them to interpret to mean his girlfriend, who he'd dumped a month earlier. So he spent the holiday alone, eating takeout and watching alien abduction documentaries on Netflix. He'd actually enjoyed himself, which worried him.

Whether in the infantry or the CID, his Army career had always required him to exist outside the rhythms of the civilian world. He'd spent Christmases in Riyadh and Tokyo and in South Korea a few miles from the DMZ. He recalled his first and most notable Christmas away from home—Baghdad in 2003, manning the mounted .50-caliber machine gun of an armored Stryker vehicle protecting a Christian quarter of the city from insurgents and car bombs.

He remembered rolling down the narrow streets at dusk. No lights or decorations, no music. Just the quiet air, thick with fear. They passed an old church, and he could faintly hear prayers, beautiful and solemn, in a language he did not recognize as Arabic and would later learn was ancient Aramaic.

He didn't miss being home. Who needed a ticky-tacky holiday when a place like this existed? A place full of history and meaning and consequence. A place where he had a mission and a purpose.

That same feeling carried him through his career. At some point he realized he'd structured his life so that he didn't have things to miss. And that was fine. It was nice to be a lone wolf. Except once you're defanged, you're just alone.

He thought about his last partner before Nick Evans. Maggie Taylor. Despite her lack of experience, she was one of the smartest and most capable people he'd ever worked with. She was also a knockout blonde, but that had nothing to do with his high opinion of her. Except that he had sort of tried to sleep with her in Caracas. But he blamed that on the stress of the mission and the strength of the Venezuelan rum. Also, she'd sent mixed signals. But they all do.

He'd struck out, which in retrospect would have been good for their continued professional relationship had there been one. But after the Mercer case she was transferred to Fort Campbell, Kentucky, where she was assigned a new partner along with—as Brodie had heard through the grapevine—a new rank of CW-2. She and Brodie hadn't spoken since, despite Brodie's half dozen attempts to contact her. He assumed she was under orders to have no contact with him, and those orders had come from either the Pentagon, which didn't like how the mission turned out, or from the spooks at Langley who were nervous about the classified intel that Brodie and Taylor both now possessed. Or maybe her Army shrink had advised her to rid herself of toxic relationships. Or perhaps Maggie Taylor figured out all by herself that Scott Brodie was hazardous to her continued well-being.

Brodie got on the northbound ramp for the I-95 and slipped into a stream of slow-moving taillights. Rush hour. He'd probably be a few minutes late, which in the Army was a crime close to desertion.

Dombroski had said it was urgent. Maybe Warrant Officer Brodie was being promoted. Maybe he was being relieved of duty. Maybe Colonel Dombroski was in cahoots with the CIA, which was going to put ricin in Brodie's happy hour nachos.

Well, it had been a while since anyone tried to kill him. That would at least be interesting.